FATAL OBSESSION
A TWISTED ROMEO & JULIET STORY

TALES OF OBSESSION
BOOK TWO

DRETHI A.

Fatal Obsession © copyright 2024 by Drethi Anis.
Copyright notice: All rights reserved under the International and Pan-American Copyright Conventions. No part of this book may be reproduced or transmitted in any form or by any means, electronic or mechanical, including photocopying, recording, or by any information storage and retrieval system, without permission in writing from the publisher.
This is a work of fiction. Names, places, characters, and incidents are either the product of the author's imagination or are used fictitiously, and any resemblance to any actual persons, living or dead, organizations, events, or locales is entirely coincidental.
Warning: the unauthorized reproduction or distribution of this copyrighted work is illegal. Criminal copyright infringement, including infringement without monetary gain, is investigated by the FBI and is punishable by up to 5 years in prison and a fine of $250,000.

❦ Created with Vellum

AUTHOR NOTE

This book contains nonconsensual sex, FF scene, birth control manipulation, suicidal thoughts, stalking, date rape drugs, gore, and other dark matters. Most described the read as morally gray with strong Wednesday Addams feels. The characters might disturb you, depending on your comfort level.

This is purely a work of fiction intended for open-minded readers. The author does not condone the content or the characters' behaviors outside of fantasy. Please read responsibly and exercise good judgment in real life.

To all the girls who want a golden boy in the streets but a walking red flag in the sheets.

BLURB

This is a dark Romeo & Juliet retelling with a *whodunit* twist and a HEA. Damon is a morally ambiguous anti-hero, willing to do anything to keep his girl.

I was groomed to hate Damon Maxwell, but he insisted I was destined to become his.

One night with a masked stranger turned my world upside down. What should have been an anonymous experience ended with me facing off against my family's nemesis.

His name is Damon Maxwell, the charismatic CEO and a beloved philanthropist. The world chants his name, but he is the last man who should've caught my attention. My family is convinced Damon is connected to my cousin's murder and that darkness lingers behind his charming facade. But Damon claims I was his destiny and refuses to leave me alone.

Desperate to uncover the truth, I play with fire by spending time with him. As his obsession with me grows, he is determined to burn anything to the ground that dares to stand between us. The closer we become, I am plagued with more questions than answers.

**Is he truly the golden boy the public paints him as?
Or is he a villain who has trapped me in his web of seduction?**

*Damon isn't a normal romance hero and, in fact, shouldn't be considered a hero at all. Check the author's content warnings before proceeding in case his actions offend you.

**This book can be enjoyed on its own, but it's recommended to read it after 5000 Nights of Obsession, Book 1 in the Tales of Obsession Series. There are spoilers from 5000 Nights of Obsession, so read Book 1 if you plan on reading it.

PROLOGUE
DAMON MAXWELL

Karens ignore trigger warnings, only to complain about said warnings. Don't be a Karen. This Romeo & Juliet retelling is only for open-minded readers exploring their fantasies in a safe space. The book contains non-consensual sex, FF scene, birth control manipulation, suicidal thoughts, stalking, date rape, drugs, gore, and other dark themes.
Most described this book as morally gray with Wednesday Addams vibes, but the threshold for content varies from person to person. Whether you consider this dark or a breezy read, please exercise good judgment in real life by differentiating fiction from reality.

"Let's see what she is hiding under that shirt."

"Grab the bitch's arms, and I'll cut it off."

"Let's start with the skirt. I want to see if the carpet matches the drapes."

Idiotic male testosterone permeated the air as the pack cautiously circled Rose. She came here for the same reason I did: to wait for her cousin Poppy Ambani while she finished her lab. These guys cornered Rose out of the blue. Classes had concluded for the day, and no one else was in the building.

Unfortunately for Rose, I had no fealty toward her. She was Poppy's best friend, on top of being her cousin, but I couldn't risk my anonymity by saving Rose. Otherwise, Poppy would find out about me, the man waiting for her in the shadows.

I absorbed the scene, undetected, with my back against the wall of the dark hallway. The altercation looked relatively civil from a distance despite the reality.

It was public knowledge in New York that the Ambani family didn't get along with the Maxwell family. People on our college campus were under the guise that we wanted them to pick a side. These boys were Maxwell supporters. Until today, I wasn't aware our lackeys attempted to gain brownie points by harassing Ambani girls. They presumed boasting about it would be their ticket into our exclusive inner circle, and Rose's timidness made her an easy target.

Weighing in at one hundred and ten pounds, Rose Ambani was a twig compared to the herd crowding her. She didn't stand a chance, though their bark was louder than their bite. These fuckers only wanted to scare her, knowing the Ambani family would tear them from limb to limb if they hurt her.

Violence would have been more entertaining than their mindless droning and empty threats. The entitled wannabes were dressed as if they stepped off the GQ runway with their Burberry collared shirts and two-hundred-dollar haircuts. I guarantee none of them had been in a real fight before.

All except one.

The biggest man out of the four knew how to fight. I picked him out of the lineup as soon as the group swarmed Rose. The man in question tried dressing the part, but the worn shoes and fake Gucci belt gave him away. He didn't fit in. The other three kept him around as their muscle, dangling their enticing life as bait.

Fake Gucci stood a few feet away from the group. It was apparent he stuck with them in hopes of climbing the social ladder and using their contacts to land a cushy job after graduation. Otherwise, he had no attachment to these snobby douchebags or respect for what they were doing to Rose.

"Please let me leave," Rose whispered, aware that she was outnumbered.

"Please let me leave," one of the douchebags mimicked.

"We are just getting started," the second one chimed in.

"What do you have in here?" The third one snatched Rose's shoulder bag and started rifling through it.

Rose stared at her brown suede boots instead of replying. An introvert with social anxiety, she never engaged. I had nothing against the girl, but she needed to grow a pair and learn to fight her battles. These guys knew it, too.

"Cat got your tongue?"

"Answer us when we speak to you," another demanded.

When Rose didn't reply, his friend dumped the bag's contents onto the ground.

"Don't you boys know better than to litter?" A new voice joined the group, shocking everyone in the hallway.

"Poppy." Rose sagged in relief at the sight of her cousin.

My mouth twitched. Fake Gucci's eyebrows rose with slight interest. Even the three entitled douchebags unapologetically bullying Rose reacted unfavorably. Poppy Ambani had that effect on people. It came with the morbid personality and the goth girl outfits. People feared it despite themselves.

Douchebag One recovered. "If it isn't Morticia."

His companions snickered at the most tired comparison Poppy had heard since starting college. Bullying had the opposite of the intended effect on Poppy. It revitalized her instead of swaying her away from her signature look. Today, she was in black leggings and an even darker sweater with decorative buttons along the side. Shiny black boots reached her knees with barely visible long socks underneath.

Expectedly, Poppy smirked. "Morticia? That's original. Did you come up with it yourself, or did someone help you?"

"You know what? Leave her." Douchebag One tilted his head at Rose. "Morticia is the one we need to teach a lesson for what they did to the Maxwells."

"What we did? Joe Maxwell took out an ad page to trash-talk my father," Rose said incredulously before remembering her fear and dropping her voice.

Rose was on the money. My ridiculous father, Joe Maxwell, took out a page in The New Yorker under the guise of advertisement. In reality, it was to trash-talk the Ambanis with insults and innuendos within the campaign. I wasn't allowed to say more. Lawsuit pending.

The men moved toward Poppy in unison. If they so much as touched one hair on that girl's head, their bodies would be found in the Hudson River tomorrow. Dropping my bag, I was about to sprint and tackle them to the ground when Poppy shocked everyone by addressing the forgotten member of the group.

"Kevin Thatcher, is it?" She asked Fake Gucci.

Fake Gucci glanced at his companions before frowning at Poppy. No one in the group addressed him unless they needed muscle. He nodded tentatively.

Poppy pulled out her phone and tapped on it a few times. "Found you." She typed something else and said, "Check your phone."

Perplexed, Kevin raised his phone to his face. He didn't bother opening it because whatever Poppy did must've come through as a notification. His head reeled back. "Whoa," he said, awestruck. "You Venmo'd me five hundred dollars?"

The other three douchebags exchanged looks, equally baffled.

"Consider it an advance payment," Poppy spoke indifferently.

"Payment for what?" he asked.

She tilted her head toward Douchebag One. "For punching him in the face."

"What the fuck?" Douchebag One's eyes bugged out, but the more shocking part was Kevin's reaction.

Taking four quick steps, Kevin reached Douchebag One and punched him so hard he went sprawling across the hallway.

Finally, the violence I had been waiting for.

Poppy did something else on her phone.

"One thousand dollars!" Kevin exclaimed, disbelieving eyes examining his phone screen.

Poppy glanced at Douchebag Two. Kevin needed no further instructions. After watching Douchebag One's fate, the second one panicked. "What the hell are you doing, Kevin?"

"Sorry, man. It's not personal. I need money for tuition."

"No, please, I have money, too," Douchebag Two pleaded.

Kevin shook his head. "Not like she does." A little-known fact, Ambanis and Maxwells were the wealthiest students on campus.

"But we're friends."

They weren't. Kevin was the token poor friend they kept around for street creds, muscle, and the occasional humiliation for their amusement. I knew their type, and I bet Kevin was sick of the typecast. The resentment came off him in waves. Kevin punched his "friend" twice, leaving him on the ground and unable to move. By the time he whirled around, the third one was shaking in his boots.

Poppy stood still, the perfect puppet master, as her minion did her bidding. Why did I doubt her? She probably took one look at Kevin and determined the same thing I had. To defeat a group, you need to find the weakest link. Kevin might be physically strong, but Poppy had sniffed out his weakness.

There was another possibility.

Poppy was the youngest person at our college, sharing a four-year age gap from the rest of the student population. For a long while, she kept herself at a distance. This was the first time Poppy had shown her fangs. Knowing she was petite and skinny at five feet, it was possible Poppy researched every student to give herself an edge. Kevin desired a better life, and his weakness was the douchebag friends holding him back.

Poppy sent another Venmo to Kevin, saving the best for last.

"Two thousand dollars," he gasped.

"You'll get another two thousand after finishing the job."

"What job?"

"Break his arm," Poppy instructed, utterly bored.

"No, please, please don't," Douchebag Three cried out, petrified. He glanced at the exit but knew Kevin would catch him before he made it. "I'm sorry. Please don't do this."

Kevin hesitated, and Rose pleaded with Poppy. "Stop it, Poppy. You can both get into a lot of trouble for this. They've learned their lesson. It's enough."

"I'll decide when it's enough," Poppy replied in a voice cool as a cucumber.

Rose should've known better than to try and dissuade Poppy. Where Rose was an insignificant Bambi, Poppy was the Bambi-killer.

"Break his arm," she repeated to Kevin. "My lawyer's on retainer. By the time he gets through, this will look like self-defense." She glanced at Douchebag Three pointedly. "And he'll be the one to get expelled for it."

Kevin needed no further encouragement. Douchebag Three ran for the exit, but Kevin moved at lightning speed. He caught Douchebag Three by the coat and yanked him back. Kevin grabbed his arm and held it between both of his.

"Stop," Poppy said just as Kevin went to snap it in half.

Like the perfect puppet, Kevin froze in place at his master's command.

"Leave him."

Kevin threw the boy on the floor without a second thought. Poppy stepped beside Kevin.

"Crawl," she ordered, pointing at the area where Douchebag Three had dumped Rose's things. "Pick up every item you threw on the floor. Stay on your knees until you're done, or Kevin will break your arm."

Douchebag Three half sobbed and half nodded, crawling toward the heap of items on the ground.

"Poppy, this is too much," Rose protested in a low voice, but a stern look from Poppy silenced her. No one dared to argue whenever she took charge. She was born to rule. *My little princess of darkness was turning into the queen of darkness.*

Douchebag Three handed the bag to Rose, apologizing in between sobs. No one asked him to apologize. Fear was more effective than what happened to his comrades, still incapacitated on the floor. Poppy knew it, too.

"Only I get to torture my family," Poppy interjected before Douchebag Three could crawl away with his tail tucked between his legs. "Make sure everyone on this campus knows that. Rose Ambani is strictly off-limits from now on. If anyone harasses her, I'll hold you personally responsible, and Kevin will come by to beat you up. I'm putting him on retainer."

Douchebag Three's lips wobbled. Not only did he fear for himself, but now he had to go out of his way to ensure Rose's safety.

I gazed upon the havoc Poppy wreaked. Douchebag Three was still on his knees, surrounded by his friends on the ground. Blood dripped from Kevin's fists. Rose appeared wretched about being surrounded by tattered bodies. Meanwhile, Poppy was undisturbed amidst the beautiful disaster as she paid Kevin his remaining balance. Like a phoenix rising from the ashes of her destruction, she was a surreal vision from a child's nightmare.

The image was seared into my brain, an indelible mark that would no doubt haunt me as she did. Even if there were a hundred men, Poppy would've found a way to defeat them without breaking a sweat and emerge unscathed. Her hardened features blended with the airy coolness she radiated, creating a combustible mixture. The regal face resembled a fierce goddess of war and the angel of death mixed in one.

I watched her, mesmerized, unable to put into words what she did to me. No matter how many times I saw her, she never failed to captivate me with how she carried herself. She was the most remarkable specimen I had laid my eyes on, and she had finally shown them what I saw every day.

The baddest, boldest bitch had made her presence known. She'd be running this place from now on because she was meant to rule.

Like a dark queen.

It was the reason I couldn't stop watching Poppy from the shadows, even though she hated me with every fiber of her being.

ACT I

The Feud

CHAPTER ONE

DAMON

"He's late," Uncle Henry decreed. "I know you were looking forward to this, but he's already rescheduled twice. Face it, Joe," he spoke haughtily, the irritation evident on his face. "Jay Ambani isn't interested in working with us."

My father, Joe Maxwell, leveled his twin brother confidently. "That's not true. Mr. Ambani knows a good opportunity when he sees one. This new interface will change everything." It was true. Our patented technology seamlessly managed client assets, a revolutionary find for hedge fund companies such as Ambani Corp. "He'll be here."

Uncle Henry shrugged back the cuff of his shirt and checked the time. "We have been waiting for almost forty-five minutes. I think it's time to be realistic and cut our losses."

"He'll be here," Dad repeated. He studied the lobby of the well-designed yacht, searching for an excuse for the lateness. Jay Ambani's assistant informed us he was conducting business from his boat while chartering it worldwide. The company's board had also flown out to join him for the week.

I mentally scoffed. Jay Ambani was too busy to meet us yet had the time to take an indefinite family vacation. It was a slap in the face. Our company exceeded Ambani Corp in valuation. They still didn't want to do business with us because our "breeding" was wrong. They were snobs, though impeccably polite about it.

"Everyone knows Jay Ambani doesn't take business meetings anymore," my uncle countered. "If our publicist wasn't friends with his wife, he wouldn't have taken this one, either."

My twin, Caledon, or Caden for short, exchanged a look with me. *Publicist?* Sure, Uncle Henry hired Jordan Banks for reputation management, though it was common knowledge they were romantically involved. Quite possibly engaged, but Henry didn't share his personal life with us.

A rigid man with a domineering personality, skin that was one shade too tan, and dyed black hair, no one would guess Uncle Henry was in his late forties. Dad was younger than Henry by a few minutes but was often mistaken for the older brother. The neglect in his health showed in his rounded body and deep-set eyes. This meeting was why his orbs were finally shining with the excitement of a younger man.

Dad met Jay Ambani through various social events and arranged this meeting with Jordan's help. This was the first time he had secured one-on-one time with the elusive mogul. "He wouldn't have invited us to Singapore just to stand us up."

Uncle Henry was unconvinced. "That's because he didn't think we'd make the trip. Ambani invited us to humor his wife. It's unlikely he'll personally attend."

Dad remained optimistic like a kid on Christmas morning. "He'll attend. I'm sure of it."

"Why is this so important to you?" My uncle raked a frustrated hand through his perfectly styled hair.

"It's an opportunity to work with the Ambanis. Everyone wants to be seen with them," Dad spoke as if the answer should be obvious.

"And what's the advantage of being seen with them?"

"How do you not get this?" Dad asked like a petulant child. "They're the real deal. They even socialize with royal families from Europe. Who doesn't want to be seen with royalty?"

My uncle threw me an exasperated look, silently begging for backup.

Uncle Henry and Dad were from agricultural backgrounds. They sold their farm to start a tech company, with Henry as the brains of the operation. Farm life hadn't prepared Dad for the shrewdness of the business world, and when the company's board noticed the inadequacies, Henry encouraged Dad to network for opportunities outside the office. It left Henry under tremendous pressure and wary about the future. His sons rebuffed any involvement past keeping up appearances at important meetings. My brother might as well be a mad scientist, focused on medicine from an early age. Henry placed all his eggs in one basket. Me.

I shared Henry's passion for the tech industry and created this algorithm to minimize the risk of investments by automatically weeding out opportunities likely to fail. The patent belonged to me, and it was ultimately my decision what to do with it. Uncle Henry wanted my father to retire so I could carry the torch as co-CEO. According to him, I possessed the temperament Dad could never master.

It wasn't Dad's fault. My cousins, brother, and I attended the best schools in the world, with etiquette shoved down our throats. Although Dad pined to be included in the inner circle of New York's high society, it was challenging. The crème de la crème of old money found Dad too crass and blunt for their taste. Mr. Ambani was the first to show my father kindness. Dad idolized him and became obsessed with joining his inner circle. To gain extensive face time with the Ambanis, Dad needed to strike an involved business deal. While I understood my uncle's position, Dad needed a win.

"This deal would benefit Ambani Corp more than us," I spoke with careful diplomacy. "It'd be stupid for Ambani to miss out on it."

"Exactly," Dad agreed with enthusiasm.

"Don't get your hopes up," Henry tsked, tapping his foot irritably on the couch. I suspected my uncle's cynicism stemmed from a personal desire to use the technology for himself. He pushed the idea of starting a hedge fund company with the technology, but I decided to back Dad's vision of integrating my algorithm with Ambani Corp's system. I owed my father a debt that might take me a lifetime to repay.

There were other reasons, too. Acquiring new clients was grueling, whereas an existing company such as Ambani Corp retained big names on their Rolodex. Our technology and their clients could make for an unstoppable duo. Jordan used the same logic to get Jay Ambani to take the meeting, though him rescheduling the meeting twice wasn't promising.

My creation landed us in this predicament. I wanted Dad to have a win, but he was unprepared. Business wasn't about a product; it was about building rapport. In preparation for this meeting, I researched Ambani Corp's clients, the board members, their spouses, and even their children. Instead of reviewing my notes, Dad was concerned with presenting us as a united front. The Ambanis were far more interested in etiquette, old money, and social standing, things Joe Maxwell wasn't known for. I worried Dad was in over his head.

Dad turned to me. "Have you talked to Jay Ambani's niece yet?"

Rosaline Ambani attended my university and constantly "bumped" into me until I realized one day that she did it on purpose. I withheld this detail about my unwanted admirer. Dad would start planning the wedding if he found out an Ambani girl liked me.

"Once or twice around campus."

"You should try harder. She's here with her family. Maybe you two can go off while the adults talk."

"It's Damon's algorithm. He needs to be in the meeting." Henry added in a mumbled breath, "If there is one."

"I'm sure it'll be okay if Damon skips the meeting."

I gritted my teeth at Dad's naivety.

First, it was my software, and I generously allowed Dad to exploit my hard work for his precious merger with the Ambanis. Dismissing me as if my presence in the meeting was optional grated on my nerves.

Second, Dad failed to recognize he was about to enter the lion's den. What were his plans if they asked him a question about the product that only I could answer?

Putting aside my resentment, I tried to help Dad. "Why don't we go over these notes while we wait?"

"I don't need—"

I spoke over Dad, cutting him off, "Jay Ambani, age fifty-two, happily married for fifteen years to Piya Ambani. They have a fourteen-year-old daughter, Poppy. Ambani loves nothing more than his daughter, so if you need a safe topic, compliment one of Poppy's accomplishments."

I read the long list of Poppy's achievements. Math Olympiad. Mensa. Graduated from high school at fourteen. Enrolling in my college for the fall semester. Since Poppy's birth, Ambani had championed his daughter to take over the company one day.

Just like me.

"If she is a math whiz like her father, then she is the perfect person to groom for CEO," I concluded.

"Like someone else we know," Caden snorted, alluding to me. "I wonder if she also has a big head."

I smirked. Apparently, I had more in common with a fourteen-year-old than anyone else in this room.

"Jay Ambani is widely known for being a family man, so always be respectful when addressing his wife."

I held up a photo of Jay and Piya. They appeared smitten with one another, just like my parents before Mom passed away. Correction. My mother, Cara Maxwell, didn't pass away; she killed herself. The weight of guilt sank in heavily at the thought.

Dad snatched the photo out of my hand.

"Holy shit, that's Piya Ambani?" Dad sputtered. "Look at the rack on her."

I pinched the bridge of my nose, imagining Jay Ambani's fist landing on Dad's jaw. There was no way Dad could pull off this meeting. He wasn't used to women exercising modesty. "That's an example of what *not* to say. They are rumored to have a strong marriage, so comments like that won't fly."

Henry scoffed. "Yeah, right."

All eyes landed on my uncle. "Something you want to share?"

"I overheard Jordan speaking to Piya on the phone."

I narrowed my eyes. If that wasn't an admission of his involvement with our publicist. "And?"

"It turns out that virtuous Mrs. Ambani was having an affair. She ended it recently and went back to her husband."

Dad's eyes widened. "What? That bitch. How can anyone cheat on Jay Ambani?"

I rolled my eyes. "Don't get carried away, Dad. It's just gossip."

"No, it's not," Henry retorted. "She told Jordan about rekindling an affair with some man she met at her brother's wedding. I looked up when her brother got married, and it conveniently lines up with Poppy Ambani's birth."

"What are you saying?" Dad asked in a stunned voice.

Henry shrugged. "That Mrs. Ambani had an affair for years behind her husband's back, and this," he pointed at a picture of Poppy, "isn't Jay Ambani's real daughter."

"Poppy Ambani is a bastard," Dad mused.

I held up two hands. "Whoa, hold up. Their personal lives are none of our business. And we need to be more careful before spreading nasty rumors about a little kid. Let's drop it."

Everyone simmered down, slightly embarrassed for getting carried away by gossip. I glimpsed at the incredibly happy couple in the photo. Mrs. Ambani, the devoted wife, gazed at her husband with adoration that couldn't be faked. No way was their marriage a sham.

I shelved the matter away when a petite brunette poked her head inside the waiting area and announced, "The board is ready for you."

CHAPTER TWO

POPPY

"Why are they here?" I asked in a low voice, my irritation rising.

"It's an important meeting, Poppy," Mom whispered. Papa was sleeping, and neither of us wanted to wake him. "Jay thinks the algorithm will set you up for the future."

For the future meant after Papa passed away, and I eventually took over the company. Mom avoided speaking the morbid truth as if pretending would make Papa's ALS go away. His mobility had decreased, while the headaches and lethargy had increased. Ultimately, patients with ALS were unable to move oxygen in and out of their lungs and passed away from respiratory failure. Judging from Mom's gloomy mood, she suspected the end was near. It only stirred my anger. We had limited time with him. Why were these people here to interrupt it?

"I don't understand why the board can't take care of the meeting. Why do they need to meet with Papa?"

"Because your father knows what he's doing," Mom explained patiently. "And he is perfectly capable of sitting through a meeting."

Lies. Mom didn't think Papa was up for the meeting, either. Doubt was etched on her face, but she rarely argued with him. They were nauseatingly in love and unconditionally supportive of one another. People often said my parents were soul mates. I presumed it was gut-wrenching to lose the love of your life and tracked her tear-stricken face. She cried in the bathroom again with the shower on to muffle her sobs. Papa's looming death would destroy my mother. His last wish was for an extended family vacation sailing to his favorite cities on our yacht. We docked in Singapore to meet with the board of Ambani Corp. They knew of the situation and were here to straighten things out before Charles Jamieson took over as the interim CEO.

No one was allowed to become CEO unless they bore the last name Ambani. The board agreed to Charles Jamieson with the expectation I'd take over in the future. It was blasphemous to eye the CEO position at fourteen, but Papa and I shared the same dream. Fifty-five-year-old Charles would be the acting CEO for ten years, giving me enough time to finish college and gain work experience. He'd hand me the reins when his contract expired and retire to Bordeaux with his wife. There were some loose ends, including a meeting with Maxwell Corp about their revolutionary software.

Papa stirred from our voices. The bed was tucked in one corner, draped in soft luxury fabrics. Mom arranged the furniture to make the most of the room. Two nightstands, a closet built into the wall, a small sofa placed at one end of the room, and a writing desk at the other, complete with the smell of the ocean wafting in through the attached terrace. The bedroom walls were painted blue, and a modern light fixture hung from the ceiling. The muted lighting and comfortable duvet made the room enticing for sleep. Mom designed it for comfort so Papa would be less inclined to work.

Papa cracked one eye open and caught us standing next to the bed.

"What's going on?" His voice was reduced to a scruff and unrecognizable in the shaky way he spoke nowadays. Most people didn't understand him anymore, so he made a point not to speak at meetings, further proving my point.

"You shouldn't attend the meeting today," I said directly. "Mom can attend for you." After Papa took a turn for the worse, Mom attended meetings as his proxy. She wore an earpiece so Papa could hear and whisper notes to her.

"They came all this way to meet me." His voice was a hoarse, raspy whisper. The simple act of inhaling and exhaling was labored.

"Who cares?" I muttered.

They were intruding on his limited time, but Papa was adamant. "Jordan set up this meeting months ago, and I canceled twice. It'll be disrespectful not to meet them."

Mom sat on the bed. "Poppy, can you check on your cousins?" she asked me. It was code for *give us a minute*.

I stepped onto the terrace, which connected to the rest of the boat. However, I didn't veer far and watched them through the slightly ajar door.

"You should let me go as your proxy," Mom said soothingly. "I've done it before."

"I can do it," Papa argued. He was stubborn to a fault. "Can you help me up?"

My frustration increased as wheezing followed his next breath. Mom moved quickly, grabbing the oxygen mask and pulling it over his face. Papa turned pale, face contorted in pain. I stood there, helpless, like an idiot, because I had no idea what to do. Mom had been a pro during these moments. She was attentive, lulling him back to the pillow with a gentle but firm stance. Papa refused to concede despite another bout of wheezing.

When he gasped for air again, he finally relented, giving Mom detailed instructions on what he wanted out of the deal. I took notes on my phone from outside in case Mom missed anything. When he finished, Papa leaned against the pillow and tested the earpiece. His laptop sat readily on the nightstand for easy reference to guide her through the meeting.

Mom pulled a blanket over him and turned on *Friends* with the volume on low before leaving the room. "Ready?" she asked upon finding me on the terrace.

I shrugged and followed her to the other side of the boat. The conference room on the yacht was immaculate. The long rectangular table in the middle was set for fourteen people, with eight water bottles on one side to identify seats for the board members of Ambani Corp and six on the other for Maxwell Corp.

I sat in the chairs against the wall with my cousins, Rose, Samar, Rayyan, and Nikhil Jr., Nick for short. My cousins and I were allowed to attend business meetings as junior interns for the company. We took notes and ran errands like fetching water or office supplies. It allowed us access to the ins and outs of our operations. I considered it a privilege because I planned to sit in Papa's chair one day. Meanwhile, my cousins thought it was forced labor.

One by one, my aunts and uncles filled the room and took their respective seats at the table. Folders were passed with the details of today's meeting, and my aunt, Sonia, laid out the agenda. Everyone listened attentively and took notes, myself included.

The only distractions were my cousins, who were more interested in horseplay. They pinched each other discreetly to get the others to squeal and get in trouble with the adults.

"Do it and lose the hand," I said mildly when Rayyan tried to pinch me.

"Relax, Pops." He retracted. Rayyan was older, graduating soon from college, but acted like a child. "It's just a dumb meeting."

"Which is why you'll never sit in *that* chair." I nodded at the seat, slightly larger than the rest. It was Papa's chair, currently occupied by Mom.

Rayyan ground his molars. He was also gunning for the coveted position, but Papa made sure I was first in the line of succession. Rayyan flipped his notepad open.

I listened carefully as my aunt spoke, taking meticulous notes about the software created by Damon Maxwell. I suddenly understood why Papa thought this meeting was necessary. If we locked down this partnership, we'd be the first hedge fund company to pioneer Damon Maxwell's algorithm. There'd be no more concerns about cash flow, further solidifying my future with this company.

Otherwise, Maxwell Corp could edge us out by keeping this technology to themselves. However, they would have to acquire a large client base, so it was mutually beneficial to merge with us instead. It would make a great partnership, though concerns were raised about Joe Maxwell. He was the co-CEO along with Henry Maxwell, my aunt Jordan's fiancé. Where Henry was collected, Joe was erratic, and taking on a volatile partner was a huge risk.

"Angela," my aunt called after we wrapped up.

"Yes?" Papa's assistant poked her face into the conference room.

"Send them in, please."

The double doors opened within minutes, and a horde of men entered the room. I stalked everyone online before this meeting to familiarize myself and matched each face to their social media profiles.

Henry and Joe Maxwell entered first with Henry's sons, Alexander and Jasper. They were followed by Joe's twin sons, Caledon and Damon Maxwell.

Twins might've stepped inside the room, but I immediately identified Damon. His dirty blond hair was slightly longer and messier than Caledon's. He commanded my attention, along with Rose's.

"Damon's here."

My eyes narrowed at Rose's small outburst. My impossibly shy eighteen-year-old cousin rarely spoke in the presence of others. It also didn't escape my attention that Rose's pupils were blown at the sight of Damon. Interesting.

"You know him?" I asked her.

Rose ducked her head. "Just a little," she mumbled. "From around campus."

I watched her quietly, then cut my glance back to Damon. My neck strained to catch his whole frame. A crisp white shirt hugged his torso, pairing well with chinos. The versatile outfit was carefully selected to transition between a business appointment and a casual yacht day in case the meeting occurred on the deck. Smart and prepared.

Broad shoulders and a solid-set jaw emanating dominance made it impossible to believe he was only twenty-one. I would have pegged Damon for the role if I didn't know Henry and Joe Maxwell to be the co-CEOs. Perhaps the enigma came from years of priming as the future of Maxwell Corp. Neither his cousins nor his brother were interested in taking over, so Damon had been groomed for the role from an early age.

Just like me.

Damon was in college but spent every waking moment shadowing his uncle to remain relative in the company's collective culture. People responded to consistency. He'd be a shoo-in to replace his father without anyone crediting it to nepotism. After all, his natural presence dwarfed his father's, who had skipped into the room as if searching for a novelty item rather than attending a business meeting.

The eight board members of Ambani Corp stood on cue to serve as the welcoming committee. This board shared a rhythm, instinctively knowing who'd speak first. One day, I'd share this chemistry with them.

My aunt, Shital, did the greeting. Shital Ambani was the epitome of poise, tall and slim, with her hair pulled back in a tight bun. Her voice was velvet as she welcomed the Maxwells. "Hello, Mr. Maxwell and Mr. Maxwell." She smiled stiffly at both Henry and Joe. "Thank you for coming all this way to meet us. How are you today?"

Joe Maxwell stopped in his tracks instead of acknowledging Shital. His gaze flickered as if searching for a rare jewel. The initial excitement in his eyes dimmed upon scanning each face on the other side of the conference table.

"Where is Mr. Ambani?" he asked briskly.

Some of my uncles snickered at the question while others exchanged perplexed looks. Henry Maxwell frowned, and Damon's face showed a hint of irritation. Their reactions were valid. Everyone meeting with this board had the good sense to research the members or at least learn their names. You should never enter a lion's den unless fully prepared. We were a family business, and our board only consisted of individuals with the last name Ambani. Five men were on the board, including Papa. All were referred to as Mr. Ambani.

Joe raised his eyebrows. "Did I say something funny?"

"They are all Mr. Ambani," Henry hissed at Joe.

No one else pointed out Joe's faux pas. The proper etiquette for conducting ourselves at work had been drilled into us since birth. Everyone in this room would rise above it instead of dwelling on being slighted.

One of my uncles, Yash, elaborated on Henry's comment, "Half the people at this table are referred to as Mr. Ambani. I'm Yash Ambani. A pleasure to meet you."

"And I'm Yash's brother, Nikhil Ambani, but please, feel free to call me Nick."

My aunt, Shital, was next and opened her mouth to introduce herself.

Joe Maxwell swiftly cut her off. "I don't need the whole assembly lineup."

Everything came to a screeching halt at Mr. Maxwell's sharp tone. The temperature in the room dropped by several degrees. Taken aback by the rudeness, the mood in the room soured.

Shital seemed mortified. "E-excuse me?"

"I was talking about Jay Ambani," the man replied crudely instead of apologizing for his outburst. "Will *that* Mr. Ambani be joining us?" he snapped, doubling down on his poor manners.

What an asshole.

Joe Maxwell interrupted our family time, the limited amount we had left with Papa, demanding an audience, yet he didn't do his homework or bother to learn our names. Although this board never did a round of introductions before, they extended an olive branch. Instead of taking it, he dared to insult them. The board members took the initiative to learn about him and his rotten family. It was evident Joe didn't know how to conduct himself professionally. The concerns voiced before this meeting were correct. The man was brash, disrespectful, and unprofessional.

Sonia straightened. She was a larger woman with broad shoulders and thick glasses perched atop her nose. I could tell she wasn't impressed, but she repressed her disdain with a plastic smile. "I'm afraid my cousin is unable to join us." She gestured to the setup across from her. "If you would kindly take a seat, we can start—"

"Unable to join us?" Joe Maxwell bellowed, extracting a couple of gasps from the room.

"Shh," Henry hushed Joe out of the corner of his mouth. Henry's sons exchanged a peeved look while Caledon appeared bored.

Damon attempted to de-escalate the situation. "Why don't we do the demo? I'm sure the board can catch Mr. Ambani up."

"The demo won't make sense if it has to be explained," Joe snapped.

Mom took charge of the situation. The inconspicuous way she brought her fingertips to her ear indicated Papa was speaking to her. As she seldom contributed during these meetings, her voice commanded attention on the rare occasions she used it. "Mr. Maxwell, I must apologize for the change of plans. My husband is feeling a little under the weather, but he sent me in his place—"

"I'm not discussing this with you." Joe's face twisted as if Mom were an annoying pest.

The plastered smile on Mom's face didn't waver. "With all due respect, you don't have to speak at all." She tilted her head toward Damon Maxwell. "Given it's Damon's product that we want to discuss."

The slightest hint of a smile grazed Damon's lips at Mom's boldness. I was also impressed by how she handled Joe, ears perking curiously to hear Damon's pitch. Considered a tech genius, Damon had already invented numerous algorithms and improved old software. I was impressed by his remarkable accomplishments. Generally, I preferred to sail under the radar. For once, I wanted someone's attention and willed Damon to look at me. I wanted to study his expressions.

Damon never looked my way or gave me a second thought.

"What do you say, young man?" Mom addressed Damon directly. "My husband tells me you're a rising star. I can't wait to see this groundbreaking algorithm. Would you like to show it to us?"

One nod from Mom, and I was on my feet. I stood beside the laptop I had set up earlier and straightened the projector. Presumably, Damon brought a USB drive for the demonstration.

"Of course." Damon didn't hesitate, wisely bypassing Joe and redirecting us to safer grounds.

Joe Maxwell didn't take kindly to being dismissed, given that he organized this meeting. He placed a hand on Damon's shoulder. "My son's not showing you anything unless we receive an explanation why Mr. Ambani dragged us to Singapore only to stand us up."

It was subtle, but I caught Damon's irritation at his father's antics.

Mom remained unruffled by Joe's hostility. "As I explained, Mr. Maxwell, my husband's health took an unexpected turn."

"We hopped two continents to meet him on this yacht, and you're telling me that he is so sick he can't take five steps out of his bedroom?"

My cousins exchanged looks, the same ones my aunts and uncles shared.

"Jay didn't intentionally fall ill to offend you, and I assure you that I'm perfectly capable of speaking on his behalf. I can help you—"

"You aren't the CEO," he spat. "You can't fucking help me, but I'm sure you know how to fuck."

The profanity elicited another gasp from around the room. In the face of utter catastrophe, Joe Maxwell unraveled.

He turned to the board, voice filled with malice. "Did you all know your fearless leader's wife has been stepping out on him for years?" He pointed a finger at me. "That's not even Ambani's real daughter." The blood drained from Joe's face as soon as the words were out of his mouth. Regret and mortification were etched in his expressions, but it was too late.

Tension crackled in the room as Henry stood frozen in shock. His sons averted their eyes, suddenly interested in something on the ground. Caledon rolled his eyes, though Mom remained unfazed. Damon's attention was finally on me. His gaze bore into me, calculating my reaction.

It took a monumental effort to keep my expression neutral and the churning nausea at bay. Joe's accusations could ruin everything I worked so hard to maintain.

It was possible Joe was disappointed by Papa's absence and, in an emotional state, made a baseless accusation about Mom. But how could he have known that Jay Ambani wasn't my biological father? My parents worked tirelessly to keep my lineage a secret. I wouldn't be allowed to take over for Papa otherwise. Joe's accusation hit too close to home to be a coincidence.

Thankfully, my parents were the pillars of the perfect marriage. No one believed Joe's accusations. Yash and Shital quickly defended my mother, their faces flushed with anger.

"How dare you?" Yash was the first to speak.

"Do you have any idea who you're speaking to?" Shital joined in. "This is Jay Ambani's wife."

"You harass us for a meeting, then insult our family," Nick chimed in. "You even bad-mouthed a child. Have you no shame?"

Watching the perfectly poised individuals turn against him solidified to Joe that he had screwed up monumentally. "I-I, I didn't mean to say that," he stammered.

Mom leveled Joe, refusing to falter at her debasement in front of her in-laws. "Mr. Maxwell, I have to conclude this meeting now," she said icily. "My husband would never work with someone who insulted our daughter. You would have known that had you bothered doing your homework. Goodbye." With her back ramrod straight and head held high, Mom exited the conference room with as much class as the situation allowed.

Joe followed Mom in a last-ditch effort to salvage the situation. "Wait, Mrs. Ambani, please. I didn't mean it."

Henry had the good sense to stop him. The board was rattled and followed Mom out of the room.

"Angela!" Dev shouted. "Call security."

It wasn't until Mom was almost out of sight that I noticed the subtle way she touched her right ear before taking off on quick feet.

Shit. Papa overheard Joe's vile accusations.

One person stayed behind in the conference room. Our eyes locked as Damon watched me with apprehension, pity, or both. Perhaps he expected me to react more dramatically and didn't know what to make of it when I didn't. The juxtaposition of his calm clashed with his father's recklessness.

"Listen, kid," he started as I rushed out of the room.

Security arrived by the time I exited the conference room. Chaos ensued because Joe refused to leave, demanding another audience with Mom. Getting past the crowd was impossible. When I made it through and returned to Papa's room, he was propped against the headboard. He fell asleep watching *Friends* in a seated position, head leaning back on a pillow. I was relieved to find Mom next to him. It seemed she came to check on him and dozed off with her head pressed against his shoulder in a similarly seated position. By the looks of it, they were fine, and Papa didn't believe Joe's lies about Mom's affair.

As if Papa's health wasn't bad enough, there was now the added stress of his wife being humiliated in front of everyone. I wanted to comfort him, but this was an area I severely lacked. In the end, I went with a small gesture. I climbed onto the bed to sit beside him and rested my head against his other shoulder.

When I woke next, Papa had passed away in his sleep, and there was only one thing I remembered from the worst day of my life. Papa claimed his greatest achievement was his two favorite girls, his wife and daughter. The last words my father heard before passing away were the Maxwells redacting the credibility of both.

CHAPTER THREE

DAMON

"Leave it alone, Dad. Haven't we done enough?"

"Leave it alone? This is our opportunity to make things right," Dad refuted, his tone firm and resolute.

I scoffed. "They can't stand us, and I don't exactly blame them."

It was ironic how quickly life could change. A few weeks ago, Jay Ambani was on my shit list for being an elitist snob who couldn't be bothered with a measly meeting. I felt nothing but remorse since the news broke about his untimely death. The latest gossip suggested he organized a family trip after receiving a fatal diagnosis. Not only did we interrupt their precious time with the demand of a meeting, but we also ruined it by hurling insults at his wife and questioning his daughter's parentage. Talk about pouring salt on a wound.

Dad sent flowers and fruit baskets to the family members as if that would salvage the blow we delivered. To his dismay, the goods were returned. The Ambanis sent a clear message: they weren't interested in mending this rift. Dad should put this to bed, except he wasn't dissuadable.

"They'll come around after we pay our respects." Dad fiddled with his tie in front of the mirror, perfecting the Windsor knot. He stood determined in his funeral attire, a black suit with a crisp white shirt, adamant he could fix things by being proactive with fruit baskets. The expectation couldn't be further from reality.

Jay Ambani was recently cremated, but I was unsure if his ashes were scattered. Everything until this point had been kept private. The family felt obliged to organize a public wake in Chicago, allowing their vast network to pay their respects. Despite the open-door policy, it was safe to say they didn't want my father in attendance. Unfortunately, Dad didn't know how to take a hint. Given how we left things with them, Dad attending Jay Ambani's funeral was cringeworthy. I practically followed him to Chicago, hoping he'd give up this pursuit. As the clock ticked forward, it became painfully apparent he had no such intention. Dad was incapable of following social norms or leaving things alone. He was adamant about showing up with more gift baskets and flowers.

Kill me, kill me now.

Falling flat on my back on Dad's king-size bed, I exasperatedly stared at the hotel room ceiling. "Don't do this, Dad. They don't want you there."

Dad grunted dismissively. "It's all about timing, Son. Jay Ambani wasn't the only way to get your foot in the door with these folks. It'll start a new era when they see we are willing to put aside our pride to help them through this difficult time. Who knows? They might let go of this silly feud and consider the previous proposition we discussed."

I wanted to scream, 'No, they won't,' but I already knew arguing with Joe Maxwell was futile. Instead, I pushed myself off the bed and followed Dad as he opened the door to the hallway. There was no way I was letting him go to the funeral alone. After what happened at that meeting, I didn't plan on stepping foot inside the Ambani home, but I could at least stay by the car if Dad pulled any stupid stunts.

I clicked the fob for the rental car and unlocked the vibrant red Lamborghini parked outside the hotel. According to Dad, the sleek model was the perfect rental for our two-day visit to Chicago. In reality, he liked it because it was flashy, even though the flashiest thing we had done thus far was drive to the store for more fruit baskets.

I started the ignition as Dad settled into the passenger seat. I couldn't help muttering, "Remember to keep your cool. Repeat what you'll say if someone asks why you're there."

"I'll say I'm here to drop these off." He pointed a thumb at the back of the car. Earlier, I watched Dad play Tetris to fit all the flowers and baskets in the back seat.

"And?" I pressed.

Dad rolled his eyes and spouted the rehearsed response. "And to pay my respects."

Pushing him to recite the "keep your cool" mantra seemed ridiculous. I might be mature for my age, but he was still my father. He should be teaching me life lessons about rising above it, not the other way around.

"Remember, if they get agitated, leave. Don't say anything stupid, okay?"

Dad waved a dismissive hand. "You're just like your mother. She used to worry too much."

That's because you talk too much, I wanted to shout. Bringing Mom up in this inopportune time did nothing except sour my mood.

After Dad's rapid rise to success, Mom found herself in a glamorous world she didn't fit into. She often missed the simplicity of farm life, and her only joy came from her sons. But we got sidetracked by the attention we received in high school for our achievements in science and technology. Girls threw themselves at us even though we were only fourteen. Our extracurriculars were extensive. Suddenly, numerous invites to the headmaster's inner circle, interviews for magazine articles, and fancy dinners were thrown in our honor. Those things gave Mom crippling anxiety, but she attended to be supportive. The academic society judged her for her 'farm' accent, not having a higher education, her taste in clothes, and even her vocabulary. She had no friends, only frenemies, the mean Moms of other overachieving students. They taunted her passive-aggressively for being different. Mom turned to prescription drugs to cope, eventually overdosing.

No one knew of her struggles because Mom never burdened us with her problems. She used to beg Caden and me to stay home for dinner or to spend time with her, but we always had something more important on the schedule. We were selfish pricks. We should've spent time with our mother instead of dragging her into our world where she didn't fit in. Whenever I thought about it, I gave Dad free rein to do as he pleased. After all, we were the reason he lost his wife. I owed him.

Dad knew how Caden and I felt and had no problem exploiting our guilt.

I swerved onto the empty street, determined to get through this ordeal while keeping a watchful eye on my impulsive father. We booked a hotel five minutes from the Ambani residence, but I drove slowly to prolong the inevitable.

"Everything will be fine," Dad insisted while I shook my head.

We were met with bumper-to-bumper traffic once we reached the long driveway to Ambani's giant mansion. Hundreds of cars flooded onto the property, and though the house sat on numerous acres, parking was limited.

I wasn't bothered by it. The guest count gave me solace because Dad might be able to blend into the crowd without attracting attention.

"Remember our conversation," I spoke absentmindedly while searching for a parking spot.

Once more, Dad promised to be on his best behavior. He'd drop off the gifts, pay his respects, and leave without making a scene. If it were anyone but Joe Maxwell, I'd believe it to be a doable task.

Since most of the guests had parked along the long driveway, and the valet service was bombarded by the excess cars, I had to pull up closer to the house and create a makeshift parking spot.

Whatever. We weren't planning on staying long, and I was in clear view of the wake to keep an eye on Dad.

The entrance to the wake was marked by two large shepherd's hooks with white twills and lilies hanging off them. It was a simple yet elegant way of directing the hushed guests to the gardens. There was a welcome table displaying photos of Jay Ambani with his family and a small guestbook. White banquet tables with modest centerpieces and garden chairs were spread across the lawn. Servers in black vests walked around with hors d'oeuvres and drinks. White roses made their sporadic presence known. It was an elaborate affair, yet the Ambanis' trained event planners made it appear effortlessly tasteful and appropriately somber for the sad occasion.

With his arms weighed down by gift baskets, Dad made his way to the lawn and disbursed into the crowd. Hopefully, he'd speak to one of the more forgiving Ambanis, share his condolences, and leave without making a peep. I leaned against the rental car and watched more guests trickle onto the lawn. They made consecutive lines to pay their respects to each family member. The Ambanis were easy to spot as they were dressed in white today.

The crowd parted, leaving an unmistakable loner in the middle. Poppy Ambani's petite frame was dwarfed by the grieving adults surrounding her. She was dressed in white, a long tunic of sorts with leggings. Her hair was spun over her head, and her face was fresh with no makeup. She looked like an entirely different person, all except the brown eyes.

I remembered watching those eyes when Dad practically called her a bastard in front of her relatives. It made me wish I had never created the stupid algorithm or let Dad use the product to further his gains. I must've replayed the moment a thousand times in my head, thinking of a million different scenarios where I comforted the kid instead of letting her run away. I kept expecting her to break down in tears after Dad's horrid accusations, but there was no emotion in her eyes. Blank. Those eyes were still wide and inexpressive, except there was now a hint of sorrow Poppy couldn't hide.

Did I cause that? Was it the aftereffect of my father's ambitions, which I backed with my stupid algorithm?

The pit of guilt harboring inside me returned like a storm. Poppy was the same age as me when I lost Mom. If the situation were reversed, I would hate the people who humiliated my dying mother. I didn't want to be the cause of that kid's sadness. The same helplessness I felt at Mom's funeral ate at me because there was nothing I could do to take Poppy's pain away.

I stared at her momentarily, then moved closer. I promised myself I was merely here as Dad's chauffeur to keep him in check. Instead of entering the manicured garden, I sought refuge under a large tree. I watched Jay Ambani's daughter from the shadows, surveying how she grieved her late father.

Poppy stood on her own like a statue, a dignified face of solemn beauty as she stared into nothingness. Occasionally, people came up to speak to her. She accepted their condolences with her back rod straight. She didn't shed one measly tear. There were no expressions on her face, nor was she entertaining herself with her phone or chit-chatting with others.

I watched as Piya Ambani walked to Poppy. Red eyes brimming with tears, Mrs. Ambani leaned over and hugged Poppy tightly, her face pressed into the young girl's hair. I could tell she wanted to comfort her daughter, but it was impossible to do so with someone as frugal with their feelings as Poppy. Poppy stood motionless in her mother's embrace until Piya released her. Then, she walked away, her footsteps inaudible from this distance.

I watched Poppy go, my heart squeezing because I knew the feeling. She was drowning in sorrow but didn't know how to express it. It was lonely.

I didn't know what to make of Poppy. It wasn't like she was so scarred she'd do something stupid like Mom, right? Other kids dealt with losing a parent, albeit it wasn't as dramatic as what happened to Poppy or specifically what *we* did to Poppy.

The pit in my stomach grew, and I followed her, keeping a respectful distance as she walked along the back of the house. An equally manicured garden rested on the other side of their mansion, though this one lacked guests. Poppy stood in a pool of light, the air heavy with grief and loss. She looked up, taking a deep breath of the crisp, fresh air.

Why was she grieving alone instead of with her family? Was it because she was too numb to share her sorrow with others?

Or perhaps it was because she was the future face of Ambani Corp and had to maintain a façade? I also acted a certain way in public, knowing what my future held. In the oddest way, Poppy and I shared a commonality no one else could understand.

There was an urge to reach out and comfort her. With her back to me, Poppy had no idea I was there. I still wanted her to know she wasn't alone in this. Unthinking, I took a few steps forward. Small twigs crunched under my feet, snapping Poppy out of her reverie. She twisted her neck to the side, but I took cover behind a tree. I was positive Poppy heard me. The moment stood still as I waited for her reaction. When it didn't come, I peeked between the branches and realized Poppy had returned to her former stance.

Odd.

Despite ascertaining she was no longer alone, Poppy didn't demand to know who was there. A stranger intruded on her space and private time to mourn, yet she didn't seem perturbed or ask them/me to leave.

Not that I could force myself to leave. The look on her face, the heavy pain with no outlet, was the same one I felt when Mom died. It was worse for Poppy since she didn't know how to verbalize her emotions or accept kindness. So, I remained behind the tree, allowing her this moment of privacy while being there for her non-verbally. She wasn't alone, and that was all I could do for her.

We stayed this way for God knows how long. The sun was dipping by the time Poppy turned my way. Safely tucked behind the tree, I rounded it when she passed by.

Poppy paused a few feet away from the tree. With her neck slightly bent, she whispered in a voice clear as day, "Thank you."

Poppy was already walking away by the time I processed the words. *Thank you.*

She knew I was there but allowed me to stay anyway. Why? Perhaps she didn't want to be alone but didn't know how to accept public sympathy. Maybe the only way she could grieve was through silent support.

I couldn't drag my eyes away from her retreating figure. There were many things I wanted to say in return. As I watched her go, I realized it was better this way. Poppy couldn't confront the feelings inside her, but the comfort provided by a stranger on the worst day of her life made the day tolerable.

When Mom was alive, I did nothing to save her. I was a selfish teenager wrapped up in my world. Even after Mom's death, I never contributed to her cause. I made algorithms and advanced my career, but nothing to improve my humanity. But today, I made a difference. I gave someone a tiny ray of comfort instead of pain.

A euphoric feeling grabbed me in a chokehold. It was far more enticing than the usual bullshit I did by drowning in work. Who knew comforting someone else could be exhilarating, especially someone who wasn't easily susceptible to emotion? I brought Poppy a moment of peace. Though it might seem minuscule to others, it was the victory of a lifetime to me. All I had done was stand in the shadows, yet it was everything we were both searching for.

She felt like my purpose, and by God, I wanted to feel it again. I wanted to be helpful to Poppy again to make this shithole life a little better for both of us. I followed Poppy back to the wake but stopped upon hearing a commotion.

"Haven't you done enough?" A small herd led by Nick Ambani surrounded Dad, their seething eyes tearing him apart.

"I'm here despite what you said to me last time. It's a gesture of good faith. Doesn't that count for something?" Dad asked plainly, trying to ignore the audience they were attracting.

Poppy also paused midway.

Shit. I couldn't let this be her lasting impression at her father's funeral.

I sped up to get to Dad before he created more of a scene. It was impossible to get through the crowd. Hushed murmurs broke out around me, catching me up with the drama. From what I gathered, one of the Ambanis located Dad in the mix and expressed his discontent. Dad initially said he was there to express his condolences, which quickly turned into snide remarks when the Ambanis didn't receive him with open arms.

"You can't be serious. This is my cousin's funeral, Mr. Maxwell, and we don't want you here. Please leave."

"I'm merely trying to fix the situation, Mr. Ambani. There is no need to insult me when all I have done is try to be nice. Have you seen the fruit baskets I brought?"

Nick huffed. "You think a few fruit baskets will fix how you spoke to my cousin's wife?"

"Well, I wasn't exactly wrong about her," Dad snapped, triggered by the jab about his precious fruit baskets.

Poppy's head reeled back from the remark. From a distance, I watched Piya Ambani stiffen as well.

Un-fucking-believable.

Dad didn't handle rejection well or have a filter when scorned. Due to his shortcomings, he made things worse. Instead of mending the rift, he might have sunk the ship by dredging up the worst possible topic. Things might still be salvageable if I could remove him from the grounds. I sifted through the crowd to get to him, only I was too late.

Nick Ambani had steam coming out of his ears. "Security!" he yelled. "Where the hell are the security guards? Get this man off our property."

Before I could reach him, a security guard emerged from the crowd and grabbed Dad's arm to escort him out.

"Get off me!" Dad shouted, trying to tug his arm away. "I'm an important man to have in your corner, Mr. Ambani. I promise you. This will not end well for you."

"Are you threatening me?"

"My God, these people are uncivilized," I heard the murmurs of judgmental guests. Eyes bored into us as I reached Dad and yanked him out of the security guards' hold.

Nick Ambani's eyes glossed over me before returning to Dad. "Leave," he ordered.

The security guards advanced on us. I held up a hand. "There is no need for that," I cautioned them coolly. "We are leaving."

I didn't give them the chance to exchange more words. Grabbing Dad by the arm, I tugged him behind, walking at intense speed toward the car before a fistfight could erupt.

My eyes paused on those big, inexpressive brown eyes amid the crowd. The momentary euphoria I found and the peace Poppy experienced was gone. It was replaced with the hatred brought on by our families.

Her accusatory glare bored into us. Dad had done the unforgivable. After wrecking her father's last moments on earth, he ruined her father's memorial.

Poppy would never forgive us, and I wondered if we'd ever feel that moment of peace again, the one we experienced while neither of our families was looking.

CHAPTER FOUR
DAMON

Tragedy struck young Poppy's life once more, a mere sixty-five days after her father's funeral.

Maya Ambani, Poppy's grandmother, passed away. Poppy harbored immense respect for the old lady. Upon hearing the news, she flew to India, where the late Mrs. Ambani resided.

It turned out I was addicted to being a part of Poppy's worst days in life. I took the next flight to Mumbai before I could call on my rational senses.

I was known to be reasonable and mature. After the quasi-run-in with Poppy at her father's funeral, I championed several drug and suicide prevention programs. People skewed reality to make it fit their romanticized version. To them, I overcame the loss of my mother and created something meaningful out of it. An influx of grateful families dubbed me wise beyond my years and a savior of lost souls. Dad became a Stage Mom, and Jordan was tasked with capitalizing on the momentum. After the embarrassing incident at Jay Ambani's funeral, Dad became obsessed with being affluent so no one could make him feel small again.

Suddenly, I was the face of suicide prevention campaigns. I couldn't save my mother, yet I walked around like I had the answer. I hated it.

I could've fought Dad for exploiting his wife's death, but my guilt trumped the loathing. It was hard not to pity Dad. The Ambani's badmouthed us to their vast network, burying his ambitions six feet under. Nothing made him particularly important except for his sons' fame, so I let him pimp out my cause. The occasional article turned into the norm, and I became the press' flavor of the week.

Poppy didn't regard me as some jewel of the crown, though. I was the guy who fucked up the crucial moments of her life. Attending another Ambani funeral was a terrible idea after what went down at her father's wake. So, why was I trolling the posh neighborhood of Colaba in Mumbai?

I couldn't shake her haunted look at her father's funeral. It made me wonder whether she'd do something rash on days she felt the most alone. I couldn't save Mom, but I could ensure Poppy didn't go down the same rabbit hole. A selfish part of me also hoped to recreate another peaceful moment for her, one that felt euphoric to share.

Poppy's grief seemed to be my calling. Her life had turned morbid. The familiarity with grief and macabre had no place in a fourteen-year-old's life. She should enjoy being a spoiled heiress, spending her parents' money with a credit card she didn't earn or stuffing her room with pink decorations.

Instead, Poppy was once more accepting condolences, and I hoped to steal a glance through the wrought iron bar gates that stretched toward the sky.

I stood across the street from the late Mrs. Ambani's residence. Luckily, Colaba was a touristy neighborhood in a cosmopolitan city, and a healthy mix of foreigners were invited to Maya Ambani's funeral. My presence didn't stand out. Decked in white to keep with tradition, I added sunglasses as an extra layer of protective armor. When another horde of guests filtered through the gates, I followed them inside.

I discreetly searched for Poppy around the lavish property. After combing through every room inside and walking around the exterior twice, I found the stream at the back of the house. As predicted, Poppy was alone by the water. Being jet lagged from the long journey made her seem like a mirage dressed in all white. I wanted to tell her there was more to life than sadness. Drill it into her brain so she wouldn't make a hasty decision. As the blazing sun settled over her hair, I approached her quietly. When the muscles on the back of her neck tensed, I crouched behind the trimmed bushes.

She heard me.

Like clockwork, Poppy made no demands on her intruder and returned to her trance, looking out onto the water. It took all my willpower not to go to her and comfort her. History repeated itself as we remained dormant while she grieved. When dusk settled, I watched her walk away.

The walk back to the hotel was unmemorable. Poppy's haunted eyes plagued my thoughts that she wasn't strong enough to handle all this grief at once. This was none of my business. Not to mention, the situation with the Ambanis had further escalated after high society boycotted Dad. It fueled Uncle Henry's ambitions. He used my program to start a competing hedge fund company. It was sucking Ambani Corp dry, just as we predicted. Things were about to get worse, so I needed to stay away from the Ambani girl.

I didn't keep the promise.

Last month, Charles Jamieson, the interim CEO of Ambani Corp, passed away from a sudden heart attack. Not only had Poppy lost her father and grandmother, but after Charles' death, her future as the CEO of Ambani Corp was also in jeopardy. Everything she loved and worked for was gone.

Unable to help it, I followed Poppy to the funeral. After confirming Poppy wouldn't throw herself off a cliff, I stumbled upon more disturbing news. Poppy's mother, Piya Ambani, was remarrying only months after her husband's death.

Unbelievable.

Poppy lost her father and grandmother. After Charles's death, her future as the CEO of Ambani Corp was also in jeopardy. Everything she loved and worked for was gone. Then, her mother got engaged to Zane Trimalchio, a retired musician formerly known as Axel, during his active years in the business. As a celebrity, his wedding was the toast of the town, with more than six hundred guests in attendance. I wondered if it was an intentional snub to Piya Ambani's first wedding. Apparently, she had five hundred guests attend the previous one. This had to be a brutal blow for Poppy.

Every time something terrible happened to her, I worried it'd push her over the edge. So, I got myself invited to the wedding. Jordan, Uncle Henry's fiancé and my soon-to-be aunt, was the bride's best friend and was in the wedding party. Despite their budding nuptials, Henry refused to attend an Ambani event, and I persuaded Jordan to take me as her plus-one instead. If I was reading the situation right, Jordan was relieved. I was even-tempered, and she preferred to avoid making a scene at her best friend's wedding. Jordan merely assumed I tagged along to network since this wedding was crawling with press, celebrities, and agents.

I grabbed a pre-ceremony drink and scouted the tented area for Poppy when I overheard Jordan and Piya. They were behind a curtain fashioned to be the bridal room.

"I told Axel we should get married after Poppy had time to process, but you know what he's like. He refused to hear it." Piya Ambani, soon to be Trimalchio, toyed with the edge of her lace veil. She wore a giant white wedding dress and stood inside a giant white tent. "This was a bad idea."

"No, it wasn't," Jordan replied without missing a beat.

A large vanity and a floor-length mirror stood next to them, along with a couple of ivory adjustable salon chairs. They were sharing a bottle of champagne inside the heated tent. Meanwhile, the catering staff set up the chairs for the ceremony in a choreographed routine. The servers were dressed in black tuxes, so it was easy to blend in while peeking through the curtains and listening in on their conversation.

"But it's only been five months since Jay—"

"I see where this is going, and I'm going to stop you right there," Jordan cut her off. "I understand this seems fast, but based on everything you told me, Zane has been waiting years to be with you."

Years?

Jordan tutted. "You have both suffered long enough. Don't make him wait again just because other people might judge you for remarrying quickly."

"I don't care what other people think of me."

"Then what is this about?"

"I'm worried about Poppy."

Me too. For the hundredth time, I found myself wondering how Poppy must be processing this transition. She lost everything within the span of a few months. It sucked that her mother was remarrying and moving on despite all the tragedy. It was one thing for death to take you from your loved ones; it was another for your alive loved ones to abandon you. This wedding was worse than the funerals because it was an intentional choice to abandon Poppy. How could her mother not see that?

"Did she object to the wedding?" Jordan asked soothingly.

"No," the soon-to-be bride replied unsurely. "Not really."

I was surprised by the answer. No teenager would be okay with their mother remarrying so quickly. There had to be more to the story.

Jordan shrugged. "Then you have nothing to worry about."

Piya shook her head. "I don't know."

"Poppy is a straight shooter. Trust me, she would have made it known if she had a problem with this."

Piya was reluctant. "Poppy has become so closed off. I have no idea what she's thinking. She never shares her feelings."

I understood her frustration surrounding this topic. Poppy was impossible to read. I noticed how the mother-daughter duo interacted at Jay Ambani's funeral. Poppy was much too reserved with her emotions.

"To be fair, Poppy has never been big on sharing her feelings to begin with."

"True. But I can't shake this feeling that she can't stand Axel, and he isn't making things any easier. He planned this big wedding without telling me. I know Poppy is going to hate it, and I don't want to make my daughter sad. This was a bad idea, Jordan—"

"Shh, take a deep breath," Jordan cooed, putting her arms around her frantic best friend. "You need to stop worrying so much about Poppy. You're an empty nester, babe. It's not like Poppy lives with you and will have to deal with Zane, so it's okay if they aren't best friends. You've done a great job raising Poppy, but she is off to college, living her own life. It's time you do the same."

Piya sighed defeatedly. "That's a valid point."

No, it wasn't. Poppy might be off to college, but she had no one else other than her mother. If Piya remarried, she'd move on to happy-go-lucky land, leaving Poppy behind to suffer alone.

Jordan set her champagne glass on the vanity and dropped her voice. "Look at it this way. If you guys are married, Poppy won't have a choice but to develop a relationship with Zane. If she is in the market for a father figure down the road, who better than her biological father?"

Biological what?

The hold around my beer glass tightened. Trimalchio was Poppy's biological father. Did that mean Piya Ambani had an affair for the entirety of her marriage? Despite Dad's assertions, I had been certain Piya Ambani loved her husband, and the cheating accusations were nothing but frivolous rumors.

Were the speculations correct?

There was a pause. "I do want them to bond, but Poppy is paranoid people will find out about Axel. I don't know if she'll ever let herself get close to him. You should've seen her after Joe Maxwell's accusation in the board room."

A punch landed in my gut. From the sounds of it, Poppy knew of her origins and hated it. She lived in fear of being discovered, and Dad outed her darkest secret.

My hands shook with fury over what Dad had done. I had been waiting for the other shoe to drop, wondering what might push Poppy over the edge. I didn't know it had already been done, and I played a part in it. I set my glass down and dragged myself away from the conversation. I didn't want to hear more. I wished I hadn't heard it because now I felt worse than ever for Poppy.

I walked toward the ceremony area and waited as guests filed in. I sat in the back to watch Poppy from a distance. She wouldn't be able to spot me with hundreds of guests in attendance. It was for the best, as I was the last person she wanted to see.

The music started, and the chit-chat stopped. I watched as Poppy walked down the aisle in a long black tulle dress, holding a bouquet of roses. My breath caught in my lungs. I could tell her mother picked the black bridesmaid outfit with Poppy in mind. She looked striking with her high cheekbones, shapely brows, and raven-colored hair framing her shoulders. Poppy looked like a transcending beauty even while sad.

Between the funerals and the weddings, Poppy had transformed into a grown woman. The only thing that hadn't changed was the deep brown eyes. The ceremony was inside a beautiful, heated tent sprawled on a long-running beach with a view of blue water. Still, the harrowing look in Poppy's eyes could have convinced you that we were in an alternate dystopian reality.

My chest tightened at the sight of her, and for a moment, her sadness was too much to take. I expected her anger over the wedding, not the melancholy loneliness in her eyes.

Poppy's hands tightened around the bouquet when she saw Trimalchio at the end of the aisle. Something told me nothing about being here was her choice. Suddenly, I was covered in the same black cloud as Poppy.

This was awful. Poppy was forced to have a front-row seat in losing her mother to the man who wrecked their home. I wanted to reach out and hold her hand, but mine wasn't the one she wanted to hold. I wanted to tell her she still had one more person who cared about what *she* wanted, one person who'd look out for her.

Though I sat far away, I swore I could hear Poppy's shallow breaths while Piya and Zane exchanged vows. Her house of horrors was coming true before her eyes, and she could do nothing to stop it. Right after they announced the newlyweds, Poppy's inexpressive eyes finally gave themselves away. It was only a flicker, but I read her emotions loud and clear.

She was devastated.

As the guests left the ceremony, I wondered if life had finally pushed Poppy too far. And I knew without fail that I wouldn't stop watching over her until I could confirm it. The world had deserted Poppy, but I never would. After finding out what I did today, I'd never abandon Poppy.

ACT 2

CHAPTER
FIVE
POPPY

4 Years Later

~

Half-lidded hazy eyes peeked at me from between my thighs as Sophie trailed her tongue to my clit, or so I assumed since I couldn't see anything past the blindfold. She talked me into it, promising me a night I wouldn't forget. So far, she was on the money. With my vision taken away, my other senses were heightened, and I climbed a peak I craved to summit.

"Fuck, you are hot," she whispered, yet her words sounded loud and clear due to the aforementioned heightened senses.

My head rolled back as Sophie pushed my bikini bottoms farther to the side and parted my lips with her fingers. Fuck indeed. Getting entangled with Sophie was the plan, although it didn't hurt that she was easy on the eyes.

I must admit this had turned into a "two birds with one stone" situation. Sophie was privy to valuable information I needed and was notoriously infamous for pillow talk following intoxicated promiscuity. Christmas came early when she asked if I'd be interested in a threesome with a vetted third. If tonight went well, I'd uncover the intel I'd been searching for. I also needed to unwind, as pointed out by everyone. Sophie was rumored to be amazing in bed and was proving the gossip with each flick of her tongue.

I sat at the edge of the bed with my legs spread wide while Sophie knelt on the ground with her head bobbing between my thighs. Delicate fingers stroked me, engulfing me with the warmth of her mouth. My eyes rolled back behind the cloth covering them. "Faster," I whispered.

Her lips hovered over my sex. "So eager."

My back arched, and I pushed myself farther onto her tongue. I didn't care for talkative lovers, not unless the words got me hotter. Her voice did nothing; it was her tongue I needed more of, and I ground harder against it. Though I initially protested the blindfold, I suddenly saw the appeal. It built anticipation.

"Harder." The word sounded harsh as I rode her tongue. I expected Sophie to back away, but she leaned into it, and I could've sworn she enjoyed it more than me.

My suspicions were confirmed when she murmured, "Oh God."

"Suck on my clit."

Sophie slurped and sucked. Her tongue plunged inside and scraped my walls before returning to the original spot. My hips almost flew off the bed, only to slump back onto the mattress.

"Again. Lick me harder."

Sophie didn't hesitate to oblige. She preferred a dominant partner in the bedroom, and something told me being on the serving end got her off.

My hips moved in rhythm with her mouth. My fingers tried to find purchase on the bedsheet when Sophie flattened her tongue against my clit. I presumed she was touching herself when her hand left my waist. As predicted, I heard her urgent moans rise in volume. Sweat beads, moisture, and fluids, hers and mine, intermingled and rolled down my thighs. The bedsheet underneath me turned damp, intensifying my crescendo.

"I'm coming," she gritted, her mouth momentarily coming off me as she spoke. I squeezed her head between my thighs, forcing her back on me while I rode her mouth. Sophie cried out against my pussy as I ground against her until my body took off with the same euphoria. The moment the orgasm washed over me, I let go of her head in a snap.

I fell back on the mattress and blew out a shallow breath. I had to hand it to Sophie. I rarely got off during sex, oral or penetration, so any orgasm, small or big, was a win.

Sophie placed her hands on my thighs for leverage and stood.

"Can you take off the blindfold?" I kept my voice complacent like a thoroughly satisfied lover. In reality, I was itching to take off the blindfold. The orgasm had subsided, and so had my interest in heightened senses.

"No can do. We're still waiting for one more person," she replied. "Remember what I told you about him. He is a big deal and would rather maintain his anonymity."

I suppressed the urge to complain. The goal tonight was to be amicable, and I wouldn't accomplish the objective if I let out my general surliness.

Sophie was an acquaintance from college. She recently approached me about a fantasy of a threesome with me and an unnamed man, insisting on exercising discretion where his identity was concerned. No exchanging names, no photography, and we used serial numbers when swapping health information, along with a blindfold for me throughout the night.

I hated giving up control. I stifled my bubbling grouchiness because it was crucial to make Sophie happy. Instead, I tried a lighthearted approach. "How about we turn off the lights, and I promise not to peek?"

Sophie laughed. "Trust me. This is simpler than an NDA. He doesn't want to involve lawyers for a one-night stand. It's easier if you keep the blindfold on."

Truthfully, a blindfold wasn't the oddest request I'd heard. We were acquainted with numerous celebrities, my stepfather included. NDA was practically a party favor in this house, though she was right. A blindfold was easier.

To Sophie's credit, she didn't strike me as someone with strong moral values, yet she had diligently protected her friend's privacy. Not to mention, she waited until after I was eighteen to approach me about her salacious desires. I started college at fourteen. No one else seemed to give a shit that I was four years younger than them. Her moral compass and skilled tongue were Sophie's saving grace. However, she hid dark, gruesome secrets, and I needed to know why. It was unlikely for Sophie to change her deposition. So far, she spewed a carefully revised version of the truth crafted by her lawyers. I had to interrogate Sophie while her defenses were down to unearth the reason behind her lies. If the rumors were to be believed, she was vulnerable after sex, especially while consuming alcohol.

So, I eagerly agreed to her proposition, unwilling to let this opportunity slide. The only nuisance in this threesome was the third person. Sophie needed to let her guard down before he entered the picture. I doubt she'd discuss a horrific, bloody murder in the presence of another.

Heat amplified the effects of alcohol. Naturally, I grabbed a handle of Grey Goose and suggested we go into the hot tub. By the third vodka shot, Sophie's inhibitions fell away, and she dragged me to bed. She insisted on the blindfold in case our mystery celebrity walked in at an inopportune moment.

The unidentified male had yet to make an appearance, and time was of the essence. If Sophie didn't retract her deposition soon or if I didn't at least understand her reasons, we'd lose our biggest client, and hundreds of people would be laid off. Perhaps two more shots and one more round of sex would pave the way.

"One more shot while we wait?" I asked casually.

Sophie playfully bumped my shoulder. "You don't have to get me drunk. Having sex was my idea."

My patience was running seriously thin. "Oh, come on," I prodded in a voice so syrupy even I cringed. "I'll stay blindfolded, and you can feed me the shot. It'll be..." Holding back the rising bile at the next word, I spat out, "Cute."

Sophie trailed a finger down my chest. "Let's not get sloppy before he gets here."

I internally groaned. "He's late. What better way to pass the time than with more drinks?" She had me blindfolded. Considering how much I hated giving up control, the least she could do was get drunk and spill her guts.

I heard Sophie's relented sigh. Just as I silently thanked Satan, the bedroom door creaked.

Our mystery man had arrived, and he had terrible timing.

CHAPTER SIX

DAMON

The thumping music vibrated almost half a mile away, and my car slowed onto the long driveway. The party was in full swing.

"This is a bad idea," my cousin Jasper muttered from the back seat.

"Don't listen to him," Caden assured me. "This is the best idea you've had in years." Considering how seldom my twin agreed with me, I suspected he had an ulterior motive for tagging along.

"More like the stupidest idea he's had in years," Jasper retorted.

"Why are we doing this again?" Xander piped in. He was Jasper's older brother and the most rational of the three.

"Because the Ambanis are building a case against Damon, or did you guys forget about the murder accusation?" Caden snapped. "Whatever argument they plan on making, Poppy would've kept the notes on her laptop or somewhere in her room. A big blowout is the perfect cover for Damon to get inside and go through her things."

"Is that a good idea?" Xander asked mildly. "If things go sideways, Damon will look more guilty."

"It won't go sideways," Caden insisted. "We'll be on the lookout for Poppy while Damon searches her room."

"How are we supposed to recognize her with a mask on?"

"Look for the shortest woman at the party," Caden quipped.

"This is a bad idea," Jasper grumbled once more.

"Stop being a little bitch."

I ignored their bickering and flicked my cigarette out the window. I texted Rose after I parked the car at the coordinates she sent. She walked out onto the lawn within seconds, slinking into the darkness where our car was hidden.

"Everyone got their masks?" I turned to check. A bouncer was rumored to be at the front door, scanning the barcode on the invitations to keep out unwanted guests. Rose would sneak us in through the back of the house, but we needed to camouflage. Luckily, it was a masquerade-themed party.

I pushed the car door open, simultaneously tying the plain black Zorro mask behind my head. My brother and cousins stepped outside, binding on similar lightweight fabrics. We were dressed the same: black slacks and dress shirts, an unplanned coincidence. It was the easiest way to blend in. Black was inconspicuous and a popular color choice at these events.

Rose sauntered to the car. She was painfully shy, but tonight, she was in a tight, asymmetrical dress and platform heels that dug into the grassy ground as she walked. Breaking out of her timidness with a sexier personality and outfit was for my benefit.

"Hey, Damon," she greeted, making her voice sultry in contradiction to her naturally reserved one. "Great to see you. I almost thought you weren't coming."

I plastered on a practiced smile as she pecked my cheek. Another bold move on Rose's part. "Wouldn't miss it for the world. Thanks for the invite."

"Sorry for making you jump through the hoops of sneaking in. You know what my cousins are like. If they knew you guys were here…" She glanced around to take stock of our audience. "Oh, hi, guys." She awkwardly waved at Jasper and Xander, who greeted her in kind.

"Hi, Rose."

"How are you?"

Caden, on the other hand, said nothing, browsing his phone as if Rose's existence didn't matter one way or the other. Though the animosity between our two families had been long-standing, Rose was the only one immune to the ire. I suspected it was due to her fascination with me rather than keeping the peace. She'd invited me to numerous parties over the years, though never to events with other Ambanis in attendance. Until tonight.

Rose organized a party at Poppy's stepfather's mansion. Since the guest count was massive and everyone would wear a mask, she felt brave enough to extend an invitation. Her surprise was evident when I accepted it despite dodging her advances for years.

For once, Rose's unwavering admiration worked in my favor. She took a huge risk by letting us into the party just as we were attending it. All hell would break loose if anyone found Maxwell blood in the mix.

Rose led us through the garage and ushered us into an elevator. "Good thing it's a costume party, right? No one will recognize you guys."

Rose wasn't only referring to her cousins but our fan club as well. Xander was drafted into the NHL. Jasper played on our college team and would likely follow suit. Caden graduated from college at twenty with a degree in chemistry before becoming a doctor at twenty-three, but it wasn't the reason behind his fame. He became an online sensation after creating various patented drug formulas that changed the game.

Of the four, I was supposed to hold the least glamorous position as the CEO of our family's company, working part-time to earn my MBA. Diplomatic. Stable. Discreet. I was known for those traits and for remaining behind the scenes. A few philanthropic efforts had dragged me into the limelight. I poured money into Caden's lab to unearth formulas for incurable neurological disorders. This was coupled with my organization rehabilitating those losing hope by replacing their violent realities with opportunities such as jobs and support groups. Our programs revealed a high success rate for those unable to escape a broken system. The model was used worldwide, resulting in endless magazine features and talk show interviews. The four of us couldn't go anywhere in New York without being recognized or harassed. No good deed went unpunished.

Rose pushed the button to call the elevator. "Wish you had gotten here earlier." She ducked her head and spoke to her shoes. The sexy persona she adopted was crumbling, her real personality defying the unnatural changes.

To be honest, Rose didn't need to change. We could've been friends if she hadn't had feelings for me. As it stood, I had no interest in leading someone on, especially someone as fragile as Rose. Even my presence gave her hope. I wouldn't typically exploit her fascination, but this was a dire circumstance.

"We did a fashion show with prizes for best outfits."

"Hmm."

Rose uneasily listed more details about the party. Jasper and Xander made polite inquiries, sensing I was in no mood to converse. Caden dragged behind, the shift in his mindset noticeable.

The elevator stopped at the main floor, the doors opening to a packed room full of who's who. Entitled heirs and heiresses occupied every corner of the house. The music was loud, and the intoxicated dancing was wild.

We shoved through the masses to reach Axel Trimalchio's famous ballroom, ironically known for its infamous parties. I was shocked the former musician allowed his eighteen-year-old stepdaughter to trash his home. My eyes peeled open in search of the five-feet demon spawn. Even if Poppy wore a mask, I'd recognize her instantly.

"Let's do some shots," Jasper eagerly steered the group toward the bar.

"Fuck yeah," Xander cheered.

"Sure," Rose obliged.

Even Caden did a bored one-shoulder shrug.

I remained unmoved. "Maybe." After scanning the crowd twice, I determined she was missing on the floor. "Is Poppy here?" I asked despite my best efforts to keep my agenda hidden. An oddball, Poppy possibly decided against attending a party in her own home. Annoyed, I rubbed the tattoo on the back of my neck.

Rose frowned. "Er. Yeah. I saw her not too long ago. Why do you ask?" The edge in her voice was unmistakable.

"No reason. Come on, let's do some shots."

I needed to distract Rose before she read into my intentions and led the charge to the bar. Within two shots, she was tipsy, throwing me forlorn looks. I slipped away with excuses of using the restroom, leaving my brother and cousins in charge of keeping Rose preoccupied.

I climbed the grand staircases, stopping to scan the room from above. Poppy wasn't here. Of course, the little antipathy veered off to somewhere secluded. My phone dinged.

> Sophie: Are you at the party?

> Damon: Yeah.

> Sophie: Your surprise is waiting.

I rolled my eyes, regretting telling Sophie I'd be here. She was merely a decent decoy if things went south. Sophie, one of the few neutral parties in the long-standing Ambani-Maxwell battle, was an old friend of mine. She was also friends with Rose and, by extension, her cousins.

We used to hook up, which later changed to a strictly platonic friendship, except for the one odd conversation last week.

∼

"I have a surprise for you." Multiple students glanced at Sophie as she barged into the library and set her purse on my table, making no effort to lower her voice.

I raised an eyebrow.

Sophie placed two hands next to her mouth as if making a big announcement. "I'm setting up a one-night stand for you with the hottest woman on earth."

My eyes returned to my laptop.

Never one to flail at the sight of rejection, Sophie continued with zest, "This girl's made of dreams. Consider it a graduation present for both of us."

Finishing my MBA was hardly a cause for celebration. Though I usually ignored Sophie's antics, her wording gave me pause. "How is setting me up a graduation present for you?"

Sophie shrugged. "I'm going to be there when it happens. She wouldn't have agreed to it otherwise. Think of it as hand-delivered merchandise, custom-made to your liking."

I shouldn't be surprised by the proposition. Sophie was sex-positive, always up for discovering new things in the bedroom. Evidently, voyeurism was the newest kink she unlocked.

"Plus, I have this theory about you that I'm dying to test. As a graduation present to myself, I'm going to find out if I'm right."

"Curiosity killed the cat."

Sophie was undeterred from her cause. "If this girl doesn't blow your mind, I'll personally fuck you to make up for it." She looked me up and down. "You know what? I'll throw in a free fuck for you regardless, as a last hurray for old times' sake."

Sophie had a comically deluded sense of self-worth. "Thank you for the generosity," I drawled, pointedly swinging my eyes to the left and right. Girls were discreetly taking my photo from phones hidden between their open books. One girl was "reading" her book upside down. We both knew I didn't need help in this department.

"Sarcasm isn't a good color on you, Damon. Everyone is over this crappy mood of yours. You need to get laid, but you think everyone is a social climber. Interesting standards to have in a city like New York, by the way," she said sardonically.

I couldn't argue with the statement. It was no surprise Sophie and the others noticed my detached attitude. My mood was worsening by the day.

"I found you a woman willing to fuck you without knowing who you are to satisfy your celebrity chaser discrimination. I omitted your name and sent her your health screening, and I just received hers. She is clean, by the way. So, you don't have to do a thing other than show up." Sophie flipped her hair haughtily as if doing me the biggest favor. "You're welcome."

I scoffed. This was Sophie's way of "fixing me," though she needn't bother. If I told her what was really wrong, hell would break loose.

"So next week?" she followed up expectantly.

"Not interested." I started typing an email.

"Fine. Maybe I'll spring it on you because I think you'll fall at my feet once you see her."

I doubt it. "Bye, Sophie." And leave me alone to wallow in my forever persistent bad mood.

~

I never gave Sophie's proposition a second thought. I should've anticipated she'd concoct a plan upon finding out I'd be here tonight.

> Sophie: Don't keep us waiting.

> Damon: Pass.

> Sophie: Go to the second floor. Take a right at the top of the staircases, last door down the hallway. Merchandise is on the bed... blindfolded.

    I stiffened upon reading the instructions before my legs moved in the direction of the room, yanking the door open.

CHAPTER SEVEN

POPPY

I was minutes away from breaking Sophie and letting her perjure herself with a variation of the truth she hadn't given the police. To say I was disappointed with the newcomer's arrival was putting it mildly.

The door adjacent to the bed creaked open. Based on the faint music floating in from the party, the door was left partially open. The way his steps staggered to a halt, it was safe to deduce he didn't step inside the room. The room was dimly illuminated with soft mood lighting, and I assumed our newest arrival was taking in the scene.

This must be a hell of an introduction with my legs obscenely spread. At least the two-piece bikini covered my privates, giving a semblance of modesty despite what occurred minutes ago. Sophie was in a similar state as we never fully undressed.

The newcomer had little to say. I had never known anyone to possess such ennui at the sight of two half-naked women and the prospect of a threesome looming over his head. He hadn't said hello, nor had I heard the door shut, indicating he was watching us from the doorframe.

It wasn't like there was much to look at anyway. I disliked the idea of personalizing a room in this house. Mom still decorated it in a Gothic undertone with the bare minimums needed to function, keeping my preference for sparsity. A four-poster bed, two side tables, vintage blackout curtains lining the windows, and a desk holding the sole picture in the room. The black walls were otherwise left empty, with no photos, artwork, or even a poster. Any connection to these four walls would echo the complacency of living with the enemy, my stepfather. This was a temporary arrangement, one I planned to fix as soon as Sophie retracted her testimony.

The man watched us silently. To be precise, he was silently watching *me*. I had no basis to confirm my suspicions except an intuition that his eyes were resting on me. The acute sense of being closely watched was difficult to shake. The air in the room thickened as we collectively waited for his next move.

Hours seemed to pass in the oppressive darkness brought forth by my blindfolds. At long last, I heard the door shut and the leisurely turn of the lock.

"I knew you'd come," Sophie gushed, voice smooth like honey.

The man didn't respond.

"What do you think?" Sophie's breath lightly touched my neck, suggesting she motioned at me with a nod. She was asking if he approved of me for their threesome.

I suspected that Sophie had slept with this man before. If this were their first time, there would be no reason to only seek approval where I was concerned. She would've sought validation for herself, too. Sophie intentionally misrepresented the situation by insinuating to me she never slept with him.

Everyone in this room appeared to have an ulterior motive; I was sure of it. Sophie was the most transparent. She wanted to fulfill a fantasy around me and a past gentleman caller.

I was attracted to Sophie but wouldn't have agreed to a threesome with a stranger unless it helped me pave the way to the truth.

As for *him*, I had an inkling his purpose was to engage in more than a mere threesome. Sophie was an incredibly beautiful and sought-after woman. I couldn't think of one person who wouldn't sleep with her. His lackluster attitude, as reflected in his bored steps, indicated girls like Sophie were a dime a dozen, and he wasn't overly enthusiastic about this prospect. This wasn't an uncommon occurrence for him, nor did he have to drive to a party to get laid.

Nevertheless, I was too invested in this plan to back out. More so, I had grown curious about the identity of the man capable of prolonged silence at such a sight. I sat still as he sized me up, determining whether I was good enough. It wasn't his approval I sought; it was his voice. With my vision taken away, it was the only way to place him.

"Be my guest if you need to take a closer look at her," Sophie spoke as if she had the right to auction me off. Strike one.

A heavy weight descended upon us, and I heard Sophie's shallow breathing turn labored. Heat emanated between us, but he remained at arm's length, giving nothing away. His restraint was admirable.

"Come closer," Sophie suggested, sounding like the perfect salesgirl. "You can hardly appreciate her from over there." She ran a finger down my neck.

"Hands off the merchandise," demanded a deep, rumbling voice.

"He speaks," I couldn't help but state. I had given up on hearing the stranger's voice. The seductive sentence was too short to flicker recognition, so I tried to engage him in a conversation. "And merchandise? Did I miss the part where I was auctioned off?"

Sophie ignored the harsh disapproval in the man's voice but complied by retracting her fingers. "I just wanted to show you how much she wants you."

Sophie carefully omitted that we hooked up minutes before his arrival. Given his tone, I could see why. He had some misgivings where threesomes were concerned. This was turning into an amusing night. I had hooked up with men and women before, but never both simultaneously. This might be my first threesome, but even I knew it involved touching all parties. Despite his late arrival, this man dubbed himself the leader, calling the shots on how this would go down. It was the type of powerplay I generally employed. It'd been a while since someone's behavior had been erratic enough to intrigue me.

"So?" Sophie prodded. "Is she made of dreams or what?"

I held still, listening to his footsteps closing in on the bed. I felt him peruse me like a display item at a storefront.

"No," he finally replied. My brow arched. Before I could take offense, he whispered almost inaudibly, "She is much, much better."

My ears perked. I listened to the man's words closely this time. It didn't spark recognition.

There was pride in Sophie's voice when she spoke next, "Of course, she is. Why don't you try her out? I'm sure she'd enjoy a test drive."

Strike two.

The way Sophie kept offering me up on a silver platter was getting on my last nerve. If anyone else were to make such assumptions, I would've ruined their financial future by now. Allowing Sophie three strikes was my generosity in exchange for her upcoming confession.

"I think that's her call, not yours." His retort was husky.

It was as if he had a straight line into my brain. The subtle clarification was hot, and he articulated precisely what was on my mind. He was more interesting than I expected.

"Mind if I sample the merchandise?" His pitch indicated the question was directed at me.

The room grew silent as he awaited my answer. For the first time, I was tongue-tied by someone's forwardness. I also didn't miss how he'd called me *merchandise* again.

"Just one taste," he added softly as if speaking solely to me.

My decision was speedy, and I spread my legs farther.

"Fuck." His earthy groan mixed with the body heat enveloping me, implying he stood before me.

With my feet flat against the carpeted floor, I sat on the edge of the bed. During the shuffle, my arm bumped against Sophie, who was behind me. She leaned over and whispered, "You're welcome. Enjoy."

"You can leave." His voice turned sharp, dripping with annoyance.

He was speaking to Sophie.

"No, she can't," I replied on her behalf. Perhaps he was gun-shy about "performing" with an audience, though it made no sense since he agreed to a threesome, but I wasn't willing to be left alone blindfolded with a stranger.

Luckily, he didn't dwell on it. Warm fingers touched the waistband of my bikini bottoms, and I jumped. My reaction gave him pause. Slowly, he knelt between my thighs and slipped the bottoms down my legs.

He smelled unbelievably good. And he must be a big guy because his hot lips grazed the top of my forehead even while kneeling. Emanating body heat cloaked me in a warm hug, stopping any cool air from reaching me. In this position, he might as well be a furnace.

The world came to a screeching halt as soon as he undid my bikini top and let it fall away. Pin-drop silence dominated the room. I knew his eyes were on the most intimate parts of me, observing me fully naked. It wasn't easy to assess how much time had passed, and I wondered if he was memorizing me to bank it away for future fantasies.

His fingers trailed my bare thighs, and an involuntary sharp inhale tumbled out of my lips. I hadn't expected the immediate reaction of being lit on fire. Large hands roamed my thighs, dipping into my curves. Like liquid fire, a scorching heat shot through my veins everywhere he touched. There was no way to determine his next move with compromised vision. So, I didn't expect it when a thick, blunt finger dove inside me without priming. A gush of liquid secreted onto his finger instinctively.

"Shit," I mumbled between bated breaths. This instantaneous response was a first for me, though he seemed familiar with rousing such reactions. Gliding my arousal around shamelessly, he made a mess between my thighs. It was followed by his hot breath blowing on my pussy, and I knew his mouth hovered over my core.

"You're wet as hell," he murmured.

Anticipation spiraled higher and higher as I waited. He was driving me mad through the simple art of withholding. Just as the torture escalated, his tongue slid over me.

My thighs shook unwillingly as an explosion threatened to break out like a supernova. "Fuck."

"Get out, Sophie." I heard him speak, though it sounded like he was lightyears away. "We'll be a little while," he said casually while his face was buried deep between my pussy.

I couldn't focus on his determination to get Sophie out of the room. I didn't know the man, but he already worked me too well, burning me from the inside out.

"Merchandise here disapproves of being left alone with strangers. It's her decision if she wants an audience," Sophie argued. "Or, in this case, a witness," she added, sounding amused.

Witness?

I should be questioning the nonsensical things they were spouting, but he had me in a trance, ready to die unless I could release the storm he stirred inside me. The budding pressure had me wound up, and I was grappling to reach the finish line. My skin felt hot everywhere he licked, like the prickling sensation of being zapped by fire ants. I wanted him to do it again and again and again, but he stopped. He retracted his fingers and mouth, leaving me suspended at the edge.

No.

Oh, hell no.

The intensity of his tongue had me soaring. I teetered at the edge of an abyss and couldn't deal with being left hanging. I contemplated giving up the meticulous control I exercised by telling Sophie to get out. If this man decided he no longer wanted a threesome, I'd rather stay for the twosome.

His voice crackled with determined energy. "Tell Sophie you'd like to be alone with me."

I fought the temptation to comply. My brain's logical side warred with my body's physical part. At least I could form a rational thought now that he had stopped driving me mad. Left blindfolded with a stranger wasn't safe. I shook my head.

"Ha!" Sophie sounded victorious. "I'm staying. Take it or leave it."

There was a long pause. He wasn't happy with my decision, nor did he consent to the arrangement, barking an order at Sophie. "Stay on that side of the bed."

I didn't know why he changed his mind about Sophie. I reached back to give her a reassuring squeeze, nonverbally communicating I'd make it up to her. Hopefully, it was enough to appease her. Alienating Sophie was detrimental to my original goal, but I was too twisted up to stop, especially when his lips grazed the outer shell of my ear. "Just so you know, baby," he drawled, "someone else being here won't stop me from wrecking you."

I would have objected to the presumptuous pet name, except the slight contact with his mouth had me spiraling. I needed him to finish what he started and was glad he saw it my way where Sophie was concerned.

Before I could savor the victory, he yanked my hips forward with brute force. His overwhelming presence pinned my ass securely on the edge of the bed, forcing my back to hit the mattress. Out of the blue, his teeth sank into my inner thigh for an unforgiving bite. No warning, no notice.

"What the hell?" I hissed, my thighs shaking in a knee-jerk reaction.

Before I could adjust to the pain, his teeth scraped over my pussy lips for another punishing bite. I jerked violently in his hold, which made him yank me farther into his mouth. He parted my pussy lips and grazed his teeth over my clit. He went for the money shot and nipped my clit before clamping down.

"Are you insane?" I gritted. My knees curved inward to close my legs and protect myself from his brutal attack. His hold tightened, keeping my legs spread and refusing to let me escape the abuse. I tried to dislodge contact by twisting my body, but one of his supersized hands slid around my waist and brought me back to place.

He was doing this shit on purpose, releasing pent-up frustration and anger over the Sophie situation on my pussy. However, I realized he could've clamped down a lot harder. The trivial restraint he exercised was so the sting of the bite would be bearable if I stopped fighting.

I went lax against the mattress, melting into the pain. The burn subsided once I put a stop to the push and pull. I surrendered, letting him win, and an unexpected, odd sensation rose in its stead. Some sort of bliss, relief, and pain mixed in one exuded from the stinging sensation until his tongue finally slid over me to soothe the wounds.

"Fuck," he groaned, sounding just as out of breath.

His tongue moved unhurriedly, exploring every part of my entrance before lingering on my clit. I grew unsteady when he returned to sucking and biting my clit. I gnawed at my lip when his tongue slid inside me. The force of a tornado broke from within me, unleashing something I'd never experienced.

It happened then. An embarrassing moan sidled out as I let go. I couldn't contain myself. I never moaned during sex, not once. I hated sex noises in general. Everything with him had been unlike me.

But he wasn't done, far from it. The gluttonous strokes of his tongue curled my toes. He continued to ravage my pussy, occasionally keeping my clit hostage between his teeth.

Suddenly, he slid two thick fingers inside me, reaching up to his knuckles. My eyes rolled back behind the blindfolds. A repressed sharp inhale was no match to being stretched wider than I thought possible.

"Fuck." I broke catastrophically when he curved his fingers.

The room echoed with the noises I made, which seemed never-ending. I was lost to whatever I just experienced. My thighs wouldn't stop shaking, nor could I stifle the sounds.

I had never climbed so high, never felt so irrevocably hit by ecstasy. I screamed for so long that my voice cracked. Thirst for water consumed my dry throat. The sounds still wouldn't dwindle, nor would he let up, gorging on my pussy as if he couldn't stop even if he wanted. My pussy was aching, burning, wrecked just like he promised, and my body couldn't handle anymore. Yet he continued and had me hallucinating of a higher power. I felt drunk from euphoria, not the vodka from earlier. No matter how much I wrestled to return to earth and scramble the pieces back together, my reality remained distorted.

Oh shit, I might have a heart attack at this rate.

"That was fun to watch," someone whispered beside me.

The voice registered after numerous moments of wrestling with the haze. *Sophie.* Shit, I forgot she was still here. The orgasm I shared with her seemed inconsequential compared to the experience of seeing divinity. Nonetheless, Sophie had been patient, watching from the sidelines while our celebrity star turned this party into a twosome.

My hand slid over her soft skin to her pussy as a consolation for her good attitude. The faint smell of her Chanel perfume wafted over me as I slid inside her bikini bottoms. Sophie moved closer, lowering herself onto my fingers. She fucked herself on two of my fingers while bending over to flick a wet tongue over my nipple.

In the interim, the man between my thighs continued to extract painful slivers of carnality with his mouth and fingers. Could an orgasm last this long?

I was seeing stars behind my closed eyelids when Sophie closed her mouth over my nipple and sucked. One hand gripped the mystery man's hair as his tongue thrust back inside me, the other fucking Sophie's pussy with two fingers while circling her clit with my thumb. I was close, so close, and once more ready for my religious experience. Gasping for breath, I clamped my thighs to let out the inferno of fire.

"Fucck," Sophie groaned. Her pussy clenched around my fingers, squeezing me like a vise.

Waves of pleasure surged through my veins with urgency. My back arched as my body ricocheted at the same time, once more vanishing into the oblivion that could only be described as transcendent.

"Oh shit, I'm coming," Sophie cried out, riding my fingers harder when I thrust one more inside her. She let go with a shout and collapsed against me, her head resting between the crook of my neck. The same exhaustion hit me tenfold. Nothing else mattered except this high.

Unfortunately, this frenzied feeling wasn't shared by all members of the room.

"WHAT THE FUCK ARE YOU DOING?" someone roared so loudly that everything in the room shook in fear.

I tried to snap out of the lust haze. "Hmm?"

There was an unmistakable commotion. I was colder than I had been moments ago and realized Sophie's warmth had been ripped away. I drooped limply against the mattress, riding high from the aftershocks. The severity of the situation refused to register.

Something was placed over my ears, followed by softly playing musical notes. With great effort, I reached up and ran my fingers over a smooth, cold plastic material. My noise-canceling headphones were draped over my ears, and someone hit the play button on the side.

Weren't the headphones on my nightstand?

Were they trying to muffle their conversation by covering my ears?

Was the commotion an ensuing fight between the two of them?

I should've voiced concerns, but my dry, cracked throat was useless. The mystery man roused something dormant inside me, and my body bowed without permission. If I had an ounce of energy, I'd investigate further. In any case, the headphones were light, comfortable, and unintrusive. I breathed in the music, letting the fog drag me deeper into the void.

A pair of legs bumped against mine as they approached the bed, a large hand firmly gripping my hair. I couldn't make out what was happening, my boneless body melting further into the mattress.

Regardless, I recognized his unforgettable scent. He climbed on top of me, parted my legs, and in one brutal thrust, he was inside me. Another unfamiliar moan ripped through me. This time, it was from pain.

"Ow!" I hissed. He was big, too big. His thickness pushed inside even when there was nowhere more to go.

A soft breath rhythmically fanning my cheek implied he said something reassuring. With both my vision and hearing taken away, making sense of things was impossible, but it appeared he was trying to get me to relax so he could go deeper. He stroked my hair, a savage contradiction to the assault, and pulled back to thrust deeper, further than anyone had gone before. I struggled to breathe and fought back, but he was determined. With one quick sweep, he pulled off the headphones.

"Just a little more," he murmured.

How could he not be all the way inside? He was already splitting me in half.

"Almost there, baby. It's okay, breathe."

"I don't think—"

He pushed inside until he was buried so deep it felt like a sword had been stuck inside me. Being taken so brutally obliterated my distorted mind, leaving me fully immersed until nothing else remained. His size was uncomfortable, though it was soon overruled when he rolled my clit between his fingers.

"God," I groaned.

He ground his hips against mine, then pushed inside me without mercy. His warm skin grazed my cheek with each thrust, his bare chest pressing firmly against mine.

When did he take his shirt off?

His slick tongue raced between my breasts, and I wondered if it was an attempt to erase traces of Sophie. When he spoke again, it was with an edge of menace. "Never do that again," the dark, seductive voice breathed with lethal fury. "Not unless you want them to pay."

"Pay?"

"Never let anyone touch you again, or I'll make them pay. I'll mail you their body parts piece by piece."

The comment finally snapped me out of the hazy trance. "What is wrong with you?" I grabbed the knot of my blindfold tied neatly at the back of my head and pulled it off.

A masked face was positioned mere inches from mine. He didn't protest when I reached up and tugged at the black Zorro mask. As soon as the material fell away, recognition struck me like lightning.

"No," I whispered through my broken voice.

Ice settled over my chest, for I recognized the face. I grew up seeing this face and knew everything about the man except his voice and scent. I never got close enough to detect either.

I shook my head, not believing it was possible. "No. No. Not you. Anyone but you."

How did this happen? How did Damon Maxwell get into our party, let alone get invited into a threesome with me?

The foreign sensation between my thighs gave way to a new revelation. I jolted. "You're not using a condom. Are you mad?"

Damon didn't respond. I pushed him off to scurry away. Damon grabbed my arm and brought me back to him with ease. He pushed me onto the mattress. With renewed zeal, he pumped into me with the enthusiasm of a starved man.

My limbs strained against Damon as he hammered into me so hard the headboard rattled. He used my body for his pleasure without kindness to spare. My breaths came out fast and harsh from each effort. The indecent rhythm went on and on, plowing into me until my crescendo built alongside his. My orgasm drew closer, the intensity rising by the second.

My muscles tightened as Damon came violently with my name on his lips. "Fuck, Poppy," he groaned.

Ecstasy flooded through me on cue. The orgasm was so powerful it shook my body, my mouth opening and closing on a silent scream, forgoing the unfamiliar sensation of cum flooding my insides.

The increased heart rate put me on high alert, aware of every detail and sound. At the same time, I couldn't concentrate on any one item from the heightened sense of exhilaration. My fingers trembled, and I couldn't decide if the surge of energy or the peace of contentment was winning.

The experience was a phenomenon to behold, a euphoria lasting for hours if not days. Stress no longer existed in my life. There was a new sense of connection as if I were part of something larger than myself.

The one to invoke the unchartered territory collapsed on top of me. Sweat dripped from Damon's forehead. Instantaneously, I reached between us to pull him out of me. It had the opposite of my intended effect. Fascinated, Damon stared at his cock hardening in my hold.

"Get off me," I spoke without looking at him, my face angled away.

Damon hovered on his elbows, amused. "Are you in a rush? Because I vote for round two."

I tensed. Did he think this was a joke?

Granted, Damon was wearing a mask, and I was blindfolded. Perhaps Sophie set us up because she thought it'd be funny to watch opposing factions unknowingly have sex. It still wouldn't be enough to excuse our behavior. We could lose everything.

"Get. Off," I chewed out.

"Ask nicely—"

An earth-shattering scream pierced through the air, interrupting our lively debate. Twisting my neck to the side, I realized the bedroom door was wide open, allowing the cry to penetrate the room. Worse yet, the voice sounded a little too familiar.

CHAPTER EIGHT

POPPY

I PUSHED DAMON AND JUMPED OFF THE BED IN FAVOR OF THE oversized black T-shirt hung on the back of my closet door.

"What the hell?" Damon was also on his feet, grabbing his discarded shirt off the floor in the dim room.

I pulled on a pair of black leggings. Barely slipping on my sandals, I dashed past him and out of the bedroom.

I heard Damon chasing me. "Poppy, wait."

Drunk idiots had infiltrated this house, and screams at parties were a recipe for disaster. Running toward them never led to anything good, but I couldn't ignore the recognizable voice.

I rushed down the stairs, taking them two at a time. A crowd was gathered around something at the bottom of the staircases. The music had been turned off, replaced by the commotion of the mob. Upon finding the main attraction, I pushed through the crowd and froze in place.

"Rose!"

At the center of the crowd was my cousin, Rose, lying in a crumpled heap. There was blood around her head like a halo, and she was unconscious. Crouching over her was a masked man, rattling off the address to a 911 operator.

I craned my neck to see what was directly above us. The second-floor mezzanine balcony overlooked the foyer. Rosie fell from the second-floor indoor balcony. Or perhaps someone pushed her?

The masked man tending to Rose cupped her head to keep it elevated, balancing the phone between his ears and shoulders. I reached them and knelt beside Rose, placing my fingers on her neck to check her pulse.

"What happened?" I demanded, voice shaking with anger. "Who did this?" I looked at the crowd, expecting a response.

A few people chimed in with feeble explanations.

"We didn't see what happened."

"We were just dancing, and she fell from above."

"Do you think someone pushed her?"

Whispers of conspiracy theories started sidetracking into a pointless conversation, none of which helped my cousin. The sole helpful person appeared to be the masked man, whom I now recognized as Caden, Damon Maxwell's twin. Same build. Same hair. Same mask.

How did this many Maxwells infiltrate our party? This house was built like a maximum security prison to keep the likes of them out. Usually, we'd seek out security upon detecting their presence. However, Caden was the only doctor present at a party filled with drunk assholes. I was positive the rest of my cousins were ten shots deep or too high to help Rose. No matter Caden's feelings about us, the Hippocratic oath wouldn't allow him to leave her side. The volume on his phone was loud enough to hear the ambulance was en route. In the meantime, Caden communicated her condition to them. In a shocking turn of events, another Maxwell weeded through the crowd and came to Rose's aid.

"Here, put pressure on the wound." Damon shoved a few towels into my hands. It appeared he ransacked all the towels from a bathroom, along with a first aid kit.

Caden and Damon were known to be as different as night and day, but it seemed their twin link kicked in during crisis mode. Damon elevated Rose's head by creating a makeshift pillow with the remaining towels, so Caden's hands would be free to assess her. I tightly wrapped one of the towels around Rose's head to stop the bleeding, holding another one against the wound. The three of us worked seamlessly to stop the bleeding, momentarily blanking the family feud and anger over the mistaken identity during sex.

Caden grabbed a sterile gauze to wrap it around Rose's head when blood soaked the towels. He retook Rose's pulse, repeating the information to the operator. Even from here, I could hear his heart pounding in fear. I gave him a quizzical look. I didn't know much about Caden Maxwell but didn't expect him to be this invested in Rose's welfare.

The person on the phone said something, and Caden securely wrapped a new towel around Rose's head on top of the gauze dressing. He rose with her unconscious body in his arms, her head lolling onto his shoulder.

"What are you doing?" I jumped to my feet.

Caden moved through the crowd. "The ambulance is pulling up. It'll take too long to find her if they have to fight through this many people. I'm taking her outside."

"Good call." Damon made a path for Caden. "Out of the way."

I followed on quick feet because they were right. This humongous house was nothing short of a maze, and weeding through the crowd might add an extra fifteen to twenty minutes. From the looks of it, time wasn't on Rose's side.

My phone was out, dialing as I walked. I tried Rose's parents first. When there was no answer, I called the next person on my list.

"Poppy. Hi!" Mom's cheerful voice sounded wrong, considering the gravity of the situation.

"Mom," I whispered into the phone.

I had barely spoken, and Mom already knew something was amiss. "What's wrong, baby?"

There was a long pause as I tried to explain what happened.

"Poppy. Is everything okay?" she asked again.

"No. It's not," I answered truthfully. "It's really fucking not. You need to come home."

After a few follow-up questions, the sirens from the ambulance drowned out Mom's voice. Caden jumped into doctor mode when the paramedics brought out the stretcher.

"I should go," I told Mom. "I'll see you when you get back." I was shocked to find Damon practically glued to my side, watching me as I hung up.

"Is your mother coming home?"

"Huh?"

Damon nodded at my phone. "Is she returning to America?"

I didn't look deeply into the fact that he knew Mom was out of the country. But I was still skeptical of his intentions. "Why did you help us tonight? I thought you were required to pledge our destruction when inducted into your company."

Damon appeared entertained, though nothing about the situation was amusing. Our families never spoke to one another unless they were fighting. His help with Rose was unprecedented.

Turning my attention to the paramedics, I realized they loaded the stretcher.

"Wait. I'll come with," I told one of the paramedics, grabbing the handle before he could shut the ambulance doors.

The paramedic shook his head. "Only one person is permitted to come along. You can drive behind the ambulance and meet us at North Shore Hospital."

I caught a glimpse of Caden inside the ambulance with Rose.

"But Rose is *my* cousin—"

Damon placed a hand on the small of my back, forcing me to backpedal from the ambulance. "No problem. She'll meet you there."

The paramedic used the opportunity to shut the door and speed away. Loud sirens drowned out the spectacle surrounding us.

I twisted to get out of Damon's hold. "What are you doing? Hospitals don't allow non-family members to tag along."

"They prefer Caden since he's a doctor and has been giving them stats on her condition," he explained patiently. "We'll meet them at the hospital."

"We? If my family suspects either of you are at the hospital..." I noted my cousins coming out of the mansion, resembling a gang.

"Maxwell!" Gia, Nick, and Sam stumbled out of the house, aiming their glares at Damon. Damon's mask was no longer intact. Enough people must've recognized him and told my cousins that he had infiltrated the party.

"How dare you show your face here?" Nick snarled.

Damon appeared bored by their mere existence, though he had the good sense not to engage on their turf.

My eyes dissected Nick when he stepped closer. "Not now," I warned.

Nick gave me an incredulous look. "Not now? Are you serious? This man killed Rayyan—"

I put up a hand, uninterested in the tired argument. "We don't have time for this. Rose was taken to the hospital. Get your car; we have to go."

Gia and Sam froze at the mention of a hospital. "What do you mean she was taken to the hospital? What are you talking about?"

"She fell from the second floor. Or did the people reporting back on him," I stuck a thumb at Damon, "forget to mention that because they were starstruck? They drove off with her in an ambulance, so let's go." Ideally, I'd leave behind their useless asses, but I had a lot to drink. Getting arrested for drunk driving wouldn't help Rose right now. When none of them moved, I reiterated, "Now!"

While Sam and Gia had the good sense to shed their hatred in favor of their cousin's wellbeing, Nick mulled over the information and turned toward Damon. "He did it."

I closed my eyes, fighting the urge to pummel him into the ground.

Nick continued his rant. "The last time he showed up at a party, Rayyan ended up dead. Rose just fell from the second floor, and he happened to be there again."

I walked away, refusing to participate in this madness. Damon easily caught up, gracefully leading me to his car hidden at the back of the house. He ignored Nick's shouted accusations that followed, busying himself with opening the passenger side door for me.

"Everything will be okay," he murmured as I ducked my head to climb in.

I nodded, strapping in. It was odd taking solace in my enemy, but he wasn't the one spouting conspiracy theories propelled by hate.

Our cousin Rayyan had a heated exchange with Damon Maxwell at a party a few months ago. He was found murdered mere hours later. It was an unfortunate coincidence, but Ambanis had been on edge since his death. They were convinced Damon did it. There was also a home invasion at my previous apartment, and my family insisted the Maxwells were behind it. Mom cried and cried until I finally agreed to move in with her because my stepfather's house was built like a fortress with numerous security measures in place.

The Maxwells thought I was collecting evidence to paint Damon as a murderer. It couldn't be further from the truth. I was trying to disprove the false accusation. Of course, the CEO of a leading company and philanthropist promoting non-violent measures didn't murder Rayyan. Damon Maxwell was the poster child for "good," with many internationally recognized organizations to his name. It made him both famous and incredibly popular. The fruitless conspiracy theories, provoked by my insane family members, were disregarded by law officials. It also made us infamously unpopular for demonizing a public hero.

The claim Damon killed Rayyan in cold blood started a new era of the ongoing feud, which was previously confined to boardrooms. Somewhere down the line, this rivalry turned fatal. The unproductive accusations cost both families millions of dollars in business, clients, and bad publicity. There were going to be mass layoffs unless we could put a stop to it.

With this newest development, the Ambanis were bound to spiral further with their condemnation of the Maxwells. It was the reason I needed Sophie to retract her testimony. For some reason, she lied, asserting Damon was the last person to see Rayyan alive. Unless he was hiding something worse than murder, it made no sense why one of Damon Maxwell's closest friends would shine a poor light on him. In any case, Sophie needed to withdraw her deposition if we stood a chance at moving forward.

I glanced at Damon as he drove off the property. I was horrified to open my blindfold and find his face hovering over mine, but there was suddenly a silver lining. Damon was with me when Rose fell. He couldn't have pushed her, and it was ridiculous to peg the world's most beloved philanthropist as Rayyan's killer. Yet Damon had been shockingly quiet during the numerous accusations spouted against him. Perhaps it was time for him to break the silence. Who better to prove his innocence than the man himself?

CHAPTER NINE

POPPY

A FEW HOURS LATER, I STILL MIMICKED A HOMICIDAL MANIAC doused in Rose's blood. Bright, crimson-red painted various parts of my hair. It was smeared across my cheek and ears, down to my neck. The liquid on my arm was sticky like honey, though the smudges on my pants had dried.

While the blood stains on my pitch-black shirt weren't visible, the unmistakable stench of iron wafted through the air. I enjoyed the occasional ripe, acidic scent of blood, but not when spilled from my favorite cousin.

Meanwhile, Damon Maxwell, standing across the hospital hallway, was a sight for sore eyes. There were no signs of gore, his all-black attire also concealing any bright red liquid spilled on him. Not one perfectly styled strand of hair was out of place. Damon casually propped himself against the wall, looking every bit like the reigning hero he had been branded. Dark blond hair with flecks of brown, sky-blue eyes, a six-foot-four athlete's body, and a model citizen who loved his community. He was the all-American boy.

Inadvertently, Damon caused quite a ruckus. Nurses and doctors walked by, slowing on approach to take pictures from their phones sneakily or outright fussing over him. They were swiftly put down by dismissive hand waves. Eventually, Damon's security emerged out of thin air to stop the brave souls from approaching him. His team was deceptively inconspicuous. I didn't notice we were followed to the hospital, and they were sporadically spread out to keep lunatic fans at bay. Not a big surprise since both Maxwell brothers had become well-known over the past several years. Damon was a junior when I started college, and women were overly eager for his attention back then, too. In an unforeseen turn of events, his attention was singular tonight.

Another pair of giggling nurses walked by, only to realize Damon was watching me. With his hands tucked in his pant pockets, his well-known adaptability to complicated situations remained unparalleled. The silence stretched in the hallway, but Damon didn't seem bothered by it. He was unfazed by the events from tonight, as if we didn't find my cousin in a gruesome state. Even I was rattled, and I excelled at being unperturbed.

Damon didn't converse during the short drive to the hospital or disclose how they managed invites to the party. After rushing to the university hospital and countless hours of waiting, we found out Rose had been placed in a medically induced coma. The doctors expected her to make a full recovery if the brain swelling could be controlled. It was good news, considering the severity of the situation.

No one else seemed to agree. My cousins were running rampant on male testosterone, adamant the Maxwell brothers were behind the attack. Rose's father, Dev, flew in from Chicago. He raised hell upon arrival, insisting on pressing charges. The news of her fall was trending on social media, turning it into a public spectacle. Damon's father, Joe Maxwell, rushed over to protect their brand in case the press showed up. Caden experienced some sort of trauma bond with Rose and slipped into doctor mode, which further aggravated everyone involved.

Fearing another Ambani-Maxwell showdown, the dean preemptively showed up to do damage control and keep the press at bay. While the accident didn't happen on school property, it was the second grim incident involving his students under the dean's leadership. The dean also wanted to appease the two most prominent families and the largest donors of his university. Playing mediator between them was a dangerous role. I stepped out of the office and into the hallway, fully aware nothing good would come of it. Damon wordlessly followed suit. For once, my enemy and I agreed. Mediation was pointless.

Shouting from the office vibrated into the hallway. Nick led the charge. "It had to be Damon Maxwell. I texted everyone at the party. The bartender recognized Jasper and Xander at the bar. And Rose practically hit Caden when she fell. Only one person was missing."

"Damon pushed my daughter off the second floor," my uncle Dev angrily summarized.

"Read the incident report before throwing out wild accusations," Joe bit back. "The police spoke to everyone at the party. They said she fell out of thin air; no one saw her being pushed. There weren't any signs of a struggle, but the girl's blood alcohol level was off the charts. Even the doctors agreed she stumbled and fell. I'm sorry if you didn't teach your daughter how to be responsible about holding her liquor, but we should hardly be blamed for your incompetence."

"Are you kidding me?" Dev screamed. "Damon was the only person unaccounted for for at least an hour. He snuck in for a reason. If he didn't do it, where was he when it happened?"

I glimpsed at Damon to assess his reaction. In a disturbingly fleeting moment, I realized he was still watching me and reclaimed my famously unruffled pose.

Technically, Damon had an alibi. If anyone discovered who it was or what he was doing with them for an hour, my career would be over before it began. The board of Ambani Corp was made up of my family, and none of them would speak to me again. I stared at Damon expectantly to set the record straight.

Meanwhile, the screaming match intensified in the office. "Just because something bad happened doesn't automatically make it our fault."

"Except something bad only happens when one of *you* is in the picture. What reason could those boys have had for breaking into our party if not to commit a crime? I'm going to have your son locked up."

"This is ridiculous, Chad," Joe addressed the dean. "Damon had nothing to do with this."

"Mr. Ambani," the dean cooed. "The doctors did a thorough inspection of the injuries, and we have pictures of the position Rose was found in. If someone shoved her off the second floor, the force needed to push her would have caused different bruises and impact. We are all emotional, but we urge you to read the report. Rose's BAC indicates an impaired state. The police will suggest putting her in rehab, and our doctors are considering a psych evaluation once she's awake."

Dev's temper threatened to break. "My daughter isn't suicidal, Chad. This was attempted murder, and it wasn't the first attack on our family. The same man was involved in both instances."

My head snapped in Damon's direction at the mention of attempted murder. "They think you tried to kill my cousin," I announced, breaking the suffocating silence.

As soon as I said it, a soft chuckle slipped from him, and his gaze flickered to the wall beside me. I followed his line of vision. A framed picture of Damon hung on the wall. Underneath it said Damon Maxwell, Humanitarian of the Year.

A barely-there smirk grazed my lips at the irony. Even if he weren't with me at the time of Rose's accident, this man campaigned against violence, drugs, and suicide. To peg him as a killer was beyond ridiculous. Before returning for his MBA, Damon received multiple awards for the charities he initiated on our campus. As the most respectable alumnus of this university, he was bestowed the honor of the keynote speaker for my upcoming graduation.

However, there was no arguing with emotional fools. Instead of acknowledging Dev's accusation, Damon said, "She'll be okay."

My head skewed into a questioning look.

"Rose," he explained. "There were no indications of major damage. She'll recover."

Damon was the only person to utter words of reassurance other than the doctors. Everyone else was focused on the *whodunit* instead of Rose's health. For a moment, there were no more sides or alliances. There was only us, without them. The two people who understood this juvenile feud were distracting us from the real concern, Rose.

With a curt nod of acknowledgment, I asked, "Aren't you going to tell them you have an alibi?"

A shadow crossed Damon's face, and he returned to his silent composure.

"I'll be obligated by law to back up your claims," I clarified in case he thought I'd deny it. Sure, I wanted to keep our tryst a secret, but this escalating madness needed to end.

I expected Damon to march inside and set the record straight, only he didn't move. There was only one logical reason behind his reluctance. He was willing to take his chances, knowing no jury on earth would indict him on a trial remotely resembling attempted murder.

On the other hand, his position as CEO would be in jeopardy if they found out about our recent sexcapade. Sleeping with the heiress of your rival company violated numerous morality clauses. It was Damon's decision if he wanted to entertain a criminal charge for job security. However, he needed a reality check because Dev didn't make empty threats.

"I suggest you go in there before my uncle takes it further. Your gorgeous face won't survive in jail longer than a week."

Damon's mouth twisted into a devious, wolfish grin. "Gorgeous?"

"That was your takeaway from what I said?"

Damon pushed off the wall, eating the distance between us with a few long strides. He faced me, bracing his hands against the wall on either side of my head. The move was unexpected. The big hallway suddenly felt small, and I was hyperaware of the large frame towering over my petite one. I unwillingly scanned the limited space between us before schooling my features.

"You should go in there and set the record straight," I suggested.

Damon didn't heed the advice. "You think I'm gorgeous, Ambani?"

Men and their egos. "According to the standard definition of beauty in our society, yes. You have desirable qualities. Does that make you happy to hear?"

Damon's steely gaze moved over my face. "Most definitely. What are my other *desirable* qualities?" The way his lips moved to enunciate *desirable* changed the meaning of the word. Was this the same Damon Maxwell who'd never made the mistake of glancing my way?

"Your facial structures are proportionally balanced and symmetrical. Straight nose, high cheekbones, generous lips." My gaze rested on his lips for a moment.

Darkness boiled in his eyes, but I couldn't decipher what it meant. I cleared my throat. Instead of taking the hint and stepping back, he leisurely perused my body as if taking mental photos. His eyes slid down my face, neck, chest. The chiseled face showed no remorse as he lewdly ogled me. A roguish smile played on his lips, and I knew he was reliving the events from this evening. Somehow, it was cruder than the actual act.

The unnerving gaze was meant to intimidate me. However, if he expected a reaction, I had none to show him. Indistinct threats from the office spilled into the hallway during our imaginary stand-off. The wall clock ticked away, and our harsh breaths worked in unison.

"You can stop this fight with one simple word..."

Damon purposely leaned forward, the spicy notes in his cologne rendering me speechless. "Why did you agree to a threesome with a stranger?"

I searched his expression for traces of humor. How in the hell could that matter in the face of attempted murder? "Why did you?" I countered.

"I had my reasons."

"Ditto."

"You're young," he observed in an accusatory manner. "Sophie must've tricked you into it."

"Is that why you kicked her out of the room? No. That happened before you found out it was me. Why did you kick Sophie out?"

"I don't like sharing."

"Coming from a guy who agreed to a threesome."

"I didn't like sharing *you*," he specified, causing my brows to rise. "Why did you agree to a threesome?" he repeated the question.

"Lots of people experiment in college."

A muscle clenched in his jaw. "Did you agree to it because you were interested in Sophie?"

I shouldn't show my hand, but something in his scrutiny told me not to lie. "No," I answered truthfully. "It was a meaningless experiment."

The answer did the trick. His features visibly relaxed. "Good." He brushed a thumb against my cheek. "Because you are done with her." Damon leaned in. His five o'clock shadow grazed my cheek, lips ghosting over my skin as he wrapped his arms around my waist. Heat emanated from the big, muscular body, blocking the cool air from the vent above my head.

"What're you doing?" I asked, noting an unfamiliar croak in my tone.

"Hugging you," he groaned. "Looked like you could use one."

Except it was no ordinary hug. Decency left the hallway for a non-embrace so intimate it bordered on dry humping. A shameful scene from our earlier encounter flashed in my mind, and I pushed against his chest, but he was an unmovable brick wall.

Stormy blue eyes watched me, impatient and ready to devour. Under my palm, his heart was beating erratically. On a whim, I counted the number of beats in ten seconds and multiplied it by six, one hundred twenty, well above a resting heart rate. Damon was either experiencing an adrenaline rush or having a stroke. I suddenly realized it was neither; Damon was aroused. I pressed my lips together when an unmistakable bulge bumped against my abs.

My eyes widened, but Damon was unconcerned. Not leaving an inch of distance, not even a slim gap to take a breath, he crushed my body between his and the sterile white wall.

"Are you insane?"

I tried to push him off, sensing his intention. Damon caught both my wrists with one hand. His other slid to the back of my thigh and lifted it. One strong leg pressed between my inner thighs.

"Stop." A barely audible protest escaped my lips.

He paid no mind and moved in closer. The pounding in my veins threatened to erupt as the tempo sped up, grinding roughly against me. A low rumble of appreciation reverberated in his chest when my eyes fluttered.

This was dangerous territory. Damon was universally accepted as the golden boy. I was widely accepted as the demon child. People were drawn to him like a magnet, whereas I had no outstanding friendships to boast about. We were the future of competing organizations, battling it out for survival, and while he represented all that was good, I was considered abnormal. One more bad move on my part, and our remaining clients would flock to him. He'd wipe Ambani Corp off the map and our legacy along with it.

The reminder drained the lust right out. I wrenched my thigh away, managing a slight distance from him. In the interim, the argument in the office gained volume.

"You'll hear from my lawyer."

"This isn't over."

"You're insane."

Damon didn't react to the voices.

"They'll be coming out of the office any minute," I warned.

"So?"

"There'll be consequences if they find us like this."

"So?"

Like any good nemesis, I had researched Damon extensively. The famously levelheaded CEO was betraying his usual characteristics. This vulgar proximity bordered on maniacal recklessness with our families in the other room.

The door burst open, shattering the imaginary bubble surrounding us. I ducked under Damon's arm before anyone stepped into the hallway and marched toward the Intensive Care Unit. Nick caught up with me, stopping to throw daggers at Damon with his eyes. I allowed myself one glance to find Damon's eyes steadfast on me. He mouthed, "*Later, Ambani.*"

I turned away, yet the feeling of his eyes crawling over my skin followed me for the remainder of the night.

CHAPTER

TEN

POPPY

> Unknown: Eyes.

I STARED AT THE TEXT. EXACTLY ONE PERSON WAS NEWLY introduced into my life, so an unregistered number could only belong to him. He didn't bother introducing himself, nor did I bother asking.

> Poppy: I need context, Maxwell.

> Unknown: Big, wide eyes are a desirable quality.

I paused, thinking back to our conversation at the hospital.
What are my other desirable qualities?
Your facial structures are proportionally balanced and symmetrical. Straight nose, high cheekbones, generous lips.
I memorized Damon's features while his face hovered inches from mine.

> Poppy: You don't have big, wide eyes.

> Unknown: No, but you do.

I stared at the phone.
I always knew I was different. As a child, I didn't join the other kids in frivolities such as laughter. My adolescent years were spent in a rat race toward my goals.

When boys on campus hit on me, the words sound generic to me, their compliments hollow. Maybe it was because he was older and more experienced than those boys, but Damon's specification, as if he were submitting concrete evidence of my beauty, suddenly made an impact. He extracted something from me that Mom or Rose couldn't despite years of trying. People rarely unnerved me in this manner, yet this man had done so repeatedly, and he was supposed to be my archenemy. Before last night, I didn't think Maxwells and Ambanis could consummate. We might as well be different species with body parts that didn't fit.

I scanned the foyer of the mansion, packed with people investigating the crime scene. Instead of wallowing over his daughter's critical condition, Dev, the man of steel, hired independent crime analysts. They reenacted numerous possible scenarios, using a doll and a stuntperson to simulate Rose's fall. The evaluations matched the incident report. While there was a possibility someone pushed her, the piling evidence suggested Rose likely stumbled off the second floor.

Dev disagreed. Deeming the conclusion unacceptable, he restarted the process until he found an outcome where Rose could've been pushed. My uncle was in a dark place and only cared about the truth if it fit his version.

I studied the madness unfolding in front of me, determining a distraction might be in order.

> Poppy: What are my other desirable qualities?

The phone lit up with a steady stream of incoming messages.

> Unknown: Smooth skin

> Unknown: Long dark hair

> Unknown: Upturned nose

> Unknown: Pink lips

> Unknown: Phenomenal body

> Unknown: Perfect tits

I hit the lock button and pocketed my phone when someone snuck up on me.

"Did Dev eat anything today?" Mom greeted me with a strained smile, attempting to maintain that everything would be okay.

I shook my head. "He refuses to let it go."

"He's hurting," Mom offered sympathetically. "Why do Maxwells ruin everything? How did they even get past our security?" It was the million-dollar question, one Damon evaded last night when asked.

My mother and stepfather, Piya and Zane Trimalchio, went away for their anniversary. Rose asked if she could throw an end-of-semester rager while they were gone. Mom agreed, hoping it'd force me to socialize with the peers I had ignored for almost four years. The party didn't bother me once I learned Sophie was excited about the masquerade theme. Sophie was supposed to have the time of her life and be seduced until she sang like a canary. She was supposed to clear the Maxwell name and end this bitter rivalry. Instead, Damon showed up, and Rose fell off the second floor.

Mom feared the Maxwells, convinced they were behind the unfortunate chain of events. She flew home as soon as I called her. Despite the exhausting overnight flight, she spent the day cooking enough food to feed a small army. She believed food cured all ailment and invited everyone from our community to be together in solidarity. Even though Dev hijacked Mom's home for a real-life crime drama reenactment, she greeted the unraveling with compassion. Mom was one of those likable people known for her kindness to all... even those who didn't deserve it.

Speaking of which, Zane entered the foyer and stared up. "Is he still forcing people to jump off our staircase?"

Zane Trimalchio, my evil stepfather, only cared about how things affected him, not the girl suffering in the hospital. Emotionless, manipulative, and cold-blooded, Zane possessed all the traits I generally admired in a person. Yet I couldn't suppress this constant wish to wipe his existence off this earth. You could chalk it up to my neurodivergence, though I had no interest in torturing others. This emotion was reserved for Zane.

"Don't worry, Zane," I said coolly. "Rose is doing fine and will recover within a few months. Thank you for asking about my cousin."

Zane ignored me. "Piya, how long will that man stay with us?"

"Be nice, Axel," Mom chided. She was the only one who still referred to Zane as Axel, his alias from his professional music days. "Dev nearly lost his daughter last night. He's processing."

Processing was putting it mildly. Dev was on a warpath.

My phone buzzed in my back pocket, but I ignored it. Dev was out for Damon's blood, insisting on acting the part of the stuntman. The contractors decided it was the last straw, forcing Dev to retire the pursuit for now. Considering my family was leading a witch hunt against Damon, seducing me with flirtatious texts was a lousy play. Or perhaps he was waving a symbolic white flag while our families acted like buffoons? Once the dust settled, we'd return to the opposite ends of the war we were expected to lead.

As the buffet-style dinner commenced, some people scattered around the grand ballroom while others opted for the dining room. Guests came and left at will, dropping off flowers and cards for Rose. The compassion was a cover to further their ambitions. Funerals, birthdays, weddings—any occasion at Zane's house was an opportunity to network. Business cards were exchanged, interviews scheduled, and someone even asked me if "Roseanne" was still alive.

I spent the night at the hospital, though we weren't allowed to see Rose until her condition stabilized. The all-nighter, followed by the meaningless drama, had me teetering at the edge. I avoided people, made myself a plate from the buffet, and snagged an empty chair at the long dining table.

Mom tried to seize the chair next to mine.

"Don't sit there." My grandmother strode up and forced Mom to give up her seat. She stopped by to pay her respects, though she had other nefarious reasons for visiting. "Paris will sit next to Poppy."

"Ugh." Mom voiced my feelings on the matter, not bothering to sugarcoat her opinion of Paris.

Because it hadn't been a shitty enough weekend, Paris, a family friend of ours, tagged along with my maternal grandmother, a.k.a. Nani. A stern woman by nature, Zaina Mittal dripped of class and old money. She made peace with Mom marrying a new money ex-celebrity DJ because it would have been difficult for a widowed single mother to remarry. However, she'd never allow the repeat of such blasphemy and appointed herself my matchmaker the moment I turned eighteen. A preemptive measure so I wouldn't have the opportunity to meet the wrong man.

"Didn't I tell you to stop setting Poppy up?" Mom sat across from me, and Zane joined her within seconds. Where Mom was, so was the bane of my existence.

Nani waved a dismissive hand. "I'm not setting her up. I'm giving her the opportunity to meet a suitable man."

Mom tilted her head as if searching for someone. "What suitable man? The only person you brought along was Paris. I don't know how that garbage person keeps getting inside, but tonight is about Rose. Get that trash out of my house."

I eyed Zane as they fought, leaning across so only he could hear my whisper. "You heard Mom. Get out."

Zane narrowed his eyes while Nani said indignantly, "Excuse me, young lady. Paris is a catch. Anyone would be lucky to have him."

"Paris is closer to my age than Poppy's. He's what, thirty? Thirty-two?"

"Thirty is the new twenty."

"The only person who'd say that is a thirty-year-old," Mom retorted.

Zane smirked around his forkful of pasta. "Good one, Princess."

Nani cast him a distasteful glance. "At least, he's a better choice than marrying someone off the streets."

"Great to see you, too, *Mom*," Zane sardonically drawled, fully aware of how much being related to him pissed off my grandmother.

Nani glared him down in response.

"My husband is a celebrated musician who built a reputable empire with hard work," Mom defended, her anger rising. "Paris is an entitled prick who has earned neither his reputation nor his status."

My grandmother scoffed. "That's ridiculous. What good is status and reputation if it's earned? It should be passed down by generation."

Laughter bubbled in my chest, though it was Zane who broke the tension first with it.

Meanwhile, Mom's head threatened to explode. "W-Wha... that's so ridiculous. Do you hear yourself?" She took a deep breath, deciding it was a pointless argument. "You know what? I don't care about your archaic beliefs. Just stop trying to brainwash my daughter. Poppy, don't listen to your nani. She hasn't taken her crazy pills today." Mom pointed an index finger at her temple and twirled it.

Nani ignored Mom's jab, adamant about having the last word. "You once told me to stop interfering in your life. Maybe you should take your own advice and let Poppy decide if she wants to talk to Paris."

At that, Mom pursed her lips.

Meanwhile, my grandmother fussed over the hem of my long-sleeved black dress. "I wish you'd wear more colorful dresses, Poppy. This is so morbid."

"Poppy looks good in black," Mom muttered sulkily.

My grandmother examined my hair that was pulled into two low braids. Milan, Mom's brother and Zaina Mittal's favorite offspring, disrupted the attempt to pull out the plaits.

"Poppy. Where is Poppy?" A hysteric Milan strolled into the dining room with his two-year-old son, Neil, tucked under his arm.

My grandmother lit up. "Milan, you made it. I didn't think you were coming."

My uncle walked past Nani, moving toward me with purpose. "I've been looking everywhere for you."

"Hi, Uncle." Robotically, I held my hands out for Neil. There was only one reason my uncle sought me out. His wife, Dahlia, was indisposed, and he was unwilling to take care of Neil for a few hours.

Milan's eldest was fifteen, which made two-year-old Neil an accident. He had presumed the phase of caring for a baby was over, and he could return to his two former great loves: designer brands and himself. My uncle had never met a reflective surface he didn't like. Self-image preservation clashed with taking care of a two-year-old, and Neil was fussing in the haphazard one-handed hold, slung sloppily against his father's hips.

Milan unceremoniously dumped Neil onto my lap. "Here you go. That child only stops crying when you hold him."

I bounced my legs a little, and my cousin stopped whining on cue. Neil stared at me with wide eyes, clasping onto the ribbon of the black choker around my neck and almost strangling me in the process. I coughed a little and pried his chubby fingers off the necklace. "Nice to see you, too, cuz."

"I'm exhausted," Milan wheezed. "I have been taking care of that baby since I got here."

"Didn't you just walk through the door?" Mom asked unironically.

When he noticed the decorative mirror on the wall, Milan forgot to retort and brushed out his bangs with his fingers. Then he recognized someone more important across the room and made himself scarce, utterly abandoning Neil without a backward glance.

Milan's undue resentment toward his youngest solidified my connection with Neil. Unwanted souls sought each other out. The feeling must be mutual because my cousin never fussed around me, and my uncle used it to his advantage. I might not appear kid-friendly, but children deviated toward me. In turn, I must admit their company was acceptable. Children had all the qualities I wished adults would embrace. They were viciously honest, blind to discrimination, and uncanny judges of characters.

Neil grabbed a handful of spaghetti off my plate and chucked it at Zane across the table. As I said, they were uncanny judges of characters.

"What the—" My stepfather looked ready to blaze Neil with his eyes but caught himself at the sound of Mom's melodic laughter.

"You naughty boy," Mom halfheartedly scolded her nephew as she laughed, using a napkin to wipe the spaghetti off Zane's face. "Who's a naughty boy? That's right, you are."

"Don't listen to them, Neil," I cooed next to his ear. Nudging my plate in front of him, I prayed for a repeat. Maybe this time, I could get it on video. I took my phone out in preparation.

Neil appeared camera-shy and turned his face away. I tapped the message icon when I noticed an excess of unread texts. The unknown number sent more messages naming my assets. I scanned the table to find Mom and Nani in another heated argument and quickly typed my response.

> Puppy: That's an impressive list.

The reply was instantaneous.

> Unknown: I was starting to think you didn't like my list.

> Poppy: ?

> Unknown: It's been dead silent on your end for hours.

> Poppy: Got sidetracked by mayhem.

> Unknown: Mayhem surrounding Rose, I presume. How is she doing?

The message gave me pause.

Rose's parents were preoccupied with proving the Maxwells did it and exacting revenge instead of meeting with doctors to discuss a recovery plan. Everyone else was busy using this dinner as a networking opportunity, setting people up on dates, and turning Rose's trauma into their gain. Ironically, the only person to express genuine interest in her welfare was the man accused of pushing her.

> Poppy: Visitations won't be allowed for a few more weeks, but she's expected to make a full recovery.

> Unknown: That's good news.

> Unknown: What was the mayhem about if it wasn't about Rose?

> Poppy: The house has been raided by relatives. If that wasn't bad enough, my grandmother set me up with some guy.

Three bubbles graced the text exchange screen before they disappeared. The phone buzzed as my grandmother exclaimed, "Okay, everyone, shh. Paris is making his way over."

I hit the lock screen as Mom mumbled, "Joy."

"Here, I'll take him." Nani snatched Neil off my lap in preparation for Paris's arrival, an arrangement that didn't suit either of us.

"It's fine. I don't mind watching him." I extended my arms, and Neil leaned over, all too willing to return.

"No. He'll distract you from Paris." Nani gave me her back, taking away the one relative that might've made his insipid presence bearable. If I weren't positive Nani would stop coming over for directly snubbing her choice, I wouldn't let Paris near me with a ten-foot pole. The small control over my future was the only reason my grandmother was malleable and civil toward Mom (yes, it could be worse, and it was when she first married Zane). It'd be long before Mom was forgiven for the transgression of marrying someone below her station.

My feelings toward Zaina Mittal were contradictory. I liked her ambition and work ethic as a mogul. On the other hand, she had no respect for the middle class. Her extreme dislike of Zane was admirable, though our reasons were worlds apart. She shared a complicated relationship with Mom while admiring my academic pursuits and reserving a soft spot for me. Nonetheless, Nani displayed her affection in the oddest way: pushing Paris on me for basic reasons.

One, Paris had an Ivy League education and came from old money. He was considered an appropriate match for the future CEO of Ambani Corp even though his father got him admitted into Cornell and created a made-up position at his company so Paris could earn a cushy salary without working.

Secondly, my grandmother thought men with old European city names were sophisticated, so she named her firstborn Milan. Paris, however, disproved Nani's theory within ten minutes.

CHAPTER
ELEVEN
POPPY

"Hi, beautiful." Paris pulled up the chair next to mine. A slightly protruding midsection grazed the edge of the table when he plopped down. His yellow shirt might have cost a pretty penny, but it wasn't made of magic.

Paris looked me up and down, throwing some of his infamous smoldering my way. It was meant to be alluring because he thought girls found him deep and mysterious. The pretentious poems he wrote supported my theory. He wanted to appear profound, though he had nothing insightful to share.

"Hello." I leaned away to escape the scent of heavily doused cologne, pretending to rifle through the breadbasket. Perhaps Paris could've been good-looking were it not for his personality.

Mom's eyes were steadfast on Paris. She buttered a piece of bread with sharp stabs, likely imagining his face. The loathing was justified.

"I can't believe what happened last night."

I nodded, foreseeing the direction of this conversation. A narcissist at heart, Paris had the uncanny ability to make everything about himself. I bet he'd do the same with Rose's accident.

First, he'd mention how upset he was about Rosie's misfortune. Then he'd complain how no one was at his million-dollar penthouse to console him, leaving him emotionally fragile. Finally, Paris would write a poem about his mental state. If people declined to hear it, he'd claim starving artists were always unappreciated in their time. By the end of the conversation, he'd be the real victim, his emotional distress surpassing Rose's ailment.

"Imagining Rose's pain and what she must've felt..." Paris shuddered as if it were involuntary. "It created a pain inside me that I didn't know existed. It was awful. I haven't been able to sleep since I found out."

I spread butter on my burnt focaccia. "You mean since you found out about it ten hours ago?"

Paris made a face. "I found out thirteen hours ago. I've been up ever since."

"Thirteen hours ago would've been six o'clock in the morning," I pointed out.

"I think worrying about Rose gave me insomnia."

"Hmm."

"Do you know there is a type of insomnia called FFI, Fatal Familial Insomnia? I googled it. I bet that's what I developed from my anxiety."

"Oh yeah?"

"If you think about it, Rose is lucky. She only hit her head, but she'll recover. Whereas FFI is an ongoing sleep deprivation that eventually leads to death."

A half smile greeted my lips as I bit into the dry bread. Mom scorched the end pieces for my benefit.

"The worst part was lying in bed and waiting for death in my big, empty condo. Do you know the place I'm talking about, my penthouse?"

It was a non-rhetorical question. "You might've mentioned it once or twice."

"Three thousand square feet, overlooks Central Park, built-in elevator. Anyway, I was lying there and dealing with Fatal Insomnia—"

"Fatal Familial Insomnia," I corrected.

He frowned. "Right, Fatal Familial Insomnia. No one was there to hold my hand, and I could have died alone. How do you come back from emotional trauma like that?"

I nodded. "It's impossible, I imagine."

"I kept thinking, what if I died and no one knew my last thoughts? So, I grabbed a pen and paper and put my feelings into words. Ended up writing my best poem yet. It's what happens when your emotions are raw from seeing death up close."

Paris was three for three. A personal best since it took him less than five minutes to turn Rose's misfortune utterly and entirely about himself. Paris acted like a petulant child at thirty, unlike a particular twenty-five-year-old CEO dripping with maturity. Unable to help myself, I unlocked my phone under the table.

> Unknown: The word mayhem should never be used when referring to a date.

> Unknown: Don't suffer through a date because your grandmother says so. Ditch him.
>
> Unknown: You there?
>
> Unknown: Are you talking to him? Is that why you aren't responding?

I glanced at Paris and realized he was still talking, simultaneously checking his reflection on a metal knife. At least conversations with him required very little energy. He could start and end a conversation by speaking only of himself. I quickly typed a message.

> Poppy: I never said it was a date.

Damon responded as if he were waiting on the other side of the phone.

> Unknown: Mayhem and 'some guy' still sound like a terrible combination.
>
> Unknown: Ditch him.

The texts possessed a jealous undertone that once more clashed with what I had learned of Damon Maxwell. I was momentarily lost in them.

"Are you listening?" Paris snapped his fingers in front of my face.

Nope. Didn't like being snapped at. By the icy glare emanating from across the table, Mom caught the motion and didn't like it, either.

I pocketed my phone instead of breaking his fingers. Exercising this much restraint might cause a brain aneurysm. "Yes, Paris?"

"I said, let's go somewhere private, and I'll read you my poem," Paris said suggestively. "You'll like this one."

Hardly able to suppress my groan, I focused on escaping the predictable. Rejection was around the time Paris went from a harmless narcissist to a douchebag. Although I repeatedly hinted at my disinterest, Paris kept coming around, hoping it would stick if I saw him enough. "No, thank you."

"You don't want to hear my poem?" Paris asked incredulously, hardly believing his ears.

"I'm afraid your... masterpiece will be wasted on me. I'm sleep-deprived from my night at the hospital."

His face twisted into a grimace. "I'm sleep-deprived, too, Poppy. You don't hear me complaining about it. Do you know most artists aren't appreciated in their time? If I die from FFI tonight, this poem will become my last thoughts on earth. What if you could go back in time and meet Van Gogh? Would you have turned down the opportunity?"

If Paris bothered listening to anyone but himself, he'd know I wouldn't care. I was into facts and math, not arts and literature.

Placing my unfinished bread on the plate, I eyed my slightly burnt chicken parmesan. I was starving but also put off by Paris's company. "Sorry to hear about your upcoming death, but as you know, I have a strict policy against being alone with strangers," I stated firmly.

The facade withered, along with the smoldering. "We aren't strangers," he muttered, annoyance coloring his words. "You know what your grandmother expects of us. There isn't exactly a large pool of acceptable men for someone in your position," he said pointedly. "So, I suggest you stop acting so self-absorbed and show some interest in my interests. The world doesn't revolve around you."

The tendons in my neck strained. Not because Paris, the king of narcissists, accused me of the same, but because there was some truth to his statement. The board of Ambani Corp was made up of my relatives, and to them, image and family values were everything. I had to marry within the next few years and not just anyone. My spouse had to be Indian, part of the upper one percentile, and come from old money. The qualifications limited the pool to the likes of Paris.

Mom warned me about this predicament and suggested pursuing the top role if it were a sacrifice I was willing to make. I never blinked twice at the face of the adversary. But suddenly, spending a lifetime with Paris seemed too big a price to pay.

I blotted the corners of my mouth and stood, dropping the linen napkin on my seat. "As charming as this has been, I should get going. I have a friend who lives abroad. He's going to FaceTime me to recite a poem he wrote."

The last sentence hit home. His jaw dropped, and I left the accelerating madness of the dining room on a high note.

Entering the grand ballroom, I located the three-tier trays with appetizers. The displays were placed strategically on coffee tables around the room, accenting the sitting areas. My stomach rumbled loudly, but before I could reach the first platter of mozzarella bites, a sea of bodies materialized out of thin air, blocking my attempt. The second platter had less of a crowd safeguarding it, but as I reached the other end of the giant ballroom, someone swooped in for the last deviled egg. Gritting my teeth, I contemplated setting this house on fire to get rid of these people. Fortunately, real mayhem overshadowed my plans.

The hum of conversation was suddenly interrupted by the piercing wail of the fire alarm. Guests searched the room to locate the source of the blaring sounds and the white strobing lights.

"Fire!" someone screamed, setting off the panic.

Startled, one person jumped to their feet, face white with fear. Another tripped over his feet and spilled a soda on his shirt. Some ran, eyes bulging as they searched for the nearest exit, while others yelled for their partners.

I found the nearest couch and nicked the tray of finger sandwiches, abandoned because of the fire. The beautiful anarchy resembled an old horror movie. A dinner and a show. I could have soaked in it for hours, but Zane's irritating voice from the dining room snapped me out of it.

"Everyone, stay calm and exit in an orderly fashion," he stated, sounding thrilled at the prospect of kicking guests out without upsetting Mom. He'd happily burn in a fire than deal with unwanted relatives.

"Where is Poppy?" I heard Mom's obscure voice. It sounded like she was being evacuated as well.

"Go outside. I'll find her," Zane informed her, though we both knew he'd never come to find me.

I took a bite of my mini sandwich, immediately spitting it out on a cocktail napkin. Gross, peppers.

An older gentleman walking toward the courtyard at a snail's pace gazed back at me in disbelief. I fought an eye roll. Did he expect me to die on an empty stomach? I barely had two bites of my dinner. Evidently, eating without the detested company of others could only be achieved through the help of a fire.

The brittle man was small enough to disappear behind a grain of rice. Unsurprisingly, he couldn't pry open the heavy door separating the courtyard from the main room, nor was he agile enough to walk to another exit. It had already taken him several minutes to cross the grand ballroom. Realizing everyone else had fled the scene, he looked back at me with hope. His incredulous stare burned a hole into my skull when I separated the bread, picked off the peppers, and popped it into my mouth. I did the same with two more finger sandwiches.

I stood once I finished chewing, mostly because he wouldn't stop gaping with doe eyes. "Alright, alright. I'll rescue you."

Unbelieving eyes followed me when I grabbed a chair to stand on instead of advancing toward him and fiddling with the alarm. Simultaneously, I texted Mom that I was fine and there was no fire. One of the smoke detectors must be malfunctioning. It was better to find and defuse it instead of having the old man walk outside. He didn't seem equipped for the cold or the exercise.

The state-of-the-art extinguishers would have doused us with sprinklers if there were a fire. The sensitive technology reacted to any traces of smoke. Zane was aware of this feature but used the fire alarm as an excuse to get rid of guests. It was one of those rare instances in which we put aside our differences for a greater cause.

When the alarm didn't shut off, I reset the remaining ones in the vicinity.

The Cinderella slipper fit the smoke detector nearest the courtyard exit, and the earsplitting sounds and flashing lights ended.

The old man mumbled a thanks, though he didn't bother returning to his previous seat. He dropped his butt on the nearest couch, turned sideways, and propped his feet up.

I shrugged. "Good call."

Examining the alarm, I checked for malfunctions. Nothing. The nearest door opened to the courtyard. There was no one around. The only incriminating evidence appeared to be something that didn't fit the picture-perfect yard. A small portion of the ground next to the exit was covered in a gray film of dust. At a closer look, it appeared to be ashes from cigarette butts. The ash felt warm between my fingers. Some asshole lit a cigarette under one of the smoke alarms, then took off.

"False alarm, everyone. Let's go back inside," someone shouted, and I could've sworn I heard Zane grit his teeth from a distance.

Although I'd heard engines revving, not all the guests evacuated the premises. Brushing the ashes off my hands, I took off. I would've investigated further, but my interest in a false fire alarm paled in comparison to avoiding murder conspiracy theories and setups.

Jogging up the stairs to my room, I locked the door behind me. I stripped off my dress, undid my hair, and changed into black sweats and a tank top. I eyed my balcony before stepping out and turning on the lights. It was otherwise indistinguishable from the outside.

This was my favorite part of this house, though the weather was disappointing tonight. The heated enclave turned the freezing cold conditions into crisp, fresh air. A bird on a nearby tree chirped happily, and the moon shone brightly without a cloud in sight. Damn. I wished the sky was beautiful tonight, maybe a downpour of rain, perhaps some tornado-like wind. Hell, I'd even settle for a bit of lightning.

I leaned my elbows against the balcony railing, scrolling through my phone for updates on Rose. Rubbing my cheeks, I stared at the fountain in the middle of the courtyard when I saw the unmistakable shape of cigarette fumes twirling from behind a tree.

Someone was watching me. The same someone who set off the fire alarm.

CHAPTER TWELVE

DAMON

The smoke from my cigarette curled and twisted, giving the illusion of warmth. In reality, the night was full of shadows and chills.

Set on the farthest corner of the house and overlooking the courtyard, Poppy's room was subjected to minimal attention. The balcony attached to her room was barely visible in the moonlight. A light came on, followed by Poppy's silhouette. She stood with her elbows against the stone railing covered in vines. Head bowed, she scrolled through her phone before pocketing it and studying the fountain instead.

"Message me back, little demon spawn," I willed her, fingering the tattoo hidden underneath my shirt's collar.

I checked my messages for the hundredth time. Texts from my uncle about work. Texts from girls I didn't know. Texts from my PR company. Nothing from Poppy. Frustrated with her lack of response, I wondered if she was messaging the man her grandmother had set her up with.

I could understand why her grandmother fixed her up. Poppy was expected to marry someone who fit the expectations of their company's board. While I empathized with the significance of tradition, I couldn't allow it. Poppy wouldn't marry out of love, but she would marry for her career. If the douchebag had her family's stamp of approval, it would close the door on us forever. The thoughts sent me into a downward spiral. This savage reaction to a woman I officially met last night was unprecedented. An imaginary string pulled me back to this property. I didn't resist the festering insanity. Instead, I embraced the darkness and went off the deep end.

I was already in their courtyard, surrounded by tall, whitewashed walls, when Poppy told me about the little date. I somewhat disguised myself by pulling my cap lower onto my forehead. Luckily, a zillion people were in the house for Rose's vigil. It was still a suicide mission, considering Ambanis outnumbered me. Thirty more seconds, and Poppy herself would've caught me red-handed. I saw her striding into the grand ballroom as I lifted my lit cigarette. Good thing I was tall. Swirling the cigarette under the smoke alarm was the easiest way to break up the non-date. Everyone flooded outside except for Poppy. She was too smart to be cold without a good reason.

If their grand ballroom hadn't been so large and crowded, sneaking out unnoticed would've been impossible. Tall trees with colorful fall leaves encompassed the insides of the courtyard, providing me with the necessary cover to remain hidden. Lurking around the yard was still a bad idea.

I finished my fifth cigarette, putting the bud out with my shoe. The wind picked up, along with the sound of waves from a distance. The minutes passed slowly, but I waited until I was positive the premise was clear. Finally, I advanced toward the fountain underneath her balcony.

Poppy didn't flinch when I stepped out of the shadows. "You know how to make an entrance; I'll give you that." She sounded bored. "But returning to the scene of the crime is indicative of serial killer behavior."

"We need to talk." I got straight to the point.

"About?"

I shook my head. "Not going to shout it from here. I'm coming up."

I expected Poppy to protest, refusing to be alone with a stranger. Poppy preferred calculated risks, and being this close to a Maxwell wasn't in her favor. However, she said nothing. There was no change in her expression, either.

The balcony stood on two large stone columns decorated with intricate carvings and vines. Tossing my bomber jacket over my shoulder, my fingers curled around the cold iron bars of the trellis on one of the columns. It must be what the gardener used to upkeep the plants. I grabbed the stone railing when I reached the top. Pulling myself up, I landed on the expansive terrace. It was encased in a wrought iron balustrade. The walls were painted black and covered in more ivy. Several fabric benches and café tables with matching chairs were scattered across. In one corner was a hot tub. On the other side, a spiral stone staircase led to the tiled roof, topped with a windowed cupola overlooking the ocean at a distance.

The Gothic balcony, better identified as a terrace due to its size, was an extension. It differed from the rest of the modern house. Someone poured love into designing this veranda to Poppy's morbid old-fashioned taste so she could enjoy a spectacular view.

Nonetheless, the best view in the house was currently mine. My eyes devoured Poppy. Her typically braided hair was loose in gentle waves, framing her shoulders and black tank top. Her flawless skin shimmered in the soft light, her wide brown eyes expressionless. It was taking all my self-restraint not to kiss her pink pillow-like lips off.

For years, I saw her around campus from a distance. Being this close to her should come with a warning sign. It was downright dangerous because I may never get my fill.

Poppy pushed off the railing, dissecting me with similar intensity. I was suffering from the insatiable need to know what she was thinking. She was shocked upon discovering my identity last night. But did the disappointment stem from my last name or a lack of attraction? Astonishing. A small person I could pick up with one hand provoked a crippling self-doubt I'd never otherwise experienced.

I frowned once we were a couple of feet apart. "Where is your coat?"

"This balcony is heated."

"So what? It's the dead of winter. You're going to catch a cold."

"Men in glass houses." She pointedly stared at my sweater, my jacket slung over my shoulder.

"It's different for me."

"Why?"

"Because I'm hotter than you."

One side of her mouth tipped upward. An overwhelming possessiveness coursed through me at the hint of her smile. Poppy wasn't known to smile, and I was dying for another.

Pulling the jacket off my shoulder, I extended it to her. "Here."

Her gaze drifted from the bomber jacket to me. Once more, I expected her to protest. What I didn't expect was Poppy to shrug on the coat. It fell heavily over her, reaching her thighs. Our height difference was significant and reflective when she wore my gear.

"Why did you set off the fire alarm?" she asked abruptly. "More importantly, how did you get past security?"

This place had better security lockdown than most prisons. Access was impossible unless someone from the inside opened the main gate. Breaking in was difficult, but I only had to do it once. I had guaranteed entry into these grounds from now on since I stole one of the staff's key fobs.

I didn't regret it. Extreme measures had to be taken after I found out about Poppy's date. The girl meant to be the bane of my existence had evoked something unparalleled. I replayed last night in my head over and over. Watching Poppy impaled on my cock, her efforts to stifle the moans of pleasure, her inability to hold it in, all the stolen moments were ripped away too soon. When Poppy looked back at the hospital hallway, I almost marched over. I composed the madness she inspired because her mind was on Rose. The last thing Poppy wanted was to fight the world for a new, undefined connection with her archnemesis. With the news of her cousin's gradual recovery, walking away for a second time was impossible.

"I waited until the main gate opened for a car and snuck in before it could close," I told her.

"And the fire alarm?"

I shrugged. "Thought you could use some assistance getting out of an unfavorable situation. You're welcome."

I braced myself for Poppy's reaction to the display of several borderline stalkerish behaviors. But Poppy appeared amused. "That's quite the gallant effort for someone you barely know."

"After our night together..." My eyes dawdled on Poppy's lips. "What man wouldn't put in a gallant effort?"

Brown eyes stared back. "Sex is hardly a cause worth dying over. Or perhaps it's the thrill of getting caught you like." She gestured at my body with a wave. "Sex is freely available to someone in your position, possibly even with a person whose family doesn't threaten your mortality."

"I'm not interested in celebrity chasers."

"Then you shouldn't have picked New York as your residence."

A humorless laugh tumbled out, recalling Sophie's reproach. "I've found exactly what I'm looking for here in New York."

Poppy studied me quietly. "You would've been exonerated from attempted murder if you told my family we were together when Rose fell."

"Careful, Ambani. It's starting to sound like you're worried about me," I mused.

Her gaze lowered. "Why didn't you tell them?"

"There would've been anarchy if word got out about us."

"Jailtime surpasses the shame of sleeping with your enemy, wouldn't you agree?"

"I meant anarchy for you. Your relatives wouldn't take kindly to us sleeping together, and you'd never be considered for CEO. I understand you're currently a shoo-in."

"Last night was the first time you even looked my way. What interest is my career to you?"

"I told you. Last night was something else. Don't pretend you didn't feel it, too."

As expected, Poppy remained unconvinced. She assumed my interest stemmed from the thrill of sleeping with my enemy. She was partially correct. There was a thrill of getting away with it under everyone's noses, but there was more. "We barely know each other," she argued.

"What would you like to know?"

"You and Caden went to boarding school in Switzerland. Why?"

I laughed. "That's what you want to know about me?"

She shrugged. "It was the only thing I couldn't find out about you."

I nodded. "Not many people know about it. Caden and I wanted to leave the country, and Switzerland had the best schools in the world. What about you? Why did you attend boarding school?" Poppy was expelled from two schools for notoriety before graduating from high school at fourteen. Besides my time outside the country, she knew my entire track record, too. We still performed the practiced choreography as if we hadn't obsessively researched the person pitted against us, unearthing every detail about them.

"I preferred an academic setting. Staying at home was distracting me."

"Distracting you from what?"

"From my goals. I wanted to graduate from high school as soon as possible." She allowed me to focus on her briefly before shooting back with, "Why did you and your brother attend boarding school outside the country?"

I frowned, calculating Poppy's easy stance. "Because I hated being here after Mom passed away. She used to be the buffer between us and Dad. In case you haven't noticed, my father is an idiot."

The comment bred Poppy's infamous semi-smirk. It knocked the wind out of me whenever she looked remotely optimistic. Tonight's goal was to purge her bias against the Maxwells. So, I tackled a matter I should have addressed years ago and gave her words that didn't exist in the Maxwell dictionary.

"I'm sorry for what he did to your mom."

Poppy neither acknowledged nor dismissed the point of contention igniting this ugly feud. She tilted her head and returned the apology, "I think we are even. Ambanis inflicted a lot of damage, too. We hold monthly D.M. meetings."

"D.M.?"

"Destroy the Maxwells."

I chuckled.

"What about you guys? Do you hold monthly meetings to bring us down?" she asked indifferently, looking out over the courtyard.

"No. We do it weekly."

The latest remark earned me a half smile, a truly rare sight.

"Any more questions?" I probed.

"Just one more." She looked back at me. "Why are you risking everything for me?"

"Because I haven't been able to stop thinking about you since last night." I moved toward her as if the choice to do anything else had been taken away. "And because you've been driving me crazy since we met. It's madness." One more step forward. "And one can't explain madness."

Poppy stepped back instinctively, her expression guarded. "I recommend snapping out of this madness before it becomes a full-blown infatuation."

"Too late."

All traces of apathy vanished from Poppy's face. She recovered swiftly and slipped back on the impassive mask. "Tread carefully, Maxwell. I'm not infatuation material. I'm cold and indifferent. If you died tomorrow, I wouldn't shed a single tear. Not because I don't want to but because my brain isn't wired that way. I can't love or express emotions, and I have nothing to offer you."

"I'll be the judge of that," I responded firmly.

"You do understand my family is trying to have you hanged?"

"The death penalty isn't applicable in New York," I countered.

"It'll fuel them to destroy you some other way."

"They can try. I'll still keep coming after you."

Pouty, pink lips pursed. Was she always this pretty? I did my best not to spook her more by staring, on top of coming on so strong. I took another step forward. Once more, Poppy backed away. I closed the distance with three long strides this time and grabbed her elbows before she could escape.

She glanced at my lips. For the first time, she seemed unsure of herself. "You're making a mistake—"

I silenced her by pressing my hungry lips forcefully against her soft ones. Poppy stiffened in surprise, not expecting the intense display. I couldn't focus on her reaction as my lips crushed hers unforgivingly. The taste and scent of her consumed my entire being.

A low groan escaped my lips as the subtle hint of lavender reached my senses. "Fuck, you smell good." I bit her bottom lip, pulling it slightly between my teeth. "And taste even better." My hand moved to her neck, gripping it firmly while my thumb massaged her pulse. Slowly, I licked down her throat, savoring every moment. "So fucking good."

Poppy remained unresponsive, causing me to return to her mouth and grip her throat firmly. A sharp inhale escaped her as she finally caught on to what we were doing.

I pulled back slightly, my lips hovering above hers. "Was that...?" I paused, closely assessing her reactions. "You've never kissed anyone before."

Instead of denying the accusation, a blank mien greeted me.

My brows knitted. "How's that possible? We've had sex, and you weren't a virgin."

She shrugged as if never having given it another thought. "Kissing seems like a waste of time. Never wanted to engage in it."

A craving stirred deep in my soul, constructed by the surge of possessiveness washing over me. At least no one was before me in one arena of her life.

My lips swooped down once more, my tongue urging her to part her lips. "Open your mouth," I instructed.

My fingers dug into her hips to bring her closer, each of them acting like barbed hooks meant to keep her rooted in place. Her resolve melted with each swipe of my tongue, and she parted her lips.

"Stick your tongue out," I groaned.

Reluctantly, she complied, and I licked her tongue with my own for an open-mouth kiss. The kiss grew rough and wild, my tongue exploring hers so lewdly that Poppy shook in my hold.

Encouraged by her reactions, I surged forward, the kiss increasing in intensity. Dropping my hands, I pushed her thighs up, forcing her legs to coil around my waist. I pressed her against the stone railing, realizing Poppy's hands were fisting my sweater. Our tongues intertwined languourously, shooting radiating electricity between us. The atmosphere was charged with energy in the face of something extraordinary.

Evidence of this strange intensity brewing between us hit me right in the groin. Suddenly, Poppy reared back, her gaze fixated on the bulge brushing against her. I followed her gaze. My cock throbbed painfully, demanding entrance to her wet warmth. I had jacked off countless times since last night after sleeping with her once. The memory was speared into my soul, and I needed another taste.

"Last night was a one-off," Poppy spoke when I grabbed the waistband of her sweatpants. She pulled my hand away with a shake of her head. "I wasn't planning on having sex again until next year."

"You've met your quota for the year, have you?" I asked, voice thick with amusement.

"Something like that," Poppy panted, though her stern expression remained intact. "And you came inside me last night," she accosted. Unwrapping her legs, Poppy slid down my body. "You were supposed to use a condom. It's a good thing I'm on the pill."

Interjecting impassiveness in my expression took an unsurmountable amount of effort. *She was on the pill.*

Before we could continue the heated exchange, the phone in Poppy's hand came alive, distracting her from berating me.

"That's Nick's ringtone. He was supposed to call me with an update on Rose." She turned away to answer with a curt, "Talk."

Nick said something over the phone that made Poppy tense. The conversation lasted mere seconds before she slowly lowered the phone.

"What's wrong?" I asked cautiously.

"Nick found a video of Rose falling," Poppy revealed.

"How is that possible?"

"I don't know," she replied, her eyes darting between the phone and me. "But he's sending it to me."

Just as she finished speaking, her phone chimed with a new message. Poppy unlocked it, and I moved beside her as she played the video. A drunk girl stumbled into the frame, belligerently swaying to the music and declaring her inebriated state. Someone pointed the camera at her, possibly intending to document the provocative dancing.

"There." Poppy zoomed in to the top right corner of the screen. "It's Rose."

The video turned slightly grainy when enlarged, but we could make out enough details. Rose stood on the second floor in the backdrop, her side profile visible as she shook her head at something not captured on film.

"What is she looking at?" Poppy mused aloud.

I tried to place Rose within the layout of the house and decipher what might have caught her attention. Nothing came to mind. Tears streamed down Rose's cheeks, and she stifled a sob with a hand over her mouth. "Or who is she looking at? They clearly freaked her out."

"No," Poppy contradicted softly. "Rose isn't spooked. She is devastated. Look at how she backed away as if hoping whatever she saw wasn't real."

Poppy was right. Rose's face was raw with pain. In her devastation, tears blurring her vision and judgment, Rose walked backward to distance herself from the distressing situation. There was a fateful moment of realization when the railing hit her lower back. Rose had backpedaled too quickly and lost her balance. Her mouth opened wide in a scream just as she stumbled over the railing and fell to the floor below.

"Shit," I cursed under my breath.

"It was an accident, after all," Poppy concluded. The phone beeped again, prompting her to tap on the message icon. "Nick unlocked Rose's phone. Her last few texts were..." Her eyes searched the screen before looking up at me. "They were from you."

I stiffened. The phone beeped persistently with more incoming texts. Poppy quickly glossed over the new messages, searching for the truth. I braced myself because I knew what was coming.

"There were so many texts between you two." Poppy held up the damning evidence, face contorting with ire. "Some of these are from years ago."

The accusation was true, though Rose's intention and mine differed. "I didn't respond to most of her messages." My voice was measured as I spoke.

"She wouldn't have pursued you this hard, not unless there was history between you two."

I shook my head. "I was never interested in Rose, nor did I encourage her advances."

Poppy scanned the texts. "But you did encourage it for an invitation to this party."

I knew where this was headed. "I can explain before you jump to any conclusions."

"Let me guess. You flirted with Rose to get into the party," she surmised. "That's how you got through security. Someone from the inside let you in."

The assessment was spot-on. "Yes, however, the messages weren't flirtatious, at least not on my end," I explained delicately. Rose was the closest Poppy had to a sister. Making Rose look bad to defend myself would work against me.

Poppy's gaze returned to the phone. Her expression morphed as if another piece of the puzzle clicked. "You didn't shut the bedroom door," she stated, her voice filled with realization.

I tried to comprehend the abrupt change of topic. "Excuse me?"

"Last night," she clarified, gesturing toward the video. "You didn't close the door after kicking Sophie out of the room."

After catching them in the act, I furiously hauled Sophie off the bed and shoved her out of the room. A blindfolded Poppy waiting for me on the bed had obliterated my reasons. I wasn't thinking straight, let alone worried about shutting the door.

Poppy pulled up the video from before. She rotated the phone, studying the spatial configuration of where Rose stood and the layout of the scene. The truth hit us simultaneously like a ton of bricks.

"If Rose was standing here, and my bedroom door was open, she was probably staring inside my bedroom when she fell," Poppy decreed. "She must've come to find me and caught us in bed together instead. That's why she was upset. Because she has been in love with you for years."

This couldn't get any worse. "I tried my best never to lead her on," I admitted instead of denying Rose's feelings.

"I'll need Rose to confirm that."

"That's not exactly possible at the moment. You have to take my word for it."

"Take your word? You selectively omitted to mention Rose's feelings for you, though you clearly knew about it. In fact, you took advantage of her feelings," Poppy accused. "After flirting with her to get into the party, you slept with a random girl, then left the door open for Rose to see."

"It wasn't intentional."

"Doesn't matter. Rose backed away so fast that she fell. She wasn't thinking clearly because of you." She paused, contemplating her words before adding, "And because of me."

"No," I spoke sternly, leaving no room for argument. Few people held a place in Poppy's heart, and Rose was one of them. Poppy was ferociously protective of her cousin. I couldn't let her shoulder the blame for Rose's tragedy. "It's not your fault." I instinctively reached for Poppy to comfort her, but she withdrew from my touch.

"Except it was my fault," Poppy argued. "She thought I betrayed her."

"You didn't."

"You should leave."

My jaw clenched. "Are you sure that's what you want?" I shifted closer. "I feel bad for Rose; I do. But whatever's happening between us, it's bigger than her. I know you feel it, too. Otherwise, you wouldn't have let me come up."

Poppy was unmoved. I used Rose to gain entry to the party, and as far as Poppy was concerned, we were both complicit in the accident. There was no convincing her otherwise or reversing the damage. Frustration swelled within me at the knowledge I had lost Poppy for the night, with no recourse other than giving her space.

"Fine. I'll give you until tomorrow to think it over," I said without moving. I might be seething, but my legs had a mind of their own. They were rooted in place, feeding off the vision before me. With determination I didn't know I possessed, I backed away. "Later, Ambani," I murmured before descending from the balcony.

ACT 3

CHAPTER
THIRTEEN
DAMON

My trusty old Louisville slugger took out the passenger side window of Sophie's cherry-red Rolls Royce, the sound music to my ears. It took making two more dents before Sophie emerged from the house, her screams piercing the air.

"Damon! What the hell?" Sophie shouted, running to the driveway. "Oh my God. Stop it, stop it." She threw her fists against my back as I kept whacking, my cigarette hanging loosely from the corner of my mouth. The big bangles around her wrists dug into my shoulders. Even at home, Sophie never missed the opportunity to dress up, accessorizing her one-shoulder sweater wrap with large pieces of jewelry.

I was positive her flashy clothes no longer held any appeal for Poppy, who was draped in my clothes when I left last night. Despite that small consolation, my anger demanded retribution, and it focused itself on Sophie's cherished car. Sophie had escaped my wrath for the past few days while I was preoccupied with Poppy. Unfortunately, Sophie's luck ran out when Poppy turned skittish around me. The setback didn't deter me, and I texted Poppy throughout the day, refusing to linger far from her mind. I made suggestions such as going to a movie or dinner. Both were met with radio silence. With Poppy no longer serving as a distraction, I had the sudden urge to exact revenge on Sophie.

I made another dent in the passenger side door.

"You bastard. It's my favorite car," she cried. "Why are you doing this?"

Favorite car? Wealthy heiresses and their problems.

Dragging the cigarette away from my mouth, I let out a long exhale before putting it out with the sole of my shoe. Not that Sophie deserved an answer, but I still gave her one.

"You touched my favorite thing in the world, so I'm going to destroy yours." The grip on my bat tightened at the reminder. I swung the bat over the windshield, the glass cracking from the impact. The fragmented pieces rained down onto the front console and seats.

This time, Sophie had no theatrics left to display. "Poppy," she uttered, summing up the situation in one word. Sophie thought it'd be entertaining to watch an Ambani anonymously fuck a Maxwell, then freak out upon discovering their identity. Sophie needed to learn a hard lesson. Provoking the wrong people with silly mind games had dire consequences.

There was a time when I would have vehemently denied any emotional attachment to an Ambani. That ship had long sailed, my sanity along with it. The only reason Sophie wasn't buried six feet under was because her little stunt brought me to Poppy. Destroying her beloved car was the tip of the iceberg in terms of payment due. Whistling, I circled the car and unleashed my anger on the driver's side window.

Malicious fury consumed Sophie upon witnessing the destruction of her prized possession. "For your information," she spat, "your girl came onto *me.*"

A fresh wave of anger surged within me, prompting me to stab one of the tires out with a pocketknife.

Sophie crossed her arms defiantly. "Would you have preferred if I turned her down? Because I don't think Little Miss *Unsunshine* would have slept with you otherwise."

I glared at Sophie, despising the truth in her words.

"I did you a favor, and we both know it," she continued, her voice laced with bitterness. "So how about you get off your high horse and shower me with gifts of gratitude instead? I saw how you looked at her; you were infatuated with her. You kicked me out during a threesome so you wouldn't have to share her. You got what you wanted, so why are you acting like I did you wrong?"

Because if Sophie deduced my obsession, she should've understood Poppy was off-limits. The realization refueled my rage. "If you saw how I looked at her, why didn't you leave?" I barked. "Why the fuck did you touch her?"

Sophie arched an eyebrow in challenge, ticking off the reasons on her fingers. "I didn't think it'd be a problem since we'd shared the same girl before. As far as I understood, you were taken enough with Poppy to fuck her. How was I supposed to know you planned on pursuing an Ambani girl outside the bedroom?"

The reasoning was plausible, though it didn't matter in my current state of irrationality. She had the audacity to lay her hands on Poppy, and I couldn't let such an offense go unpunished. Moving to the next tire, I deflated it with a swift motion.

Sophie huffed in frustration. "Come on, Damon. It wasn't my fault. Poppy researched me to find out when I'm the most vulnerable."

"I don't care."

"No?" She quirked her brows. "She kept feeding me shots before seducing me."

I whirled around so fast that Sophie backpedaled. Even in this manic state, she couldn't comprehend the depths of my darkness. Pushing me wasn't in her best interest.

When she spoke again, her tone held a hint of diplomacy. "All I meant was Poppy obviously got me drunk to pump me for information. It's well known that I exercise poor judgment while drunk off my ass."

The shockingly self-aware assessment gave me pause. Sophie was right. Poppy would only slip someone shots if she had an ulterior motive.

Sophie took a deep breath. "I'm sorry. I shouldn't have touched her." Her gaze swung to the bat resting over my shoulder. "It won't happen again. I won't even message her back, okay?"

"Message her back?" I tilted my head. "Poppy texted you?"

"Er, yeah," she admitted unsurely. "She wanted to meet up, but I won't respond if—"

"Give me your phone," I ordered, cutting her off sharply.

Once more, her eyes darted toward the baseball bat. Reluctantly, Sophie handed over the phone. I read through their texts, fist clenching and unclenching. The flirtatious exchanges between Poppy and Sophie made my blood boil, and I contemplated wrecking the rest of Sophie's cars.

I rubbed the tattoo along the back of my neck, taking in the calm it brought me at these kinds of moments. Another consolation safeguarded Sophie's prized possessions. Poppy sounded genuine in our exchanges, while her responses to Sophie appeared fake. As I scrolled through the thread, it became abundantly clear Poppy crafted the flirtatious responses with the help of an AI app. An elaborate ruse to trap Sophie in the web she'd weaved.

No longer was I worried about the petty jealousy where Sophie was concerned. Something worse was at play. There was only one reason to go to these lengths. She was digging into Sophie's testimony, searching for intel about Rayyan's murder. I thought Poppy had shelved the matter, but her interest seemed far from over. This was bad.

"What did you tell Poppy about your testimony?" I stalked forward, a death glare emanating from my eyes.

Sophie gave me an apprehensive look. "Nothing. I swear, Damon."

I dropped my voice. "If I find out you're lying to me, I'll come back to light the rest of these on fire." I pointed my bat at the lineup of cars Daddy Dearest bought her. "Do you understand?"

Sophie eyed me warily. "Why are you taking my phone?" she asked when I pocketed her phone.

"You're gifting it to me as a thank you for not killing you," I explained coldly. "Wait three days before you get a new phone. Until then, I'm in charge of your correspondence." Specifically, her correspondence with Poppy.

Sophie rolled her eyes in frustration. "How am I supposed to get ahold of people?"

"Not my problem." With that, I turned away from her.

Sophie stomped inside, but I had no sympathy to spare. No matter who initiated it, Sophie was a friend of mine, and touching Poppy was a betrayal. Damaging one car wasn't enough of a hefty price. She was addicted to social media. Not having a phone for a few days would be equivalent to torture.

I marched to my car and sped off to Poppy's house, making a quick detour to gather a few items. Silencing Sophie was just a temporary solution. I needed to gain Poppy's confidence and understand why she was determined to overturn Sophie's testimony.

The key fob I stole last night granted me access to Poppy's home through the staff gate. Switching off my headlights, I parked my car near the courtyard, using the moonlight as my guide. I retrieved the large bag from my trunk and climbed up to Poppy's balcony for the second night.

The frosted glass doors obstructed my view into her room, though the darkness confirmed she wasn't there. At least the heated floors and heat lamps created a cozy atmosphere, keeping out the cold.

Unzipping my bag, I assembled a projector and screen, an attached stand, and my laptop. There were blankets on a lounge chair. I placed them on the ground with the throw pillows from the accent chairs to create a makeshift spot.

Last night, the defiance was evident in Poppy's body language. She was torn between her mixed feelings for me and her loyalty to Rose and her family. Unsure how she'd react, I froze at faint footsteps from the bedroom. Eons seemed to pass in waiting, and I mentally willed Poppy to move faster.

Finally, the glass doors slid open, revealing Poppy's perplexed expression as she took in the setup. I expected her to be angry and make demands that I leave immediately. A subtle thrill coursed through me when Poppy stepped onto the balcony instead.

CHAPTER
FOURTEEN
POPPY

"Ms. Ambani. These were delivered for you." Rachel, one of the housekeepers, presented an opaque cylinder vase with an arrangement of black dahlias nestled in greenery.

A fork clattered onto a plate, disrupting the tranquil room as Mom gaped at the stunning arrangement. Zane studied the flowers from across the table, quickly grew bored, and returned to his meal with mechanical precision. My eyes were also on the oversized bouquet, instinctively knowing they were from *him*. Sending flowers to my house was unprecedented, but at least the unwanted relatives were gone, and they didn't bear witness to this.

A sigh escaped the lips of my two-year-old cousin, nestled contentedly in my lap. With his parents spending the night in the city, I offered to babysit Neil, hoping his presence would alleviate the gut punch I received last night. Guilt wasn't something I succumbed to, but this felt damn close to it. Damon was meant to distract me from Rose's accident, not the person I needed a distraction *from* for Rose's sake.

I cleared my throat. "Thank you, Rachel. Was there a card?"

"Yes."

Rachel extended a tiny envelope. My fingers hesitated before pulling out the engraved note concealed within.

To your many firsts

My lips throbbed with the memory of Damon's assault on them. Kissing always seemed frivolous to me, a pointless indulgence that delayed gratification. I already limited distractions such as sex to once a year. Although, since Damon bulldozed into my life, the notion of his tongue stroking mine more than annually didn't seem so bad.

There was only one rational explanation for deviating from my usual frame of mind. I was experiencing a psychotic breakdown.

I always assumed going mad would at least be entertaining, but so far, it had brought forth unwelcome emotions. Damon's incessant stream of texts didn't help. My resolute loyalty to Rose wavered under the weight of his unfaltering attention.

Perhaps I wasn't giving Rose enough credit. She might've acted irrationally on the night she fell because she was drunk. Maybe she'd be happy I finally found someone who intrigued me.

It was wishful thinking. No one had such a strong reaction unless they were hopelessly in love. Damon might not be at fault for encouraging Rose's advances, but she still fell for him. Who could blame her?

Despite the disappointing men I had encountered, Damon was a good apple in a bushel of rotten ones. His contributions to suicide prevention programs and generosity as the leading benefactor for countless ALS research facilities testified to his integrity. The widely acclaimed philanthropist had covertly turned me into a fan of his. I was supposed to be his enemy but reluctantly admitted long ago that Damon was exceptional. Unbeknownst to him, Damon embraced a cause holding deep personal significance to me. His pursuits resonated with the core of my being, embodying the morals I lacked.

Unlike Rose.

Rose was a better choice for Damon in every way. She was kind and possessed endless compassion. Rose would mold into his life and could give him the one thing I couldn't. Love.

Mom waited for me to acknowledge the elephant in the room, brimming with curiosity. Unable to hold back, she blurted, "Please tell me those aren't from Paris. They're too beautiful to be burned."

My lips tilted to one side. The last time Paris sent me flowers, I burned them in the sink, inadvertently setting off the fire alarm. That day, I learned a valuable lesson: the extinguishers dispersed solely for real fires.

"Someone did their research," Mom added slyly, hoping for a hint about the secret sender of flowers.

Yes. Damon had gone to great lengths to procure my phone number and favorite flowers. The name paid homage to my favorite aunt and Neil's mother, Dahlia. Black was also the only color that didn't make my skin crawl.

"Piya," Zane drawled, "If you want to know who they're from, ask her." He had a habit of speaking about me as if I weren't in the room, often referring to me in the third person rather than addressing me directly.

Mom chose not to pry. "Poppy, it's up to you if you want to tell me who they're from."

"A friend," I replied dispassionately.

My eyes strayed to Rachel's retreating figure as she set the vase in the other corner of the room. Zane's irritating voice interrupted the beautiful haze.

"Did you make up your mind about the casket?" He slid a brochure to Mom.

"How about this one?" Mom pressed an index finger onto the booklet.

Zane wrinkled his nose. "It's pink."

"It's cute."

"We aren't getting buried in a pink casket."

My eyes twitched from across the table. *What?*

Mom's bright eyes danced with amusement. "What if only my side of the coffin is pink?"

Piercing a piece of broccoli with my fork, I twisted the utensil against the fine china. "Did I miss an invitation to your upcoming murder-suicide pact?"

Zane's dull eyes drilled into me, face set in the same discontent whenever he remembered my existence.

"It's this silly thing we're doing," Mom explained. "Our lawyer recommended making a will and figuring out things like power of attorney and burial plots. Axel suggested a mausoleum for our final resting place."

Of course, he did. It wasn't enough to monopolize every waking minute of Mom's life; he wanted to do the same in death.

"They sell custom-made joint coffins so we can be buried together," Zane added airily.

"But you're Hindu," I reminded Mom. "You believe in cremation."

"Er. It's just an idea," Mom offered. "We haven't made any commitments."

Not true. Mom did commit but to another man.

When I was young, Mom and Papa discussed having their ashes scattered in Lake Michigan after they passed. It was so *they* could be together in death. At the time, my parents seemed nauseatingly in love. I held onto Papa's ashes so I could reunite him with Mom one day and rectify their story that was cut too short.

I shouldn't have bothered. Mom had long forgotten about her first husband. It was as if Papa never existed. Nothing existed for her anymore except for Zane.

I perused my mother, decked out in a hot pink jumpsuit with long sleeves and sparkling tassel earrings. *Piya Ambani* wouldn't have been caught dead wearing something so bright and bold. *That* woman would've opted for cremation and preferred to be put to rest with Jay Ambani, the love of her life.

On the other hand, *Piya Trimalchio, dressed head to toe in pink,* wasn't someone I recognized. The name came with a brand-new personality. Zane had systematically erased all traces of my father from this persona. We weren't allowed to reminisce, miss, or celebrate Jay Ambani's life. All hell would break loose if Mom dared to grieve him even on the anniversary of his death. The only thing Zane couldn't erase about Jay Ambani was me, and he begrudged it daily.

"It's not just an idea," Zane argued on cue. "We'll be buried together."

"Hmm." I leisurely chewed. "But what if you die first, and Mom meets someone younger? She might prefer being buried with him."

Zane's fist clenched around his fork, nails digging into his palm. The thought had crossed his mind.

Mom laughed nervously. "I don't know about you guys, but this morbid topic is starting to ruin dinner." She lifted a dish. "Truffle mac 'n' cheese?" Mom made a show of offering her famous casserole to redirect the conversation to neutral territory. Food was her go-to distraction during tense moments.

Zane didn't take the bait. "I wouldn't worry about it. When the love of your life dies, you mourn it forever. Meeting someone new only happens if you were with the wrong person to begin with."

I stilled. The attempt to taunt me by putting Papa down was working. Mom's speedy remarriage to Zane made it difficult to dispute the allegations. How could she have forgotten her first husband so quickly if she cared about him?

Zane placed his elbow on the table and leaned forward to drive home his point. "Trust me, if I died, she'd be mourning me for the rest of her life."

"Why don't you die and let's find out if she does?" I retorted.

"That's enough," Mom intervened in the heated argument with a rare stern tone and a pointed glance at Neil.

I pressed my lips together, not wanting Neil to witness this heartwarming "family moment." Everyone returned to their meals. Mom offered to take Neil while I finished my dinner, but his company was therapeutic. Oblivious to the unfair world, Neil picked at a piece of bread, engrossed in the cartoons playing on my phone. He didn't protest when the YouTube app paused, alerting me of an incoming text.

> Sophie: Can't meet up atm. In Vegas for New Year's.

> Poppy: When are you coming back?

> Sophie: I'll be staying here a while. Join me if you want

Given our complicated history with Damon's family, it was apparent Sophie orchestrated the anonymous threesome to push our buttons. Bored rich girls went to extreme lengths to entertain themselves. But confronting her about the setup would be futile. I had to maintain an amicable facade as Sophie was indispensable until she retracted her testimony. I reached out in a renewed effort, but it seemed she was indisposed. I contemplated whether a trip to Vegas was manageable.

"Bad news?" Mom inquired, reading into the furrowed lines on my forehead.

I shook my head. "A friend of mine invited me to Vegas."

"That's exciting. You should go." Mom encouraged me to loosen up and embrace the last year of college life. Las Vegas was also special to both of us.

Papa attended a conference in Vegas once, prompting Mom and me to join him. Despite our differing personalities, Las Vegas resonated with us. The city's degenerate vibe was the decadent embrace of darkness I sought, while Mom found solace in its bright lights adorning the Strip. The allure of gambling captivated me the first time I stood beside a blackjack table and discovered my knack for counting cards. Meanwhile, Mom immersed herself in various popular shows, such as Cirque du Soleil. The city catered to good and evil, allowing us a space to find common footing.

"Maybe. But we don't have an update on Rose"

"It might do you good to get away and take your mind off her," she gently said. "Until they approve visitations, there is nothing more you can do."

My shoulders lifted. "There's also the matter of security. You'd have to spare someone from your team," I spoke inattentively, preoccupied with fixing the front of Neil's shirt.

The last thing I wanted was to owe Zane any favors, but my security team belonged to his payroll, and safety was non-negotiable. After the break-in at my old apartment, the board was convinced a lunatic was after me. They reminded me that callous actions put everyone in jeopardy. If I were kidnapped due to a lack of a competent security team, I could be held for ransom or used against the company.

I had never considered employing bodyguards before and feared it might be too late. Vetting a security team took an excruciating amount of time, longer with an active threat in place. The perpetrator searched for opportunities, so a newly put-together team would be vulnerable and easy to infiltrate. By hiring security now, I'd welcome more danger into our lives.

Mom's face fell at the mention of security, recalling the looming threat.

"One guard won't be enough, not if the Maxwells are behind the recent attacks," she mumbled, voice tinged with apprehension.

"They are not," I bristled. "You saw Rose's video. Damon had nothing to do with it."

Mom caught on to the defensiveness in my tone and frowned. "All I know is that Damon Maxwell seduced her, and he must've had a reason." She made a meager sound, her words more apprehensive than venomous. "Poor Rose. She's too nice for her own good."

Everyone was convinced Damon toyed with sweet Rose's heart for nefarious reasons, though the video absolved him from physically pushing her. A war had been brewing since Nick uncovered the messages on her phone. Dev insisted the board withdraw from another project involving the Maxwells, a boycott that'd be detrimental to our company.

"I have an idea," Mom exclaimed, bypassing the morose topic. "Why don't *we* go to Vegas together for the remainder of your break?"

I knew where Mom's mind had wandered. She believed I was in danger and would only find solace if she were nearby with an army of guards shielding me. Honestly, spending a few days with Mom wasn't entirely revolting. We hadn't taken a trip or even hung out alone since Mom remarried.

"I can keep myself busy while you meet up with your friend. We can hang out after," Mom suggested. "We always talked about going back, and now we can make it happen."

Eons ago, we discussed returning to Vegas for a mother-daughter trip. Putting the plan in motion at long last didn't repel me. I enjoyed my mother's sense of humor. She was the perfect person to help me overcome this fixation with Damon because I needed to move on. After regaining consciousness, Rose wouldn't rejoice in my relationship with the man responsible for seducing her. The mere notion of seeing us together might put her into another coma. I might not consider myself a good person, but I had no desire to ruin Rose's life beyond what I already had. I needed to leave Damon in the rearview mirror, and this impromptu girls' trip was the doctor-prescribed remedy. No Zane, uninterrupted time with Mom, counting cards, and some detective work in my downtime. An emotion adjacent to optimism dared to flicker. It was the closest I had taken to a positive stance in years.

I slanted my head, accepting her offer.

Mom cheerfully clapped her hands. "It'll be so much fun."

"Sounds great," Zane piped in, scrolling through his phone. "I'll charter the plane. Let's leave on January first. Vegas is a nightmare on New Year's."

I froze. Mom and I had forgotten about the obstacle in our relationship for a moment. Zane would never allow his wife out of his sight. The trip I envisioned didn't include the evil stepfather. I'd much rather stay home if it meant spending more time with him.

Mom caught the drift. "Er. I think this trip will just be for Poppy and me. A girls' trip, you know?"

As expected, tension emanated from Zane. He stared at Mom for several moments before stating a firm, "That's not a good idea."

The temperature in the room dropped by several degrees. The toddler's presence in the room restrained Mom's desire to lash out. My focus immediately shifted to the two-year-old.

"Stop it, Neil. Why are you being so fussy?"

He wasn't. Neil was a perfect gentleman and watched me with accusatory saucer eyes for throwing him under the bus. *Sorry, little dude.* We had to leave before the matter escalated. A cranky baby was the perfect pretext to escape unwanted situations. Add that to the growing list of reasons babies were superior to adults.

I dropped my napkin on the table and rose to my feet with Neil cradled in my arms. "I'll take him for a walk in the hallway. Maybe it'll calm him down."

Growing up, my parents never fought. There were no raised voices, passive-aggressive behavior, or even a whispered argument from the other room. Our home was the perfect concoction of tranquility, encouraging intellectual growth, the expansion of minds, and lively political debates.

Meanwhile, Mom and Zane were addicted to the drama. They met in their early twenties, parting ways after a short-lived romance. Mom later discovered she was pregnant. She could have taken the easy way out, the path most twenty-one-year-olds would've chosen. Instead, Mom kept me, eventually falling in love with Papa and marrying him. Following Papa's death, Zane pursued a romantic relationship with Mom and hasn't left her side since.

I grew up knowing Zane was my biological father, though my childhood was spared from his existence. I had never been more grateful for the fact. Witnessing their endless cycle of "fight and make up" as a child would have altered my personality. If I were raised in a household run by Zane, I would've led with my naturally self-destructive tendencies. Twenty-one-year-old Piya Mittal had enough sense not to raise a baby with a tumultuous man like Zane. So why couldn't thirty-nine-year-old Piya Trimalchio see things more clearly?

Mom was silent when I exited the room, angrily jabbing at her food with a fork. They waited until we were in the hallway to start fighting.

"You can't stop me from spending time with my daughter."

"She's my daughter, too," Zane shot back.

Mom huffed while I snorted. Zane had no interest in me, only in keeping his wife glued to his side. "Poppy isn't exactly your biggest fan."

Understatement of the century.

"That's because you don't force her to spend time with me."

"I'm not going to force her into something she doesn't want to do."

"And that's why she isn't my biggest fan."

Mom exhaled in frustration. "Oh, please. If you want her to like you, all you have to do is try harder when you're around her."

"Good idea. I'll start when we go to Vegas as a family."

I heard Mom's defeated sigh. The outcome of this fight was predictable. I made the mistake of being preemptively optimistic, reminding me why my *unsunny* disposition deserved more merit.

Mom tried again. "You're not coming with us, Axel. This trip is supposed to be a mother-daughter thing."

"That's precisely the problem. You keep telling me to try harder, but Poppy won't warm up to me unless we create bonding experiences for all three of us. Instead of facilitating it, you act like a gatekeeper between us."

"I don't do that," Mom denied before pausing to reflect on her behavior. "Do I?" she asked unsurely.

Zane was a master manipulator. He exploited the vulnerabilities of his opponents to disarm them, then effectively used his words to gain the upper hand. A respectable trait, I must admit. What a shame it was wasted on him.

The gaslighting worked. Mom didn't want to keep me from "bonding" with my biological father, and he planted the seed that she was keeping us apart by excluding him on a family vacation. A small part of me resigned, hoping Mom would get out of this, but I knew the answer before stepping into the room.

I returned to the table without taking a seat. Instead, I gathered Neil's scattered toys.

Mom broke the awkward silence. "Poppy. I think it'll be nice if we go on a family vacation to Vegas and save our girls' trip for another time."

My best childhood memories revolved around vacations with my parents. One trip with Zane would ruin the preserved perfection of family holidays. Stomaching him within the confines of this home was already a challenge. We barely held back our tongues for Mom's sake. We weren't capable of tolerating each other for an extended time. Glancing at his smug face solidified my two options.

If I continued pushing for a girls' trip, another fight would ensue between them, making Mom unhappy in the long run.

However, if I went on the trip, Mom would be traumatized after witnessing the depth of loathing between Zane and me.

"Vegas is a no-go. Sophie texted while I was in the hallway," I spoke stiffly, keeping my gaze on the toddler propped against my hips. "Next time."

Disappointment coated Mom's face. "Oh. But we could still go"

"If it's okay with you, I'll pass." I grabbed Neil's safety blanket with my free hand. "I should put Neil to bed."

Mom's expression mimicked a kicked puppy. I knew she was looking forward to it, increasing my resentment toward Zane. He had taken something valuable not only from me but also from her. I despised him, and I hated living in his house.

~

"One more." Rayyan thrust his empty beer bottle at the server.

"I think you've had enough," Rose spoke between pressed lips as the waiter managed to get a solid hold on the bottle.

"And I think you should mind your own business."

"Great comeback." Rose rolled her eyes at Rayyan. He was being an idiot as usual, stumbling around drunk at a funeral.

Death had become my new best friend. Everyone around me was dropping like flies, Charles Jamieson being the latest victim. He was supposed to serve as interim CEO before I took over. Charles took me under his wing, and I had come to respect the man. So, of course, he had to die from a sudden heart attack. Something poisonous in the air was taking out the few people I liked.

Mom picked me up from college and brought me to the wake, hosted at Charles' upstate home. Everyone from Ambani Corp drove up as well, though most harbored a hidden agenda. They were vying for the newly available CEO, with Rayyan Ambani as the top contender.

While Charles would've handed over the reins after holding the temporary CEO title, Rayyan would weasel his way into a permanent position. Despite being older and graduating early from college, Rayyan had a major substance abuse issue. If my calculations were correct, based on the increased bathroom visits and the redness around his nostrils, he'd overdose in years. But not without first digging the company into an early grave.

A waitress passed by, holding a black service tray over her right shoulder. Rayyan tried to grab her ass, but I seized his wrist and spoke in a voice loud enough to turn heads. "I highly recommend against doing that."

The waitress in the black pants and white button-down was unaware, and I released his hand as soon as she vanished inside the house.

Rayyan's sneer curled into a frown. "No one asked for your opinion."

"Why don't you take a walk and cool off?" Rose kept her voice sweet, but the disapproval seeped through.

I tolerated my cousins just fine but was in no mood for Rayyan's brashness. On top of losing someone I respected, I had to watch vultures drool over my birthright. Everything Papa and I worked toward hinged on what happened next. Though Rose aimed her comment at Rayyan, it was my chance to escape. "Good idea."

Rose was taken aback. "I didn't mean you, Poppy."

"I'll go anyways."

"Poppy—" Rose called after me, but I was already walking away.

I left the lavish mansion and went down a beaten path. Charles once mentioned a hiking spot he liked near his home. After careful surveillance, I found the hidden trail among the tall trees. I trekked the gravel path, detesting the beautiful, sunny day. At least I could finally relish in solitude. That was until I heard the rustling of leaves.

The deliberately light footsteps halted when I glanced behind me. A figure slinked away behind an oak tree. The trail was supposed to be a safe place with only snakes and bears for company. But instead of calling security patrolling these grounds, I considered calling out to the man in the shadows. I was curious. This ghost watched me twice at my lowest point without hurting me. Maybe it was one of my father's assistants, paid in perpetuity to watch over me after he passed. Per his instructions, numerous staff carried out tasks such as sending me potential investment opportunities or gifts on the first day of college. Though this was the only man who didn't reveal his face, he was my favorite. His quiet company was the closest to peace I had gotten.

Letting him be, I turned away and gazed out at what Charles must have looked at every morning. That was when I noticed something worse than a funeral. My mother was kissing my biological father, Zane Trimalchio.

Without thinking, I sprinted down the steep trail to catch her red-handed. Zane had parked his car by the hill, and it seemed Mom met him there. At least the house was at a distance, so no one could witness this wonderful family reunion.

"What's going on?" I snapped, my generally even tone in shambles.

Mom jumped out of his embrace. "Poppy." She held out her hands as if they were caught inside a cookie jar. "This isn't what it looks like."

I suppressed an eye roll. People only said that when it was exactly what it looked like. "No? You weren't kissing another man four months after Papa died?"

Moisture gathered in Mom's eyes while red, hot anger blinded mine.

Zane was underdressed in slacks and a T-shirt, but you wouldn't guess it in the self-assured way he spoke. "It's time she found out," he informed Mom.

"Axel, no," she pleaded. "Now isn't the time. I told you not to come here."

Zane was unimpressed by her tone. "And I told you never to take off without telling me."

"This was important to Poppy."

"In that case, Poppy deserves to know." He took a step forward. "Your mother and I are together."

Zane went on to reveal two more vital pieces of information.

One. Mom had been dating Zane for a few weeks.

Two. They were getting married in a few weeks.

What the hell? Zane was supposed to be a mistake she made at twenty-one, and Papa was supposed to be the love of her life. If my parents were these detestable cute soulmates, how the hell could she have moved on within months?

Joe Maxwell's words echoed in my mind, taunting me. No. There was no way Mom could've cheated on Papa.

"Do you want to talk about it?" Mom asked, voice shaking.

I turned around to leave. Mom was getting remarried FIVE months after Papa died. I wouldn't have known about it if Zane hadn't driven upstate because he couldn't bear to be apart for a few hours. The time for conversations ended when she didn't consider me in her life-altering decisions. Without turning back, I announced, "Rose will take me back to the dorms. Thanks for the update."

"Poppy, please don't leave," Mom called out desperately. "I'm sorry."

It was too late for apologies. I heard Zane holding Mom back when she tried to follow me. I walked toward the house, their faint voices trailing behind me.

"Give her time. She needs to cool off."

"She was already having a hard enough day." Mom whisper-yelled. "You had no right to unload that on her."

"But I do have the right. She is my daughter, too."

I gritted my teeth, and my footsteps quickened to drown out the truth I hated.

∽

CHAPTER
FIFTEEN
POPPY

I carried Neil to my sanctuary, breathing in the freedom it offered. I might hate living in this house, but not my room.

Mom poured countless hours into transforming every inch of this room. It was unrecognizable from the original version. The previous eggshell walls were painted over with a beautiful shade of soul-sucking pitch black. Mom stripped the old carpeting, replacing it with a large, worn-out, vintage rug that stretched across the floor, reaching all four corners. Drab curtains hung from the ceiling, giving it a Victorian edge. The modern furniture was discarded for the essentials needed to function. The four-poster bed had a mattress so firm only a human-machine would find comfort on it. All in all, this room exceeded my wildest expectations.

No sooner had I changed Neil's diaper and dressed him in pajamas when a knock sounded on the door. I laid Neil in the crib and opened the door to find an unwelcome guest leaning against the frame, the pose suggesting it had been practiced to perfection.

"Paris?"

Leering eyes greeted me, lacking the allure of a certain archnemesis from last night. "I Ii, Poppy."

I scanned the hallway behind him. Even if Paris coasted past the guards at the gate, Mom wouldn't have allowed him upstairs. "What are you doing here?"

"Your grandma put me on the list of approved guests with your security, and they called one of the staff members to let me in the house."

I awkwardly skirted around the door. "I see. How are you?"

"Not great. I felt bad about how our conversation ended and wanted to stop by. You ran away so fast I didn't have a chance to apologize," he accused.

With narrowed eyes cast in doubt, I acknowledged his words skeptically, "Hmm."

This was the part where Paris attempted to apologize for being a douchebag while simultaneously trying to wheedle his way into my room. Except, he never makes it to the apology part; rather, he pats himself on the back for attempting it. I wasn't convinced this time would be any different.

"It's a good thing I don't let pride get in the way." Paris would have clapped for himself if he could. "Some men never think to apologize."

I was positive Paris believed an apology lay somewhere between the lines of complimenting himself. I didn't care. "Of course," I replied dismissively.

"Since I'm already here, why don't we start our date over?" he suggested.

Our community came together after my cousin's accident, and Paris essentially invited himself. It was far from a date.

Sensing my hesitancy, Paris continued, "I'm just asking to hang out. No need to be rude about it. I mean, you haven't even asked me how I'm doing."

It was the third thing I asked, but arguing with Paris was pointless. The thought of him tattling to Nani was worse. "How are you, Paris?"

"Devastated." He sighed dramatically. "This whole thing with Rose happened before my big New Year's party. It put a damper on everything. She could've at least been considerate enough to jump after the holidays so it wouldn't bum everyone out."

Scorn was displayed on my face, acting as armor to shield Rose. "Rose didn't get hurt on purpose."

Paris brushed off my remark. "She should've known her actions would affect empaths like me. I always prioritize other people's emotions before mine and end up suffering for it."

I took a deep inhale. Smoothing out my features, I said, "Oh, you must not have heard. The doctors concluded Rose fell because of a muscular disease and diagnosed her with plasmaosis."

"What?"

"Plasmaosis," I repeated, relishing how quickly I came up with a name for a fabricated illness. "It's a disease that makes your legs unsteady. It made her collapse. I'm surprised you don't know about it." I cocked my head questioningly. Paris was so conceited he'd never admit to not knowing a made-up ailment.

He coughed awkwardly. "Of course, I know of it, but you mispronounced the word. It's pronounced P-l-a-a-s-m-a-o-s-i. The last *s* is silent."

"Of course, it is."

Paris abruptly changed the subject. "Anyways, let's hang out since I'm already here. I'll read you my latest poem," he suggested as if it were a reward to be earned.

"It's not a great time. I'm babysitting my cousin." I tilted my head toward Neil, who was peacefully sleeping in his crib. "Thanks for stopping by. I'll see you later." I began to shut the door, but Paris blocked it with his foot.

"Your cousin's asleep. It's not like you have to do anything for him."

With a steely glare directed at his foot, I firmly stated, "That's beside the point. As I mentioned numerous times, I don't like to be alone with strangers."

Paris chuckled. "Oh, okay. I don't like to be alone with strangers," he imitated, the mocking tone grating on my nerves. "And technically, we do have a chaperone tonight." Paris nudged his head toward Neil. "We'll hang out in your room. You can keep an eye on your cousin, and I can—"

"No." It was an innate response. My stomach churned, and not in a good way, at the mere thought of Paris's proximity to Neil without anyone else to act as a buffer. It was a prospect far worse than a date.

"Why not?" Paris gripped the edge of the door so I couldn't slam it in his face.

"Let go of the door or lose the hand." My voice was eerily calm even as my stomach rocked from an unsettled feeling.

His demeanor shifted from amusement to annoyance. "Spending time with me is to your benefit, Poppy."

"Keep your voice down, or you'll wake the baby," I warned in a soft but unyielding tone.

His hand transferred from the door to my bicep, squeezing tightly. Pain shot through me, but we both knew he'd never see it etched on my face. "I'll be doing him a favor," he whispered through clenched teeth, "because if things go well tonight, it'll be an educational experience for him. Your little cousin will learn how he was made."

My eye twitched at the insinuation, and I stared at the grip on my bicep. Paris had officially pissed me off.

Lifting my eyes to meet his boorish ones, I laced my words with dripping honey, "You want to spend time with me and read me a poem. That's all, right?"

"That's right." His gaze dropped between the V of my black-and-white checkered sweater, lazily trailing to my black leggings. "I just want to read you a poem I wrote about you."

I smiled, and for the first time since I'd known Paris, it was a genuine one. "Of course," I replied seductively. "But we have to be quiet. It wouldn't be appropriate if Neil woke up while you were... reading poetry. Why don't we go to the other room?"

"Other room?" Paris questioned, confused.

I pointed at the adjacent wall, finger tracing an invisible path at the mahogany door leading to an adjoining room. "My room opens up to another one."

I turned and sashayed toward the door, pulling up the baby camera app on my phone to keep an eye on Neil. Narcissists didn't question sudden changes of heart where the effectiveness of their charm was concerned. Paris eagerly followed me next door.

The sterile room mimicked a doctor's office. The walls were painted white, with a barren desk in the corner. The windows were draped, with another balcony connected to the room. The most interesting thing about the room was the steel walk-in vault.

Curiosity sparked in Paris's eyes. "What's this?" he asked, fixating on the metal surface gleaming softly in the dim light.

"It's a panic room," I replied matter-of-factly. "Lots of celebrities have them."

Except Zane didn't have a panic room. Mom had it built for me when rumors circulated about Damon murdering Rayyan to eradicate the Ambani line. Mom put numerous safeguards in place after I moved in, fearing I might be the next target. One of them was a panic room in my adjoining room.

The vault was larger than a walk-in closet with a bathroom off the side. It was minimal, with a bed, a television, a shelf with ration, a mini fridge, and a phone to call the authorities. The walls were made of malleable polymer, and the floors were hard plastic. It could be barricaded from the inside or outside if you knew the pin to the door.

I stopped at the propped-open steel door. "So you have a poem you wanted to recite?"

Paris's eyebrows lowered. "I have something better for you," he replied, his voice husky with anticipation. Instead of fishing out the poem from his pocket, he aggressively thrust his hips forward for an outline of what I imagined was a teeny weeny. Despite claiming he wanted to recite poetry with deep meaning, the first thing Paris did once we were alone was lunge for me.

With agility, I moved out of the way before his chubby hands could lock my arms into place. "I told you I'm not interested in you." I gave him one more chance, my voice lined with a formal warning.

"I know you like to act tough," he sneered, frustration etched on his face. "But stop fighting your feelings, Poppy."

He charged again, fueled by delusional arrogance and entitlement. This time, I twisted my body sideways before he could make contact. I clenched my hand into a tight fist, reared back, and punched him square in the face. Paris reached to grab onto me, but his arms flailed in a futile attempt to regain balance. He stumbled backward and fell onto the cold floor of the panic room with a resounding thud. Without hesitation, I slammed the heavy steel door shut. The panic room served the dual purpose of a jail to hold intruders. Without the code, Paris couldn't escape its fortified walls. The room was sealed off, and cell service didn't penetrate its sturdy exterior either.

Good. I didn't need Zane or my mother to find out about this. Mom detested it when I exacted retribution, and I doubted Paris would keep quiet about being taken hostage. It would also cause a massive scandal about how I was mentally unstable.

Whatever. I'd figure out a way to keep a lid on taking a prisoner. For now, I needed to keep Paris from calling the police. It'd be rude to wake Neil with unfriendly sirens.

Retrieving the phone from my back pocket, I opened the app for the panic room. I turned off the ability to make outgoing calls from the landline inside. Then, I opened the surveillance feeds to keep an eye on him.

A plethora of curse words sounded from behind the metal door. "You fucking bitch. Let me out. I'll sue you and your entire family." Blah, blah, blah. He continued cursing at me, his words echoing through the confined space.

I watched him for another thirty minutes to confirm his cell service remained weak. After realizing it was fruitless, Paris tired himself out like a spoiled brat and retreated to the bed. He kept cursing me as he took off his shoes and jacket, crawled under the blanket, and broke down in sobs.

I had no pity to spare. I allowed Paris every opportunity to redeem himself, but he proved vile on all accounts. If the likes of Paris were the most eligible bachelors, I shuddered at the thought of the less suitable matches.

There had to be a curse on me. Between my overly emotional male relatives, my heavy-handed stepfather, and Paris, the men around me continued to fall short. The man who didn't fall short bore the last name meant to be my downfall. And, oh yeah, Rose put a claim on him.

A heavy sigh escaped my lips as I left behind my captive and the sweet melody of his cries. I walked back to my room and closed the adjoining door. I checked on Neil, who was still fast asleep but stopped short upon turning. There was movement outside, but the glass was imperceptible to see through. Several moments passed before I made out Damon Maxwell's form.

After learning about Damon and Rose, I wanted to lock myself in the panic room. But with the harsh reminder of my home life and the run-in with Paris fresh on my mind, Damon's presence seemed like a reprieve even as I chided myself.

Why couldn't you love someone else, Rose? Why did it have to be Damon?

In a few short days, he demonstrated more knowledge about me than anyone in this world. It rendered tedious small talk useless, leaving more space for my preferred comfortable silence. I had never experienced such an unspoken connection, and having to say goodbye to it sucked.

I tiptoed outside. As if sensing my presence, Damon glanced at me when I opened the sliding doors. He looked like a dark angel descending from above in black slacks and a dark gray sweater fitted over his broad chest, and I was so screwed.

CHAPTER SIXTEEN

DAMON

THE OBJECT OF MY OBSESSION STOOD BEFORE ME, AND I hungrily drank in the vision. Poppy's dark hair was undone, giving her a vixen-like quality. Against her black-and-white checkered sweater, the tan hue of her skin appeared soft. The unusual display of a light color, though blended with the black of her sweater and leggings, imbued her with a rare brightness.

I swallowed, stuck somewhere between lust and ire. It had been twenty-three restless hours since I last saw her. A crushing weight sat heavily on my chest the entire time. I was filled with resentment, but at least I could breathe now.

"Hi," I spoke in a steady voice despite my apprehension.

Poppy didn't seem surprised by the unannounced intrusion. "Hello."

One word from her lips could stifle the torment keeping me up all night. But instead of wrapping my hands around her neck and suffocating her mouth with my tongue, I let my hands fall to my sides. Poppy wouldn't let her guard down unless I convinced her we could be something that would supersede her loyalty to Rose. Good-faith gestures, such as this date, were necessary to show my understanding of her. Poppy didn't believe anyone shared her interests. I had to disprove her because the little time we spent apart had me craving her so much I couldn't see straight.

It wasn't a figment of my imagination that the hunger was mutual. Her eyes traced the veins on my exposed arms, revealed by my rolled-up sweater sleeves, before wandering to my chest. Fame accustomed me to attention from women. I always found it remarkably ordinary until Poppy because she didn't care about fame, nor was she easily swayed. Provoking desire in this unshakable goth girl was something else. I needed this after last night.

When Poppy caught my self-satisfied grin, she cleared her throat. "What are you doing?"

"Setting up a home movie theater," I replied as if my presence was warranted, and Poppy forgot that we arranged to meet.

"Why?"

Unrevealing eyes followed me as I walked past her to set up the floor stand. "To watch a movie."

"I'm not in a position to spend time with the man Rose is in love with."

"Do you want caramel popcorn or butter?" I paused, extending the stand to the perfect height.

Her restraint with indifference crumpled. "I'm capable of many things, Damon, but not intentionally hurting Rose. Please leave."

"I know you'd never intentionally hurt Rose." Undoing the rolled-up projector screen, I hung it on the stand. "I also know you'll watch this movie with me."

"Let me prove you wrong."

When Poppy moved toward the door, I went in for the kill. "I know Zane is your biological father."

Even without watching her out of the corner of my eye, I knew Poppy heard me. The cozy balcony was suddenly cold. I ignored the escalating tension and set up my laptop on a nearby table.

Poppy watched me tinker with it for minutes before asking, "How?"

I faced Poppy, having completed the setup. "I have my ways."

For the first time, Poppy displayed a vivid expression. Angry and shaken. The wheels were turning in her head. She suddenly saw me as a threat, the guy holding the key to her future. "What now?" she quipped. "I do whatever you ask, or you tell everyone about me. Is that it?"

I shook my head. "I'd never broadcast your business."

"Why did you bring it up if you didn't plan on using it against me?"

"To build trust."

Poppy seemed stuck between disbelief and rage. Watching her flabbergasted would've been satisfying if she hadn't looked sick. Rightfully so. If word got out that Poppy wasn't Jay Ambani's biological daughter, it would ruin her future.

"I know what would happen to you if word got out about this. I want you to trust that I'll never use this against you."

"Until you want something from me." Poppy looked away. "You're not the first person to blackmail me with this information."

My intent to gain her trust had misfired. This situation was spiraling fast, and I needed to de-escalate it.

"This isn't coercion, Poppy," I attempted to reconcile. "I have known for years. Haven't told a soul despite the million times my family pushed me to dig up dirt on you."

"Your family will have a field day if they find out about me." She frowned, the insinuation sinking in. "And they'll be pissed at you for withholding this information."

"Exactly. But your secret's safe with me," I declared firmly. "I hope that's enough to trust me and find some common ground."

"What about Rose?" Poppy forced the words out as if they were too painful to utter.

I let out an impatient sound. "This doesn't affect Rose." I speedily revised my tone and continued in a gentler voice, "I meant that Rose won't find out about us until after she recovers, which will take some time. Hang out with me in the meantime and figure out if this thing between us stands a chance."

"And if I don't?"

"Then you'll never find out who told me about Zane." I forced my eyes to be insouciant. "If this is worth fighting for, we can help Rose come to terms with it. If not, you can walk away."

Distrustful eyes roamed my face. "Why are you going to these lengths to see me?"

"I already told you why."

Because I haven't been able to stop thinking about you. Because you've been driving me crazy since we met. It's madness, and you can't explain madness.

"I want to watch a movie with you, that's all. I'll answer any more questions afterward."

Doubt clouded Poppy's resilient eyes, but I knew she was considering it. Her attention shifted to the screen, shielding her eyes momentarily against the glaring light from the projector. Poppy studied the blanket next, along with the pillows on the floor. A different person might have been thrilled with the romantic gesture and gushed over it.

Oh wow. This is beautiful.
I can't believe you set up a home theater for us.
You are so thoughtful. Thank you.
Etc., etc., etc.

I harbored no such fanciful expectations. I expected Poppy to put up further objections surrounding Rose or interrogate me about her coveted secret, demanding answers before agreeing to a movie. Imagine my surprise when Poppy appeared relieved.

Did having an external reason to hang out with me take away feelings mimicking guilt over Rose?

Perhaps something else was bothering Poppy, for only distress could make her overlook Rose's feelings.

Maybe it was both.

Poppy approached the setup. "Keep your hands to yourself." Lowering onto the blanket, she nestled against the pillows. "I assume we are watching a movie, not an educational video."

Cautiously, I nodded. The warmth in her reception caught me off guard because while she didn't fuss over the gesture, there was also no more hostility in her features. A lack of suspicion was Poppy's love language.

I straightened the laptop until the video mirroring onto the screen wasn't tilted. Poppy refrained from striking up any further conversation and patiently waited for me to press play. The caption on the screen read, "*Twelve Gruesome Murders, The Explicit Edition.*"

Curiosity danced on her face. "*This* is what we are watching?"

"We could do something else." I eyed the blankets suggestively.

Poppy stared at me for several moments before mumbling, "The only thing better than watching *Twelve Gruesome Murders* is watching it in the explicit edition. I asked because the banned version isn't available online."

A hint of pride laved through me at her words. The explicit copy was banned due to controversial content and was nearly impossible to find. It was worth it, though, when Poppy's inexpressive eyes came alive at the footage of torture weapons laid out on a sterile table. "I have my ways."

Poppy blew out a breath of approval as I pulled a blanket over her lap. With only a finger's width between us, she was close enough for me to smell her intoxicating perfume. Poppy didn't react to the proximity. Traces of bitterness between us evaporated at the scent of her vanilla and lavender shower gel, leaving me consumed by her. We watched the movie in comfortable silence, with horrified screams and blood baths projected onto the screen. I was impervious to everything except her.

The moonlight illuminated Poppy's face, and I ogled, taking full advantage while she was too distracted by the gruesome murders to notice. The way she was engrossed in the gore, the way her back remained ramrod straight, the scent of her barely-there perfume, everything about this woman drove me crazy. My hand grazed hers, and an electrifying shock jolted up my arm at the contact. She felt it and stilled at the touch, though her attention remained on the screen. Our mutual silence hung heavy, both aware this poorly veiled facade of platonic friendship never stood a chance, just like my control.

Every fiber in my being warned me to slow down. Initiating physical contact might set off alarms for someone still weighing the risks versus rewards, but surely, exercising forty-five minutes of restraint was good enough.

Maneuvering her, I sat behind with Poppy plopped between my legs. Gently brushing her hair aside to expose the vulnerable curve of her neck, I played with the strands. My other hand banded around her chest. I palmed her breasts, my thumb circling the nipples over her sweater. Her body instinctively responded to my touch, her heart beating violently against my fingertips. A rhythmic drum playing an erotic tune. I shoved my hand inside her sweater, but Poppy grabbed it.

I groaned. "I need to feel you, Poppy."

"No. This is too messed up. My cousin might die thinking I betrayed her by sleeping with the man she loves. She is obsessed with you."

"That's too bad because I'm obsessed with *you*," I breathed.

Poppy shook her head. "I can't do this to her."

I knew Poppy wouldn't disregard her cousin's infatuation with me. It was difficult to dissuade her loyalty. Instead of pushing, I tried to ease her into it.

"You're not doing this to her; I am. Enjoy this without being in cahoots with me. Let me shoulder the blame because I'll do anything for you, Poppy." An overpowering thirst took over, one only she could quench, and I dug my nose into her tresses. "You always smell so fucking good."

I kissed the back of her neck before dragging my tongue across her skin. The chill in the air mixed with my hot tongue as I licked and sucked the back of her neck. Her lips parted, and an involuntary shiver raced through Poppy.

Once more, I grabbed at the hem of her sweater. "I'm going to take this off, okay?"

Poppy didn't object when I pulled the top over her head this time. My hand returned to her chest, pulling at the cups of her bra to reveal her tits. She sat facing away from me, but I could see them over her shoulders. Round and inviting breasts sprang free, accompanied by a flat stomach toned from hours of running.

Before she could react, I dipped two fingers inside her mouth, pressing down on her wet tongue. I retracted them just as swiftly and drew them to her nipple. Poppy shivered at the cold contact, her bare nipples hardening as I rolled them between my fingers. My other hand skated past her belly button down to her leggings.

I spun her body, pushed her onto the blanket beneath us, and stretched out on top of her. Indecision encompassed her, caught between Rose and me. In the end, Poppy turned her face to the screen as a defense mechanism. She was taking me up on the offer to exonerate herself from the situation, pretending this wasn't happening.

My eyes took their fill of her body with untamed wildness. Fortunately, Poppy faced the screen, so she didn't catch the animalistic lust on my face. I sucked on her nipples, hollowing out my cheeks until Poppy panted for relief. I continued to lick and suck every inch of her skin before dipping my tongue into her belly button. No skin was left unturned under my attention.

Grabbing onto the waistband of her leggings, I slowly pulled down her pants. Her harsh breath could be outlined in the air as I dipped inside to trace the outside of her panties. Poppy's head lolled back when I moved my fingers inside her underwear to find her dripping.

When I tried taking off her underwear, she grabbed my wrist. "Don't take them off."

I didn't. It was pertinent this was Poppy's decision to allow her the illusion of loyalty. Instead, I lowered to her pussy, and my tongue swiped her core over the black panties.

"Shit," Poppy hissed. Glossy eyes fixed on the screen, almost as if she wouldn't be in collusion with me if she didn't witness the act.

The panties were covered in dark spots, soaked from her arousal and my efforts. I kept licking over the damp material until Poppy seemed ready to lose it.

"Fuck, baby," I groaned. "Can I eat you out raw?"

"No." She found her voice and immediately clamped her legs shut.

"Don't close up on me, Poppy. I won't if you don't want it, but you seem stressed out." I rubbed a thumb up and down her covered slit, refusing to let her close all the way. "Don't you want me to make you feel better?"

With her teeth clamped onto her bottom lip, Poppy shook her head at the screen.

I swiped my nose against the wet spots. "You were so relaxed after you came for me the other night. I can do that for you again."

When Poppy didn't deny it, I hooked my thumbs over the waistband.

Her eyes fluttered. "Stop."

I internally cursed. My control was seconds from shattering, making me wonder whether I could stop. However, it was vital for Poppy to have a say in this. "Please, baby. Let me take these off and make you feel good." My teeth grazed against her clit through the cloth.

Poppy quivered. I kept at it for several moments, waiting patiently. Poppy covered her eyes with both hands, once more avoiding being held accountable for her involvement.

I didn't miss a beat. Instead of pulling her underwear down, I pressed her knees to her chest and pushed her underwear up, leaving it banded around her thighs. My gaze dropped to her glistening pussy, smooth from a recent wax. Butt, pussy, everything was wide open and indecently exposed with her knees drawn to her chest. Poppy could smell her arousal on the underwear resting near her nose from the position.

Drawing a line from her thigh to her core, I let my tongue rest outside of where she needed it. Poppy cheated on the screen for only a second and stared down at me. She quickly looked away as if any more eye contact would be a bigger betrayal. I immediately buried my face between her thighs and swiped up with my tongue. Poppy's hand fisted the blanket underneath her, warding off whatever overwhelming ecstasy consumed her.

"You taste just like I remember," I groaned between licks. "So. Fucking. Good."

I let a bit of saliva dribble out to create added moisture, eyes on Poppy as she writhed under my mouth. A low moan ripped through her, hands resting on my shoulders. I stabbed my tongue inside her, and her hips moved instinctively, encouraging my tongue to push deeper.

"I'm coming," she whispered, body convulsing.

Poppy came violently, jerking in rhythm with the ecstasy pulsing through her. The veins on her neck strained as she fought the louder cry generating in the back of her throat. I kept licking her, but she garbled any further sounds by biting her fist.

Leaving a trail of wet kisses on her inner thigh, I sat back on my heels. Her knees were still drawn to her chest, her chest crudely bared, with small hickeys forming around her nipples. I ran a thumb up and down her slit, eliciting another low grumble.

"I want to be inside you so fucking bad."

"No." Poppy turned her face back to the screen.

She was fucking adorable. It made me smile, and I returned to her pussy.

"Wait, not again," she objected.

Poppy was mortified when I made her ride my tongue until she shattered two more times. After the third orgasm, she was faster to yank her leggings up her hips. I made my way up as she fixed her bra and sweater. Our eyes locked, her heavy eyelids struggling to remain open. Her chest heaved, breaths coming out in short, shallow spurts. She was dead on her feet, eyes unfocused.

My fingers wrapped around Poppy's neck to drag her limp body up and meet my lips. Her soft pink mouth parted in anticipation so my tongue could delve in for a taste. I smeared her with her own taste, strategically licking every last drop off her lips, then diving inside her mouth to chase any lingering remnants.

Raw and passionate, the intoxicating kiss turned messy. Our bodies moved in fluid motion, her fingers bracing against my chest while mine yanked at her hair. With my lips locked onto hers, my left hand cradled her nape while my right rested lightly on her hips. I pulled away, savoring the final taste of her by running my tongue over my teeth.

Her fingers trembled along with her body, and I realized the quivering was her body's inability to calm down post-orgasm. Resting my forehead in the crook of her neck, I covered her with my body. It was partly to keep her warm but mostly to breathe in the relief of having her back in my arms.

CHAPTER SEVENTEEN

DAMON

Poppy pushed me off her as soon as she recovered, scrambling to the other side. "The movie is over," she announced, trying to make it sound like this date was over, too.

"Oh."

The movie credits were rolling, making me frown. I blacked out even though Poppy was the one who came numerous times. She was quickly becoming addicting. What was she made of, cocaine?

I strolled to the laptop to turn it off. "Did you like the movie?" Someone should, considering I clocked in five minutes of screen time.

"It was perfect," she confessed. After a moment of contemplation, she added, "Thank you."

My brows knotted. "You're welcome?" I responded tentatively.

The rare vulnerability nagged at the back of my mind because Poppy had been acting uncharacteristically all night. I knew her reservations about Rose were far from erased. The way she still accepted my intrusion, putting up a limited fight, had set off the initial warning bells. Instead of demanding answers, I decided to tackle the problem later. Whatever troubled Poppy was a more significant stressor than choosing between Rose and me. It had pushed Poppy right into my arms.

In another wildly implausible gesture, Poppy initiated a conversation while I packed the laptop and projector. "We talked a lot about my family, but what about yours? How would they react if they knew you were romancing me with violent movies?"

"Unhappy, I presume," I replied flatly, putting away the remaining items.

"That's an understatement. They'll have you committed."

Amused, I considered the prospect. "I've been thinking about taking a vacation."

"It might be a permanent vacation if they find out," Poppy prodded.

"Then we better make sure they don't find out."

"That's impossible," she argued. "You're a celebrity with no privacy. Someone can follow you here or leak our texts. Any restraint exercised against us would be considered disloyal if your family caught wind of it. They'll say you can no longer perform your job because you're compromised and fire you as the CEO."

I blew out a breath defensively. "Or they'll look the other way once we get married and merge the two biggest companies in our industry."

Disconcert replaced Poppy's cynical expression at the mention of marriage. The surety of it had slipped out after being cornered by Poppy's devil's advocacy.

Sure. My family would be ruthless in their dealings. I wasn't offended by Poppy's insinuation of their viciousness, merely irked at the suggestion I'd allow outside influence to dictate my decisions.

"I meant, *if* we got married and combined our assets," I tried to rectify the impulsive slip of the tongue. "No one would be stupid enough to challenge the mega player monopolizing the field. Or turn down the pay bump from eliminating each other's biggest competition."

The sound argument was met with Poppy's pensiveness. She was debating whether I proposed a business plan or simply proposed. Money wasn't an incentive for people who had no need for it, and Poppy suspected I knew as much. The bad blood between our families was too deep-rooted and incurable.

Our silent pondering in the dark ended when Poppy suddenly leaped to her feet with the phone in hand.

"What's wrong?" I asked.

"You have to leave now."

"Why?"

Poppy pointed at her room with a thumb. "My cousin's here."

Fighting Ambanis wasn't how I envisioned ending the night. My back straightened with tension until I caught a glimpse of Poppy's phone. A baby camera app on the screen displayed the video of a little boy.

"You are babysitting?" I asked somewhat incredulously.

She tilted her head.

"How old is he?"

"Two. And he might be waking up any moment." Poppy pocketed the phone and rushed inside. "Thanks for the movie. Feel free to let... climb yourself out."

Poppy shot me an irritated look when I trailed behind her instead of leaving, and I concealed my surprise when she didn't lock the doors on me. She opened her mouth, presumably to ask me to leave. Before she could speak, I placed a finger over my lips, signaling her to keep quiet and not disturb the baby at the cusp of waking up. She snapped her mouth shut but continued to glare. I paid no attention to her, taking stock of her room instead.

Poppy's bedroom was how I remembered it, gloomy but interesting, with a few new additions. A foldable crib sat next to the bed adorned with baby paraphernalia and a diaper bag that said, *Neil's Shit.*

I joined Poppy by the crib. Inside was the two-year-old, shifting restlessly from side to side and kicking off his blanket. He wore black onesies that read "Stop texting and change my diaper" across the chest. No doubt a satiric gift from Poppy.

Poppy hovered by the crib on the fence whether the toddler was waking up or lulling himself back to sleep. When Neil stirred again, she picked him up and patted his bottom to check if the diaper was dry. Neil gave a soft cry, prompting Poppy to carry him to her bed.

The dark linens on the mattress were meticulously tucked into the corners with military precision, indicating Poppy had made her bed rather than relying on housekeepers. Neil made disgruntled noises as she lay on the bed with him, pulling a pillow under both their heads. Tiny fingers clutched at her strands, but Poppy didn't pull away. A warm body seemed to alleviate the little boy's abandonment issues, and I wondered if Poppy possessed the ability to comfort him due to personal experience.

As if the scene weren't astonishing enough, Poppy did the unthinkable. With my arms folded across my chest, I watched in fascination as she sang a lullaby to rock Neil back to sleep. "Monday's child is fair of face. Tuesday's child is full of grace."

She sings?

Captivated, I found my legs involuntarily moving toward them. I settled on the bed with Poppy, separated by Neil in the middle, and savored the unconventional scene.

"Wednesday's child is full of woe," Poppy continued in an unexpectedly melodic tone, her eyes drawing away once to glower at my bold move of sitting on her bed. "Thursday's child has far to go."

The sight triggered an unexpected foreign emotion, catapulting irrational ideas to the forefront of my mind. The feelings were far from contrived, nor could I suppress the images conjured by my imagination.

When Neil's breathing evened out, Poppy drew the covers over him. Her head reeled back when she caught the intensity shooting from my eyes. "Why are you staring at me like that?"

My gaze burned into her with the fervor of a wild animal ready to break out of its cage. I was on the brink of going mad and moments from losing control to pave the way. My prolonged silence embellished what I desperately desired. The wild hunger could barely be warded off, but I had to focus on the bigger picture.

"It was a bad idea to let me see you that way," I finally confessed.

"What way?"

My gaze flickered to a sleeping Neil. "The way you're right now."

"Why?"

Because it does things to me that might scare you. My head hit the pillow beside Neil's, and I stretched out, one arm snaking under my hair. "You're not ready to find out."

She scrutinized me without pressing further, perhaps realizing the answer. Neither of us indulged in serene moments with our ridiculous families. Since Mom passed away, I couldn't remember a similarly peaceful instant despite the countless hours spent with them. This humble domestic experience had evoked similar thoughts in her. Ideas such as leaving behind our family's bullshit in exchange for something resembling happiness.

Yes, Poppy, I understand you better than you think. You're reminiscing about the last time you felt this content. It was before your father passed away.

"Will you do me a favor?" Poppy asked out of the blue.

"Hmm?"

"Will you ask me about my father?"

I lifted my head from the pillow and studied her impassive face.

Poppy's attention was on Neil as she stroked his dark hair. "Zane doesn't like it when we mention Papa, so no one talks about him. It's starting to feel like he never existed."

"Tell me about your father," I asked right away. "What was he like?"

Falling back on her pillow, Poppy stared at the ceiling. "Warm. Nice. The man was a genius. A legend," she thoughtfully recounted his qualities. "I idolized him. He was a good person. Perhaps too good of a person. He never thought about himself, only about us. Everything he did was for his family. He was the glue who held Mom and I together."

"What is it like with your mom now?"

She turned onto her side. "She is different around Zane. I don't recognize her."

"And what is it like with Zane?"

Poppy distractedly picked at a loose thread on the sheet beneath her. "We used to go on cruises when I was young. Every year, Mom insisted on taking the same professional family photo onboard. She safeguarded the framed pictures because she always forgot to request digital copies. After Papa passed away, she gave me the entire collection. Said it was our family documented over the years. I organized them and displayed them by the year. But when I moved into the dorms, there wasn't enough space. Mom suggested choosing one photo and storing the rest here until I could clear out some space."

"I don't follow. What does that have to do with Zane?"

Poppy let out a heavy sigh. "By the time I made room and returned for the picture frames, Zane had found the photos and cut Papa's face out of them." She pointed at her desk; it was a picture of Poppy and her parents in a frame decorated with seashells. "It's the only one still intact."

"That's very cruel," I murmured.

"When I confronted him, Zane told me never to bring that filth inside his house again. Does that answer your question about my relationship with Zane?"

"He's a sadistic asshole," I said bluntly. "Did you ever tell your mom?"

Poppy lay on her back, and I mirrored the pose. Out of the corner of my eye, I watched her shake her head. "Mom used to cry a lot after Papa got sick. If I ruined their relationship, she'd go back to being depressed. What would be the point in making her sad?"

I wanted to kill Zane for what he did to Poppy. He didn't deserve to breathe the same air as her. However, she'd never be able to maintain a relationship with her mother if things weren't mended with him.

"He deserved better," she suddenly murmured.

"Who?"

"Papa," Poppy replied, voice somber. "He deserved a daughter who loved and mourned him. Did you know I didn't shed a single tear at Papa's funeral?"

Yes.

"It's not in my genes," Poppy explained. "Crying, that is." Her eyes lifted to mine, assessing if I understood the passive reference.

It hit me then. The real reason behind Poppy's resentment toward her biological father wasn't his cruelty. It was the genes he passed down. They both had anti-social personalities and didn't feel empathy or remorse for their actions. The behavior made it difficult to sustain long-term relationships, especially when unable to control their anger. While Poppy's traits were more obvious due to that inability, Zane did a better job of hiding his demons. Poppy believed she was missing out on a profound life experience due to her emotional limitations. Whereas she exercised immense control over her goals, she couldn't alter DNA to make it fit her life.

"You have never cried?"

Poppy shook her head. "I can sense grief after losing someone, but ultimately, any sadness is tied to my needs. I needed Papa because he was my mentor and role model. My sadness stemmed from my loss of those things. Papa deserved better, someone who loved him and expressed sadness, regardless."

Her words hung in the air as I let their weight settle into my thoughts. "I believe that's true for neurotypical people as well. They mourn and cry over people fulfilling a need for them, whether it be love, kindness, attention, attachment, or whatever it is. Humans are selfish creatures. We don't grieve people unless they impact our lives."

Poppy gave the impression she wanted to argue the logic, her eyes silently challenging my words.

"But," I added thoughtfully, "if this is about the outward expression of mourning, enough people openly grieved your father. I'm sure your mother loved your father and cried for him."

Poppy let out a scoff. "Mom also remarried five months after Papa died. How much could she have loved him?" A tinge of bitterness coated her words. Poppy looked away and said, "Maybe your dad was right all along. Mom cheated on Papa."

CHAPTER
EIGHTEEN
DAMON

Nothing could have prepared me for Poppy's announcement. There were no words of consolation to negate the accusation, either. Poppy stared at the ceiling, silently conveying she wouldn't delve deeper into the topic after dropping the atomic bomb.

I badly wanted to return Neil to his crib and pull Poppy close. Hold her. Comfort her. Feel her heartbeat against mine. I wanted to do many things to her, both dirty and romantic. But she wouldn't respond kindly to comfort. All she wanted now was a change of topic.

I exercised restraint like I had never known, distracting myself with my surroundings. Lifting myself onto my elbows, I allowed my gaze to wander across the room, examining the antique pieces. I settled on a model of the Grim Reaper on Poppy's nightstand. It matched the overall theme of the room.

"Quite the collection of antiques here," I mused, breaking the heavy silence between us.

Poppy skimmed the item in my hand. "I like the style."

I carefully returned the figurine to its rightful place, ensuring it wasn't even an inch off the original location. Poppy appeared pleased by the effort, the heavy cloud dissipating some.

A playful tone crept into my voice as I dragged a finger across her old, wooden nightstand. "By any chance, did you spend more money on previously used crap than you would have on new furniture?"

"Vintage costs money," was her nonchalant explanation, voice filled with a hint of pride. "But it's worth it."

Next, I elbowed the lump of a mattress beneath me. "I'm sure it was worth paying double for a bed made of rocks. Are you trying to bring back the Stone Ages?"

She lifted a shoulder. "I like a firm mattress. It keeps me from oversleeping. It took some practice, but I've learned to function with five hours of sleep. It leaves me with more time for productivity."

I nudged the mattress again, deeming it suitable for a cold dungeon. Nope. Compromising on sleep wouldn't do it for me. "Psychopaths like rock-hard mattresses," I concluded.

"Did my cheerful disposition mislead you about my personality?" she retorted.

A lopsided grin tugged at the corner of my mouth. "Not a chance, little demon spawn. I'd believe it even if you had someone locked up in your basement."

She lurched back as if offended. "That's irresponsible kidnapping," she declared, voice dripping with disdain. "Basements are far too easy to escape. I locked him in the panic room."

Ordinarily, I'd presume the remark was a joke. Except her delivery lacked all traces of dark humor. "Excuse me?"

"I'm just saying, psychopathy doesn't equal stupidity." She spoke matter-of-factly. Poppy continued staring at me with an unyielding straight face.

I lifted to seating when her expression didn't morph. "Explain the *locking him up in the panic room* portion."

Without hesitation, Poppy launched into a detailed account of her citizen's arrest. She opened an app on her phone and showed me a video of Paris. He sobbed uncontrollably against his pillow, chest heaving from the desperate effort. "I don't think he is taking very kindly to the kidnapping," she determined.

Long black hair cascaded around her shoulders like a curtain of shadows as she assessed my reaction. For some reason, Poppy appeared to be awaiting my judgment, as if I couldn't stomach her actions.

"I'll let him out as soon as I figure out how to keep him from creating a scandal or going to the cops," she justified when I didn't speak. "Paris is filthy rich, so it's not like I can bribe him. The only thing he might want..." She let the gravity of the insinuation sink in. "That's never going to happen."

A surge of jealousy coursed through me, threatening to consume my senses. Did she think I'd let her entertain the option even if she were willing? Was she worried my prolonged silence was a condemnation of her revenge and allowing the fucker off the hook would appease me? My silence was an effort to contain my wrath so I wouldn't reveal how much it killed me that someone dared to touch her or thought they could take her from me. My hands shook with uncontrollable rage.

Earlier today, I learned about the mystery date set up by Poppy's grandmother. My head of security tailed numerous guests from last night's vigil and paid them handsomely until someone pointed him toward Paris. The pieces fell into place soon after. Poppy tolerated Paris because she didn't want to create further rifts in her mother and grandmother's fragile relationship. Poppy's relationship with her mom and her grandma, to a certain degree, was important to her. I wanted to protect their bond. However, I also knew I'd murder Paris in cold blood if he dared to come near Poppy again. Since I didn't relish serving life in prison, I planned on paying him a "friendly" visit tomorrow. Yet it seems the asshole beat me to the punch by showing up here.

I should have predicted it. Poppy didn't object to me tonight because her environment posed threats bigger than her enemy. This house was crammed with overbearing relatives, a stepfather she hated, and fuckers like Paris. I couldn't take the thought of him having access to Poppy. I wouldn't allow it. This madness would end tonight. I'd ensure it right after taking care of a dirty street rat named Paris.

Rising from the bed, I charged toward the adjoining room.

"Where are you going?" Poppy jumped out of bed and trailed me.

"To take care of Paris. Stay here," I ordered, opening the door that separated the two rooms.

Poppy must have noticed the brooding and remained at my heels as I stampeded into the next room. I doubt I could contain myself upon seeing the fucker's face. This might be the moment I finally snapped.

Poppy faced me when I reached the steel door. "What are you going to do?" she asked in a soft yet determined voice.

"I'll handle it so it won't trace back to you," I replied in a tone colder than ice.

Poppy didn't press for more details. The big brown eyes looked at me intently, somewhat dulling away the fire. The fact she could disarm me while I was in a manic state was stupefying.

Though her presence subdued the murderous rage, it didn't smother the jealousy gnawing inside me. My mind raced much too fast with possessiveness. I couldn't let this go on, not after Paris entered her room.

Unthinking, I punched in the code harder than necessary. Poppy caught the action but wisely chose against questioning it. She could tell I was in a mood and banked away my knowledge over her pin for a conversation to be had later.

"You can't be here for this. Go back to your room," I said sternly.

Poppy hesitated for a moment. "Don't do anything rash. You have a lot to lose," she warned gently before stepping away.

As soon as she left, I threw open the steel door with a resounding thud. Motion sensors activated the lights inside, and the sleek interior shone under the brightness. Paris was sprawled on a twin bed and gasped at the intrusion. The asshole dared to rest after coming into this house to disrupt Poppy's peace.

"Wha" His head whipped toward me in confusion. Paris seemed to question his sanity, wondering if he had been transported into a different person's panic room. Recognition flared in his eyes, and he scrambled out of bed. "Aren't you Damon Maxwell?" he asked, his voice filled with astonishment and relief.

I wasn't in a rational enough state to answer.

"What are you doing here?" he rambled, trying to make sense of the situation. "Oh my God, are you here as part of a rescue mission? Is saving hostages one of your philanthropic efforts? Thank God. I have been locked in here for hours. No water. No food. It's been traumatizing."

He reclaimed a seat on the bed, casually lacing his shoes. I glared at the man who could only be described as a cartoon character.

"I finally understand why great poets are made in captivity," he conversed lightly. He thought nothing of the reason he was shoved inside the box. Fucking privileged asshole. Paris rose gingerly, slipped on his coat, and moved to stand in front of me. "So, is Poppy Ambani in custody? Who called in the tip about the kidnapping? That bitch is nuts"

The blow I delivered landed square on his jaw, sending him backward onto the cold ground.

"What the fuck?" he wailed, clutching his injured mouth. "Ow."

"Keep your voice down," I advised in a measured tone. "A baby is sleeping next door."

Paris stared at me in stunned disbelief. The man known worldwide for his philanthropic efforts had punched him in the face. Violence wasn't supposed to be a part of my DNA, according to the magazine articles and the staged interviews I gave on late-night shows. My organization promoted a peaceful life of fighting drugs and suicide. The anti-violent paradigm had been copied across the nation before going international. I was expected to become a future Nobel Peace Prize laureate for my work, not a scathing hypocrite succumbing to basic emotions like anger.

The way I saw it, both personalities existed within me. One thrived in the light, dedicated to helping others. The other reveled in the dark, drawn to *her*.

Paris realized my PR team featured Jekyll in the spotlight while he was receiving a rare glimpse at Hyde. For I was no savior; I was his motherfucking worst nightmare. "I thought you were here to save me," he muttered, dumbfounded.

"I'm here to chat." A chat involving my fist. I rolled my shoulders, the first impact barely satiating my bloodthirst.

Paris glared at me, holding a hand over his busted lip. The pressure didn't stop the blood from oozing out. "I don't understand. What is this about?"

"This is about Poppy," I replied coldly. The detached demeanor probably made me appear more possessed. "I heard you've been snooping around my girl."

"Your girl?" he asked, dumbfounded. "B-but you are a Maxwell." That was all he could muster as if the explanation should suffice. Perhaps it did for many. "Is that even allowed?"

"Allowed or not, she belongs to me."

"But you can have any woman in the world. Tell me you aren't stupid enough to catch feelings for the only one you can't," he sneered, momentarily regaining his bravado. "On top of being a Maxwell, you aren't Indian. The Ambani board will never approve of you. There is no future with her other than a few casual fucks."

That earned him a kick in the stomach. I questioned my mental stability when I reveled in the sight of him hunched sideways, clutching his abdomen.

Paris swallowed, fear returning to his eyes. "W-what do you want from me?"

"First, I want to hear your thoughts on an important matter. Who does Poppy belong to?"

He looked away. Paris loved making things difficult for himself. I landed a kick to his chest, eliciting a screech. "Okay! Okay! She belongs to you."

"I'm glad you see it my way. And in case there is any confusion, I'll clarify a few things."

I circled him while he lay on the ground. Fear had him tracking my feet like prey, predicting the next move.

"Poppy is mine," I spoke from behind, making him jump. "If you look at her again, I'll remove your eyes from their sockets. If you touch her, I'll chop off your hands. If your dick gets hard fantasizing about her, I'll cut it off. If you even think about her, I will sever your head from your body and keep the brains on my nightstand."

"You are sick," he spat without thinking.

The comment made me laugh and deliver one more kick. This time, he coughed up blood and held up a surrendered palm.

"Paris," I tutted. "This brings me no joy." It was a bald-faced lie. Even burying him would bring me joy. He had no idea what I was capable of. "Help me, help you," I reasoned.

Petrified, Paris vigorously nodded.

I completed the circle and stood in front of Paris. "I'll ask again. Am I making myself clear about Poppy?"

Red blood stained his previously white teeth. "Yes," he gurgled.

I reached for the phone in my back pocket and pulled up my email. "I have a little gift for you in case you ever need a refresher." Scrolling through, I found the email my head of security sent and read aloud a bank account number and the balance.

"What the fuck?" Paris roared when he recognized the figures.

"Shh," I hushed, placing a finger over his lips. "We have a baby sleeping in the next room. I told you that," I chided. "This is a bank statement for an offshore account."

"How did you find it?"

"It wasn't difficult. After all, it's one of the oldest tricks. You embezzle a small amount from your father's company every quarter so no one would notice. Then, deposit the money into an offshore account."

"You can't prove jack shit," Paris seethed. "There is no paper trail."

I tapped my lips thoughtfully. "Maybe not. Although, I doubt it'll matter when the deposits in this account match the amounts missing for the last several quarters."

Paris paled.

"Oof, stealing money from your own father?" I made a face. "That's cold. How will your father react if I forward him this email? I'm guessing Daddy Dearest will stop paying your salary and mortgage."

Paris said nothing, the gravity of the situation sinking in. The physical pain I inflicted would heal. The financial hit wasn't salvageable.

"Maybe he'll understand once he knows it's for a good cause. How else will his son pay for his little sex addiction?" I scrolled through more emails and turned the phone to show him the incriminating photo. It was of Paris bent over the hood of a police car, handcuffed next to a woman in a similar position. "I believe that's a picture of you getting arrested with a sex worker."

Paris stared at me blankly. "Oh fuck. You're insane."

I nodded solemnly. "I have come to terms with it."

"Don't. Please," he snapped out of his anger and resorted to begging. "Please don't show those to anyone."

"I won't have to if you remember everything we discussed today." I pocketed the phone. "I'll hang onto them in case you forget. Oh, this goes without saying, but if you breathe a word about Poppy locking you up, I'll pursue all the avenues we discussed tonight. Understood?"

He nodded vehemently, not daring to hesitate.

"Glad we agree." I glanced at my watch. Our chat took longer than expected. Poppy went to sleep at midnight without exception, and dealing with this asshole ruined my last remaining moments with her. As if I needed more reasons to erase Paris' existence from this planet. Grabbing his collar, I yanked him off the ground with one hand.

"Ow," he yowled as I dragged him out of the panic room. "Where are you taking me?"

"This has been nice and all, but it's best if you get going. Leave through the balcony. It'll be rude to wake everyone."

Paris struggled to keep up, holding his side. "You can't be serious," he protested once I shoved him onto the connected balcony. "I could get seriously injured jumping off the second floor."

"You'll get more hurt if I *throw* you off the second floor." It wasn't a high jump, and he'd probably survive. The fucker would limp to his car as long as he landed on the soft ground. This was generous, considering my earlier murderous mood. "This way, you have a chance at making it."

Paris shuddered. "Chance?"

"I'd say fifty-fifty." I shrugged indifferently. It should worry me how little I cared whether he survived or not. "Avoid getting hit on the head."

Paris gulped and looked below. "How am I supposed to do that?"

"Not my problem."

"Please don't do this."

Boredom seeped into me. I menacingly stepped forward to pluck him off the ground and make good on my promise. Having read my intentions, Paris quickly climbed the railing, then jumped off without giving himself a chance to reconsider.

A thud was followed by overabundant whining. I skimmed with mild curiosity to find Paris lying on a rose bush.

Hm. He survived. Good for him.

Paris remained flat on the bush, moving his head from side to side. I let out a sigh. Guess I should drop him off at the hospital. It wouldn't look good for Poppy if he died on the property. However, I had one small matter to attend to first.

Leaving the balcony, I walked through the door connecting the two rooms. Poppy was under the blanket, having changed into a black tank top. As predicted, she was fast asleep with Neil in her arms. There was an ache to return to that bed and hold her for a few hours, but it had to wait.

I went through Poppy's desk drawer but didn't find what I was looking for. Next, I searched her nightstand drawer and found the birth control pills shoved inside. I pulled out the packets and pocketed them.

Next, I took a selfie with Poppy and Neil sleeping soundly on the bed, ensuring her desk was innocuously visible in the background. Before texting her the photo, I picked up her phone, bypassed her PIN, and toyed with the settings. I laughed upon noticing that she'd saved my number as *Bad News*.

Tearing myself away from them, I strode to Poppy's desk. It was time to initiate the next phase of the plan. I had hoped to ease Poppy into it, but her grandmother left me no choice by sanctioning Paris's entry into this house. The asshole returned after I intervened and after Poppy turned him down. Playing interception would no longer suffice. Her mother hosted too many events for their tight-knit community while banning outsiders. If not Paris, one of her family's other picks would replace him, and unfortunately, it wouldn't be me. I would never be their choice for the reasons Paris cited, which didn't leave me with many options.

Never again will fuckers have access to what's mine because it's Poppy's last night in this house.

With careful deliberation, I popped open the frame on her desk and took out the picture of Poppy with her parents, looking miserably happy. It was the last surviving memento from their yearly vacations. Taking it away brought me no joy, but I had to pour gasoline on the fire to ignite Poppy's wrath. It would break the restraint she exercised around Zane and Piya.

Careful not to wrinkle the old photo, I slipped out of Poppy's room with one last glance at my serenity.

One more night.

CHAPTER NINETEEN
POPPY

It was five a.m. when I blinked awake to a toddler and a text from Damon.

> Damon: Paris is handled. Didn't want to wake either of you. Night.

He attached a selfie with Neil and me sleeping peacefully on the bed.

I was a person of habit. Every morning, I woke up at five o'clock to run, followed by an hour-long meditation, email correspondences, and stock portfolio review. Every night, I read before bed and fell asleep precisely at midnight. Last night was the first time I made an exception to my sleep schedule.

Damon Maxwell possessed incriminating information about me. He could ruin everything I worked toward and turn my future into ashes if he so pleased. The looming threat should've been tearing me apart, but it wasn't what kept me up past my bedtime.

I planned on handling Paris without involving Damon, but he didn't leave room for an argument. The last thing I wanted was to involve Damon. He was the face of a humanitarian campaign and would lose credibility for engaging in aggression due to a momentary lapse in judgment. The unprecedented rage behind Damon's eyes had me fighting off sleep. I lost the battle.

After Neil's parents picked him up, I went for my daily run, showered, and threw on shorts and a tank. An hour of meditation failed to center my mind. How did Damon resolve the matter? His inspirational words on peace wouldn't have subdued Paris.

I waited until eight in the morning, deemed the earliest time appropriate to call someone, before dialing Damon's number. Or did others regard it as okay to call after nine o'clock?

I didn't have the chance to change my mind. Damon picked up before the end of the first ring, sounding as surprised as I felt for making the call. "Poppy?"

"Yes. Hello." I sounded unnatural. Phone calls were a normal societal means of communication, except I rarely partook in them. Once more, I didn't recognize myself where Damon was concerned.

"Hi. I'm glad you called." His rough voice sounded huskier over the phone, the gravelly tone leaving a peculiar electricity in its wake. "I hated leaving last night without saying bye, but I didn't want to wake you."

Of course, he didn't. Damon didn't admonish me for kidnapping Paris. Instead, he was concerned about my sleep health.

I cleared my throat. "What happened with Paris?"

Damon's easy mood disappeared. "He won't be a problem again."

My skepticism questioned the easy win. "Paris agreed not to call the police just like that?"

"He has no choice. Otherwise, he'll be charged with harassment."

"Harassment?"

"He came to your place unannounced, didn't leave when you asked, and made a move after you asked him to stop." Damon spoke with an edge to his tone, barely keeping out the bite.

"He is not even filing a report for assault and battery?" I hesitated, disbelieving Paris could be easily persuaded.

"No." The calm in Damon's voice was reassuring. "Why would he?"

"Because I punched him."

"Even if you shot him, he'd be the one at fault." A dark undertone was woven into the words as if wishing I had done just that. I'd chalk it up to my imagination, except I'd never been accused of having one. "Paris knows he's at fault, so keeping quiet is in his best interest."

It was remarkable, indeed, how a little perspective could turn a situation around. I counted on a scandal for taking a prisoner. Perhaps some jail time as well. To not face any consequences sounded too good to be true. What was more astonishing was that rather than being scared off by glimpses of my evil, Damon sounded like the same golden boy and helped hide my mistakes without batting an eye.

"My security team will keep Paris under surveillance to be safe." The timbre in his voice embraced my insides for a warm hug. "If he changes his mind and spreads gossip or contacts the police, they'll take out a restraining order on your behalf. It'll invalidate any defense about him being the victim."

"You covered up my crimes," I spoke satirically. He couldn't be more perfect if he tried.

"Yes, but don't let your grandmother set you up again," he warned. "I'll run out of security keeping you out of jail."

I glanced at the mirror. A barely-there smile was planted on my face. I had never known this face with genuine smiles, only sarcastic smirks. It looked odd, as if a stranger were staring back. No one had been so nonjudgmental about my personality before, not even Rose. Perhaps Damon had a valid point with his suggestion.

If this is worth fighting for, we can help Rose come to terms with it.

I shook my head. No. Rose wouldn't go for it, especially after reacting so poorly to seeing us together. Choosing Damon meant losing everything I had worked toward, including my relationship with Rose and my family.

Plus, Damon was unequivocally perfect. How long until the faultless man figured out how far removed I was from perfection? It was one thing to be aware of my issues, but another to live the experience. Like everyone else, he'd tire of my inability to reciprocate his feelings and display compassion. Eventually, he'd abandon the pursuit after uncovering my personality's unsavory bits. All the sacrifices I'd make would be for nothing.

I put the phone on speaker, setting it on the obsidian-colored comforter while rummaging through my closet. Nodding occasionally as Damon spoke, I absentmindedly grabbed an outfit Rose had gifted me for my eighteenth birthday. It never crossed my mind to wear it since the dress seemed too bright. Unthinking, I slid it over my head. My fingertips hovered over the collar of the black dress with large white prints. The cuffs of the sleeves were also white with clear buttons. Looking in the mirror, I realized it was the most illuminated version of myself I had seen in years. I thought I'd hate it more, but the aversion was lukewarm at best. The miracles kept coming.

Damon rattled off his jam-packed schedule, though it was a Sunday. They were working a half-day to ensure everything was in order before ringing in the new year.

I checked the time on my phone, realizing we had been talking for over twenty minutes. "Sounds like a busy day. Shouldn't you leave for work?"

Damon chuckled. "I'm already at work."

I frowned. "You said there was a business meeting first thing in the morning."

"Yes," he negligently agreed. "I'm in the meeting."

I stilled, picking up the faint sound of shuffling paper for the first time. Uncomfortable coughs and muted chatter of employees about passing a pen or a file became apparent in the background. They were patiently waiting for their CEO to wrap up a call that was clearly personal.

"You're talking to me on the phone in front of your staff?" I asked.

"Don't worry." Damon was unfazed, his voice collected as he spoke into the receiver. "They have NDAs. Anything said here is kept private."

"That's not what I was worried about." There were a million Poppies in the world. They'd never guess it was Poppy Ambani speaking to Damon on the other line. However, spending a business meeting on the phone was cavalier. "You can't put your staff on standby while you take a personal call."

"They don't mind," he said flippantly. It sounded like Damon lowered the receiver to address his team. "You guys don't mind if I talk to my girlfriend, do you? She missed me and couldn't stand the separation."

"I'm not your girl"

I was overruled by the voices on the other side of the line. A unanimous, *no sir, not at all, go ahead, we are happy to wait,* sounded throughout the conference room. At least fifteen to twenty people must be awkwardly watching Damon chat away. What was he thinking? More importantly, *girlfriend?*

I didn't know what to address first since he bypassed my gripe about the girlfriend comment. I went for the problem needing an immediate solution. "Go back to your meeting. I just called to thank you for covering for me."

"Always," Damon replied without hesitation. As if he had done this a million times when I created trouble in the past and would continue doing so in the future. "I'll swing by later. Bye." Damon's deep voice echoed through the phone. He hung up before I could argue.

I heaved a sigh. Reprimanding Damon's heavy-handed nature procured inadequate results. There was zero hesitation in his pursuit. We were too alike, and I couldn't put a brake on something I didn't know how to stop myself. Plus, we had things to discuss. Such as how Damon knew the pin to my panic room and *girlfriend?*

At least one thing was accomplished with the call. Damon didn't jeopardize everything because of me. The relief was short-lived.

Throughout college, I'd worked at Ambani Corp as a part-time analyst. I was knee-deep in a work project when something caught my eye. My desk was different from last night. Abandoning my laptop, I immediately grabbed the empty picture frame off my desk.

What the hell?

The remaining family photo from our vacation, the last souvenir I had of Papa, was missing. My hands shook with rage. I brought that picture into this house after Mom assured me no one would enter my room. She never understood why I insisted she had a talk with Zane. My floor was strictly off-limits to him. No one had access to this room except Mom and our housekeeper, Rachel, both of whom knew better than to touch my things.

Technically, Paris entered my room last night. But I showed Damon the picture *after* locking Paris away. I pulled up my phone, veins pumping with fury as I tapped on the photo Damon sent me. Zooming in, I confirmed the picture was on the desk, untouched when Damon left with Paris. I examined the time stamp. Someone must've entered my room between one and five o'clock.

Only one person had a motive to steal the picture, someone who'd done it before with access to my room. Zane's signature move was to cut out Papa's face and leave behind the photo. If he took the picture, it meant he was using it as collateral, most likely holding it in case I changed my mind about going away with Mom.

Calm, murderous rage boiled within me. I was going to lock Zane inside that panic room for years to come until he was nothing more than a pile of bones. I'd kill him with my bare hands if need be. Last night's near-prison sentence meant nothing because I was willing to risk it again. I'd happily go to jail for killing Zane.

∼

An elegant winter wedding in beautiful Sands Point, New York, taught me an important life lesson. I preferred funerals.

Morbid violinists were significantly better than wedding guests hopping on the dance floor. I'd happily trade the cheerful people for the solemn ones bowing their heads in respect. I'd gladly give up the fall-inspired terracotta cloth napkins in favor of handkerchiefs to blot tears. And I'd rather be anywhere but here.

Unfortunately, the option wasn't available.

"You are staying for the reception," Zane, aka my new evil stepfather as of ten minutes ago, informed me stoically.

Zane and Mom officially tied the knot at his over-the-top house in Sands Point. The ceremony took place inside a heated tent on the beach running alongside his property, and the reception was being held inside in the ballroom.

They had to have known it was inappropriate to have such an obnoxious wedding five months after my father's death. Wasn't ten years the customary mourning period, or was that wishful thinking? I knew my mother was young and beautiful. Papa mentally prepared me for such a possibility, but did she have to marry the worst human being on earth?

I pushed my chair back and grabbed my phone off the six-foot marble table decorated with tall vases. "The deal was that I stayed for the wedding. The ceremony is over, you're officially married, and I'm out of here." I have had enough of this charade. It was bad enough to suffer alone in this never-ending cesspool of misery, but was it also necessary to throw their PDA-filled love in my face? I wasn't stopping them from being happy, so why couldn't they leave me alone to be miserable?

"The deal is that you stay for as long as your mother wants you here." Zane was dressed to the nines in a sharp, black tux. Everything about him was welcoming except for his eyes. Cold, dark eyes told me that he didn't give a shit how hard this day was for me to endure. "You're not ruining Piya's day by leaving before the reception is over."

Ruin her day? I wanted to scream she ruined my life by marrying the worst person in the world. For the last couple of weeks, Zane had systematically blackmailed me into bending to his will while simultaneously reassuring Mom no one would find out he was my biological father. My life had gone from a loving family to a shitty stepfather and an oblivious mother parading around her happiness. I never considered myself sensitive, but was it presumptuous to expect my neurotypical mother to be?

Apparently so.

At least Mom had the good sense to try and keep things on the down low. Zane, on the other hand, invited the entire world to their wedding. He insisted she had a big dress, a wedding party, a giant cake, and a zillion people to witness the spectacle. He had exercised zero shame in flaunting this inappropriate celebration with a widow supposedly still in mourning.

Before Mom could ask me if I was okay with this circus, Zane, the snake, got to me. He showed me a DNA test proving his parentage. If I held back my blessing, he'd post it on social media to out me. Since then, he'd held that card over my head and been strategic about his manipulations. I thought about outing him to Mom, but a part of me wondered if it was best that she moved on instead of drowning with me. While misery loved company, I had never been much for company.

Nonetheless, being forced to celebrate their happiness still sucked. "I have a bunch of projects due on Monday."

"It can wait until tomorrow," he said curtly, voice dripping with distaste. It was a window into my new life. There was no doubt in my mind Zane regretted the day I was conceived. He was the opposite of Papa. Papa looked at me as if his world revolved around my happiness. Zane looked at me like I was the pest he was forced to deal with but would much rather squash.

"Unfortunately, it can't," I replied coolly and tapped the Uber app on my phone.

"Okay. Then we should take a father-daughter selfie before you leave," he spoke in a syrupy voice, though the words were sardonic.

Before I could protest, Zane took out his phone and snapped a selfie of us. A cold smirk pulled on his lips, boiling my blood. "Adorable. Let's post this one on the Gram. How about 'father-daughter finally reunited' for the caption?" He thrummed two fingers over his lips as if in deep contemplation.

Asshole.

Zane owned me, and he knew it, too. Obediently, I placed my phone on the table and took my previous seat.

I had finally found the thing I hated more than death—love.

CHAPTER TWENTY
POPPY

By the time we gathered for "family brunch," I was seething. I'd burn down this house if I didn't get my picture back. Tapping my foot under the table, I kept my glare steadfast on Zane.

"Poppy, do you want a croissant?" Mom held out the breadbasket, cutting into my limitless rage with another blindingly colorful pink sundress. "I made your favorite. Burnt."

I silently shook my head.

"Are you sure, baby? Look, I toasted them the way you like it. The bread's completely dry and impossible to tear."

They looked lovely, but my appetite was scarce. The eggs and baked beans on my plate hadn't been touched, either. I bode my time. Mom usually forgot something in the kitchen and excused herself midway through breakfast, giving me a small window to confront an unaccompanied Zane.

The one thing Zane and I had in common was protecting Mom's feelings. I never told her of the horrible things he did because it would shatter her picture-perfect world. Making my mother miserable wasn't my priority. The same philosophy didn't apply to Zane.

Zane coughed, suspiciously eyeing his breakfast before his lids slanted to me.

"You okay?" Mom set the breadbasket down to pat his back. When Zane indicated he was fine, she returned her attention to me. "Poppy, how's your winter project going?"

I spent my winter break working remotely as a hedge fund analyst, coining new ideas with a substantial short-term payoff. I invested macro amounts in thousands of risky companies, assessing when the rates would mature. Once the semester started, I'd resume my position in person, but with an impressive portfolio. Upon graduation, it'd jumpstart my career as a senior analyst at Ambani Corp.

However, I undertook another project this winter. An experiment. If I must live with the enemy, it was mandatory to learn their weakness. Through a process of elimination, I figured out Zane was allergic to the herb *anise*. As predicted, he hadn't consumed the rare spice before and wasn't aware of the allergy. On the days he pissed me off beyond measure, I added a small dose to his meals. Not enough to be fatal, but enough to cause moderate discomfort.

I directed a smirk at Zane. "The winter project's going better than I expected."

Opening my notebook, I recorded Zane's reaction to today's amount. A quarter gram of anise triggered a red hue to the skin, flared nose, and coughing. I had to keep thorough notes so I didn't accidentally kill him. Mom would frown upon that. Not to mention, if Zane had a near-death experience, he'd find a way to somehow make it my fault.

"You don't like your oatmeal?" I asked innocently when Zane pushed away his bowl, unceremoniously avoiding his breakfast.

"You barely touched it." Mom looked hurt. "I thought it was your favorite." She made fresh chia jam for Zane's oatmeal topping every day. I hated ruining her hard work. I wouldn't have to resort to such measures if Zane hadn't touched my things in the first place.

He reached over to hold Mom's hand. "It is, Princess," he spoke to her warmly before his distrustful eyes found mine. I raised my eyebrows in challenge. "I'm just having an off day." He made excuses to placate her. "Couldn't even get out of bed this morning."

"Aww. Did someone leave a big rock on top of your coffin again?" I mumbled under my breath, but Zane caught it and glowered.

"I can make you something else," Mom offered.

"Don't worry about it."

"It's not a problem. I'll whip something up five minutes."

"Not that hungry."

Mom threw up her hands. "Poppy doesn't like her burnt croissants anymore. You suddenly don't like the oatmeal I make from scratch. I don't know why I bother." She rose from her seat, frustrated. "I'll get the orange juice. Everyone seems to be on a liquid diet anyway."

Mom dramatically huffed and puffed out of the room, leaving Zane and me to our glaring contest. He shrugged back the sleeves of his black sweater, getting ready for battle.

"What did you lace the oatmeal with?" He got straight to the point the moment Mom was out of earshot.

"You're paranoid, old man." I reached over and scooped up a spoonful of his oatmeal. I shoved it in my mouth and chewed. "See? There is nothing laced in your food."

Zane narrowed his eyes. "Piya has made the same oatmeal for years. It never tasted like that before."

"If you don't like Mom's cooking anymore, say so. I'm sure she'll understand. Wait, no, she won't because cooking for her family brings her immense joy. In the future, might I suggest completing every meal she places before you?"

"We both know I'm not stupid enough to do that," he chewed out.

I shrugged. "Papa ate her cooking and never complained a day in his life. Maybe that's why she liked him better"

Zane slammed his fist against the dining table so hard it vibrated. "That's enough. Stop trying to turn my wife against me."

Unperturbed, I studied the notes in my book. "If you need a quality assurance manager so your food tastes like it used to, I'll happily take on the position. All you have to do is return my photo," I spoke into my journal.

For the first time, Zane appeared at a loss. "Am I supposed to understand the reference?"

"Don't act dumb. I know you took that picture from my room."

"What the hell are you talking about?"

What pissed me off more than Zane stealing the picture was him lying about it. *Up the ante*, I wrote in the entry for tomorrow's breakfast. His suffering would increase daily until he gave back what was rightfully mine.

I opened my mouth with a comeback when Mom strolled in with a jug of orange juice. The short walk to the kitchen had simmered down her irritation. She hummed, unaware of the hostility festering in the dining room.

"Poppy, you never told me if you saw a return on your winter investments. The project's supposed to determine your plans after graduation, right?" she asked, pouring juice into Zane's glass.

I nodded. "If everything goes well, the company will offer me the senior analyst position after graduation."

"That's amazing," she gushed, filling my empty glass.

No doubt, Mom woke up early to squeeze a zillion oranges and strained the pulp, too. She cast an irritated glance when she caught Zane staring at the cup instead of taking a sip. It was a wise decision. Anise might've made its way into every item in the kitchen.

What? He took my photo.

I took a long sip of my juice and asked for more. It made Mom smile, and Zane seethe.

"It'll still take another six years before I can apply for the CEO position," I told Mom as she refilled my cup. "Less if I get married and have kids."

The jug halted midair at the mention of marriage. Mom appeared stupefied while Zane burst out in laughter. "Kids? You?"

My expression remained stoic while Mom scathed him. "Stop it, Axel," she admonished, returning her attention to me. "Where is this coming from, Beta? You've never talked about marriage or having kids before."

"Past Ambani Corp CEOs were expected to marry and have kids." The thought came to me recently, a concept that no longer repelled me. "If I get married, it'll show the board I share their values; I'm stable and interested in representing a family business. And it makes perfect sense to have kids before becoming CEO. I won't be able to afford to take time off for maternity leave after assuming the position. Better to get it out of the way."

"Poppy," Mom said incredulously. "You don't have kids to *get it out of the way*. Having a child is a serious commitment."

I lifted my shoulders and let them fall away lazily. "I'll get a nanny to watch it." Not to mention, I was great with kids. No way was I giving Zane more ammunition to laugh over by admitting it in front of him.

"It? You mean the baby?" Mom appeared flabbergasted. "Poppy, you shouldn't jump into things because the board expects it." She stilled when a horror-struck expression crossed her face. "Oh God, are you thinking about marrying Paris? Before you make any rash decisions"

"It's not Paris." I cut her off so her hysteria wouldn't spiral.

Mom sighed in relief before another school of thought clouded her emotions. She scanned through my limited list of acquaintances for possible alternate candidates. When none presented itself, she asked, "Then who?"

Zane looked smug as he announced, "I believe a certain flower sender inspired her sudden interest in marriage." My gaze narrowed. There was no way he knew, right? Zane shattered my illusion of safety as he boasted, "Did you think Damon Maxwell could send flowers to my house without me finding out?"

"What!?" If Mom was horrified at the thought of Paris, she nearly fainted at the mention of Damon Maxwell. "What is he talking about?"

"Nothing." I silently willed Zane to shut up.

I fired a warning shot to scare Zane into returning my photo. I made the grave mistake of underestimating him by pulling the trigger halfway. I should've either poisoned him to death or not laced his food at all. The little display ignited his wrath, and he was coming for me. After all, we were cut from the same cloth. I should've known he was also collecting dirt on me. My poison turned out to be Damon Maxwell.

"Levi traced the flowers from yesterday to the original sender," Zane explained to Mom matter-of-factly, eyes grazing over the bouquet in the other corner of the room. "It was paid for by Damon Maxwell. You know, the one accused of killing her cousin."

Mom clutched the jug of orange juice to her chest, warding off the devil.

My fingers tightened around my utensil. I couldn't believe Zane was telling on me. What are we, five?

"I have to hand it to him," Zane's disparaging tone droned on. "Maxwell knows exactly what he's doing."

"Shut up." Zane had no right to say Damon's name. It was the equivalent of a demon taking the lord's name in vain. "You know nothing about him."

"I know he's eliminating his biggest competition by pursuing you," Zane shot back. "If he can get you to marry him, he'll acquire Ambani Corp's clients, then dissolve your company."

The comment made my eyes twitch. Damon brought up marriage yesterday. Could there be a grain of truth in Zane's assessment?

I vehemently dismissed it. No. I saw the look on Damon's face when I held Neil. It could only be described as longing. The innocent exchanges we shared in bed were honest. It trumped our ambitions.

"That's ridiculous. Damon knows I'll never get married without an iron-clad prenup," I said flippantly.

Mom blanched. "So, it is true?"

Dammit.

"I-I don't understand. I thought Damon Maxwell was in a secret relationship with Rose."

My chest iced over.

The texts Nick uncovered from Rose's phone had become common knowledge within our family. They knew of Rose's infatuation with Damon Maxwell but there was no way to prove the feelings weren't mutual.

"Poppy, this seems like a really bad idea," she spoke slowly, paralyzed with fear. "Maybe I didn't give Paris enough of a chance. Let's revisit him as an option." Mom gagged, unable to finish the sentence. "Nope. Can't say it with a straight face. Please don't marry Paris. And definitely don't marry Damon."

I threw daggers at Zane with my eyes. "Don't let him instigate and blow this out of proportion, Mom. All Damon did was send me some flowers. It's not a big deal."

"Not a big deal?" Mom forced out the words, hardly believing it possible. She counted off the cons. "Damon Maxwell is too old for you. Our families hate each other. And, oh yeah, the man was accused of murdering your cousin. Not to mention, he seduced Rose, probably for the same reasons Axel mentioned. And now that she's indisposed, he's going after you. How do you expect me not to be concerned for your safety?"

I must admit Damon didn't come out looking good. But as a person exercising immense caution around men, I trusted my gut instinct. My judgment was sound where Damon was concerned.

"Damon wasn't involved with Rose, nor is he a murderer. Why would a future Nobel laureate murder a no-good drug addict like Rayyan?"

Mom gasped. "Poppy, don't speak ill of the dead. And we don't know the full story about Rose. Even if he didn't physically push her, what if he had a hand in it? No one saw Damon for over an hour. He was the only one missing from the party"

"He wasn't the only one missing from the party. We were together," I burst out, immediately eyeing Zane. He grinned arrogantly because I'd shot myself in the foot, and he didn't have to do anything except pave the way.

The room turned pin-drop silent. It took Mom several moments to recover. "What do you mean you two were together?" Her voice was almost inaudible. "Why were you alone with Damon Maxwell for over an hour?"

I didn't respond, waiting for Mom to put two and two together.

Understanding dawned on Mom, followed by the disappointment she couldn't mask. "Rose is in love with that man, and he strung her along for God knows what reasons," she whispered, voice coated in sadness.

I could see it in Mom's face. It was covered in pity. She thought Damon was taking advantage of her little girl, distracting me with his pretty face.

"You can't marry someone who'll profit from your fortune and might kill you after taking possession of it." Mom shifted restlessly from foot to foot as if her worst nightmares were coming true.

I fought an eye roll. "This is ridiculous. No one's getting married."

"So, you'll stop seeing him?" she asked hopefully. "Until the allegations against him are cleared, you must consider that Damon is a very dangerous person," Mom asserted.

Her normal composure was shredded. Mom was imagining the death of her only child. After dealing with Papa's ongoing illness, Mom would have to be institutionalized if anything happened to me. I understood the sentiment and why Damon represented a threat.

Nonetheless, I fell silent, unable to verbally commit to her request.

Damon was the first person to witness the vile parts of me, and instead of running away, he dove in headfirst. It was ridiculous to never see him again based on unproven fears. In any case, only Rose had the right to demand this of me. After she recovered, I fully intended to give her the courtesy and explain what happened. Technically, there was nothing between us out of respect for Rose. I still couldn't force my lips to vow never to see him again.

Mom pulled out the big guns at my refusal. "If you keep seeing him, I-I," she stammered, the jug of juice still clutched at her heart. Her fear of the Maxwells surpassed more than what I anticipated. "I'll tell the board members of Ambani Corp about your relationship," she blurted, unable to think of other ways to keep me away from Damon. "They'll never let you become CEO if they find out."

I caught myself before exposing my reaction to Mom's unexpected threat. "Even if I can't be CEO, Papa left me enough stocks to sit on the board," I shot back.

"No. He left *me* those stocks." Mom's voice turned apprehensive. She spoke quietly as if hating every moment of this conversation but doing what she thought was necessary to protect me. It was misguided good intentions. "I planned on signing them over to you, but I'm wondering if I should implement a clause revoking your inheritance for marrying Damon Maxwell."

I struggled to grasp how my sweet, sensitive mother could concoct a plan remotely conniving. Her years with Zane had paid off.

"I'm sorry, Poppy, but this is for your own good. You might feel strongly right now, but don't confuse sex for the great love of your life. Damon isn't a good man. He is a placeholder."

The middle of my chest squeezed tightly at the face of Mom's unforeseen betrayal. This discussion had taken a bitter turn. "A placeholder?" I weighed the word against the tip of my tongue. "You mean a placeholder like Papa. You didn't even wait six months to remarry after his death."

Mom gasped, not expecting such a forward attack. I had never confronted her before, but I exceeded my threshold today. They drudged up the past by taking away the last piece of Papa, then threatened to take Damon away, too. Pandora's box was open and on full display.

When Mom remarried, I gave the benefit of the doubt to a whirlwind romance with Zane instead of a preexisting one. I never asked her about Joe Maxwell's accusations, believing she wouldn't cross that boundary.

But now... "Joe Maxwell was right, wasn't he?" my voice soft but menacing. "How else could you have moved on so fast?"

My mind refused to believe my mother was an adulterer, and I silently begged her to refute the accusation. Her silence was nothing short of confirmation.

My eyes inclined to Zane's conceited mien. "*He* would've made a disastrous father. So, you used Papa to raise your bastard child, then cheated on him when *the great love of your life* came back."

The jug of orange juice dropped from Mom's hand, the glass shattering on the wooden floor. Zane and I jumped out of our chairs. Zane instructed Mom not to move so the glass didn't cut her. Mom stood on shaky legs, barefoot amid the spilled juice and broken glass in her knee-length pink sundress. The shards on the floor mimicked our shattered bond. For the first time, I was disgusted by the truth.

Her bottom lip quivered. "Poppy"

I shook my head. "Papa loved you. He would've never done that to you."

"I know," was all she could muster, extending her hand to reach for me.

I recoiled, stumbling back. "How could you do that to Papa?" I pointed at Zane. "How could you choose *him* over us?"

A painful look crossed Mom's face, and she unthinkingly stepped forward. Her foot landed on a piece of broken glass. Zane cursed and scooped her into the air, the glass piercing his feet as well.

A sob tore out of Mom's mouth. "I'm sorry, Poppy," she whispered. "I'm so sorry. You have to believe me."

Believe her? Our entire lives had been a lie. The bullshit soulmate label everyone gave my parents was a facade. In reality, she had been biding her time for Papa to pass so she could return to *him*, the true love of her life.

The glint in Zane's eyes was cruel and unforgiving. "Stop," he snapped when Mom broke down against his chest. "You're upsetting your mother."

"I'd rather not take advice on family matters from a homewrecker."

"Drop it. It's not like I tried to replace Ambani in your life, and Piya stayed with him until the end. What more do you want? She did her best, especially with raising someone like *you*," he spat with disgust.

"Someone like me? That's rich coming from you," I bit back. "I don't dislike you because Mom moved on too quickly or because I worried about you replacing my father. I can't stand you because I hate having anything in common with someone like *you*. Every time I look at myself, I see you, and it makes me sick."

I was a byproduct of Zane. People like us struggled with relationships because we weren't moral or compassionate. Someone like *me* didn't belong with a good person like Damon. All I could give him was my destruction, and as soon as someone sweet like Rose came around, he'd see it, too.

My chest rose and fell with anger. "Papa was the best man I knew, but *you* are the reason I'm rotten. My brain isn't wired for anything good because of you." *I'll never know love or have anything good like Damon because of you. Thanks a lot for your screwed-up DNA.* "So why are you being rewarded after ruining everything for the rest of us?"

"As I said," he spoke through gritted teeth. "Piya was with him until the end, and your father knew about us. Everything was done by his choice. No one ruined anything for him."

I momentarily flailed. Mom had her face buried in Zane's chest and was in no condition to speak. I still directed the question at her. "Papa knew you cheated on him?"

Why the hell couldn't they have let the man die in peace, ignorant of his wife's betrayal? It was the least they owed him.

I stared at Zane, stunned. "This is sick. You are sick."

"If that's how you feel, then get out."

"Gladly." I slammed my notebook shut and stormed off with it.

CHAPTER
TWENTY-ONE
POPPY

Under the weight of defeat, I sought solitude in my refuge. The truth was supposed to liberate me, but it had become my bitter enemy. With everything out in the open, fresh blood poured freely from forgotten wounds.

Although I was supposed to make decisions sparked by logic, not emotions, I tossed clothes into a duffel bag without a destination in mind. I frowned when I couldn't find my birth control pills inside my nightstand drawer. I turned the drawer upside down and swore. I must be losing my mind.

The reasonable thing to do would be to first calm down and find a place to live behind fortified walls or ask one of my relatives if I could crash with them. However, if Mom followed through with her threat, I'd be out on my ass regardless.

I could go to Las Vegas, though I wasn't supposed to travel without guards. The board drilled into me countless times about doing everything in my power to remain safe. It was protection in name but a shackle in reality. They were paranoid that key players of the company could be used to gain intel. We had a lot of enemies and placed safeguards in our residences for that reason.

The soft patter of footsteps on the balcony sliced through my dilemma. A shadowy figure emerged from outside. I couldn't properly make him out through the glass doors, but it could only be the man. Whereas I had previously been wary of his presence, I didn't object when he slid the door open today.

Damon stepped inside, and I was momentarily punch-drunk at seeing him in a professional getup. His tall stature commanded more attention than usual in a fitted dark charcoal suit with two buttons on the front and notched lapels accentuating his broad chest. The crisp white shirt underneath had zero wrinkles, highlighting his chiseled features and tapered waist. Even the styled messy hair somehow matched the professional look.

The custom-made suit was fancier than any office wear I had seen before. If that was how he dressed at work, I had no idea how his staff got any work done. The outfit was as immaculate as his strong jawline, but his piercing sky-blue eyes, filled with intensity, stole the show. They speared into me.

"Hey—"

Before another word could escape my lips, Damon backed me against the cool wall. My gaze briefly fell on his full lips before he swooped in for a kiss. The fabric of his suit grazed against my fingertips as his right hand locked possessively around the base of my neck, the other cupping my cheek. There was a hint of something mint-flavored on his tongue that wrestled mine with fevered desperation. As if we had been apart for a lifetime instead of ten hours.

I planned on pushing him away; I did. But the ferocious attack had forced the faint whiff of his cologne into my lungs. The subtle blend of sandalwood and musk heightened my senses, turning me scatterbrained.

Wrapped in Damon's strong embrace, I couldn't remember why I shouldn't be in it. The kind of affection I resisted suddenly had me surrounded. No. He had me drowning. Damon had become the exception to my every rule, for he wouldn't do the heinous things people in this house were capable of.

My hands migrated to his shoulders, and he tensed, his hold tightening so I couldn't push him away. That wasn't my intention. Instead, my fingers tangled in his tousled hair to draw him closer. He groaned against my lips as if it were the last thing he expected. I ran my fingers through his unkempt hair, then traced the contours of his face, feeling his clean-shaven jaw against the warmth of my hand. His hands roamed my back and hips before returning to my face. Damon was all over me like he couldn't stand not to touch me. He refused to let me pull away even when we struggled for air, preferring suffocation to breaking the kiss. The charged electricity between us grew each time I saw him, and my commitment to Rose lessened. I wasn't sure how much longer I could fight off his advances. I half expected to have my dress bunched around my waist and was surprised when Damon let me withdraw.

His fingers grazed lightly over my cheek, assessing me. "What's wrong?"

Sometimes, I wondered if Damon possessed x-ray vision goggles for my mind. How else could he read my mood so succinctly? "Don't worry about it."

His deep voice dropped for a soothing one. "Tell me what's wrong."

I didn't need much persuasion. The events from today unfolded like an unstoppable torrent. Damon knew my truth, so I could disclose the entire matter without holding back information. He didn't offer empty reassurances and merely glimpsed at the packed bag on my bed.

"You were going to leave without telling me," he said in a slightly accusatory tone after I finished.

I tilted my head, not understanding the insinuation.

"If my father cheated on my mother, then married his mistress months after her death, I wouldn't be able to stand either of them, let alone live under the same roof," he explained with unwavering conviction. "Isn't that why you packed your bags?"

I stared at his Adam's apple.

Damon skimmed over the bag on my bed, then spotted the backpack containing my laptop and charger. "I understand your reasons, but I don't like that you were going to leave without telling me the destination. I don't like you running from me."

"Couldn't run even if I wanted to. The board sent me multiple warnings about how the security measures at my old apartment weren't good enough. It justified their paranoia when someone broke into my old place."

A faint flicker of tension crossed Damon's face, but the expression cleared before I could read into it.

"I was thinking of going away while I look for a new place. But I don't have a security detail, so that's out."

"Where would you go if you had a team?"

"Las Vegas."

"That's surprising."

"Why?"

"Most people are generally drunk and happy in Vegas." When he noticed my scowl, Damon clucked his tongue. "Don't worry, Little Spawn. It's the holidays. There'll also be plenty of degenerates gambling away their life savings this time of the year. Vegas will be morose."

"You think?" I asked hopefully.

Damon chuckled. "Never mind. Why Las Vegas?"

"Sophie is in Vegas."

His jaw ticked. I knew Damon threw Sophie out of the room the first night we were together and adding fuel to the fire wasn't my intention.

"I'm not interested in Sophie," I quickly added, taken aback that I was offering him an explanation. "I need to ask her a few questions." I needed to clear Damon's name.

"What about?"

"I can't tell you. It's between her and me."

Damon gave me a tight smile, then grabbed the duffel bag off the bed. "Let's go."

I stared at him blankly. "Where?"

"I thought we were going to Vegas," he spoke like the answer was obvious.

A scoff fizzed in my chest at his bold haste. "You can't come to Vegas with me."

"If we leave now, we can still enjoy most of the day with the time difference." Damon hardly acknowledged my refusal, busy picking out a coat from my closet, the same bomber jacket he had left me with.

"You..." *You belong to Rose* was on the tip of my tongue.

Or at least Rose believed that Damon belonged to her. Some of her texts were challenging to read, outright confessing her feelings to him. I didn't know if anything happened between them, but after this morning, perhaps illusion was better than reality.

I wasn't sure how to articulate the thought and went with, "You come to Vegas with me, and paparazzi will take a million pictures of us together."

"Paparazzi only take pictures of me in New York because they know I live here. Vegas is different, especially on New Year's. The place is crawling with celebrities. They won't notice me or if we are together."

"Or pictures of us will be the headline tomorrow, and we'll be jobless the day after."

Damon disregarded the concern. He draped the giant jacket over my shoulders, humming appreciatively at the sight of me swimming in it.

I grappled with another concern. "What about your work?"

"I was supposed to take time off to be committed, remember?" When I didn't move, Damon let out a sigh. "Tomorrow is a holiday."

I tried to think of more obstacles. "New Year's is the biggest night in Vegas. All the hotels will be booked."

A wolfish grin appeared on Damon. "Getting a hotel isn't a problem if you want to spend the night with me."

"There'll be none of that."

Damon shrugged indifferently. "Then we'll meet with Sophie, ring in the new year, and take a red-eye back on my plane."

I huffed. "Of course, you own a plane."

"It belongs to my company." His gaze appeared bored. "There is Wi-Fi on board. You can find a listing on the flight to Vegas, and I'll drop you off at your new home in the morning."

More time would help me find a suitable new place. It wasn't a bad plan so long as Damon kept his hands to himself.

No one dared to take care of me; Mom and Rose were the only ones to try. Meanwhile, Damon catered to my whims, even a last-minute trip to Las Vegas. Recently, he seemed to be the solution to every problem I had.

Damon slung my laptop bag over his shoulder and added, "It's your best option. I have a vetted team who can keep an eye on you. They are discreet but good at spotting danger from a distance."

Security on Maxwell dime? The board wouldn't approve, but it was better than the alternative. They'd throw a fit over my recklessness if something happened to me while unaccompanied. Work-wise, the board of directors found me impressive. Temperament-wise, not so much. It often made them question if I was fit to be a future tycoon.

It was either staying with Zane while I searched for a new place or going away under Damon's protection. I went with the lesser of the two evils. I never considered a partner-in-crime before, but everything sucked less with Damon around.

"Ready?" I asked.

"Ready for what?"

"I thought we were going to Vegas," I replied like the answer should be obvious.

Damon didn't react. He simply turned and strode toward the balcony with one of my bags in each hand. I hurried after to keep up with the distance he covered with his long legs. He effortlessly climbed down the railing in his fancy suit. Damon waited patiently at the bottom, strong hands grabbing me before my feet could touch the ground. Together, we made our way to the staff entrance, where a sleek, metallic car was parked.

"This is your car?"

Damon nodded, placing my bags in the trunk.

I couldn't resist admiring the polished exterior of the Aston Martin, the flawless gunmetal finish gleaming in the sunlight. Especially since this car had caught my attention at a sales lot for those very reasons.

"I own the same car," I declared.

"Oh." Damon held open the passenger side door, unperturbed. "Cool." I couldn't read his reaction at all.

Alarms blared in my mind. Damon always possessed information he shouldn't have access to, with a knack for articulating my thoughts verbatim. Not to mention, his urgency to leave was startling. It was the first time he prioritized getting me out of the house instead of stripping me naked.

Damon looked me over when I didn't move toward his car. "Something wrong?"

"We should drive separately so I can have my car."

"Parking's a bitch at the airport, and if we get separated, it'll be impossible for you to find the tarmac for chartered planes. I'll bring you back here tomorrow so you can pick up your car." Furrowed lines appeared on his forehead when I still hadn't moved, searching for a reason behind my hesitation. "Don't tell me you're scared after coming this far."

I raised an eyebrow. "Should I be?"

He said nothing, narrowed eyes landing on my face, the silence stretching.

My paranoia was unfounded. This was Damon we were talking about, dubbed the best human on earth by literally everyone except my family.

Not to mention, Damon and I were extremely similar, except for our morals on the account he had some. Was it so shocking he owned the same car as me? Tons of people drove this car. It was a mere coincidence.

In hindsight, I ignored the red flags to escape my predicament. Because either I trusted Damon, or I had to keep living with that damn homewrecker.

"Never mind. Let's go."

Damon didn't budge until I folded myself inside the car. He closed the passenger side door and activated the lock while rounding the vehicle as if I were a flight risk. Was he preventing my escape attempt?

Argh. I was letting my family get in my head. These weren't legitimate concerns. I shook them away, checking out the sleek interior and the black leather of the heated seat. Same as mine.

Damon slipped into the driver's seat, quickly shifting the gear to drive off before I could change my mind.

∼

DAMON

A new habit took root in my life after Poppy's mother remarried. What started as lightening my guilty conscience turned into watching out for Poppy around campus. I used to wonder if Poppy was suicidal or perhaps an adrenaline junkie who welcomed the danger. Or maybe it was the grief blinding her from her otherwise rational personality. What other reason could there be for walking home alone after dark in a big, bad city? No one seemed to care about irreversible damage to her, Poppy included.

The part of me that was still riddled with guilt refused to let anything else bad happen to her. During Poppy's first year at college, I walked behind her every night until she reached her dorms safely.

It was remarkable how much you could learn about a person by simply observing them. People's inhibitions were exposed when they thought no one was looking. The uninterrupted observation allowed me to grasp Poppy was neither suicidal nor an adrenaline junkie. She had done extensive research to confirm the path she took wasn't riddled with past crimes. Poppy knew it was safe to walk the route and, as an added measure, carried a taser. I found out when she pulled it out one night upon hearing my footsteps.

It was ironic. I inadvertently ended up stalking Poppy while paying a small fortune to keep stalkers away from me. Per my publicist's prodding, I partici-

pated in dozens of magazine campaigns, television ads, and outreach programs. The exposure brought forth all kinds of crazy. With the rising fame and exponentially increased attention, I was forced to move out of the dorms and into a penthouse, with security patrolling my building around the clock.

Women presumed they had a claim to me if they collected my magazine articles or taped my televised ads. People waited in front of my building for an autograph or picture. Students on campus followed me for a chance at fame or to share in the limelight. Magazine articles flooded the stands with my "good deeds." Despite the monotony of my new life, there was one routine that didn't irk me.

Walking behind Poppy had turned into a routine, and I was a person of habit. By the start of my senior year of college, I altered my schedule so my first class would fall near hers. I also changed my garage to the one closest to Poppy's dorm. After walking her home religiously for a whole year, I realized she was a person of habits as well. She was also overly cautious, constantly weighing risk versus reward. So, imagine my surprise when one day, she took a new route. Poppy looked different today, as well, with makeup and high heels. Her raven hair was in a messy bun, giving her a slightly older look. For the hundredth time, I found myself thinking she was beautiful. The thought resulted in immediate admonishment.

You sick fuck, she was fifteen and too young for the ideas playing on a loop in your dirty mind. My job was to make sure she survived, nothing more.

Lighting up a cigarette, I put distance between us with the pre-measured number of steps. Poppy was too observant, and I perfected the routine to ensure she couldn't discover me. I was shocked when Poppy pulled open the door to a tattoo parlor. The makeup, the high heels, the hair, all of it finally made sense. It was a ruse to appear older because she planned on getting a tattoo.

Flicking my cigarette to the side, I pulled my cap down and slid inside the parlor. I pretended to study the art on the wall like a potential patron about to be inked.

A bulky man covered in a sleeve of tattoos approached me. "Can I help you?"

"Just browsing," I dismissed him, never taking my eyes off the wall, simultaneously listening to Poppy's conversation with the girl at the front desk. I had become a pro at multitasking, watching Poppy out of the corner of my eye while appearing outwardly busy.

The front desk gave Poppy a once-over. "ID?" she asked cautiously.

Poppy dropped a driver's license on the counter. Without a doubt, she procured this fake for the purpose of getting a tattoo.

"Do you know what you want?"

"Here." Poppy slapped a piece of paper on the counter.

The woman glanced at the design. "That's simple enough. It'll take less than fifteen minutes. Where do you want it?"

"The back of my neck."

"Follow me."

The woman led her to the other side of the counter. There were various massage tables spread across the floor. She led Poppy to her station.

What the hell, Poppy? This place better be sanitary. At least it appeared posh, but I opened my phone to check their online reviews. It was rated high on Yelp and accredited. clearly, Poppy had done her research. As I was about to hit the lock button, I froze upon noticing today's date on the screen.

It was the day Poppy's father died.

Since his funeral, there has been no other commemoration surrounding Jay Ambani. Even on the anniversary of his death, Poppy was alone at a tattoo shop.

Fuck, this sucked.

I couldn't leave now, nor could I bear the thought of her getting a tattoo by her lonesome self. There was nothing I could do other than what I had always done for Poppy, being there for her non-verbally.

I walked up to the new girl covering the front desk. She had numerous piercings and strands of deep red hair sticking out.

"Hello there." The girl's pupils dilated like I was on the menu, but she quickly composed herself. "May I help you?"

My eyes flicked to the side. Poppy was flat on a massage table while the tattoo artist prepped her skin with a swab.

Despite the promise I made to my dead mother, who hated body art, I declared, "I need a tattoo." God, the lengths I went to for a girl who hated me and my entire family.

"Sure thing," she spoke breathlessly while I suppressed an eye roll. "What would you like?"

I pointed at the abandoned piece of paper Poppy left behind on the counter. The woman appeared confused as to why I wanted to imitate another's personal artwork and etch it permanently on my skin. I gave her my most charming smile.

"I'm not the most imaginative. This looks nice enough." It was a stylish artwork of a Roman numeral for the number one. I presumed it was a permanent commemoration of her father. It better not mean Poppy planned on getting the same tattoo annually, marking each year to pass after his death.

Belatedly, I realized that was exactly what she planned on doing.

"Where do you want it?"

I pointed at the back of my neck. At least, it wouldn't show in business meetings, and I could maintain the professional façade. I had an inkling Poppy had the same thought. Hair, collared outfits, or suit jackets would hide the small numeral on the back of the neck.

Poppy's shenanigans didn't end there. A couple of months later, she drank herself into a stupor on the anniversary of her grandmother's death. Instead of *leaving herself vulnerable, she brought along Rose and a trusted security guard from her mother's roster. Rose and Poppy strolled into a bar, the security guard sitting five seats down so boys couldn't take advantage of them while intoxicated. Not that she knew, but Poppy needn't worry about it. I would never let that happen in a million years. Make that a zillion years. Pride still thumped in my chest because she thought of everything.*

She was my good girl. My good girl who started ordering drinks with her fake ID and pounding shots like a pro. Just like everything else Poppy did, she did it a little too well. Rose vehemently discouraged the binge drinking, but Poppy got sloppy drunk. The guard ensured they were safely returned to their dorms. Of course, I still snuck into her room, watching her throughout the night to ensure she didn't have alcohol poisoning.

The slight recklessness should've made me angry, but it had the opposite effect on me. I found it endearing. Part of me was proud that Poppy could throw back drinks despite steering clear of socialization during her time in college. The other part simply loved it when she lost herself to the moment. Poppy rarely let her guard down or made mistakes. She was always in control, aware of herself and her surroundings. The rare occasions when Poppy gave in to her grief by doing something bad was my favorite window into her soul.

It made her human.

I liked it when Poppy was human.

In the perfect Poppy fashion, she celebrated the worst days of her life. By my calculation, however, there was one more day that deserved a reckless celebration. The day her mother remarried. I saw the look on Poppy's face; she was broken.

Nonetheless, I didn't know what she did to deal with her grief on the day of her mother's anniversary since it fell over winter break. Classes were out of session. Much to her mother's chagrin, Poppy opted to leave town for a winter internship at Cornell.

I must've gone insane because I drove to upstate New York. It was a closed campus, and outsiders weren't allowed in. The irregularity of seeing her left a restlessness gnawing under my skin. Poppy was safe and not suicidal, yet each passing day signified a slow agony for unanswered questions.

Did she still finish crossword puzzles at super speed?

Did she still yell at people for littering?

What new enigma did Poppy Ambani come up with today?

By the end of the break, I was snapping at everyone over trivial shit. My friends stayed away in apprehension, my twin was fed up with my bad mood, and even Dad gave me space. I was the only senior itching for classes to resume.

I waited for Poppy on the first day of classes, leaning against her dorm building with my usual baseball cap pulled low. The giddiness in my chest could only compare to some middle school bullshit. At long last, Poppy strolled out in her signature all-black get-up. Other than not seeing her in weeks, there was nothing special about the day. It was cold and dreary outside. Poppy's outfit matched the morbid weather. Be that as it may, something was different in the air today.

I watched her from afar, my eyes eating her up like she was my last meal on earth. With one glance, she fixed the problem I had been struggling with for weeks. The impatience was gone, and so was the irritation. It was as if she was the ticket to end my suffering.

Poppy walked to campus, and I stalked after her like a man possessed. She was beautiful and witty, with a surprisingly strong moral compass that she'd picked up from her father (the one she liked). Poppy hid those things under her dark personality, but she couldn't hide from me.

And that was when it hit me like a train wreck.

I missed her.

I missed her so fucking much.

The time I spent ensuring Poppy didn't off herself in her sorrows left me hooked on her. Somewhere down the line, my feelings for her transformed from protectiveness to possessiveness. A few short weeks away made me realize I was downright addicted to Poppy.

I had no idea how I let it progress this far, but the truth was irrefutable. I craved these moments. Moments where I could watch her, and she didn't hate me or my family for tarnishing the famous Ambani name or publicly accusing her of being a bastard.

I took the measured steps to put enough distance between us, but I made several mistakes today, barely containing myself in my excitement. This girl had me twisted from the inside out. I had been obsessing over her whereabouts and forgot what it was like to look at her. It was blowing my fucking mind the things I missed about her until they were no longer in front of me.

Was she always this beautiful, or did she seem different today?

Fuck, what was I doing? She was fifteen, and I was twenty-two. Even without our families in the mix, this obsession of mine was downright sick. If I pursued her, if I did anything with her, I would fuck up her childhood worse than I already have. That wasn't me. I didn't hurt children.

Like the devil, my mind whispered that she wouldn't always remain a teenager. She'd transform in a few short years. Everything about Poppy had already changed in the weeks I didn't see her. She was more beautiful, more sexual. There was a sway in her hips that didn't exist before. I was probably making this shit up in my fucked-up head, but I couldn't stop the thoughts from forming. All because I forgot how great it felt being near her.

My fingers itched to touch her, though pining after her was useless. The competing company, fueled by my uncle and the damn algorithm I created, plummeted Ambani Corp over the last few months. I tried stopping it, but

Henry asserted the company owned my intellectual property. There was nothing I could do about it until I took over as CEO.

Never had another man hated his creation more. It took away the only woman who mattered to me. Poppy hated my rotten family for systematically ruining her father's untouched legacy and her birthright, me most of all for creating the software. She loathed this face. If I could take it off, I would do it for her in a heartbeat. I'd do anything to lessen her suffering.

Nonetheless, no matter how much she hated me, Poppy was already mine.

So, over the next few years, when Poppy returned to the tattoo parlor and added another line to the back of her neck, my skin was also permanently marked. Every time she wasn't around, I couldn't help rubbing my neck as if touching the tattoo brought me closer to her.

It was the same every year. She tattooed herself on the anniversary of her father's death, and she drank herself silly on the anniversary of her grandmother's death. Which left me with the same burning question.

How did Poppy find comfort on Zane and Piya's anniversary?

CHAPTER
TWENTY-TWO
POPPY

It was late afternoon when Damon's company plane touched down on the tarmac of Las Vegas Airport. Before boarding, I texted my cousins to crash with them in case I couldn't find a rental by tomorrow.

No response.

Maybe Mom followed through and told them about my recent liaison with a Maxwell, so they were shunning me. The betrayal only fueled my fire, and I spent the journey seething and looking for a new home using the terrible in-flight Wi-Fi. My search yielded limited results.

Damon was also busy emailing and coordinating details on the phone about something. I was sharing his space, yet it felt strangely natural and a window into life with this man. Our focus only deviated when Damon's eyes landed on me, which happened often. They were constantly undressing me. The way he watched me between his laptop screen and multitasking, you'd think watching me was second nature to him. There was a heat simmering between us that seemed ready to blow the lid of the boiling pot.

Three men also joined us on the flight, each introducing themselves as part of his security team. Bodyguards protecting Damon was like flushing money down the drain. Those men couldn't have a more pointless job, given that Damon was bigger and towered over them. I suspected he would've forgone security had I not been on this trip with him. The "bodyguards" disappeared when we landed, but I knew they followed us in a rental car.

Meanwhile, a sleek limousine picked us up. We surrendered our bags to the chauffeur, who introduced himself as Miguel and informed us the car was at our disposal for the evening. He drove us to the hotel Sophie pinned for me when I texted her about my impromptu trip. Miguel skirted past the main entrance, veering toward a clandestine area with three imposing letters: VIP.

Every aspect of this excursion seemed meticulously preplanned, superseding a spontaneous trip. Yet Damon had a statement prepared whenever I pointed it out. He had a pre-packed bag in his trunk, which Damon claimed was a byproduct of his unpredictable travel schedule. When I mentioned it was impossible to charter a private plane so quickly, Damon insisted the plane was always on standby for him and Caden.

Eventually, I dropped the subject.

The elevator doors revealed a gigantic hotel lobby vibrating with Vegas energy. The air was thick with anticipation and chattering voices, punctuated by the occasional jingle of slot machines. As we walked through the maze of flashing lights, I pulled my phone out of Damon's bomber jacket, still draped around me. My thumbs swiped across the screen to the text thread with Sophie. She hadn't responded to my last two texts.

Me: I'm here.
Me: Where are you?

"What's wrong?" Damon asked, watching me tinker with the phone.

I glanced up at him, neck craning at the reminder he was freakishly tall when compared to my five-foot frame. "I messaged Sophie before we took off. She texted me the hotel address but hasn't responded since."

Damon didn't appear the least bit surprised. "She's probably getting drunk at some day party. Try calling her."

The phone on the other end rang once, twice, repeatedly, before going to voicemail. I stared at the device like it was my enemy. "Don't tell me we came all this way, and now she's too drunk to meet up."

Damon tried to hide his amusement. "What did you expect? It's Sophie."

Damn. He was right.

As if to soothe my disappointment, he suggested, "Do you know where she's celebrating New Year's? We can meet her there."

I looked through my texts with Sophie about mentions of her New Year's plans. "She is going to Xtasy. It's a club inside Paradise Hotel." Sophie was ringing in the New Year with some friends and suggested going in with them on the table. Suffice to say, I didn't take her up on the offer.

"There you go. We'll meet her there before she starts having too much fun."

"What do we do until then?"

Damon turned toward me and moved closer, our bodies nearly touching. He left his suit jacket in the limousine and just wore the fitted white shirt. Heat emanated through the thin material, accompanied by an undercurrent of danger. "The same thing," he said suggestively. "Fun."

"What did you have in mind?"

He brushed a strand of hair away from my face. "I hear you're an expert at counting cards."

Not what I expected him to say.

"A little gambling never hurt anyone," he added when I didn't jump at the suggestion.

"Addicts would argue it hurts a lot of people."

His smirk remained intact as he leaned closer, his lips inches away from mine. "Gambling never hurt *you*."

What I should've asked was how he could've possibly known that. Instead, I made another round of excuses. *This man lived inside my brain.*

"So? Should we put your gambling skills to the test?"

"Lead the way." Just as I said it, I realized something. "My fake ID is in my bag in the car." I grimaced, remembering Damon was much older and not prepared to deal with this problem. Another arena that wouldn't be a problem for Rose.

"You don't need it." Damon took my hand.

"Where are we going?"

"You'll see."

Damon led me to an area separate from the casino floor and spoke to a lady with decorated strings of pearls in her bun. Whatever he said to her, the eloquence had the woman complying without argument. She showed us to a private room behind a set of closed doors.

The place was packed with numerous tables on each side, but the seas parted when Damon entered. We quickly found a blackjack table, its shiny surface reflecting the eager faces of the players surrounding it. Damon bartered with the croupier, handing over a wad of cash. I sat beside him at the half-moon table as he set a pile of chips before me. Belatedly, I realized he had exchanged chips for the both of us.

"I have money"

A busty server in fishnet stockings interjected me, looking like she walked out of a femme-fatale photo shoot. Damon and I sat side by side, but she maneuvered into the minuscule space between our seats, positioning herself so her knockers would inadvertently brush against him. "Drinks?" she purred rather than asked.

Damon asked her to bring their driest bottle of champagne, dry was my favorite as well, and handed over his credit card.

Femme-Fatale flipped her hair and examined the card, the curled auburn strands hitting me in the face. She had yet to acknowledge my presence with her back turned to me. "Anything for you, Mr. Maxwell."

I inwardly snorted. Must be nice to be Damon fucking Maxwell.

The bottle arrived before the dealer finished shuffling the decks. Femme-Fatale poured the champagne, but Damon pointedly motioned at me when she tried handing him a flute. At long last, she was forced to accept my existence and resentfully offered me the glass instead. I sarcastically raised it to her "excellent" service. The server wasn't flustered by my mock solute, offering Damon the other flute before placing the half-empty bottle in an ice bucket stand.

"She didn't check my ID." I studied the room. "Neither did anyone else here."

Damon gave a husky laugh. "People look the other way in this room because only a select few can afford to enter it."

"How do you know about this place?"

"Does it matter?" Damon raised his glass. "Cheers."

I only drank a select number of times per year. It was rare when I sought a state of relaxation, but who better to partake in it with than my new partner in crime?

We toasted. I waited until Damon drank his before tasting mine. It was an old habit. If I didn't serve the alcohol myself or left a drink unattended, then my companion needed to be the poison taster, especially if he was twice my size and could easily overpower me while my defenses were down. Yes, my paranoia was out of control. Years of lectures about the safety of the Ambani clan had rubbed off. It was drilled into our heads that people wanted what we had.

The bubbles tickled my throat from the long sip. I set the glass down on the blackjack table but felt Damon's scorching hot gaze crawling over my skin as if watching me was his greatest pleasure in life. It was the same during the short drive to the hotel and on the plane.

The dealer asked us to place our bets, forcing Damon to retreat. He reluctantly turned his attention to the table, taking another sip of his drink. I followed his example, my mind wandering.

We played numerous hands, and before long, I caught onto Damon's skillful strategies. I wasn't the only one counting cards. Damon knew the number of decks in play and which cards had been dealt, staying or hitting on the dealt hands accordingly.

Never in a million years did I expect Damon Maxwell to have a dark side. Or perhaps this side always existed, but he only allowed me a glimpse of it.

I leaned over and whispered, "I wasn't expecting this from the golden boy of New York."

"I have no idea what you're talking about," Damon replied innocently.

I pointedly eyed his mounting pile of chips.

"It's called beginner's luck."

It wasn't. "Sure." I raised my glass. "To your hidden talents."

He clinked our flutes. "To our many skills."

The trepidation where Damon was concerned lessened a little with his playfulness. Our eyes locked, the electricity intensifying even during a good-humored moment.

Damon sat back in his chair the same way he did everything else, shoulders relaxed, one hand on the blackjack table like he owned the place. Other men at the table felt innately threatened and unconsciously mimicked the pose, desperate to master the aura Damon possessed without trying. His commanding presence filled the room and drew attention, especially from women.

Femme Fatale returned and placed a hand on Damon's shoulder with a sultry, "Can I get you something else, hun?" The question left little to the imagination whether she was offering a drink, a phone number, a quickie in the bathroom, or a combination of all three. She didn't bother asking anyone else at the table for their drink orders.

Damon gave her a flippant, "No, thanks," before pulling my chair closer and grabbing my waist until I was practically sitting on his lap. The subtle letdown was evident in his actions since she could no longer stand between us and hit on him with her back to me. It didn't stop her from leaving a napkin with her phone number. She placed it next to Damon's chips, and when an older gentleman at our table covered his mouth and nose to sneeze, Damon extended the napkin to him, letting his snot ruin the heart drawn next to Femme Fatale's number.

Were this an isolated incident, it would've been fine. But several other servers tried their luck with Damon, causing my traitorous ears to perk for his answer. Some of them didn't even work for the hotel. Women flat-out asked Damon if he wanted a drink or to join them at the bar.

Curiosity finally got the better of me. "Do these women know who you are?" Photography might not be allowed near the casino tables, but people would've still discreetly taken pictures of Damon if they recognized him.

"No," Damon replied curtly.

I frowned because he was telling the truth. People in our city were familiar with Damon's face because he was from the area. Many might be familiar with the name nationwide, but I doubted they'd recognize him in person. Theoretically, only a select few could pick out a philanthropic CEO from a crowd.

"So women are obsessed with you regardless of celebrity status." This shouldn't have been news to me.

Damon appeared uncomfortable with the question and tried to downplay his effect on women. "They are just trolling for tips."

"Some of those women aren't even servers," I pointed out when another discreetly folded a cocktail napkin and slid it to Damon. He immediately brushed it off the table as if it were contaminated, the tissue falling dramatically on the ground. The sly woman looked hurt.

"It has nothing to do with me."

"Except for how you look and dress and your body." I let my finger slice vertically through the air, motioning at all of him.

"Exactly. Women become infatuated with an outer package because of what they think I can give them. Those feelings aren't real. They don't know anything about me." Damon leveled me, needing me to understand an important distinction.

It dawned on me why the topic made him tense. Damon was referring to Rose. He wouldn't speak poorly of her in front of me, but he wanted me to identify her feelings as superficial. I blocked the thought with great effort and diverted my attention to the table.

Time slowed as Damon played in synchrony with me. He mirrored my choices, and I realized he intentionally lost or won so it would work out in my favor. The unspoken connection grew stronger with each hand.

Just when we were on a roll, Damon suggested, "Let's go to the next table."

I gave him an inquisitive look.

He lowered his voice to state, "We've won too many hands at this table."

Good point. If we wanted to remain unnoticed, exercising discretion was important. We cashed out our winnings, and Damon pulled me toward another room. I glanced at our empty champagne bottle. "That was a good choice."

"We'll order the same one later tonight, then."

"What's tonight?"

Sky-blue eyes watched me, studying me, dissecting me, like always. "New Year's," he finally replied. Something about his ominous tone told me there was more to the story, but instead of prying, I simply watched him in turn.

CHAPTER
TWENTY-THREE
POPPY

FLUSHED WITH VICTORY, WE VISITED NUMEROUS ROOMS, constantly rotating tables. We won hand after hand because we knew when to hit. Better yet, we knew when to quit.

"We need to move on," Damon suggested. "The casino will catch on if we keep winning."

My stomach growled in response. I hadn't eaten since the disastrous breakfast. Although the flight attendant served a full lunch on the plane, I didn't have an appetite. Damon had scowled at my unfinished plate but let it go on account of my foul mood.

The courtesy no longer applied. "We are getting some food in you before we do anything else," he declared.

We ventured beyond the confines of the hotel in search of Miguel. I wasn't surprised when the limousine dropped us off at a restaurant just abhorrent enough to suit my taste. Of course, Damon picked a place custom-made for me, from the worn-out menus down to the God-awful yellow wallpaper. I found myself staring at a dry sandwich with buns slightly burnt around the outer edges. It was horrifically perfect, but others didn't often share my taste.

"Do you not like yours?" I skimmed Damon's plate, which had been mostly neglected.

"It's fine." Damon watched me shove food down my throat as if it was the most endearing thing he had seen in years.

"I thought you'd be hungrier."

"Oh, I'm definitely hungry." His tongue darted out to lick his bottom lip.

My eyes followed the motion. The double entendre left a dipping sensation low in my abdomen, and sitting still was suddenly a challenge.

The smell of Damon's expensive cologne and a hint of his sweat had tortured me for hours, and I was finally at my limit. His presence was worse. Damon carried himself with a quiet confidence, making his magnetism impossible to ignore. The man was incredibly built with broad shoulders, toned muscles, and warm, golden skin. If his stature managed not to captivate people, the masculine aura dripping with sex did the trick.

Damon caught the way I shifted in my seat. He wore a cocky grin and leaned back, a hand over his mouth hiding the amusement as if he knew exactly what got me worked up. The effect he had on me was absurd.

"You feeling okay, baby? You look a little flushed."

"I don't flush."

His eyes lazily perused me from top to bottom. He leaned closer, the taut muscles under his shirt contracting. "You do. Your face is all red."

"Impossible."

"And you look restless." His voice was low and smooth, eliciting an embarrassing response between my legs. "If you need something to help you relax, all you have to do is ask."

"I'm fine," I managed.

"Sure, baby," he said with a knowing grin.

The infuriating smile loitered as I pushed my meal away. The perfect sandwich tasted like ash in my mouth. I needed to work off the abrupt edginess and was relieved when Damon suggested a walk on the Strip.

The unexpected detour of strolling past iconic hotels and landmarks wasn't as bad as I expected. For once, I wasn't bothered by a bustling crowd, lively streets, or cheerful performers. Whereas the bright lights casting a vibrant glow on Las Vegas should've made my blood boil, it felt like background noise next to Damon. The swagger in his graceful movements oozed with control and self-assurance as he grabbed my hand.

Eventually, we reached the Bellagio fountains. The rhythmic rise and fall of water danced harmoniously with the lights in the dark of the night. Even I wasn't cynical enough to deny the tranquility.

When the cold settled in, Damon pulled me to his chest, a hand resting on my hip. The other trailed up my side, wrapping around my neck. He studied me intently, face inches from mine. "You are beautiful, Poppy."

No one spoke my name the way it rolled off his tongue. "What are you doing?"

"What you were thinking about doing in the restaurant." He pulled me closer by the nape. "You were squirming because you needed me to fix what was broken."

"No, I wasn't."

Damon laughed under his breath. "You're killing me," he breathed, pressing a surprisingly soft kiss on the corner of my mouth.

"Get a room," a bystander griped.

My head lurched back at the unexpected voice.

"Ignore them. They don't know us." Damon tried to find my lips again, but I turned my face away.

"Everyone knows you," I reminded him. What was I thinking? I forgot we were no longer within the confines of my balcony but out in public. Even his security team was watching us from a distance.

Damon made a frustrated noise at the back of his throat, his free hand raking through his hair. "Maybe it's time they know about you, too. Then everyone will know you're mine."

Was that how I wanted Rose to wake up? Was that how I wanted to destroy my remaining relationships? I lived my life forgoing conventional bonds, and now I had burned too many bridges. There were two people left on my side; one was in a coma, and the other was a two-year-old. It wasn't exactly a promising outlook. Even my mother turned her back on me, handing me over to the board for violating the morality clause.

An overwhelming tightness gripped my throat, and my voice dropped to a whisper. "Let go!"

"No." His fingers tightened around the base of my neck.

"People are watching."

"Do I look like I care?" For the first time, Damon seemed pissed. Until now, he'd never denied me, catering to my every wish. The abrupt personality transplant was an unchartered territory.

I stared at him with wide eyes, ambushed by the change in tone. I tried to yank away once more. "Let go."

"No," he roared, grabbing my elbow harder than necessary.

Before I could take another step, Damon dragged me back with a roughness unlike him. Our lips collided. He kissed me hard, too hard, as if he was tired of waiting and at the end of his rope. My legs were weak from the ferocity of it, but he held me up with an arm wrapped around my middle.

His tongue glided past my lips and pushed inside my mouth. Damon groaned like he might die, exploring my mouth as he pleased. It was challenging to keep my eyes peeled open. It was all too much.

The tension between us was volatile, our bodies ready to explode without immediate release. His thumbs made circles on my back, causing a wild beast inside me to rattle the bars of its cage to escape.

Is this what drugs feel like?

A quiet moan escaped my lips when he licked down the column of my neck. Damon returned to my mouth, taking my bottom lip between his teeth for a harsh tug.

"Stop fighting me, Poppy," he whispered against my lips. "We'd be so good together; it'd be worth fighting the world for it, not me."

A hand traveled to my breast over my dress, squeezing firmly. He thumbed my nipple until I shuddered, utterly past the point of giving a shit about who was watching us. I was in no state to think clearly. My fingers wrapped around his messy hair as I bit back another moan. His hand slid down to my ass, gripping me tightly under the bomber jacket, lewdly bunching the material of my dress to pull it up with no care for onlookers.

Just then, I heard the murmurs in the background.

I know him.

That's Damon Maxwell.

Who's the girl?

For a moment, I still relented. The shutter sound from a phone camera went off, finally snapping me out of the haze. I opened my eyes and pushed at Damon's chest, averting my face so it wouldn't be captured in pictures.

We weren't surrounded by paparazzi. Instead, a group in their twenties had recognized Damon. Fortunately, they read the intimate scene and didn't approach us. Unfortunately, all of them had their cameras out.

"Damon, stop. People are taking pictures of us."

The kissing stopped, but his grip remained firm, his eyes liquid fire. This was a different man than before. "Who cares?" he hissed through clenched teeth.

"I do."

His eyes widened enough to give away their fury. "This is ridiculous. You don't care what other people think. You're just hung up on Rose even though I've been telling you for days that you've nothing to worry about."

I shook my head. "I've got to talk to her first."

"No, you don't. Nothing happened with Rose."

"I still need her to tell me it's okay."

"Why?" he demanded.

"Because I don't want to be this awful of a person."

Using every ounce of strength, I pushed Damon away from me. He wasn't receptive, and it seemed he wanted to argue more. Eventually, Damon released the grip.

Glancing at my phone, I realized it was almost nine thirty. "It's getting late. We should head to Xtasy."

Damon watched me quietly. His frosty expression left no room for diplomacy, shredding his wholesome persona. He spoke in a tone made of ice. "I'll call Miguel."

DAMON

"Surprise!"

"Happy Birthday!"

I stepped inside the bar to ear-shattering screams, flashing lights, and one too many cameras for a birthday party.

Caden gave me a one-shoulder hug. "The big two-five. You can rent a car. Can't wait to join you tomorrow."

Despite being twins, Caden and I didn't share a birthday. I was ten minutes older, born at eleven fifty-five at night. My brother was born after twelve, and his birthday was tomorrow.

I wished it weren't the case so Caden could take the attention off me because I was ready to punch someone. My morning was jam-packed with meetings, and Poppy's evening was predetermined by her weekly visits with her parents. She recently gave up her dorm room and moved into an apartment in the city. Every Friday, Zane sent a town car to her new apartment, demanding she drop by to make her mother happy, and to make matters worse, Zane's property had more security than the White House. I couldn't access it, and Poppy wouldn't be home until ten o'clock, which meant it had been twenty-four hours since I laid eyes on her.

I wanted to burn the world to the ground.

I tried staying busy. After graduating college, I started working as co-CEO with my uncle at Maxwell Corp. Within a week of not seeing Poppy consistently, I was going out of my mind. I bartered with my uncle to return for a part-time MBA.

"Why do you need an MBA? You are the fucking CEO," he had said incredulously.

It was a valid question without a logical answer. I needed an excuse to access the campus on an ongoing basis. Only students could access places like the library where Poppy studied every evening or the cafeteria where she often grabbed lunch or dinner. I couldn't wait until the weekend to see her. I chose the longest part-time MBA program and signed up for it. Even that was ending in six months.

The thought further dampened my mood. Everything pissed me off nowadays, and I was in no condition to socialize.

For years, my brother suspected my feelings, though he never confronted me. He was tired of my grouchiness. When he asked to meet up for a birthday drink, I agreed, thinking I could kill some time before Poppy returned.

Apparently, Dad made other plans. The bar had been transformed into a PR circus.

"Happy Birthday, kiddo." Dad hugged me, but not before turning sideways so someone with a camera could capture this million-dollar father-son moment.

I replied with a curt nod.

"Look who finally showed up to their own birthday party." Jasper slapped me on the back.

I replied with my signature cranky look.

Caden caught sight of my torture, and the fucker smiled. Sometimes, I wondered if he deliberately did things to make my life miserable.

I marched straight to the bar and ordered a shot of vodka. I was antsy as fuck. This was the worst day of the week, the day she went to Sands Point. I needed something to get me through the next few hours.

"One more," I told the bartender.

"Make that two." Caden joined me at the bar.

My twin watched me quietly as I downed the shot and ordered another.

"You're in a good mood," he said sarcastically. "Want to talk about it?"

"No."

I focused on the burn sliding down my throat instead of her. Poppy hated going home and spending time with Zane, which increased my erratic thoughts. She must be going stir-crazy, hating every minute of her visit. It would be another three hours before she was dropped off and another two until she fell asleep.

My thoughts were heavy by the time we took the third shot. Caden eyed me apprehensively.

"What?" I snapped. It wasn't his fault that I became short-tempered whenever I didn't see Poppy regularly. It was no different than someone not taking their prescribed dose of medication to keep themselves balanced.

Caden sipped his beer and told the bartender to hold off when I asked for one more round. "Try this instead." He slid me a bottle of craft beer. "This way, you'll still be standing when you visit your little girlfriend."

My head tilted to ensure no one was listening. The paparazzi snapped away but maintained a respectful distance on the other side of the red velvet rope.

My twin was the only one who knew about Poppy. Even then, he guessed it, but I never confirmed anything. The situation had worsened between our families. There was another pending litigation over clients and lost business.

"Relax." Once more, Caden pushed the beer my way. "I'll never tell anyone about your fascination with the five-foot demon child."

I wondered if he'd feel the same upon discovering how deep this "fascination" ran. My life now revolved around my extracurricular activity.

I said nothing and sipped on my beer, frustration gnawing under my skin. I looked at my phone. Fuck. Two hours and fifty more minutes. I banged on my phone to get time to move faster.

I set the beer on the bar counter with a thud. "Everyone's going to freak out when they find out. So, why don't I care more about how they feel?" It was as close to an admission as I had given Caden.

Caden blinked, taken aback by the unexpected confession. "I hope you know what you're doing. If you pursue this, there will be a full-blown war."

I was ready to go to war for her. "I don't care."

"She is only seventeen."

"About to be eighteen," I argued immediately. "Doesn't matter either way. I'll wait for her. She is the end game."

Caden's head lurched back.

"What?" I snapped again.

"It's funny to witness the great Damon Maxwell whipped. Should I sound the news to your stalkers?"

The hold on my beer tightened, but I didn't contest the observation. It made Caden's shit-eating smile bigger.

The next couple of hours passed by in a blur with more photos. I glanced at my phone and realized it was finally time. I shouldn't leave a party meant to be a PR stunt in my honor, but my legs had a mind of their own and pulled me toward Poppy's apartment. It was the only place where my life didn't feel like a circus. There was nothing pretentious about Poppy. She never tried impressing anyone, nor did the superficial aspects of my life enamor her.

Poppy equaled peace.

I stopped in front of her building and pulled out a pack of cigarettes. I smoked during my four years abroad. Everyone smoked, drank, and fucked like bunnies in boarding school due to a lack of parental supervision. When I started college, I tampered down my bad habits. Alcohol was for the weekends, and cigarettes went out the window.

However, cigarettes were a stalker's best friend.

Cigarettes allowed me an unassuming activity while waiting outside Poppy's apartment. Bystanders witnessing someone with a cigarette didn't question their motive other than partaking in a bad habit. They wouldn't call the cops if I loitered outside for two hours, smoking. And if Poppy were to discover me, I could puff away, and she'd dismiss it as a coincidence that I was out for a smoke at the same place as her.

Once the lights in Poppy's apartment dimmed, I pulled the hood of my jacket over my face. The last thing I needed was a horde of screaming girls recognizing me.

The fob I copied months ago gave me easy access through the doors. Luckily, the night doorman didn't know every tenant by face. As far as he was concerned, I was another resident returning home.

There was one more obstacle to get through after crossing the lobby. Two security guards roamed all corners of this building, courtesy of Piya Trimalchio. They worked in shifts, one guard at night and the other in the morning. They received special permission from the apartment building and were smarter than the night doorman. They memorized every resident in the building.

Worse, they were given pictures of potential threats to the Ambanis, including me. The same men used to monitor Poppy's dorms. Luckily, Poppy limited security to her living quarters only, and I memorized their routine. I knew which areas would be patrolled this time of the night: the hallway around the elevators.

Taking the marble spiral stairs two at a time, I reached the eighth floor without passing anyone. Stairs were safer than elevators, anyway. There are no security cameras and fewer chances of running into people.

Poppy lived in 8J, the farthest apartment at the end of the hallway. Maintaining distance from others was an intentional move when Poppy moved out of her dorm in favor of living alone. Pulling out the copied key, I turned the lock to her apartment door. I memorized every rhythm of Poppy's nightly routine.

Over the last two years, Poppy forced her body to turn into a machine through sheer control. There was dedicated gym time and meditation, training her mind and body to feel things as she pleased. Poppy considered sleep a waste of time and only allowed herself five hours a day so she'd have more time to be productive.

I'd done the same because it was easier to follow her if we were on the same schedule. After two years of rigorous training, our bodies now operate on cue. We didn't feel the pain of running ten miles every morning. There was no exhaustion during our busy days, either. Best of all, both of us slept like a rock due to sleep deprivation. The moment our heads hit the pillow, nothing could wake us until five hours had passed.

Generally, I'd also be sleeping at this time, but I miss her too much on Fridays. The longest I went without seeing her was during my workday or when an unfortunate business trip popped up.

As predicted, the two-bedroom apartment was dark. Slivers of moonlight seeped through the cracks of the window blinds. I gently closed the door, letting my eyes adjust to the dim lighting.

This apartment reflected Poppy's taste. It was nice, overlooking Central Park, but not over the top. Upholstered sofas, tufted armchairs, and a pedestal dining table decorated the space in a minimalistic fashion.

Once my eyes adjusted, I felt my way to her bedroom. The door was left open, and the faint sound of Poppy breathing filled the space. The moonlight cast a glow around her body, letting me make her out on the four-poster bed. Dark, long eyelashes fanned her smooth cheeks, and her tidy, plaited hair was now messy and wild. Throughout the day, Poppy fought every instinct to bare her vulnerabilities, but inside this room, Poppy was soft and vulnerable.

All I wanted was to crawl into the old-fashioned bed with my soft, vulnerable girl and hold her while she slept. For a torturous number of years, my thoughts revolved around sliding my hands around her waist, touching her smooth skin, running my fingers along her curves, letting go at long last, and gorging on her body.

No matter how deeply she slept, I couldn't risk giving in to my temptations. This tiny interaction got me through the worst days. It'd be snatched away if Poppy found me here, and I'd return to the miserable nights with nothing to look forward to.

Instead of touching her, I watched her with my hands by my side. It was hard to look away even though this was wrong. It was wrong to break into her home. It was wrong to be in her room while she was unconscious. Everything about this was wrong, so why didn't it feel that way? I'm hooked on her like an addict. Nothing seemed to matter other than being with her and getting my fix.

A suffocating sense of ownership rushed through me. Poppy is mine, yet I couldn't touch her or climb into bed with her. It was ridiculous in all senses of the word. All night, people asked me what I wanted for my birthday, a milestone according to many. The only thing I wanted was to hold Poppy, and it was the only thing I couldn't have. I had the world at my disposal, but without Poppy, I had nothing.

The need for her hit me harder than ever before. If I couldn't hold her, I would do the next best thing and coat myself in her essence. Deciding to give myself a birthday gift, I stretched out on the uncomfortable bed beside her.

Poppy's scent, today she smelled like vanilla, wafted into my nostrils. My cock jumped to attention, pushing painfully against my pants. The feeling came on strong and suddenly, tugging at my insides and refusing to leave. I had never been so hard for her, nor had I experienced this kind of desire for anyone else. It was the closest to her I'd allowed myself, and I was ready to burst from the proximity. This lust was infinite and never-ending, and I couldn't function unless I acted on this impulse.

Keeping a careful four inches of distance between us, I opened the button of my jeans and slowly unzipped, sighing with relief when the pressure depleted. I never pushed the envelope this far, but if I couldn't hold her tonight, I'd at least live out this fantasy.

I turned my face to her, grabbed my cock, and stroked myself, imagining it was Poppy's hands wrapped around the base of my shaft or, better yet, her lips wrapped around me. Despite my best efforts, a groan of pleasure slipped out. The mattress shifted, and I stiffened. I waited on bated breath, sure that I had been caught. However, Poppy merely shifted to her side.

My hand moved over my cock in slow strokes once more, precum dripping at the image of Poppy getting on her knees. Fuuuuck. My breathing grew heavy, and I sped up. I made a fist with my other hand and bit into it as I came, cum shooting out and drenching me.

I kept my hand over my mouth until the erratic thudding in my chest simmered down, but I was hard again within seconds. I left a party with hundreds of people waiting for me, press, camera, action, you name it. Yet, this was how I chose to spend my night. Next to an unconscious seventeen-year-old, coming on her bed to lewd fantasies of her. It was a new low.

I never climbed into her bed or jerked off while she slept. I always maintained a sliver of moral. My thirst for any contact with her was getting violently out of control. There was no resuscitating my soul after crossing this last boundary, so what the hell was I waiting for?

It was time to make Poppy mine.

CHAPTER
TWENTY-FOUR
POPPY

"Why did you ask Miguel to wait? It might be hours before we head out."

"We might need the car sooner," Damon replied vaguely. He led me to the elevators, hitting the button for floor forty-eight.

"It's on standby, just in case." It wasn't quite a statement or a question.

Damon's only acknowledgment was a small smile that didn't quite reach his eyes. The elevator journey was marked by silence, though his eyes were trained on me, and I allowed myself to wonder if the night was salvageable.

After Miguel picked us up, Damon maintained his glacial expression as he rattled off the address to Xtasy, located inside Paradise Hotel. The hostility between us remained until Miguel dropped us off. Damon slipped Miguel some cash and instructed him to wait in front of the hotel.

It made no sense. Limousines weren't allowed in the standby area on such a busy night. However, Damon was in no mood to explain his behavior, shrugging on his black suit jacket to follow the club's strict dress code.

I handed over my thin cardholder with my credit cards and fake identification for Damon to hold in his jacket pocket. Standing next to him made me feel like a schlep in comparison. The ridiculously expensive dress Rose bought for me was versatile enough for the club, but the Converses I paired them with weren't in style. I ditched the bomber jacket, which made Damon's eyes twitch, and dug out a pair of black high-heeled boots from my bag, which made his pupils dilate. They remained strained on my shoes while he led me to the club as if he visualized seeing me in nothing but them. Heels weren't my usual go-to, but Mom bought them for me last year. Generally, items Mom or Rose bought me fit into these places.

At this point, Las Vegas was packed shoulder to shoulder with people. Damon bypassed the long queue of overdressed patrons. They groaned when Damon walked past them like he owned the place and leaned down to whisper something to the hostess.

Initially, she giggled at the idea of them sharing a secret but wised up at Damon's stony glare. Damon Maxwell might be a man of few words, but he didn't have to speak for the air around him to radiate authority. On the rare occasions he spoke, his deep timbre vibrated with dominance.

The hostess, who went by Francesca, turned into the most professional woman in Las Vegas and led us through a different set of entrances than the general public and VIPs. She set us up at a table upstairs on a mezzanine balcony overlooking the main floor. A chilled bottle of the same champagne from earlier was already on the table, along with a selection of water, mixers, and a bottle of vodka. Everything was sealed.

Since the club's main floor was visible through the balcony, we could easily spot Sophie upon her arrival. The reserved tables on the main floor were off to one side. Nonetheless, it looked like a mosh pit. Too many humans packed in a compact spot, and I wanted no part in it.

Damon must've dropped a lot of cash to secure a fairly private room on such short notice. The mezzanine balcony held only six tables, and everyone here looked important or an escort to someone important. This wasn't just any other VIP room. It was an extreme version of it.

Damon popped the champagne and passed me a flute when I joined him at the table. His good mood had been restored, and he raised his glass to clink it with mine. The déjà vu had me staring at Damon until he took a sip before I did the same.

"This whole day has been a wild goose chase," I commented.

"Why?"

"Because of Sophie."

Damon straightened. "What about her?"

"We still haven't seen her."

A sly smile crossed his face. "*Harold and Kumar Go To White Castle.*"

I immediately understood the reference. It was an old movie about two guys on the hunt to find White Castle, but they never seemed to reach their destination. It was quite fitting.

Shaking my head, I downed the contents in my flute. My glass was topped off the moment it was empty. Damon's fingers laced mine as I sipped on the last of it. Alcohol swam through my veins, the warmth of it spreading up my arms. Considering the intensity with which Damon watched me, I wondered if he knew I was past my limit. He must have because Damon shrugged off his jacket and pulled me to the dance floor.

I stumbled a little. Something was off. I didn't drink often, but a few glasses of champagne had never done the trick before. Damon caught me, drawing me against his body.

The small number of the super VIP guests danced like drugged-up zombies to whatever music was droning on. Normally, I wouldn't partake in it, but an especially eerie song with a haunting beat came on.

I swayed to the music with my head slumped forward. Black strands fell around my shoulders as I moved my face from side to side. My limbs flailed to the side, dancing like no one else was watching.

With each movement, my dress brushed against my hand, and my ears tried to pick up the soft rustling. My head tipped into the air. Disheveled hair accentuated my wide eyes, which were often referred to as disturbing.

My body contorted in unnatural ways, the sharp steps appearing choreographed. People around us looked freaked out, wondering if I was having a seizure. My lips curled, the bitter taste of alcohol lingering on my tongue as I twirled and spun, practically floating in the air.

While others on the dance floor thought I was summoning spirits, Damon stared at me with adoration, mesmerized by my odd dancing. His fingers curled around mine. The warm touch of his skin against mine sent shivers down my spine. My long, slender fingers between his thick, large ones looked childish, and I started laughing hysterically before I could stop myself.

That was the dealbreaker, and the guests surrounding us had finally had enough. The dance floor cleared out, but Damon didn't notice. The singular attention remained on me for two more songs before my feet started hurting from the heels, and we returned to our table.

After we settled in, Damon's attention finally diverted to something else. He fiddled with his phone over a message he received. It seemed important because Damon tensed when the reply he texted bounced back.

"I'll be right back. I have to make a call, but I'm not getting reception inside." He reached out and ran the back of his fingers across my cheek as if soothing the pain of the momentary separation. "You'll be okay for a few minutes?"

I nodded. "I'll use the bathroom while you're gone." I pointed a thumb at the restroom sign.

Damon rose to his feet. "Okay. As long as you stay in this section."

I shrugged.

He eyed me carefully before leaning down to press his lips against my temple. "I'm serious, Poppy. Stay here until I'm back. This is the only section of the club being monitored by my security."

How? We were in an enclosed area. Did they set up cameras before our arrival? It was too late to ask since Damon had already walked away.

I followed the bathroom signs, but I seemed to be moving at a glacial pace. Padding to the bathroom took an excruciating amount of time for some reason. It must be my natural clock fighting off sleep. With the time difference, it was past midnight in New York. I hadn't stayed up this late in years. After using the facilities, I tossed water on my face to wake myself up.

I sought our table, only to realize I was standing outside the super VIP room.

The fuck? How did this happen?

It seemed I somehow stumbled out of the private room and ended up in the staff restroom. Except, why didn't I have any recollection of this? One moment, I was lucid and alert of my surroundings. The next, I was out of it.

At least I was wired for now.

A muscular gentleman blocked my path when I tried to reenter the room. With a thick neck connecting his bald head to his broad shoulders, he had the natural looks of a bouncer.

I raised my eyebrows.

With a stern expression and arms crossed over his chest, he asked, "Can I help you?"

"Yes, you can by opening the door behind you so I can walk through it."

The bouncer was unamused, disbelieving I belonged in the super pretentious area. However, he couldn't deny my access in the odd chance I was an elite. He chose a tactful approach instead. "Happy to, as soon as you show me some ID."

Well, he got me there. I looked younger than twenty-one because it was the truth.

"My ID is in my..." What was the correct way of describing my relationship with Damon? Friends? Lovers? Enemies? Potential boyfriend if he didn't sleep with my cousin? "Companion's jacket," I drawled.

Muscles rippled beneath the man's tight black shirt, silently communicating he didn't buy the story and there was no way I was getting past him. "Call him. I'm sure he won't mind bringing it to you."

"My phone's not working," I informed, holding up my cell to show him I had no bars. "And he stepped out to take a call. I'm not sure if he's back."

The man was unmoved. "Sucks for you."

"Does it? The way I see it, you have two options. You can go to my table and grab the black jacket there. I'll show you my ID, and you don't risk pissing off an exclusive client that can afford a table in there." I pointed at the closed door behind him. "Or you can call Francesca from downstairs. She is the one who booked us the table."

A serious expression was etched onto his features. He pulled a walkie-talkie from his back pocket and explained the situation to someone. As luck would have it, Francesca was out on a smoke break.

"If I'm lying, it won't be difficult to throw a five-foot woman out of this club," I tried again.

After thinking about it momentarily, the bouncer considered I might be telling the truth. Not wanting to get into trouble with one of the club's exclusive guests, he accepted my description of Damon's jacket and our table.

"Wait here," he grumbled and marched through the doors.

He retrieved the coat reasonably quickly, but the expedition was in vain. A frantic Francesca came barreling through the hallway. "I'm so sorry it took me so long to get here," she gasped, sounding out of breath from the jog, holding onto her side for support. "Please accept my apologies for this inconvenience." She started a frenzy of explanations.

From what I gathered, identification wasn't necessary for me. If anything, Francesca was deeply embarrassed by the bouncer's behavior.

"He is new," she glowered at the man twice her size, making him also apologize. "He didn't know you were Mr. Maxwell's guest." She sheepishly added, "If possible, c-can we keep this between us."

As in, don't mention the snub to Damon Maxwell.

"Only on one condition." I held her gaze. "Tell me why you're scared of Damon."

"Because he told me he'd fire me if I made one more mistake tonight."

"Damon is your boss," I guessed.

Francesca looked taken aback as if the answer should be obvious. "He is all of our boss. He owns this club."

Of course, he did.

"I'm so sorry for flirting with him. He told me I was being disrespectful to you. I didn't mean to be."

Damon told her off for giggling?

"It won't happen again." Francesca stared at the ground, fighting back tears, but I couldn't focus on her dilemma, not with my brain power already at capacity. "P-please don't mention this to Mr. Maxwell. I need this job."

"Only on one condition. Don't tell him I know he owns this club, and I'll keep this between us."

They exchanged a confused look but didn't argue. They weren't worried about customer service but rather about losing their jobs. Meanwhile, I was only concerned about one thing. I had to get to the bottom of this before my mind fizzed out again. It wasn't a coincidence that Sophie chose the same club Damon owned, a fact he had conveniently omitted.

With Damon's jacket in hand, I pushed past them and hobbled to the correct VIP bathroom this time. I glance at our table from a distance. Good. He was still gone.

I locked the door of the lush bathroom with scented diffusers at every corner. Another swinging door separated the hallway from the two stalls on the other side. The small lounge area in the hallway was meant to give off a luxurious vibe, a place for women to wait or touch up their makeup. With a couch, a tiny coffee table in the middle, and a soft white rug covering the area, it exceeded the expectations of a club bathroom.

Grabbing hold of my uncomfortable black boots, I pulled them off and parked my butt on the couch. My feet sang at the sweet freedom, my toes wiggling inside my socks. Whoever created heels did it to torture women.

Feeling somewhat sane without those monstrosities on my feet, I went through Damon's jacket pockets, turning them inside out and dumping the contents onto the table.

Wads of cash from our winnings fell on the marble table with a thud, but I stuffed it back into the pockets. It wasn't the only item to emerge. An iPhone fell out, though I succinctly remembered Damon taking his phone, along with some folded-up stapled papers and a piece of stock paper. The paper floated lazily onto the rug, resting face down. I believed it was a picture.

What photo could have been so important that Damon always carried it?

Hunching over, I grabbed the picture and turned it over, only to be graced by my own face. The picture I had been searching for, the reason I left home and burned all my bridges, stared back at me.

CHAPTER TWENTY-FIVE
POPPY

I couldn't tear my eyes away from the photo. I needed to snap out of it. This was Damon's club, and he could hunt me down at any moment. Glancing over my shoulders periodically to ensure the bathroom door was still locked, I sorted through the rest of the items.

I grabbed the iPhone that fell out and turned it on. There was no passcode, but according to the wallpaper, the phone belonged to Sophie. A plethora of texts popped onto the screen. The new messages were from me, asking for her status. My old texts were replied to with ambiguous wording. The nondescript language was intentional so that I couldn't pick up on the voice behind the messages, and the personality could fly under the radar.

Damon used Sophie's phone to ask me to meet in Las Vegas. When it didn't work, he manipulated me into sharing my triggers and used them to orchestrate a rift between me and Mom. Damon knew the fight would've made me act irrational enough to leave my impenetrable fortress and swooped in to save me from the very situation he created, acting like a damn knight in shining armor.

Every detail of this trip was meticulously planned because Damon plotted against me. He played me like a marionette. The worst part was that he proved my family right despite how vehemently I defended him.

I experienced numerous disappointments in life, but this gut punch landed the hardest. Alarming red signs had piled up against Damon throughout the day, but I ignored it. I placed him under the good guy category because I desperately needed a hero. His deviation from the role was a more significant betrayal than anything else. The person who was supposed to be an idealist had shown his fangs, like everyone else.

What a rookie mistake. The incriminating evidence had blown up in my face. If Damon purposely lured me out of a safe zone and isolated me from my family, it was because he intended to do something they'd prevent him from accomplishing.

Without thinking, I grabbed the papers, unsure what to search for. What I didn't expect to find was an application for a marriage license. It was filled out with both of our names and information.

I couldn't believe Zane was right. What else was Damon capable of if he had been lying to me thus far? Did he plan to marry me for my inheritance, then kill me as suggested by my family?

It was challenging to process the abrupt stream of information while my mind was scattered. That was when the last betrayal hit me like a train. Despite my vigilance to avoid such a predicament, Damon drugged me. My mind was slipping, refusing to play ball.

I exposed my vulnerabilities to another person for the first time in years. I didn't cherish losing my inhibitions in the company of others but trusted Damon not to take advantage. In turn, he betrayed my trust, slicing right through me with a knife. The small amount of warmth he had invoked in my ice-cold heart withered away at the thought.

With cathartic solace, I grabbed the edge of the couch and stood to height. I didn't have time to lick my wounds. I needed to get the hell out of here.

Rummaging through his jacket, I grabbed my cardholder, some of the cash winnings, and the photo Damon had stolen. I stuffed them into my bra. My bags were in Damon's car, but I didn't care. He could keep them as a parting gift.

I tucked my shoes under my arms. I'd run better in my socks than in those torturous heels. I could put the boots on once I was inside a cab to the airport.

"Poppy!" The door banged behind me, Damon's voice wafting through. He sounded wild instead of his usually leveled tone. He must've lost his shit at my prolonged absence and asked Francesca or the bouncer for my whereabouts.

The evidence of Damon's crimes lay in plain sight on the table. So, I couldn't open the door and pretend to make nice until another opportunity to run presented itself. He'd immediately realize I had unearthed too much. I ignored the call, scouting the bathroom for an escape route. As I searched, I carelessly shoved Damon's things inside his jacket and threw it haphazardly on the couch. He'd still realize the truth because I wasn't in the headspace to put things back in the correct order, but at least this would buy me time if he barged in here.

My eyes landed on the air vent in the ceiling. I was small enough to crawl through it. Climbing onto the sofa, I reached up and tapped until the lid popped open.

"Poppy, open this door." The shouting intensified, and my mind went momentarily blank again. Damnit.

I slapped my right cheek. Hard. *Wake up, Poppy*. Roofied or not, I got myself into this mess. It was time to crawl out of it, literally and figuratively.

I grabbed the space in the ceiling and began pulling myself up just as Damon burst through the door. "What the hell are you doing?"

Before I could hoist myself up completely, two freakishly strong hands wrapped around my thighs and yanked me down.

I fell against a hard chest. His ensemble was still in place, the white shirt crisp as ever, the designer belt looped around his snug pants and wrinkle-free. The perfectly sculpted torso could be easily made out under the material of his thin shirt, reminding me why I had been complicit with the enemy. A beautiful monster made me lapse on my rational senses.

Despite the rough manhandling, Damon set me down on the ground surprisingly gently. He kept me in place with an arm wrapped around me and eyed my shoes tucked sloppily under my armpit. "Going somewhere? I told you that I don't like it when you run from me."

I met him stare for stare, holding the intensity. The hunger behind his eyes was the only guarantee he wouldn't spot the jacket on the couch because Damon never looked away from me. But a ruthless man desiring me didn't mean he wouldn't kill me for his gain. I had to catch him by surprise to make a run for it.

It took immense control to maintain my neutral composure. "I thought I smelled smoke."

He gave me an odd look. "You thought there was a fire, and your first instinct was to climb into a tight space instead of opening the door I've been banging on?"

I went with the truth. "It's stupid, I know. But I can't seem to think straight or hear things properly."

Jackpot.

It was the first thing I said that Damon believed. The asshole drugged me and knew my mind was playing tricks on me.

I scowled as if irritated. "So, I freaked out over nothing? There is no fire?"

Damon continued to stare at me, giving his head a slight shake. He was trying to figure out if my behavior was an aftereffect of the drugs he fed me or if I knew more than I was letting on.

"Let's go back to our table then," I suggested.

"After you."

Damon released me, and I held his gaze as I backed away. I needed enough distance between us for a head start. The moment I gave him my back, I dove for the door and turned the handle.

Locked.

When I initially locked the door, I used the deadbolt. But now, turning the deadbolt did nothing. There was a keypad above it, which was previously inactive. Angry, flashing red lights blinked on the pad, indicating Damon activated it to gain entry.

I assessed my options for escape and realized there were none other than the vent. Phones didn't work inside the club, either.

There weren't any noises coming from behind me. I was certain Damon was looped in by now after finding his disheveled jacket on the couch and knowing I must've uncovered the hidden items. He took his glorious time approaching me. It was the smug declaration of a checkmate.

"How many times do I have to tell you that I don't like it when you run from me?" Damon spoke from behind but didn't sound angry. Instead, he tried to engage me in a conversation.

Unable to turn around and admit defeat, I stood facing the door. How did I let this happen? How could I be so careless?

Damon read my mind. "Don't beat yourself up, Poppy. I bested you because I know everything about you. The odds were stacked against you from the moment I entered your room. There was nowhere to run from me because you've only ever had the illusion of freedom, never the real thing." He almost sounded sympathetic.

I stilled when his imposing presence touched my back. His lips grazed against my neck.

"I planned on returning the photo to you. But it doesn't matter now, does it?"

"You came to the bathroom because you knew I found the picture," I guessed. "How?"

When Damon didn't speak, I glanced over my shoulders. In a trance-like state, his face filled my vision. *Stay sharp*, I scolded myself.

Damon pointed at the potted plant off to the side of the room. "World's smallest camera. These were implanted today in the waiting room of the bathroom and every section of the VIP area. I told you that you were being watched."

Despite the ominous threat hanging in the air, a sudden calm descended upon me, the warmth of it coursing through my veins. Somehow, I managed to spin in place to face him. I watched him, mesmerized, as his features shifted before my eyes. I swayed a little, and Damon preemptively gripped my hips.

"The GHB is kicking in. Don't fight it."

GHB? The cobwebs cleared momentarily, and I scanned my brain for the name. It was a party drug meant to relax people, right?

"All the drinks were sealed," I accused rather than stated, refusing to believe I was bested this way.

"The drug was injected with a needle through the cork," he explained unapologetically. "I brought the bottle with me. Miguel dropped it off so my staff could set it up at our table."

"But I watched you drink the champagne."

Damon nodded. "I have taken this drug before in Caden's lab."

My head reeled back. "Caden's lab? Your brother helped you drug me." Family of psychos. "How long have you been planning this?"

He ignored the question. "Caden didn't know what it was for. He needed a human volunteer to find ways to counteract the effects of GHB."

"And why would you volunteer?"

"So, the effects could be monitored in a controlled environment before giving it to you. I wanted to determine the dose to administer without causing you any critical side effects."

I huffed. "If that isn't the most romantic thing I've ever heard. Yet I'm slipping in and out while you are standing upright."

I winced when he kissed my hair, unruffled by my words. "I took trace amounts of it until I built up a tolerance. Consuming a small dose of GHB no longer affects me."

My jaw dropped. It was ridiculous yet preposterously genius, like in *The Princess Bride* when Westley gave Vizzini the illusion of choice, telling him one of the glasses was poisoned. It was never a fair duel. Westley had grown a tolerance for poison, so Vizzini would've died no matter which glass he chose.

"You drugged yourself so that you could drug me?"

Damon smugly looked me straight in the eye. "I knew you'd never drink the champagne otherwise. I told you. I know everything about you, Poppy. We are the same."

"We are nothing alike," I spat. There were no more pretenses left, no civilities needed. "I know what I am. I'm bad to the bone. But you... you are the worst kind of evil. You act like a big savior, only to lull people into a false sense of security before you strike."

Sky blue eyes mimicked two bottomless pools. "We are exactly alike. I just hide my demons better than you. Except your demons don't scare me or chase me away. I would never run from you."

"Pity. Seeing as I plan on running from you at every chance. Whatever you're trying to do, I won't go down without a fight."

My feet felt like they were made of lead, and I staggered. On impulse, my palms fell flat against his chest. Without missing a beat, Damon wrapped an arm around my waist.

"Shh." He stroked my hair. "It's best not to get so worked up right now. Relax."

Everything slowed down after that, my body refusing to cooperate with my threats about sobering up. I glanced at my fingers, unable to remember how long I had been staring at them.

When I blinked, I was sitting on the couch, and Damon kneeled in front of me, putting on my boots one foot at a time.

"I gave you the smallest dose needed to lower your inhibitions. There'll be some impaired judgment, difficulty forming thoughts, slowed reactions, and a distorted sense of time. Eventually, you'll feel like you're on ecstasy," he explained, his hand lingering on my bare skin as if he couldn't wait until that phase kicked in. "It should be out of your system by tomorrow, and the side effects afterward should be minimal," he spoke gravely, though it sounded distant and unimportant. "You'll be the most present during the first hour. By the second hour, you'll be just coherent enough to exchange vows. So we've got to leave soon."

"Vows?" I was losing the battle against my mind. Everything faded away except for the sound of Damon's voice.

"Yes, our vows," he clarified nonchalantly, a thumb brushing over my cheek. "We are getting married tonight."

CHAPTER
TWENTY-SIX
POPPY

Damon pulled me to stand on my heavy legs, pressing his lips to my mouth. I felt uncoordinated, but he carried me out of the bathroom as if I were rock steady.

I had no idea how we got to the hotel lobby, weeding through unfamiliar people. It was confusing and overwhelming until the arm around my waist tightened. A wave of relief washed over me when I glanced at Damon striding beside me. I would've fallen if his iron-clad grasp weren't around my waist.

"I got you, baby," he whispered on cue.

"Where we goin?" I asked, hearing my words slightly slur.

He smiled devilishly and took my hand, exiting through the front doors. "Downtown Las Vegas."

The cool air on my heated skin was refreshing, though I didn't get to bask in it for long. Damon pulled me inside a limousine that had the rear door already held open. The driver stood next to it, greeting us like old friends.

"Good evening, Mr. and Mrs. Maxwell."

Mrs. Maxwell?

"Good evening," Damon replied. We climbed into the back, and he pulled me to his lap, wrapping his arm around my waist. "We'll be there soon, but we need to make a stop before the chapel."

Shredded memories slowly returned to my hazy mind. He was forcing me into a marriage without a prenup while I was docile and cooperative under the influence.

"Stop."

"I took care of everything on the flight and throughout the night," he bypassed my protest, explaining his determined focus on the flight to Vegas and the numerous calls he had taken throughout the night. "The chapel's booked. We'll pick up our outfits on the way there. I've got the jeweler bringing the rings to the chapel. The photographer, videographer, and musician are meeting us there, too. The bakery couldn't make a pitch black cake on short notice, but the florist said she could cover the cake with some black dahlias, so at least the pictures will turn out okay."

I stared at him, gobsmacked. "We can't geet married," I slurred.

He shook his head, the displeasure coming out in waves. "Always running from me, aren't you? Cold feet won't get you out of this one. It's happening, baby."

"No."

I felt his eyes staring at me for a long while. A part of me badly wanted to melt in his arms until everything got better. The other part, the woman scorned, wanted to set the world on fire.

"I know you're angry right now," he murmured against the shell of my ear. "But you'll see that this is for the best. I'll make you understand."

"You ruined everything between us."

"No, I haven't," he growled. "This is the only way we can be together."

Damon didn't speak for the rest of the ride, seething silently. I wanted to fight but couldn't remember how to argue. My eyes closed, and I slumped against him, the powerful arm acting as a warm blanket. The cityscape blurred against the window before the limousine came to a screeching halt.

Damon tugged at my elbow.

My lids flapped, refusing to remain open. "Whattu doin?"

"You need a dress." Damon yanked at my arm, dragging me out of the car with a lot more force than he exercised moments ago.

We were in front of a dress shop. It looked all wrong for a place this fancy to be open in the dead of the night. A shopkeeper fumbled to greet us, holding the door open. She dragged me to a rack with her best selections, talking too fast for my slow-moving mind.

"No dress," I stuttered when she thrust a long white dress into my arms.

Damon was displeased. "If you don't pick something, I'll buy the pinkest dress in this store and make you wear it."

"I choose what I wear," I retorted. It wasn't a clever comeback.

"Not if you're going to wear black."

As if through sheer suggestion, my gaze landed on a black satin dress on the mannequin by the window, most likely meant to be a bridesmaid dress.

Damon drew in a long sigh. "Fine, if it makes you happy." He pointed at the mannequin. "That one. No need to wrap it; just get her in the dress."

"That's a bridesmaid dress"

"Just do it," he snapped.

The next moment, I found myself in a fitting room, tucked into a dress that was a perfect fit because of the seamstress working at manic speed.

"What?" I mumbled. How did I get here? Why did I keep losing time? Instinctively, I patted my chest. My bra was missing, my cardholder and photo with it. "Where is my bra and my things?" I asked whoever was willing to listen.

"We gave it to your fiancé," someone replied.

Someone else announced, "She is ready!"

My stomach tightened. Ready for what?

I was jostled out of the dressing room and pushed toward a man in a tuxedo, waiting at the front of the showroom with his back to me. The fabric hugged his muscular physique, and for a moment, I wondered how they found an outfit to dress a giant. He was broad-shouldered, incredibly tall, and muscular, like an Adonis overlooking his subjects.

The man turned to spear me with his sky-blues.

Damon.

His dirty blond hair was slicked back for once, a few strands falling carelessly over his forehead. It seemed he had selected an outfit and changed into it as well.

Damon examined me closely, hungry eyes undressing me before eating up the distance between us. Two supersized hands grabbed my face, firm lips covering mine for an unexpected kiss. His tongue thrust inside my mouth, kissing me punishingly hard. My body alternated between numbing cold and burning heat until he released me.

"We'll finish this later." The promise in his eyes sounded like a threat.

Once more, I was shoved into the limousine and onto Damon's lap. He was on the phone, something about the rings. His hand landed on my thighs possessively, and I stared at it.

"Damon." My voice sounded small. "What are we doing?"

"We are getting married, baby. I told you this already."

"Stop." I tried to smack his hand, but he interlaced our fingers.

"Behave." The words were quiet but angry. It was as if he'd had a personality transplant within a matter of a day.

His lips were on my shoulders, traveling up to my neck. Where it had been thrilling mere hours ago, now it made me recoil.

"No." The word didn't come out right. I tried to scurry away, but his hand held me in place.

"I told you numerous times I don't like it when you run from me." His fingers trailed along my thigh before resting dangerously close to my intimate area. "You'll stop running once I put a baby in you."

"You were supposed to be the good guy," I garbled.

"Sometimes you have to be the bad guy to get what you want." He dragged a finger along my bottom lip. "But now that I have everything I want, I'll try to be *your* good guy. I'll restore your faith, Poppy."

When we pulled up to the chapel, Damon stroked my cheek.

"Baby, I know this isn't how you wanted it to happen, but it's still our wedding. Try to make the best of it."

My eyes closed to savor the comfort from the calloused hand before the words seeped in.

Wedding?

I had repeatedly forgotten throughout the night. Damon was forcing me to marry him so he could take everything from me, and he wanted me to make the best of it? I wrenched away, which made Damon blow out a frustrated exhale.

The car door was thrown open, and I was hit with an ice bath of reality. Damon carried me out bridal style and explained to a passerby that the bride drank too much. Half the people getting married in Las Vegas were drunk. No one questioned it. Not the people inside the church, not the photographer, or the person who brought the rings. Not even Elvis, as he declared, "I now pronounce you husband and wife. It's also officially midnight. Happy New Year."

Black flower petals and the sound of bottles popping went off at the same time Damon grabbed me for a soul-stealing kiss.

"You married me at midnight," was all I could grumble against his lips.

"Can you think of a better way for a new start? Happy New Year, Wife."

∾

I must have blacked out for the rest of the celebration because when I came to, Damon was carrying me outside. His tux jacket was draped around my shoulders, but the frigid air cut into my exposed skin like tiny, sharp razors.

My hand was splayed on his chest, feeling the taut muscles under his shirt flex. In the back of my mind, I knew it was the drugs heightening my senses. I didn't care. It felt so good to touch him.

Damon set me down on my feet to open the door, pressing me against the side of the limousine. The crowd had thinned, and the car was parked in a deserted alleyway. Being alone with Damon reminded me of the most pressing matter.

"Are you going to kill me?"

A cruel laugh tumbled out of his lips. His lips crashed onto mine instead of confirming or denying the accusation, for a kiss that was every bit as brutal as the man. I attempted to resist, even as he held me firmly, trapping me between his muscular body and the car. His tongue moved aggressively against mine, leaving me breathless. As the kiss deepened, restless fingers moved along the curve of my neck and down my side, his touch gentle until he reached for the halter of the dress. With a harsh tug, he pulled down the fabric, exposing my hardened nipples.

I swatted at his hand. "Don't."

"Why not? You're my wife," he explained as if it was justification enough for whatever he planned.

Damon kneaded my breast. Skin-on-skin contact felt phenomenal, and my mouth dropped open. It hurt to deny this pleasure, so I tried to reason with him instead.

"Someone will see us."

"No one's around." Not to mention, Damon's broad body shielded my puny one from passersby. I was still paranoid.

"Miguel's around."

"Miguel's inside the car. He can't see us from the driver's seat."

"But he is still here. He might hear us. Please, Damon, I don't want him to hear me."

Something resembling a growl escaped his throat at the thought of someone hearing me, and he opened the car door. Swearing under his breath, Damon took off the tux jacket that was wrapped around me. He tossed me onto the leather seat along the long side of the limousine. My butt bounced against my will, my body too lethargic to otherwise move.

"Get out of the car, Miguel," Damon shouted.

My head tipped up. The upside-down view was slightly disorienting, but I could make out that the partition was up. Damon was speaking to Miguel through the intercom.

I gripped the sides to steady myself from a sudden bout of dizziness. Damon maneuvered me into pulling my legs straight, handling me rather roughly as he gave Miguel further instructions.

"Put your headphones on and some loud music. Then take fifty steps from the car and wait there until I call you."

Miguel voiced no objections regarding the ridiculous demands. He simply said, "Yes, sir," before I heard the opening and closing of a car door.

Damon stretched out on top of me and lowered his head, covering my nipple with his mouth. My stomach clenched when his tongue traced circles around the sensitive area.

"Fuck, I missed this," he spoke with a shaky breath.

Large hands roamed my body before Damon let go of my nipple.

Hot breath tickled my cheek. "You belong to me. You're finally all mine, and I'm going to use this body over and over until you realize it, too."

"But you've always asked me if I wanted this," I couldn't help objecting. Even the first time when I was blindfolded, Damon let it be my decision.

"I needed you to trust me."

Damon no longer cared about permission or shattering my trust. I was his, which apparently meant he could do as he pleased.

A strong hand folded one of my legs to press it against my breasts. His other traced the lace of my underwear. Heat coursed through my veins when rough fingers slipped beneath the material and fought their way inside. A hot and cold sensation sparked to life as his fingers filled me, wetness gathering between my legs as he moved in and out. The thick fingers expertly grazed my walls, and I bit back a moan. A low hum still tumbled out, and I surrendered completely to the inferno whirling inside me.

"Oh, shit."

"That's it, baby," he groaned.

I knew what sex with this man felt like, yet nothing had felt so incredible before. The drugs had seeped deep into my skin, and every sensation was extraordinary. "That feels too good."

Damon pressed his lips on my breast, setting every nerve in my body on fire, tingling with desire. Jolts of pleasure shot through my body as his thumb came into play.

"Damon." I clutched at his shirt when his thumb made slippery circles around my clit. I was so wet that I could hear the liquid swishing around.

My breath caught in my throat as the heat inside me turned into liquid fire. My skin broke out into a sheen of sweat from anticipating what was to come. Each stroke of his fingers dragged me deeper into darkness, keeping me right on the cusp. I finally caved when he curled his fingers and pressed against my G-spot.

My body arched, and even as I fought the euphoria, I knew it was futile. My limbs thrashed tragically with a pathetic attempt at gasping for air.

His fingers slipped out, leaving me empty. A rush of air surrounded my ears when he dropped lower while I wheezed for oxygen.

Damon slipped off the stupid heels the women at the boutique had forced me into. He rubbed the soles of my feet, tsking at the red blisters. "I should've asked them to put you in flats." Regret laced his voice, his lips trailing the edges of my feet.

A little moan of approval sounded from my lips when his tongue moved over the sore areas, erasing the pain. I closed my eyes, wavering under the surprisingly pleasant sensation. The ruffling of fabric jolted me out of it.

"What are you doing?"

Damon didn't reply, dragging the black dress the rest of the way down, leaving me in only my underwear. My bra was missing, and I faintly recalled the bridal store attendees mentioning they had given it and other items to my fiancé.

"Fuck, you're beautiful." An appreciative voice awed from my lower half. "I'm going to pleasure this sweet pussy of yours, then bury myself so deep, you forget where you end, and I begin." It sounded like one of his wedding vows.

His mouth settled on my throbbing clit, sending shivers down my spine. My eyes drooped, caught in a battle with his blue ones. He watched me possessively, his mouth full of my pussy. I should have pushed him away, but I was in pain. It was painful to feel this way and not have someone to take away the ache. Damon pulled back, licking his lips.

"It's been days since we first slept together, and this is all I've thought about." He returned for more punishing licks, our groans mixing in the confines of the car.

My body sang for him, releasing a surge of arousal as he continued lapping his tongue over my core. When he focused on the swollen bud, I couldn't hold back any longer. Broken gasps tumbled out as waves of ecstasy crashed over me for the second time, soothing the agony roused by the drugs.

It didn't last long. The restlessness returned within minutes, and I rubbed my thighs. How long did these effects last? I might die at this rate.

"Fuck, I can't wait anymore," Damon growled.

My mind momentarily cleared for a morbid recollection. I didn't find my birth control pills before leaving for Vegas.

"Hold on. I'm not on birth control."

I tried to sit up, but Damon pressed me back to the leather with a hand wrapped around my neck. He guided the thick head of his cock to my entrance. "Good. And just so you know, twins run in our family."

The throbbing shaft entered me so roughly that I screamed. He was painfully big, but at least I was wet beyond belief and in desperate need of relief. The forceful shove caused an initial discomfort that quickly turned into intense pleasure.

Damon fucked me as if I were the answer to his prayers. He held down my wrists, the heavy boulder of a body adding to the feeling of entrapment. His features were shrouded in darkness, his tense body language conveying a sense of desperation and a bottomless pit of hunger. My toes curled involuntarily against the leather seat. I sensed myself being pulled into it, struggling in vain against the invisible force. His deep thrusts brought me closer to climax with each push, keeping me there until he was ready to join me.

"Oh, god." I spread my legs farther, making room for him.

Damon growled gibberish in between each thrust. "This is how it was meant to be between us." Thrust. "I'm never giving you up again." Thrust. "You have no idea how long I've waited for you." Thrust. "You are finally mine." Thrust. "I can't stay away from you anymore." Thrust. "Never. We'll never be apart."

With a final shove, Damon found his release, pulling me into the abyss with him. My moans were muffled when his mouth found my lips.

He spoke against my lips one final time, "You're mine."

Minutes later, or perhaps hours, Damon covered my face with tender kisses. I lay there, staring at the sunroof of the car. Somehow, only one comment stuck with me, the question slowly churning in my mind.

"How long have you waited for me?"

"Years. I've loved you for years, Poppy." Damon turned to face me. "And I'm done waiting," he growled before taking me again and again until I had no breath left to scream.

~

DAMON

Things couldn't continue this way. I'd never get over Poppy, but I couldn't keep stalking her, especially with my rising popularity. I couldn't go anywhere without the press following me. Sooner or later, I'd lead the paparazzi to her apartment. If news of my nocturnal activities got out, there wouldn't be a shot in hell with Poppy. In conclusion, Poppy had to overcome the fact that she hated me for the greater good. Our future happiness.

At least I had a segue into the conversation.

Poppy started working at Ambani Corp as an analyst and had her own set of clients to manage. The ones who weren't freaked out by her young age were impressed by her work and the results she yielded for them.

Over the last few months, I have been wooing her biggest client. Poppy knew we approached him and offered to undercut Ambani Corp fees with a massive price reduction. The new rate wouldn't be worth taking him on as a client, so I knew she couldn't match the price.

The client was biding his time, waiting for his contract to expire before jumping ship. The hit of losing her biggest client wasn't one she'd be willing to entertain, and I knew she was working on ways to keep him. I'd provide her with a solution in the name of a merger and share the client. To discuss such a big possibility, we needed to get together three, perhaps four, times a week. It was the most surefire way of forcing Poppy to see me.

Unfortunately, Poppy would never speak to me without witnesses. She was a stickler for safety, and a Maxwell was a walking red flag. The discussion had to be public.

It just so happened there was a party that a mutual friend of the Ambanis and Maxwells was hosting. I knew Poppy would attend because she turned eighteen today. Rose and her mother tried throwing a party in Poppy's honor, a plan she immediately banned. As a compromise, her mother agreed to a family dinner, and Rose settled on taking Poppy to someone else's party for two hours as long as no one mentioned birthday or cake. Rose promised her it'd be a torturous time, which seemed to have done the trick.

The pungent scent of alcohol hung in the air as I walked into the house. The house was packed, and many were already doing cannonballs in the outdoor pool.

My eyes swept the room to find my clan, my brother, my cousins, and some of their friends. They were close to the main hallway, which meant the Ambanis had claimed the other side. Both families intentionally maintained distance while on neutral turf.

My gaze flickered to the other side, unsurprised to find the Ambanis in the open living room. Rayyan and Nick Jr. were stretched out on the L-shaped sectional while Rose rested her hips against the arm of the couch. My eyes honed in on Poppy at the far end of the sofa. She was conversing with some man crouched in front of her. He hung onto her every word during the span of their short conversation, his body language oozing with appreciation.

Lava-like hot envy coursed through me. I kept the hoodie over my head and quickly moved past the crowd. The longer I remained unrecognized, the more time I'd have for a conversation. The clusters of people thickened, and I did my best to weed through it.

By the time I reached the group, the man had dispersed. At least I wouldn't have to add murder to my TTD list tonight.

Poppy sat with her back straight on the couch. She wore her signature black attire, hair in two neat pleats, with a pair of Converse to complete the look. The most dressed-down woman in the room held my undivided attention. I had no idea how she did it, but fuck, I couldn't keep my eyes off her.

"Hi, stranger," a meek voice greeted me. Two unsure hands wrapped around my neck for a tentative hug.

Fucking Rose.

Trying to keep the annoyance out of my voice, I pulled her arms down with as much politeness as I could muster. "Hi, Rose."

Rose stepped back. The rest of the Ambani clan were immediately on high alert. Rayyan leaned back on the couch, no doubt coked out of his mind. Nick Jr. stood up, ready for a confrontation. The only one unperturbed was Poppy. Her gaze flicked up and down, and then she glanced away, bored. She checked her phone for the time. I bet she put on a timer for two hours and had an Uber pre-scheduled. I internally smiled. Why was that fucking adorable?

"What the hell do you want?" Rayyan spoke first.

"Be nice, Rayyan," Rose chided, fixing her black crop top strap. "Damon's an old friend of mine."

"I didn't realize you were friends with trash."

Great comeback. I mentally rolled my eyes and smirked upon noticing Poppy did the same. It was subtle but noticeable. Poppy didn't care for verbal attacks. She attacked by hitting where it hurt, by going after something her opposition loved. She could control and ruin someone's financial history with the snap of a finger. That hurt worse than any verbal attack, as she had repeatedly proved over the years.

"Get the hell out of here, Maxwell," Nick Jr. sneered, popping the collar of his light blue polo. It was beyond childish, but I willed myself not to get into an altercation with Poppy's family.

"Guys, calm down. Damon and I say hello to each other at parties. It's no big deal." Rose spoke as if we were star-crossed lovers, and everyone else was keeping us apart. After all these years, how did she still not get it? I brushed her off at every opportunity.

"That's where you're wrong," Rayyan snapped.

Rose opened her mouth, but I interrupted. "Actually, I'm here for Poppy."

Four pairs of eyes landed on Poppy in unison. Rose's was the most curious.

"We need to talk. Privately."

Rayyan stood on cue, blocking Poppy's body with his puny one. "She isn't going anywhere with a Maxwell."

Could I kill a man for merely annoying me?

I used the thing readily available at my disposal; my height. I towered over Rayyan, letting him know that I could destroy him with a flick of a finger. He gulped and glanced back at Poppy.

Poppy was unperturbed by the concern displayed by her cousins. "How can I help you, Maxwell?" She said, sounding collected but curious. It hit me right in the groin, and I almost groaned at the pain it caused me. It was the first time she addressed me, but the way she said "Maxwell" made her feelings regarding the name crystal clear.

It made me hate my name.

No matter how she affected me, this wasn't the time to let it show. "I have a deal for you," I spoke with conviction, never taking my eyes off Poppy.

Rose and Nick Jr. appeared to be baffled little lambs. Meanwhile, Rayyan was ready to hit the roof.

"We don't deal with Maxwells."

"You heard him," Nick Jr. chimed in. "Get lost."

My eyes rested on Poppy. As far as I was concerned, we were the only two people in the room. "Do you always let your guard dogs speak on your behalf?" I challenged, knowing Poppy would take the bait.

She raised an eyebrow. "What kind of deal are we talking about?"

"We aren't talking any deals because we don't deal with Maxwells," Rayyan practically shouted. He was off his rockers on blow, and I knew continuing this conversation here wouldn't bode well. However, I also knew Poppy wouldn't walk away from the group with a Maxwell. She was a safety-first kind of girl, so the conversation needed to happen here and now.

"Equity Solutions is about to switch over to us. I was thinking something *along the lines of a merger so we can both benefit from it."*

At this point, Nick Jr. and Rayyan were shouting disgruntled words of protest. Poppy managed to tune them out and have a perfectly normal businesslike conversation over their annoying-as-fuck voices. "They are already going with you as soon as our contract expires. Why would you consider a merger? That doesn't benefit you."

"That's where you're wrong. This client is too big, and we don't have enough manpower, whereas Ambani Corp has one of the largest staff on their payroll. My technology and your manpower and it might be a win-win situation. What do you think, Ambani?" I murmured as if suggesting a bit more than a simple merger, which I was.

"Why are you bringing this offer to me?"

"Because we both know who holds the real power in your company."

Poppy's smirk was fleeting. It was magic and disappeared before I could capture it.

I was so addicted to her that I went in for the kill too quickly. "Let's go to dinner tomorrow night and discuss the details."

"W-what?" It wasn't Rayyan but Rose's voice that interrupted our private yet very public conversation. Her cheeks burned, embarrassed by the loud eruption, and people were looking at her.

Poppy's gaze fleeted in Rose's direction, studying her cousin's extremely rare public outburst.

Fuck. The last thing I needed was Rose's silly crush ruining things between us. Nonetheless, I had to keep up a polite front. Rose needed to get over her feelings but still like me enough to encourage Poppy in my direction. So did her cousins, though they sure knew how to push my buttons.

"You're kidding, right?" Nick's annoying voice joined the bandwagon, but Rayyan took the cake.

"Let me guess," Rayyan drawled, voice dripping with venom. "You're bored of all the desperate women throwing themselves at you, and the easy pussy is no longer cutting it. Now, you want the challenge of fucking an Ambani."

Rose hung her head. A single tear slid down her cheek, unable to hide the hurt. Fuck, this was spiraling.

"It's just like a Maxwell to act with no class," Nick Jr. bit out.

"Let me save you some time," Rayyan added sharply. "Poppy isn't interested in having dinner or making any deals with you."

I raised an eyebrow. "Then I'd like to hear it from her."

"I don't know how you guys roll, but family comes first for us," Rayyan snapped. "Poppy would never betray us by having dinner with you. How little do you think of her?"

The tactic of putting words in Poppy's mouth was purposeful, making it impossible for her to refute the claim. I got the distinct impression Poppy was seconds away from agreeing to meet me before Rose's public meltdown. The wheels were turning in her head, and I couldn't blame her. People hadn't done right by Poppy. Her life was full of deception and abandonment, and she didn't know how to trust.

My gaze returned to Poppy. All I wanted was to hold her, own every part of her, and be with her all day, every day. Others might label my feelings as red flags, but to me, it was the most natural thing in the world. My mood, my happiness, everything revolved around her. But the tense crowd surrounding us told me the journey wouldn't start tonight.

Rayyan's theory of fucking Poppy as a challenge was more realistic than offering to share a client when I clearly didn't need Ambani Corp to retain them. Poppy had listened carefully to his words and fortified her walls. Little did she know I'd break down every barrier she put up and every obstacle in my way.

"Goodbye, Maxwell," she said impassively.

Rage and disappointment clashed at her response. "Not for long," I countered.

"That's it." Rayyan moved toward me with his fist raised.

Normally, I'd refer to diplomacy and my rational senses. However, Poppy's rejection churned my stomach. I couldn't digest it and chose a different route.

I clocked Rayyan square in the jaw.

Nick shouted slurs, Rose gasped, and Poppy glanced at the injured Rayyan on the ground, mildly curious. Only the people in the immediate vicinity saw me land the punch. Although I should be concerned if more bore witness to this PR nightmare, I couldn't find it in myself to care.

"What the hell, Damon?" Caden and my cousins were at my side in a pinch, his hateful eyes steady on a weeping Rose. It was obvious they kept an eye on the scene from a distance. "Why would you approach her in public?" he gritted out in a whisper, referring to Poppy.

"You know why." *Because she would've refused to speak to me otherwise. Not that it mattered. Private or public, they made it clear how unavailable she was to me.*

It didn't erase Caden's frustration. "You should still know better than to do this shit in public. Everything you worked for will be gone if this goes public." Caden was already pushing me out of the room while my cousins ensured no one from their group launched a counterattack.

I left with one last glance at the girl with haunted eyes and mouthed, "Goodbye, Ambani."

The one impulsive action ended whatever bridge I intended to mend. Because later that night, Rayyan Ambani was found dead. The police showed up at my doorstep, and I was the number one suspect.

DRETHI A.

ACT 4

CHAPTER
TWENTY-SEVEN
DAMON

Poppy was complacent when Miguel drove us to the airport. She fell asleep on the flight back, but I didn't wake her during the ride to my condo and carried her to our bedroom. Some adjustments, such as installing lock code pads between rooms and removing sharp objects, were implemented in my penthouse while we were away. It was temporary until Poppy adjusted to the situation.

Some might argue this was hardly the foundation for a healthy marriage. Any rational person would say I had lost my mind. But when the video surfaced of Rose falling, along with the texts she sent me, I knew Poppy would no longer give in to my advances. She could live with betraying the rest of her family, but not Rose. Poppy thought Rose was too fragile to survive such a blow. In some ways, she was right.

Rose's reaction almost cost her life. The moment she awoke, she'd be further devastated upon finding out about us. One tear from Neil or Rose could thaw, if not melt, Poppy's icy heart because she couldn't stomach their sadness. Had I not married her, she would've cut ties with me. What other choice did I have other than to deceive her?

But first, I wanted to give Poppy a day she'd never forget in her favorite city. Part of me hoped she'd fall enough in love with me to agree to an impulsive, drunken Las Vegas wedding. The hopeful wish died when Poppy ripped away from me even after sharing the perfect day. She couldn't see past the Rose dilemma, and I had to make an executive decision. Poppy's concerns would eventually fade once she was pregnant with our baby.

I knew Poppy felt betrayed. Everyone else in life had let her down, and she put me above those imbeciles. Shattering her illusion brought me no joy. The last thing I should do was impregnate my eighteen-year-old wife while she hated me. I should wait a few years, but I can't help it. I thought I'd be placated once my ring was on her finger. Instead, I had become more psychotic, consumed with the idea of fucking my baby into her.

She thought I was doing all this to merge our two companies. Technically, this marriage would solidify the futures of our two organizations. We could finally pursue the original deal when we first met, so her company didn't go belly up while competing with mine. It was also part of the reason I wanted us to marry as soon as possible. The other reason was Poppy's hesitations surrounding Rose. I worried it'd be enough to push her into a marriage arranged by her family. Big companies often negotiated such deals based on mergers; hers was no different. I couldn't risk it. I depended on Poppy to function.

If I went a day without seeing Poppy's face, others barely survived my wrath. Those were the days I wanted to fuck her so bad it was all I thought about instead of doing one lick of work. I'd blow up on people randomly. I saw the fear in their eyes and didn't know how to tamper down my anger. Since Poppy and I started up, I was once more a sea of calm. She was my reason to breathe, to live, to get up in the morning. I would do anything for her except give her up.

I needed to isolate Poppy from her family to make her mine. The answer came in the form of a photo. I had seen the picture of Poppy with her parents, but I never knew the story behind it. Poppy's loyalty was her weakness. Despite the years, she was devoted to her father. I knew she'd snap if I took the photo, and the first person she'd attack was Zane, followed by her mother. The years of resentment had built up inside her. All I did was give her a gentle shove. Nonetheless, ruining her relationship with them brought me no joy, and I vowed to fix it once our marriage was cemented.

For now, I plan on enjoying the things I have craved for years. I wanted Poppy all to myself without having to count the number of steps between us or keeping my feelings a secret from the world. I had wanted to steal her away for so long, and I finally had.

Given my philanthropic efforts, what I did to Poppy was hypocritical. I guess the line between right and wrong blurred somewhere along my patience while waiting for her to turn of age. If you think about it, she was the one who did this to me. The more I waited, the more I lost my mind.

I knew Poppy could fall in love with me given some time. She was already halfway there, with only her loyalty holding her back. A boyfriend might not trump the woman you consider a sister, but a husband would. Because I knew Poppy better than anyone else. I knew her better than I knew myself. If I could keep her at my penthouse, show her I was the only man capable of loving her despite knowing every last evil deed she had done, she'd see the light.

I lay sideways on the bed, head propped up on my elbow. Untying the plaits so her strands fanned out on the black pillow, I played with Poppy's hair. I hadn't been able to look away the entire time she slept. It was the only time she looked innocent. Watching her do mundane tasks such as sleeping or eating turned me on like I never imagined possible.

For years, I jerked off to her so much that the cum I spilled could fill not just my outdoor pool but my neighbors' as well. Nonetheless, I maintained distance. Had I preyed on her when she was a lost girl grieving her dead father, it would've fucked her up. I had to wait until she turned a reasonable age. The wait killed me a little every day. After touching her and watching her up close, I was incapable of keeping my distance again.

I waited years for this moment. The day she wore my ring, and I could finally shout through a megaphone that she was mine.

My fingers hovered over Poppy's left hand. The fresh ink glimmered under the dim lighting. It was a tattoo of her obsidian ring etched around her ring finger. I was shocked she slept through it. No doubt an aftereffect of the drugs. She'd be pissed about this new tattoo, but it was necessary.

The first thing Poppy would do upon noticing her wedding ring would be to take it off and chuck it across the room. So, I copied the design and tattooed it on her ring finger. Even if she took off the wedding ring, she'd never go a minute without people knowing she belonged to me.

After the last tattoo we got together, I nearly killed the artist when I saw his finger trailing her skin longer than necessary. I could practically see the lewd thoughts on his face and knew what he was thinking. I might've thrown on a hoodie, then met him in the parking lot to get in a couple of punches.

After the incident, I vowed no one else would tattoo her again. I took lessons and could replicate designs, including rings and lines ticking off the years (we had four of those on the back of our necks).

What I couldn't do was tattoo my own finger. One of the bodyguards who came to Vegas with us was a tattoo artist who tattooed my ring finger on the flight home after I was done with Poppy's.

Holding out her left hand, I studied our tattoos side by side, semi-hidden under our wedding rings.

A hot rush of possessiveness overwhelmed me at the sight. I couldn't control myself anymore and pulled her close to kiss her soft, pillow-like lips. I intended to kiss her once, but when I caught her enticing scent, it made me continue. She smelled incredible. Poppy's scent changed based on whatever shampoo, body wash, and perfume her mother stocked her bathroom with. Today, she smelled of vanilla. Vanilla never smelled so good before. I inhaled the scent like it was the oxygen I needed to survive.

My gaze fixated on the swell of her breasts. I kneaded her bare breasts, glancing at the black dress in a crumpled heap on the floor after I undressed her. The nipples on her perky breasts stiffened under my restless thumb.

Dropping my hand, I trailed her hot olive skin. Her soft moans drifted over us in her slumber. My cock stirred in response, and I pressed my arousal against her.

I should have put a temporary brake on this madness until she adjusted. But I couldn't stop after she was finally in my bed. My fingers slipped under the comforter and between her legs. I captured one of her nipples in my mouth that was begging for my attention. I swirled my tongue around it, nipping and teasing until she squirmed.

The effects from the drugs would no longer carry over, so Poppy might not be as accommodating as she was last night. However, she was enjoying what I was doing to her body. I kept at it until another moan escaped her parted lips. The drugs might've worn out, but sleeping on a soft bed for the first time in years kept her from waking.

Her moans continued to slip out as I explored the rest of her body. I gorged on every inch of skin I could reach with my lips and hands. Touching her this way while she couldn't stop me further fueled my craving. Wetness coated my fingers when I reached her pussy. Her lips were swollen and glistening even while unconscious.

"That's right," I murmured. "You're mine even in your sleep."

Poppy groaned, and a drop of her arousal touched my lips. Impatience took over, and my tongue darted out, tasting every bit of her as if it were the last thing I'd eat on earth. I shoved my tongue inside her and kept at it until Poppy cried out.

"What the hell are you doing?"

Part of me knew I should stop, but the rest refused to listen and kept going.

CHAPTER TWENTY-EIGHT
POPPY

A HAND KNEADED MY BREASTS, THUMB SWIPING OVER MY NIPPLE. The warmth from the touch lingered on my skin, electrifying every inch of my body. A wave of chills rushed through me, settling in my core. It felt too good to be a wet dream, but it couldn't be real, either.

Hands roamed my inner thighs, hot breath landing on my sex. A tongue trailed to my pussy, stopping right outside of where I needed it.

Oh fuck, oh fuck, my mind sang on replay.

For a moment, there was no other movement. The tongue resting in place drove me frantic like a wild animal. When I let out a breath of frustration, a groan sounded against my core. Abruptly, it started moving, devouring me with a sense of urgency.

It felt too good to sleep through this.

My tired eyes peeled open. The pounding in my head was replaced by the soothing laps circling my clit and cooling the ignited heat. Lying flat on the bed, I gazed through my narrowed slits.

A naked Damon was between my legs, his tongue buried deep into my pussy. Hazy memories of what he did returned like a storm.

"What the hell are you doing?" I struggled to speak, my voice scratchy.

His lids flipped up to me. A possessive fire burned in his sky-blue eyes, and his tongue darted out to his wet lips that were covered in me.

"Making up for lost time," he groaned into my sex. It throbbed in response, the nerves pounding with desperation. "You have no idea how many times I've jerked off thinking of doing this. I never thought there'd be an opening."

There was only an opening because I got distracted by Mr. Perfect's charms and the bubbling resentment of my home life. He found my weakness and used it to trap me.

"Get. Off. Me." I chewed out, his betrayal cutting me open all over again.

With a foot on his shoulder, I tried to kick Damon off. He ignored my attempts, determined to finish what he started. A forceful grip on the backs of my thighs pushed my legs up to bend them at the knee. Using both hands, he forced my feet flat on the mattress. His mouth descended once more, eagerly sucking on my clit.

"I said, get off me, you psycho... oh, fuck!" An accidental shiver ran down my spine, and for a moment, I forgot where I was and who I was with. My toes curled somewhere between asking him to get off me and his rough groans.

"Your sweet little pussy is driving me crazy, baby." He licked me hungrily like I was the source of his nourishment. "I'll go mad if I can't taste this every day from now on."

"You've already gone mad," I spat. "You are... ah." I jolted when he bit my clit.

My hands shot out to grab his head. I meant to push him away. I think he expected the same and licked away the sting. Distracted, my fingers curled around his soft, wavy locks instead.

"Fuck," he grunted, sounding stunned by my reaction. He gorged my pussy rather than lick it. At this point, it couldn't be considered someone going down on me. It was done with the zealousness of someone wrecking my cunt.

"Stopfuck," I grunted.

My hold on his hair tightened, unsure if I still wanted to push him off or have him finish the job. The way my back arched off the bed, it was probably the latter.

My legs shook. I practically clawed his head and neck, searching for my release. It must have been painful, but he didn't let me go. Instead, he licked me with everything in him.

Despite my attempts to stop it from happening, I couldn't hold back. My eyes squeezed shut, and my core clenched tightly. Another moan slipped out no matter how hard I tried to suppress it. With a final shout, I let go.

"God."

Damon was a sick fuck who might kill me. Getting off on him was monumentally stupid. Incredibly idiotic. But it couldn't be helped. It had never been like this with anyone else. I was the most alive with him while simultaneously ready to die.

Damon's insatiable tongue licked me into another orgasm. My muscles contracted when two of his fingers slid inside. A stream of wetness released from my body when he crooked his fingers and pressed his tongue against my clit. Damon devoured the liquid gushing out of me like it was the oxygen he needed to survive, his lewd sounds echoing through the room along with mine.

Feeling nearly faint now, I was no longer paying close attention to Damon. I vaguely noticed him grinding against the mattress, beyond turned on after I squirted. As if he could no longer wait, Damon blasted to his knees and pushed inside me with one hard thrust.

"Fuck," he growled, his face drenched in me.

"Jesus, Damon. Stop." Even after squirting, he was too big. The man was double my size, and it reflected... everywhere.

Damon responded by thrusting his hips, pushing further inside. His lips found my neck. "I can't. Every fucking time I'm inside you, it makes me even crazier. I love making you mine."

Damon didn't exercise patience, gripping my thighs hard enough to bruise, shoving them further apart. He palmed my breasts and pounded into me like he had already waited too long.

Damon slanted his head and sought out my lips. Instinctively, I turned away from him. Even though I looked away, taking stock of the room instead, I couldn't escape the intense blues piercing into me.

"I suggest getting used to kissing me because no matter how many times you turn away, there is no one else you'd be okay kissing other than me."

"My family has plenty of men lined up for me," I said stoically. "The moment I'm out of this situation, maybe I'll open up to the idea of kissing them."

Damon's body radiated with fury. He spoke calmly, even as the next words were laced with such rage that it took several seconds for them to seep in. "If you ever kiss anyone other than me, I'll kill them. And if you ever leave me to marry someone else, I'll kill us both."

My head turned back at the gory statement. Damon grabbed the opportunity by the horn and gripped my chin. He shoved his tongue inside my mouth, taking me for a kiss so deep it caused my body to shake and left me breathless.

My inner muscles tightened around him instinctively. Damon sensed the shift and groaned loudly. "Fuck."

My back arched for an orgasm so powerful that my mouth hung open, and my eyes rolled to the back of my head.

Damon followed soon after. With a final thrust, he buried himself deep inside and erupted violently without warning.

The asshole came inside me again while I was off birth control. I planned to murder him, but my fingers wouldn't stop shaking. My eyes refused to open, my body transported to a world I couldn't seem to return from. I was barely aware of Damon's cock still throbbing inside me as his body sagged. His lips lazily trailed over my cheeks.

"Where are we?" I panted with my eyes still shut. We were in an unfamiliar and undisclosed location.

"My apartment. We flew back last night," he explained patiently before shifting his weight. For a second, I thought he'd get off me when I heard him open a drawer instead.

It sounded like a nightstand drawer. My forehead creased. People kept kinky shit in their nightstands. Was Damon about to pull out a sex toy?

I should have opened my eyes and blasted him, but my mind refused to cooperate. My body was shaking as if I had the jitters. Even my fingertips were trembling. What the hell did he do to me? This couldn't just be the aftereffect of sex with him.

The clanking of two metals clashing against each other reached my ears. Something unforgivingly cold tightened around my wrist. I jerked when metal cut into my skin, a heavy item weighed down my small wrists. I tried to yank my hand away, but it dug painfully into my skin. My eyes finally shot open, only to realize the other end of the contraption was attached to Damon.

The cold metal around my wrist glinted in the sunlight streaming from the windows, the same as the ones around Damon's wrist, restricting my movement and my last-ditch effort to run.

The motherfucker handcuffed us together.

CHAPTER TWENTY-NINE

DAMON

"Seriously?" Poppy glared at the handcuff before a worse sight catapulted her attention.

Gripping the comforter to her chest with one hand, she shot up to a seated position, outraged. She held out her left hand, the one handcuffed to my right, to inspect her ring finger.

If she was already this upset, I didn't look forward to her reaction upon discovering the tattoo hidden underneath the two rings. The first was her engagement ring, with a solitaire black diamond cut in the shape of a crown. It was paired with a slender wedding ring, a white gold band dipped into black rhodium to give it the obsidian color.

My hand covered hers, the black ceramic band complementing hers. "Do you like them?"

Poppy responded by prying the rings off her finger and throwing them across the room. I raised an eyebrow, listening to the bands clash against the door and bounce off. Black diamond glinted on the ground, making the ring laughably easy to locate.

"I'll take that as a maybe."

Poppy's composure melted entirely once her attention landed on what the rings concealed: her real wedding band, the one she could never take off.

"What the hell is this?" Her eyes were unmoved, pupils dilated at seeing the tattoo in the same design as her thin wedding band.

"Your wedding ring." I only replicated the wedding band into a tattoo, not the engagement ring. I knew she'd be pissed enough about the one.

"You branded me," she seethed.

My hand grazed the back of her neck. "Is that what you think of these, the tattoos you get every year on the day your father died?"

Poppy stilled. "How do you know about that?" She shook her head as if asking irrelevant questions, having realized I knew everything about her. "Those were done by my choice. Someone didn't stamp me to prove their ownership of me."

I repositioned my wedding band to show her the fresh ink on my finger. "I got one, too."

The reciprocal gesture merely made her fume. "What the hell is wrong with you?"

"This is hardly the first matching tattoo we got together."

The comment made Poppy freeze. I'd purposefully hidden my tattoos during our encounters. The cat was out of the bag now. I was on my side, my neck exposed. Horror was etched on her face as she leaned over to check the back of my neck.

"You have the same tattoos as me," she stoically declared.

I nodded. "All four of them." Four lines memorializing each year of her father's death. Those marks also commemorated the anniversary of the first day we met.

I expected her full-blown wrath. Poppy quietly watched me instead, assessing. "How long have you been stalking me? Is that the reason you know so much about me?"

The tidbits I told her last night were returning to her in fragments. Based on my admissions, she knew my obsession wasn't just knee-deep.

I've loved you for years, Poppy, and I'm done waiting. The words didn't have the intended effect, and questions were raised about my sanity.

"That's how you learned to count cards," she surmised.

Nothing went unnoticed by my girl. "Yes. I was with you all those times you snuck off to Atlantic City."

Composing herself, Poppy slipped back the impassive mask, though another question burned in her eyes. *How could you do this to me?* She felt betrayed, nevertheless I could fix her pain with time.

"I love you more than anything, Poppy, but I meant what I said. I'm done waiting," I answered her unasked question. I didn't break eye contact, my determination growing by the minute. "I know you better than you know yourself. Because I've watched you for years, I understand everything about you. I'm the only person capable of loving you the way you need. You never have to censor yourself around me to avoid being judged, nor do you have to make dull conversations with me to fill the silence. It's what you've always wanted."

Poppy processed my words.

"I know you're angry right now, but I promise you'll see things my way."

Poppy didn't care to know more, focusing on her surroundings instead. She was thinking of ways out of this predicament. Questions tumbled out of her mouth like in the rapid-fire round in a game show.

"None of my cousins responded to my texts about crashing with them. Was that your doing?"

I nodded. "I thought you might reach out to them, so I changed their numbers to random burner phones."

"And my mom? She hasn't gone a day without calling me."

"Her and Zane's numbers were blocked."

Poppy laughed, whether in misery or at the situation, remained to be seen. "I'm guessing you're holding my phone hostage."

"I'll return it to you after our honeymoon," I replied carefully.

"You call this a honeymoon?" She tried holding up our adjoined hands. The cuffs dug into her delicate skin due to her inability to move my heavier hand. Sharp jolts of pain must be prickling her skin, though Poppy didn't let it show.

"Stop that," I said in a soft but firm voice. "The metal might leave scars if you keep pulling at it." I took her hand and interlaced it with my fingers, making it impossible to pull at the handcuffs again.

"If you knew anything about me, you must know I don't do well in captivity."

"It's a temporary measure. Until you see things clearly, you can only run by taking me with you."

Hatred seemed to consume Poppy, and she turned her face as if unable to look at me any longer.

Grabbing her arm, I turned her to face me. Poppy clutched at the comforter on instinct when I dragged her closer. She didn't stop me when I covered her face with soft kisses.

"You're already thinking of a hundred escape plans, but I know everything you might try and put in fail-safes." My voice was soothing, though the meaning behind the words was menacing. "There is no way out of this, Poppy." I held up the handcuff. It had a slot configuration with numbers in the middle. "This doesn't even have a key, just a pin. The only way to unlock these cuffs without the code is by chopping off your fingers."

If I handcuffed her to anything other than myself, she'd find a way to run. The cuffs were selected purposefully, metal instead of leather, so Poppy couldn't possibly cut through them, and the metal would hurt too much if she kept yanking at them, forcing her to stop. Part of knowing her intimately also meant I could predict Poppy's every course of action in this dilemma. As I said, I knew her better than she knew herself.

CHAPTER THIRTY
POPPY

He was a lunatic.

A damn madman who I had to keep on an even keel if there was any hope of getting out of here. Only how do you defeat someone who lives inside your head? Damon and I were the same person. It meant he was ten steps ahead of me. Throwing a fit over his deceit or baiting him wouldn't work in my favor. As far as he was concerned, I was his, and no one else was allowed to have me. Any contradiction would have him choking me to death.

I let my gaze stray to the bedroom. If I had a chance in hell of getting out of here, I needed the lay of the land. "I have to use the bathroom."

"I'll take you." Damon grabbed the comforter, forcing my hands to tighten around it.

"Can I put some clothes on first, or is that not allowed?"

"If you must."

Reaching past me, Damon grabbed two bags off the floor with his free hand. They were carelessly thrown on the ground next to the bed. I stilled when his arm grazed against mine in his effort, cheek mere inches away from mine. Inadvertently, my gaze was on his face, wishing it weren't the case. Damon must've cleaned up before climbing back into bed with me. He appeared recently showered with slightly damp hair, face freshly shaved, and body utterly naked.

Beads of sweat from our most recent tumble rolled down a sculpted torso to the V of his abs, the comforter pooling around it. It was dragged low, dangerously close to revealing more.

The vision of a naked Damon in bed was the glaring reason why I had been complicit with the enemy. It took a beautiful monster to make my rational senses lapse.

Taut muscles on his abs flexed when he caught my attention.

"See something you like?" Damon raised an eyebrow, tongue darting out to suggestively lick his bottom lip.

My mind went blank, eyes refusing to blink away.

"We don't have to get dressed at all if you'd rather"

I snatched the bag I had haphazardly packed for Vegas away from him. It made him grin like he was privy to a private joke. I shifted through the choices with my free hand and settled on a dark gray halter dress, another attempt from Rose to "diversify" my closet. It didn't require a bra and was the only thing I could put on since Damon refused to take off the damn handcuffs. I turned to the side, touching the floors with my feet, forcing Damon to follow my movements as I stepped into the dress. He'd realize within hours how much of a nuisance it was being handcuffed to someone else. To my dismay, Damon didn't complain when I jerked his hand around, pulling the dress over my hips, and even helped me with the last stretch by zipping the back with his free hand.

Glancing over my shoulders, I watched him rip away the comforter covering him. His cock was hard and curved, hitting his abdomen. When precum leaked out, I quickly turned away, listening to the erratic beating in my chest as I watched him out of the corner of my eye. Unlike me, he didn't fumble, gracefully gliding into a pair of black boxers. Damon purposefully chose to forego more clothing when he caught my deliberate avoidance, his arousal peeking out from his boxers.

He rose to stand next to me. Realizing my hand would be dragged down because of our height difference, he bent his elbow and interlaced our fingers, which escalated the heat rising in the room.

"Hungry?" he asked innocently, extending the suffocating heat we were trapped in. "We can have breakfast... afterward." He dropped the voice laced with insinuation.

I looked away and took stock of the room. The bedroom mimicked the size of my last apartment, with custom-made choices to reflect his taste. Shockingly, it reflected some of mine as well.

The walls were dark gray instead of pitch-black.

Vintage furniture such as tufted bench chairs and ottomans, though chicer than my usual.

Minimalistic with no artwork on the walls.

Four-poster bed, but the Tempur-Pedic mattress allowed the person to select the firmness for their side of the bed.

Large windows overlooking a familiar view of Central Park. I frowned. "We're near my old apartment."

He didn't confirm nor deny it, remaining surprisingly quiet while my eyes took in the surroundings.

"Bathroom?"

He held out his free hand in an *after-you* gesture. The bathroom was furnished similarly: minimal. His and Hers sink, and a skinny gray shelf with three tiers. The bottom was stocked with towels. I wasn't the least bit surprised to discover Damon used the same brand of toothpaste as me on the top tier, though it was the middle tier that caught my attention.

There were various unopened bottles of face wash, moisturizer, bath products, and lotions. I wasn't particular about brands, using whatever Mom stocked my bathroom with. Every item Damon bought was something Mom also bought me in the past. Exactly how long had he been stalking me?

He let it all sink in, nonverbally boasting the extent of his obsession. "I put some clothes for you in here." The drawers underneath the sink held some lingerie and sleeping clothes. They had tags on, forcing me to wonder when he made these plans. Technically, we officially met last week.

When Damon didn't unhand me to do my business, I grasped the appalling reality of the situation.

"I'm not going to the bathroom in front of another person," I declared, affronted.

He ogled me as if I was the one being unreasonable. "But there are no cameras in here. It's not like some perv will stumble upon a video of you going to the bathroom."

"All except one." I nodded at him pointedly.

Damon sighed. "There'll be no boundaries between us, Poppy."

"I haven't gone in front of another person in sixteen years. I'm not about to start now," I shot back indignantly.

Damon shrugged. "This isn't optional, baby. The only way I'd leave you unattended again is if you were sedated."

Of all the things Damon had done thus far, this one offended me the most. I was potty trained by the time I was a year and a half old and preferred to use the bathroom alone the following year. Mom presumed it was because the idea of soiling myself in front of others never appealed to me. This was humiliating and a dig at my repressive personality.

I crossed my arms across my chest. "Then I guess I don't have to use the bathroom, after all," I chewed out.

"Don't be ridiculous. You'll end up with a UTI."

"Then decide what's more important to you."

Damon clenched his jaw. "Five minutes. Door stays open."

"Ten minutes. Door stays closed but unlocked."

Damon considered my counteroffer, then pointed at the ceiling vent and the bathroom window. "Just so you know, those were sealed shut this morning. Don't even think about it."

He moved the numbers on the slot configuration with his eyes on me, ensuring my pupils didn't drop to register the numbers. The cuffs fell open, the momentary reprieve more than welcome.

As soon as Damon stepped out, I focused on my natural objective. My sweet, sweet escape. I turned on the shower. Damon mentioned the windows were sealed shut this morning. If caulk were used to fill it, nothing would get in the way of drying like a steamy shower. For good measure, I doused a towel in hot water and placed it against the grout. Standing on the toilet with the lid down, I realized a ledge was on the other side. I needed to open this window, take the ledge, climb one floor, and bang on that person's window.

While I waited, I relieved myself and used the unopened toothbrush he left me. Damon wouldn't let me use the bathroom again for a while if I got caught, so I needed to use facilities and steer clear of liquids. I rinsed out my mouth, the rancid taste of drugs finally washing away. Hopping into the shower, I washed my face and body down in less than two minutes, keeping count of the seconds in my head.

With my senses restored and six minutes to go, I patted down with a big fluffy towel and dug out a pair of underwear and a sports bra from the items Damon had bought. I paired it with black yoga pants and a black T-shirt with enormous white carvings of satirical words across the front. "I was spanked as a child. As a result, I suffer from a psychological disorder known as RESPECT FOR OTHERS." There was also a hoodie that zipped up.

I tossed my hair up in a messy bun, stood on the toilet, and jimmied with the window handle to pry it open. With a snap, it came loose and finally popped open.

"Yes." I celebrated the small victory.

Grabbing the edge, I put my left foot on the sill. The fall would result in my death, but luckily, the ledge was wide enough for someone my size.

With my eyes on the grand prize, I didn't realize someone was throwing the door open until it was too late. Two hands grabbed my waist and wrestled me off the wall. "The hell?"

My pulse careened upon realizing I had been caught red-handed. The evidence of my escape effort lay in plain sight. Not only had he stopped me, but I knew there'd be consequences for my actions.

Damon whirled me around and set me down on my feet. Within seconds, the handcuff was back on my wrist, and this time, I had a feeling it wouldn't come off.

He regarded the black pants and hoodie I had changed into. Meanwhile, Damon had put on a heather gray collared shirt and cargo shorts with a dark brown designer belt looped through. The perfect ensemble would fit into almost any occasion. I resembled a schlep in comparison, and for a moment, it distracted me.

Blue eyes analyzed me with their usual hunger and desire, but this time, there was anger in them, too. It reminded me of an exchange between a predator and its prey. I met him stare for stare, holding onto the intensity.

"Going somewhere?" he asked, voice slightly shaking. He was trying to control an oncoming wrath.

"It's such a lovely day," I commented sardonically. "Thought I'd go for a walk." Why was I goading him on? He could snap at any moment and wring my little neck out.

"Of course," he snarled with a glint of mania in his eyes. "What says leisurely walk like a carefree stroll off the fifty-sixth floor?"

"Better than the alternative."

"The alternative where you're in a safe, warm home and not tumbling to your death? What the hell were you thinking?" He glowered at me. "I swear to God, if you ever put yourself at risk again, you'll be tied to my bed until the day you give birth," he growled.

The tension radiating from him was more than about an escape attempt. There was something else in his gaze, too.

Anger? No.

Apprehension? Nah.

Concern? Maybe.

Or could it be... fear?

Damon was scared that I could've died. As if that were his worst nightmare. He hadn't expressed fear of anything thus far, charging ahead and taking on my family. But suddenly, he was scared at the thought of my death.

"All I've ever wanted was to keep you safe. You're making that impossible to accomplish. What if you'd fallen off that ledge? You could've died." His voice sounded panicked. Closer to terrified, in fact. "How could you do that to me?"

I was lost. "Falling to my death is hardly a personal attack on you."

His face turned beet red. "That's exactly what it is. Do you understand what would happen to me if..." He ran a hand through his wavy locks, unable to finish the thought. "Dammit, Poppy," he snarled.

The fear in his eyes stretched until he could no longer bear it. Damon shook away the images and closed his eyes, breathing heavily. I had never seen him this way.

"If you let me go, I wouldn't risk my life again."

"Is that what you plan on doing whenever I give you an inch of freedom, risk your life? How am I supposed to trust you if you run away every time I untie you?"

It took immense control to maintain my neutral composure at his ridiculous statement. "You are the last person allowed to talk about trust, my dearest husband," I retorted.

I expected further ire from Damon, but his anger abruptly dropped upon the usage of the unsavory term, husband. No matter how sarcastically I said it, it was music to his ears.

My crimes were forgotten and forgiven.

Damon shook his head, cracking a smile. "I can never stay mad at you. Come on, little demon spawn. I need to feed you. How else will you have enough energy to plot your next escape?"

I knew he was taunting me, but I didn't argue. I was lucky that something I said charmed him enough to bypass this little blunder. Damon was significantly bigger than me and could make me pay in more ways than one.

He guided me out of the bedroom. A spark of hope returned before realizing there was a lock pad between the rooms that could only be opened with Damon's thumbprint.

With my face placid, I said, "I'm guessing you own the penthouse in this building."

He nodded, leading me through a formal dining room with a twelve-person dining table and into the massive living room. There was no need to turn on the lights. The sunlight streaming through the large windows was enough. The glass displayed an even better view of the park. I bet you could see the seediest parts of Central Park at night from here. I also bet those windows were suitable for an alternate escape in case of a fire. A ledge was visible from here. I had to find a way to free myself of the cuff, shatter the glass, and climb the ledge. Jumping onto the balcony of the person living under Damon would be the biggest challenge.

"How long have you lived here?" I asked Damon to distract him from noticing my inspection.

"Long enough to know those windows are bulletproof, weatherproof, furniture-proof, and definitely Poppy-proof. They are unbreakable, so don't bother."

He glanced at me knowingly, challenging me to deny I didn't scope out every item in the vicinity. We remained in a staring contest until Damon dragged me to the kitchen.

Damon sat at the breakfast table, pulling me onto his lap. Dome basting covers were on numerous dishes on the table, though there was only one place setting. Damon couldn't have cooked all this. He had been in the bedroom with me all morning, another reason I needed to leave. The nutjob took away my contraceptives, and I needed to get my hands on Plan B before it was too late. The GHB Damon slipped me had a similar effect as ecstasy, and given my vague recollection of last night, I lost count of how many times we had sex.

If Damon had watched me for years, he knew my protective instincts and loyalty wouldn't let me make a different choice in terms of a baby. Except he was wrong in assuming it'd stop me from leaving him. I'd never stop fighting for my freedom. I didn't do well in captivity.

Damon uncovered the dishes one by one. An English breakfast of baked beans with scrambled eggs and croissants that were toasted until nearly burnt. I presumed those two were for me. There was also a bowl with fruits and yogurt and a plate of omelets with toast (unburnt, gross). I guess that was what Damon ate, and the dishes were a compilation of our staples.

My stomach growled, but when Damon brought a forkful of dry eggs to my lips, they didn't part.

"There are no drugs in the food," he announced, dissecting my hesitation.

My lips remained sealed. The last time I trusted Damon, I ended up married. Excuse me for being skeptical.

Damon rolled his eyes and took a bite of the food. "See?"

"That proves nothing. You're immune to GHB."

"I'm not immune. Trace amounts don't affect me. That's all."

I nodded at the food, indicating for him to eat more.

"Seriously?"

I stared at the meal longingly. It looked perfect down to the last detail. The moisture from the eggs was sucked dry by leaving them on the stove for a tad too long. Even the food was served on black plates.

With a heavy sigh, Damon took a few more bites. His face scrunched up with distaste, and a part of me wanted him to keep going, taking pleasure in his pain. When he cleared half the plate and held a forkful to my lips, I took my first bite. He fed me until the plate was cleared before moving on to his.

I watched him eat, enjoying the momentary silence. He caught me in the act and moved some of the hair out of my face.

"What is it?" he asked, knowing I had a question at the tip of my tongue. I might be plotting Damon's death, but I couldn't deny how nice it was never to have to express my thoughts. Damon lived inside my head, rendering conversations pointless. As a result, Damon was the only person who didn't annoy me. Ironically, it was because he was a madman who stalked me for years.

"You watched me for years but never came near me. What made you reach out to Rose and come to that party to finally meet me?"

He reached around to finger the tattoos on the back of my neck. "I saw how you dealt with the worst days of your life for years. All except for one. I finally found out how you coped on your mother's anniversary."

CHAPTER
THIRTY-ONE
DAMON

THE BUILDING WAS ON A RESPECTABLE STREET ON THE UPPER East Side. The hallways were clean and modern. I caught a whiff of pine wood mixed with a leftover Christmas smell as I approached the apartment door.

Elijah Dankworth.

9B.

I had been waiting for this piece of shit for a while. He left the country years ago for a job opportunity. I had to offer a ton of money to coax him back and accept a position at my company instead.

My head of security informed me the moment he landed on US soil. I sedated Poppy to make the excursion, but at least I didn't have to trick her again. I promised to let Poppy out of the house in a month if she willingly took the sleeping pill. I was positive Poppy would break by then, and Poppy wanted to guarantee her freedom in case she couldn't find an escape. I watched her through the cameras on my phone and had a guard on standby in case of emergencies such as fires.

I planned on a staycation with Poppy for the upcoming month. My uncle was pissed about the unprecedented time off, but I had worked like a dog for my damn family for years. They could fuck off while I enjoyed my secret honeymoon.

This unfinished business dragged me away from my new bride. My security team was not only discreet but wicked smart. They tailed the schedules of the residents on this floor and those downstairs. This was the only window when everyone was either at work or school, sans a ninety-year-old grandmother who lived down the hall. Luckily, her hearing was impaired, and she had no idea what was about to occur. The surveillance cameras in the hallways and around the building were switched off five minutes ago. I snuck in while the doorman was away on break, and he'd be lured out by a commotion when I was ready to leave.

In other words, there'd be no traces of me being here as long as I took care of this problem within the next thirty minutes. My team was on standby during the allocated time, so nothing could go wrong. This wasn't their first rodeo. They'd done this for years while I followed Poppy. Some of them thought I was keeping an eye on my biggest rival, though most were smart enough to figure out my real motives.

Raising my fist, I banged on the door twice.

Elijah opened the door, a hand rubbing sleep-heavy eyes. He hadn't expected company.

"Hello," he said, confused. "May I help you?"

He stared at me, trying to place me. My team confirmed Elijah was none the wiser about what I looked like, having only heard of me by name since he had been out of the country for the last two years.

I couldn't help the shit-eating grin to grace my face. "Yes. Mind if I come in?"

This was one of the instances where my frame worked against me. No one wanted to let a terrifyingly huge man into their home. I could crush him like a puny twig, and he knew it, too.

"Um"

I brushed past him, forcing the door to open wider with my larger body that towered over his. I took in the eggshell walls, the living room, and the adjoining kitchen. The apartment was untidy, with two black suitcases sprawled open in the living room and dirty dishes in the sink.

"Hey, hey, hey," he cried, following behind. "What the hell do you think you're doing? Get out, or I'm calling the cops," he said with a bravado he didn't own.

Dankworth was in pajamas and a wrinkled white T-shirt, clearly jet-lagged and sleeping through the day. I highly doubt he had his phone on him.

"Call them," I said easily, only increasing his fear.

We were at a standstill, and he wondered if he should run for the exit to find the doorman or run to his bedroom, where I presumed he left his phone.

I rolled my eyes when Dankworth lunged for the door.

When will people learn they can't escape their fates?

Grabbing his shirt, I dragged him back with ease and threw him on the ground. I walked to the door and closed it.

"No. Ah," he cried out, long copper hair falling over his eyes upon hitting the ground. "Please don't hurt me," he howled.

Another cliche reaction: people begging despite knowing someone intended to cause them harm.

Faint white music drifted from the Alexa in the living room, and unpacked clothes were haphazardly spread on the coffee table. One was a Cornell sweatshirt, which Dankworth attended during his undergraduate. That was where he met my lovely wife during her freshman-year winter internship.

I discovered this tidbit two weeks ago. It propelled my haste to solidify things with Poppy and force this fucker back to the country. He had to face the consequences of his actions.

"Hey, Alexa, turn up the music," I called out.

"What are you doing?" he asked, petrified.

The background music intensified until it could no longer be considered white noise. The room wasn't lit, with only the afternoon sun scarcely spilling through the gaps in the blackout curtain. I still caught the fear in his eyes. It invigorated me, and I hummed, circling him while he lay on the floor. A single droplet of water dripped from the kitchen faucet steadily with a three-second intermission, intermingling with my footsteps. Drip. Step. Drip. Step. Drip. Step.

The ominous threat of what might happen was worse than the actual action. I had a feeling Dankworth felt the same and was ready to piss his pants.

"What do you want? Please take whatever you want. Just don't hurt me." His voice quivered.

I raised an eyebrow. "That's interesting coming from you since you like to hurt little girls."

The comment startled him. "Who are you talking about?" He stared at me, trying to make out any sparks of recognition.

"The fact you don't know means she wasn't the first fifteen-year-old girl you slept with." I intentionally left out my wife's name.

To my surprise, recognition flared in his eyes. He surmised, "Poppy Ambani."

Soon to be Maxwell. I could apply for a name change after the circuit court received the marriage license.

I paused. If Dankworth immediately knew I was talking about Poppy, there couldn't have been anyone else. Perhaps it was the only time he slept with a minor.

If only that were enough to make this a pleasant visit for him. I still couldn't leave his offense unpunished, but at least I didn't have to kill him in concern of him repeating the behavior.

"You knew she was fifteen," I checked for clarity.

For some reason, he didn't try to lie. "Um. Yes. B-But I asked her if she wanted to"

The kick to his stomach cut off the half-ass excuses. "A fifteen-year-old cannot give consent, you dumb fuck. Do you know what would happen if I went to the police with this? I have evidence of what you did. Some pictures had just recently resurfaced of you two together."

He started shaking his head vehemently. "No, please, no. I can give you money. I have money. I'm starting a new job. It pays well"

I kicked him again, this time on the chest. The way he howled, I must've broken one of Dankworth's ribs. This time, I did it to shut him up. Did I look like someone starving for money?

"You seduced a fifteen-year-old girl when she was vulnerable."

"Please, please, stop. I can give you anything." He whimpered.

The funny thing was that Elijah had bypassed trying to rationalize his behavior. He knew what he did was wrong. The guilt was written on his face.

However, it didn't seem like he was a pedophile.

My team did some research. Dankworth had no taboo pornography, nor did he walk around at playgrounds. My wife simply had a way of turning heads.

While he might've had concerns regarding Poppy's age, he overlooked his conscience for a chance with the unattainable girl. Even if Poppy consented, she wasn't old enough for it. Ideally, Dankworth would've never gone near my favorite thing in the world, let alone put his grubby little hands on her. However, if I had to deal with someone else coming before me, I would've appreciated it if they handled my things with more care.

The carelessness he exercised with Poppy was a sin I couldn't forgive. I wouldn't kill him, but I wanted him to think he was about to meet his maker. I wanted him to shake death's hand and be ready for acceptance so he could genuinely regret his actions. Only then would I let him go.

I kicked him in the stomach. Leaning over, I struck him across the jaw, blood spraying out of his mouth. His head jerked to the side, and he wept when one of his teeth was knocked out.

I took pleasure in seeing him writhe in agony. I savored every moment of his torment, especially his fear. He thought he got away with it and there'd be no consequences because no one cared enough. Someone looking out for the lonely girl was the last thing he expected. The last time they saw each other, Poppy was sixteen. It had been two years, and as far as he was concerned, the entire experience was in the rear-view mirror.

Perhaps Poppy didn't think much about losing her virginity. But she was only fifteen and an emotional wreck. He was twenty-one. What she might've considered okay, I didn't. It wasn't okay.

Kneeling onto the floor, I grabbed the front of his T-shirt to raise him and land punch after punch on his face. He let out a bloodcurdling scream. Sucking in air through gritted teeth, he pleaded, "Why are you doing this to me?"

Why was I doing this? It'd be hypocritical to say I didn't fantasize about Poppy when she was fifteen, but actions differed from imagination. I waited for her, but this fucker found Poppy on her lowest night and took her virginity. Perhaps some of my anger also lay with the fact that he took what was supposed to be mine.

I wanted him to be beyond unrecognizable. I was pretty sure I broke his nose and his jaw, too. Blood covered his mouth, and one of his eyes was sealed shut. It wasn't enough. I should kill him and remove him from existence. The world would be better for it, but I knew Poppy wouldn't like it if I killed every person to come before me.

There were four before me, and they all paid the price for touching Poppy. My anger was somewhat dissuaded the longer they waited for her to be of a reasonable age. Dankworth was the only one to escape my wrath because I couldn't find him. This fucker deserved the worst of it.

A punch to his face had his head lulling to one side in the process of passing out. I stood over him, disgust and hatred dripping in spades.

In between his sputters, he managed to spit out something resembling, "Who is she to you?"

"My wife." I wasn't worried about Elijah figuring out my identity or going to the police. If he did, he'd have to divulge sleeping with a fifteen-year-old and be taken away for longer.

I wrapped a hand around his throat, cutting off his oxygen. He gagged, gripping my hands with both of his to stop me. Before the light could go out of his eyes, I let go, and he gurgled out a mouthful of blood.

It should've been satisfying, but it only made me angry at myself. Had I found a way to be with her at Cornell, I could've prevented fuckers like him coming near my girl.

CHAPTER
THIRTY-TWO
POPPY

A THICK LENGTH FOUGHT ITS WAY INSIDE ME, AND I KNEW IT WAS Damon without opening my eyes. The bastard had broken me. No matter what I felt for him, I was drenched between my legs for him every damn time.

There was a whisper in my ears. "I love you." A hand traveled to my quivering stomach. "And I'm going to love the shit out of our baby. I hope you're pregnant already."

It broke the trance.

My eyes snapped open, hands pushing against his chest. Damon hovered over me, eyes gleaming with lust and greed. The handcuffs were back. They only came off temporarily when he allowed me a few minutes of privacy in the bathroom in exchange for taking a daily pregnancy test. Today, he had also removed them after I willingly took a sleeping pill. I knew he left the apartment to take care of business, and whatever he had done must've worked up an appetite.

He worked his cock in, plunging deep inside and holding himself there for a moment. "I couldn't wait any longer. I needed you."

My core tightened, more wetness seeping out of me when his fingers came into play. This routine was the same every day, Damon claiming me as his own and me reluctantly submitting.

Sex was something I used to participate in once a year, and now I couldn't fathom going half a day without it. While Damon had turned me into a crazed nympho, I couldn't get behind his ulterior motive. If I were pregnant, this life would forever be sealed to Damon's. I couldn't do that to a baby. Damon was unstable.

Damon grunted nonsense, proving my theory. "I can't explain it. I go mad if I'm not with you, but being inside you drives me crazy, too. Fuck, Poppy. You're my kryptonite. I'm almost there, baby."

My groggy mind struggled to catalog the words, but when his eyelids drooped, I realized he was on the verge of losing control.

"Wait."

The bathroom was stocked with ovulation kits, yet Damon hadn't made me take anything except for the pregnancy tests. Undoubtedly, he knew the dates of my menstrual cycle after years of stalking me. He expected me to ovulate at the end of the week. The only saving grace was that my last period had started early. Counting the days in my head, I realized I was ovulating today. Hopefully, Damon was unaware of this fact, and I could dupe him into not coming inside me. If there was a time to stop this crazy train, it was now.

I braced my hands against his chest as his pace quickened. The pressure built inside me, and the strength needed to resist rather than succumb became overwhelming. "Wait," I repeated.

Damon frowned. I generally didn't protest this close to the finish line. "What's wrong, baby?"

If I told him the truth, he'd keep me in bed all day, trying to impregnate me. I'd already assessed all possible escape routes and came up empty-handed. The doors between the rooms were locked, requiring Damon's thumbprint for access. The large windows offered the illusion of escape without the real thing. Opting out of sex altogether wasn't an option. The only thing Damon might believe was sexual curiosity, given the limited times I had sex.

"I-I want to try something different before you finish." I glanced between us. "I've never gone down on anyone before."

"And you thought *now* would be the best time to give it a go? While I'm inside you?" A look of surprise and skepticism flickered across his face.

"I feel inspired."

A dark glimmer shone in his eyes, and he pushed off me, taking me with him. Despite using a blowjob as a decoy, my veins surged at the excitement radiating from him. I could envision Damon losing control if I got on my knees for him, his hands in my hair while he pushed himself into my mouth.

Damon growled at the lust-crazed look I must be wearing. "I know you're thinking about it. I can see it in your face. God, I could come just looking at you."

He sat at the edge of the bed, maneuvering me to stand in front of him. A damp palm rested on his shoulder with a sinking awareness; I was nervous. What if I was no good at it? He must've been with experienced women, whereas I had never attempted it before.

Many girls in my boarding school and previous dorms had raved about blowjobs, claiming it evoked unhinged reactions from men. Watching Damon hold his breath and ready to lose his cool, I suddenly understood the appeal. The rare power exchange ignited a fire within me. I relished having this control over him.

Kneeling down with our hands still bound, I beheld his cock up close for the first time. He was bigger than I imagined, skin pink with veins running down. The little bit of hair was neatly trimmed, leaving a barely-there gruff.

Damon ran his fingers through his hair, watching me intently with hooded eyes as he spread his legs on either side of me. He didn't help or rush me, simply waiting for my move. The tip of his curved dick reached his abdomen, glistening from our combined fluids. Where it should've turned me off, I was depraved enough to have the opposite reaction.

I was beyond turned on.

I took my time, knowing the mounting anticipation was killing him. The evidence of his need was etched on his face, the veins on his cock throbbing in a desperate search for attention, no matter how cool and aloof Damon appeared. More pre-cum trickled out, and I hadn't even touched him yet.

With a flick of my tongue, I licked the underside of his dick. Damon let out a deep groan, instantly surrendering and putting me in charge. I wanted to hear his reaction to everything I did, exerting the same command he had over me for days. My tongue traced the contours of his length, gaze locked onto his. He gripped my hair tightly with his free hand when I took the head into my mouth.

"Poppy, fuck," he said breathlessly, sounding like an entirely different person. One consumed by raw need.

A satisfied smile played on my lips, reveling in the intensity pouring out of him. The desperation burned in his gaze. His cock slid deeper with a forceful thrust, hitting the back of my throat. The initial gag reflex subsided when I relaxed to accommodate his size.

"Fuck, fuck. Poppy. Fuck, baby, that feels so good." He chanted, using "baby" and my name interchangeably.

My hand, which lay splayed on his abdomen, wrapped around his pulsating shaft. I held on firmly, feeling each thrust between my hands. His cock pulsed achingly within my grip.

In the past, I had been a selfish lover and never considered oral sex could be a turn-on. But his urgency made me wish I could finish myself off alongside him. Everything about Damon was twisted and provocative.

His head fell backward with incoherent words tumbling out—something to the extent of needing to stop so he could come inside me.

I knew why.

Damon didn't want to waste the opportunity to knock me up by letting his precious cum go down my throat.

Playing with my breasts was the final straw for him. Damon palmed my bare right breast, grazing a thumb over my nipple. He undressed me while I was asleep. My shorts and wrinkled nightshirt were on the floor beside my knee. He was such an ass. The thought spurred me on to suck harder rather than stopping.

"Enough, baby. Take your mouth off and ride my cock like a good little girl. I need to come inside you."

I sensed his impending climax and his deliberate effort to decelerate it. I took him deeper, giving him what he needed to finish. For years, I had trained my body to fight natural instincts. I trained it when to sleep and wake up, how to work like a dog, and I taught it control. Mind over matter. As far as I was concerned, gag reflexes were a construct of my mind. I further relaxed my muscles, taking him so deep that he was fucking my throat at this point.

"Fuck, baby." The groans grew louder, but Damon never lost sight of his goal, even in this predicament. "I need to fill you with my cum right this second, Poppy. Hey! I said that's enough."

But I didn't stop. In fact, I continued with more fervor.

Damon grabbed my hair and forcefully pulled me off him. Saliva dribbled out of my mouth as both of us panted harshly in the quiet room.

"What the hell are you playing at? I told you that was enough."

There was a momentary pause as his eyes scanned my face. My emotionless expression was no match for how well he knew me, and I was confident he had already figured it out. It clicked for him that my offer was merely a distraction.

Damon pulled me closer, his grip tightening. "Tell me, Poppy. Why were you suddenly inspired to give me a blowjob?"

Nothing got past Damon. His skeptical gaze earlier was due to my willingness to get on my knees for my enemy as a means of avoiding a greater catastrophe.

A retort was stuck in my throat when my eyes landed on his hand. The knuckles were blood red. I hadn't noticed it before, with one hand wrapped around my hair and the other cuffed. I no longer believed Damon had a work emergency. I grabbed his hand, inspecting the swollen knuckles that were likely involved in an unnecessary fight.

"What happened to your hand?"

"Don't change the subject. Tell me why you didn't want me coming inside you?"

"Whose blood is this?" It couldn't be Damon's blood. His hand wasn't busted. There were no cuts or scrapes, either.

For a moment, he didn't respond. Then Damon declared, with a hint of pride, "Elijah Dankworth."

I jerked my head back, shoving his hand aside. "You are not serious." The glass ceiling shattered repeatedly where Damon's sanity was concerned. I thought he was a peaceful man, but Damon turned out to be the opposite. "You hunted down the people I've been with and beat them up?"

"What else did you expect me to do?" He shrugged as if it were no big deal and reached into his nightstand, unlocking it with his thumbprint. He retrieved the cell phone he had hidden there, preventing me from getting ahold of it.

Damon unlocked his phone and tapped on it. I could see him piecing together the puzzle pieces in his mind.

"You're not supposed to ovulate yet. Unless your last period was early."

My jaw would have dropped if the asshole hadn't desensitized me to how much he had invaded my privacy over the years.

Realization dawned on me about what he was about to do. I instinctively leaned away when he attempted to kiss me. "What are you doing?"

"You're ovulating, Poppy. This needs to happen now," Damon replied, lacking any hint of doubt in his voice. He leaned forward, his nose grazing my hair. "You smell good. Which shampoo did you use today?"

I wanted to run from the maniac, but where was I going while handcuffed to him? I suspected that was why he had done it, imprisoning himself alongside me because he didn't like it when I ran from him. My instincts kicked in, and since I couldn't run, I went for the next best option.

I tried to knee him in the balls, both as revenge and to take him out of commission for the next few hours.

Damon grabbed my hair to keep me still. I tried to punch him in the face, but he easily captured my wrist in a grip hard enough to leave bruises.

"Enough, Poppy," he hissed. "This is happening."

His lips sought mine, but I headbutted him, moving my mouth out of reach. A growl of frustration escaped him.

"Stop fighting me." He grabbed my arm, shaking me roughly. "When will you understand that I'm the only one for you? Everyone else has turned their backs on you except for me. We belong together. The frustrating part is you know it, too. Name another person you share this connection with."

My mind went blank for a moment too long. Damon didn't give me any more time to think and lunged at me.

This time, he kissed me forcefully. I didn't part my mouth, not caring when Damon bit my bottom lip and blood trickled out. The taste of copper singed our bitter, bloody kiss together.

I twisted and struggled to break free from his hold. Turning away from him, I ended up on my hands and knees. Pushing my palms against the ground, I tried to rise. Damon pushed me forward, following me to the floor. His weight covered my back, his front pressed against me. My cheek grazed the rug when he held me down to the floor.

Damon grabbed the back of my knee and forcefully spread my legs. His hand cupped between my legs, pushing two fingers inside. His thumb rubbed against my clit until my back arched. Liquid trickled out of me, creating a mess between us, even as I tried to close my legs to stop his relentless fingers. His mouth alternated between biting my neck and kissing it, distracting me with varying sensations. Unbeknownst to me, he withdrew his fingers, his cock slamming inside me instead.

"Fuck, yes," he panted against the back of my neck, his lips hovering over my tattoos.

My mouth hung open though I ought to fight. I tried to crawl forward on my knees, but he gripped my hips, holding me firmly as he fucked me from behind.

"Don't fight me, baby," he spoke soothingly while fucking me rough, resembling an unhinged obsession.

I grasped at anything to make him see reason. "Stop, Damon. This is insane."

"I promise you; we'll be happy together. I'll fix everything else in your life, too."

Before I knew it, I did something that was a first for me. I pleaded. "Please, Damon. Don't do this."

Damon showered my back with kisses, his only response being, "I love you so damn much."

His thumb continued to circle my clit, coaxing me into an unexpected orgasm. My body pushed forward from his steady thrusts, my knees, and cheeks rubbing against the rug, leaving burns. I climaxed against my will, my thighs trembling and my body shaking as it always did for him.

Damon followed suit, emptying himself inside me. He slumped over me, his face buried in my hair, while I closed my eyes, feeling a mix of mortification and the realization that he might have sealed our fates.

There was no after-sex glow for once. Only hollow nothingness.

CHAPTER THIRTY-THREE
POPPY

"Get off me." I chewed out, my eyes fixed on the intricately patterned rug while trapped underneath Damon. Anger surged within me, and I fought the urge to claw at his eyes.

Damon complied wordlessly, peeling me off the floor and dragging us back to bed. His warm body enveloped mine from the side, his free hand sliding under the pillow and our adjoined hands resting on my torso.

It was suffocating.

I closed my eyes in surrender. When I opened them, I was met with his calculating gaze, a flicker of regret shining through.

"I shouldn't have lost my cool with you." Resignation tinted his tone. "But things can't go on like this, Poppy."

What did he expect after what just transpired between us? "Don't touch me." I slapped the hand resting on my stomach.

Damon watched me for a long moment before speaking. "I've waited years for you. I don't want to lose you after you're finally here with me."

"You should've thought about that before drugging me to marry you," I retorted.

"No matter how it happened, we are married. That's our truth. I don't want our marriage to be a colossal trainwreck without giving it a fair chance."

"This isn't a real marriage."

Damon flinched. "Then tell me what it'll take to make it real for you."

"My freedom."

There was a pained expression on his face as if my freedom was an unbearable blow to him. It nearly minimized my campaign for freedom. This had to be Stockholm Syndrome kicking in. "That's the only thing I can't give you."

"It'll never be real for me as long as these shackles are on." I lifted our handcuffed hands.

"We both know you'll run the moment I take them off."

"So, your solution is to breed me like some prized animal instead?" I turned away, fuming like a radiator about to burst.

"You want kids as much as I do," he spoke like he was placating me after a lover's spat. "And I know you want them before you get busy with a high-stress job."

But this wasn't how a baby should be brought into the world. "You forgot one important part." Defiance coated my voice. "I don't want them with you."

Grabbing my chin, he roughly jerked my face toward him, his previous gentleness replaced by a hardened expression. "Too bad because I'm the only option available to you." Anger pulsed through every inch of his being, threatening to consume him. "So, either you have them with me or not at all."

I batted his hand away.

Damon closed his eyes. His voice laced with exhaustion, "Poppy, I'm trying here. Just meet me halfway."

Meet him halfway? Damon pretended to be my savior, then broke my trust like everyone else. He wanted my body night and day, not caring when I said no or asked him to stop. When he wasn't pinning my body down to impregnate me, he was beating up other people for touching me, oblivious of his own follies. Damon wasn't at all the hero I made him out to be, the good guy meant to save my wicked, tainted soul.

"You have to believe that everything I do is for you." Damon continued, "For our future."

"Our future?" I struggled with the words. "Staying locked up in some gilded cage isn't the future I envisioned."

"I know. Believe me, I know. I'm working toward achieving the things you set out to accomplish."

"What are you talking about?" Skepticism colored my voice.

"I have a patented technology, one that's bleeding out hedge fund companies like yours," he explained, slightly rising on his elbows. "Your father recognized the potential and proposed a merger. Since I became CEO, I have tried my best to keep your company afloat by not poaching your clients. But I can't stop my uncle or the ruthless board from doing what they please. And sometimes, your clients chase us down."

It was true. Everyone had been flocking toward Maxwell Corp since they integrated the software. The number of losses we incurred over the years had been significant. If it kept up, our company would go bankrupt within a couple of decades.

"The only way I can protect you is through a merger. A marriage will solidify that because no one can dispute either party's intentions. It'll finally put an end to this rivalry, and you can become the CEO of a thriving company instead of a failing one. I'll merge our hedge fund division with yours and sever all ties with my uncle."

I stared at him, brows furrowed in confusion. "You would give up your company for me?"

"For us," he corrected.

Shaking my head, I couldn't fathom or grasp the sacrifice. "Why would you do that? Especially because the board of Ambani Corp is super old-fashioned. They'll never allow someone without the Ambani name to sit on the board."

"Then I'll change my last name to Ambani," he spoke with such ease that I would've stumbled had I not been in bed.

I was rattled, suddenly questioning everything between us.

"I don't care what name we go by. All that matters is we're together," he said, his words flowing effortlessly. "And I know you feel the same. You're just too angry right now to see things clearly."

"Can you blame me?" I held up our cuffed hands.

Damon let out an exasperated sigh. "I admit the optics don't look good. But everything I've done has been for you since you were a lost little girl. I've been cleaning up your messes for years."

My eyes narrowed, trying to detect a hint of truth in his words.

"Do you remember when a gang of boys cornered Rose during your sophomore year?"

The memory flooded my mind, recalling the time I had returned from my winter internship only to find Rose being bullied. Some of the students thought it would earn them favors with the Maxwell family. Rose had been waiting for me to finish my lab that day when a group of "Maxwell followers" surrounded her. I had caught them red-handed, and I paid one of the guys from their group to teach the rest a lesson they wouldn't forget.

"You forgot there were cameras in that hallway. Who do you think broke into the security control room to erase the footage?"

I staggered. Checking for cameras didn't cross my mind.

"The year after, you blew up your uncle's car while he was at work. There was a witness," Damon revealed.

I had completely forgotten about that incident. Uncle Milan often visited Mom after Neil was born, mostly to dump a crying baby on Mom or me if I was around. Once, he left the baby in the freezing cold car, preoccupied with bringing in his shopping bags and showing off his newest purchases to Mom.

Mom ran outside to retrieve Neil after finding out. Naturally, I soaked Milan's precious car in gasoline the next day and lit it on fire.

"What did you do to the witness?" I asked curiously.

"Paid them off," Damon replied. "The point is that you aren't always as careful as you should be." He paused for a moment before a hint of a smirk appeared on his lips. "But that's alright because I like watching over you."

Silence hung heavy between us as I processed Damon's words. Slowly, I sat up. My mind was still filled with his revelations when my gaze landed on something on his desk. The picture Damon had stolen of my parents and me skillfully restored in its original frame.

"How did you"

"I broke into your mom's house earlier today and grabbed it," Damon interrupted. "Thought you might prefer it in its original frame."

Was it wrong that I found all this to be insanely romantic?

Breaking into my house, especially while I wasn't there to defend him if he got caught, was a life-threatening risk for a Maxwell. There was an unwritten shoot-on-sight policy against them.

Plus, I didn't realize Damon had been playing the role of my fairy godfather for years, covering up my mistakes with his invisible magic wand.

I tried to poison my biological father at least once a month. I constantly locked up my cousins and family members when they annoyed me, pretending I did it by mistake. I tortured my uncle endlessly. I was the absolute worst, yet Damon covered up my messes. He enabled my terrible behavior instead of telling me to become a better person like everyone else.

No one had coddled me like this in years.

It didn't bother me that he had been stalking me. It should. Instead, I was grateful someone covered up my tracks. Besides, I stalked people whenever I needed to put them in their place. Stalking was necessary for gathering vital information on someone. The fact Damon did it for years without detection was... admirable.

My gaze shifted back to the picture on the desk. "Why did you start following me?" I asked softly.

"Because I saw you that day, at your father's funeral. You looked so damn lonely."

A lightbulb went off in my head. "You were the man hiding behind the tree."

"I couldn't let you grieve alone," Damon confessed. "At first, I just wanted to ensure you were alright."

"And later?"

"I couldn't stop watching you."

My heart slammed violently against my chest. "My car," was all I could muster.

"What about it?"

"Why do you own the same car as me?"

He chortled. "Honestly, it made me feel closer to you."

"That's all?"

"And jerking off inside the car made me feel like you were there with me."

I huffed, though an unwilling smirk graced my face. "That doesn't explain why you helped me all these years?"

Damon shrugged. "Helping you gave me purpose."

"But why?" I pressed.

He looked at me for a long moment. "You might not believe yourself to be a very good person, Poppy, but I wouldn't be the person I am today if it weren't for you. You're the reason I'm good. Helping you gave me solace, and I thought I could feel that again by doing the same for others."

Suddenly, Damon's philanthropic efforts seemed intentional rather than a coincidence. "Am I the reason you funded all those ALS research in Caden's lab? Because Papa died of ALS."

Damon nodded. "I told you, everything I did was for you. I've helped thousands, soon to be millions, live a better life. Still, nothing came close to how I felt helping you."

I was left speechless, trying to process his words. "If that's how you felt about me, why did you resort to drugging me to marry you?" The truth still stung as it escaped my lips.

Damon took a deep breath before answering. "It was the only way we could be together."

He'd echoed the sentiment numerous times. My eyes were downcast. "Maybe I would have chosen to marry you willingly if you had waited."

"I couldn't take the chance." Damon's voice was thick with determination. "I've waited too long already. After that night at the party, I thought we'd finally be together. Then those texts and videos emerged from Rose's phone."

The mention of Rose's name dropped something heavy over my chest.

Damon caught the shift in my body language. "I checked with Caden earlier. Rose was taken out of the medically induced coma, but she isn't lucid," he cautiously updated me on Rose. "She is in the ICU, but visitors aren't allowed yet."

"Oh."

A hand brushed against my cheek. "I'll take you to see her once they allow it. I know how much she means to you."

"Then you must understand why I was hesitant about this relationship," I told him honestly. "If you exercised a little patience, things could've been different. I'd already planned on speaking to Rose after she recovered."

Damon didn't appear convinced. "No matter what you felt for me, you couldn't bear to hurt Rose. Telling her about us would've broken her heart, and I knew you would've backed out. I panicked."

Damon wasn't entirely wrong. Finally, I could relate to his reasons.

"Just so you know, I'm soft on Rose because she has been through a lot," I divulged. "She was nearly beaten to death when she was young."

Damon's frown deepened. "I didn't know that."

"Not a lot of people do. She was found in front of her parent's house, and ever since, she has been scared of strangers, the dark, or even engaging in a conversation. According to those texts, you were the first person she opened up to apart from me. I didn't want to be the person taking that away from her."

Damon scoffed. "Trust me, you didn't. Because I've always been yours."

For once, I couldn't refute the truth or find it in me to disagree. Nonetheless, I doubted he'd feel the same if he found out my bitter secret and the other reason why hurting Rose was such a non-negotiable for me.

ACT 5

Whodunit

CHAPTER THIRTY-FOUR
POPPY

"One more bite." Damon brought the forkful of eggs to my lips, imitating the airplane trick parents use to feed their children.

Like every morning, I was perched on his lap while he fed me breakfast, acutely aware of his growing erection with every bite I took.

Unlike the other mornings, I was no longer plotting his death.

Turning toward him, I noticed the five o'clock shadow, which made his face even more attractive. He was shirtless, as usual, and as I shifted, my nipples brushed up against his chest, and the reaction was instantaneous. They became hard, and my panties became soaked. Ignoring my current state or perhaps because of it, I made a decision I wouldn't have considered mere days ago. "I change my mind."

Damon's gaze probed for answers as he brought a glass of juice to my lips. His stare never left my mouth as I swallowed.

I have been thinking about it since our conversation. After considering every avenue, I realized Damon was right. Perhaps this was Stockholm Syndrome talking, but there was no point in being miserable. A merger between our two families would solve all the problems, and everyone in our lives would benefit. Rose would have to accept our relationship eventually. There was no other alternative.

"I've decided to meet you halfway. But I've got some conditions."

If Damon was surprised by my abrupt change of heart, he didn't let it show. He nodded with an *'I'm listening'* mien.

"If you want me to give this marriage a fair chance, then the handcuffs need to go," I stated firmly.

Damon shook his head. "Handcuffs stay on."

"Handcuffs come off if I prove myself," I renegotiated. "There is an incentive for me not to run because then you'll never let me off the hook again."

Damon considered my proposition. "No handcuffs during the day, but we sleep with them on."

The suggestion made sense. Damon slept just as soundly as me for five hours a day and wouldn't wake up if I tried to escape in his sleep.

With a slight nod, I agreed. Damon grasped at the cuffs and played with the lock. They fell off, and I wrung out my reddened wrists.

"Better?"

I nodded before continuing with my conditions. "I also need you to arrange a private conversation with Sophie."

Damon scoffed incredulously. "You can't be serious." His eyebrows lifted in amusement as if he had heard the funniest joke on earth.

"This is non-negotiable," I asserted. "I have no interest in her; I have told you that numerous times. However, I need to have a conversation with her to straighten some things out."

Rayyan and Sophie lived in Sands Point, a few blocks away from my mother. Sophie was Rayyan's next-door neighbor. On the night of his death, Rayyan got incredibly high, and I personally delivered him home before retiring to Mom and Zane's house. There was no one else in the house, nor were there cars in the driveway.

Sophie claimed to have witnessed Damon exiting Rayyan's house. But Damon told me he never stalked me to Sands Point, and I believed him. Not to mention, Damon wasn't stupid enough to drive to Sands Point and hurt Rayyan in his own home after a public spat. Even if Damon wanted to kill Rayyan, he would've waited until the heat was off him. A public altercation with the victim automatically made Damon the number-one suspect.

"Why?" Damon pushed.

I didn't want to disclose the real reason. "That's between her and I."

"So, you keep saying."

"You can monitor us on CCTV without sound, but I want an audience with Sophie, and the conversation must remain private. If you want me to give our marriage a real chance, talking to other people comes with the territory."

Damon didn't agree or disagree. Instead, he asked, "Anything else?"

I took a deep breath. "My childhood psychologist once said that people like me had no problem lying but couldn't deal with liars." Part of the reason why Damon's betrayal stung so much. "So, I need you to be honest with me about some things."

His eyes narrowed at the threat of the foreboding questions. "I feel like you already have a topic in mind."

It was both ridiculous and a relief how well he knew me. There was never a need for childish games or trite explanations.

"What really happened to Paris?"

Damon didn't miss a beat. "I blackmailed him into never seeing you again, then I asked him to jump off a balcony. He was admitted to the same hospital as Rose."

"Hm." I didn't care what happened to Paris but used the question to test Damon's new honesty policy. "You've been following me for years but never in Zane's house. Why is that?"

"The security was too tight," he replied immediately.

"So, you didn't track me when I went home to Sands Point? Was there anywhere else I went where you didn't have eyes on me?"

He shook his head. "I also couldn't see you during your winter breaks. The internship took place in a closed campus, and I couldn't get in." A strange emotion resonated in Damon's voice, one I couldn't comprehend. "But I would've found a way if I had known how you spent your mother's anniversary."

I froze. I carefully avoided this topic when Damon brought it up the other day. It wouldn't bode well for me to grease the wheels of Damon's jealousy.

I lost my virginity during my winter internship at Cornell on my mother's wedding anniversary. It was the first holiday I spent without family, and I was feeling sorry for myself at a dorm party. The night ended with a lot of booze and a resident assistant who was acceptable under certain lighting. I was fifteen, he was twenty-one, and in hindsight, it was a terrible decision.

Since I was a person of habit, it became an annual tradition of sorts, booze, sex, and partying, and not necessarily in that order. At sixteen, I returned to Cornell and hooked up with a girl whose name escapes me. The following year, it was Tom. This year, I decided against going away and chose Sophie.

However, Damon happened instead.

I glanced at the handcuffs, then at his swollen knuckles, with disappointment rather than rage. I couldn't imagine what he did to the rest if he had beaten Elijah over something that happened eons ago. "What did you do to those people? To everyone who came before you?"

Instead of beating around the bush, he answered plainly. "Did you know Sarah Lineman was a trust fund princess?"

Sarah! That was the name of the girl I hooked up with at sixteen. I shook my head.

"Guess who manages her assets?" Damon asked.

"Your company," I responded mechanically. Of course, he did.

Damon grinned. "Poor investments might have driven down the valuation of her trust fund. A wrecked financial future is worse than a broken nose. Wouldn't you agree?"

"Is that what you did to the others? A broken nose."

"Only to Tom. His promising job offers after college might also have disappeared. He works at the university café now."

"Jesus."

"I wouldn't display sympathy for these people if I were you," Damon suggested coolly.

"They didn't do anything wrong except like me for one random night."

"I respectfully disagree," he retorted.

"And what about Sophie?" I remembered Damon had taken Sophie's phone. Technically, I hadn't heard from the real Sophie in days. Did he hurt her, too? "What did you do to Sophie?"

"I wrecked one of her cars and took her phone. She's fine otherwise."

I frowned. A wrecked car wasn't as bad as financial ruin, like what he did to Sarah and Tom. "Why did you go easy on her compared to the rest?"

"Because she waited until you were eighteen."

"So?" I asked, not fully comprehending his reasoning.

"So?" He leaned forward until the tip of his nose touched mine, his piercing blue eyes resembling ice. "On top of touching what's mine, they took advantage of you. They deserved harsher consequences. Trust me."

That could only mean the person who took my virginity suffered the worst of Damon's wrath. "Is Elijah still alive?"

"Don't say his name in front of me." All warmth from this morning suddenly vanished, his voice dripping with disdain.

"Is that RA from Cornell still alive?" I rephrased, focusing solely on the answer.

"I heard an ambulance was called," was Damon's callous reply.

My shoulders sagged.

"However," Damon continued before I could get too comfortable, "Dankworth gave up a promising career for a job that no longer exists. His health insurance lapsed during his transition between jobs, and he'll be paying off hospital bills for the rest of his life."

People thought I was cruel. Damon was on another level, he was diabolical. A broken nose would heal, but financial ruin would leave him with a dismal future. "Why do you hate him so much?" I couldn't help asking.

Damon straightened up, his anger palpable. "I hate all of them, everyone who came before me. There was supposed to be no one else because I thought I kept everyone away from you. Students on campus knew better than to approach you. Most thought I asked them to stay away from you because of some petty rivalry."

There were times when boys on campus would hit on me, but they always mysteriously disappeared. Now that I was putting two and two together, Damon must've paid them off to stay away or beat them up, perhaps both. I decided against questioning him about another topic where I could be called to the witness stand.

Damon stared me right in the eyes. "Then I overheard Sophie and Rose at a party a few weeks ago. Sophie asked if you hooked up with girls, and Rose said you didn't discriminate but suggested waiting until winter break. Until then, I didn't think you were sexually active."

Damon studied me intently, contemplating whether to delve further into the topic. He ran his fingers through my hair.

"But I get it." For once, he didn't sound merely jealous but remorseful as well. "Your mother's anniversary fell during your winter break, the day you felt the loneliest, so you sought comfort in sex."

I didn't deny his assessment. Lying to him felt like lying to myself. The first few years after my mom remarried were particularly difficult. I didn't want to bear witness to their happiness, and the furtive glances she exchanged with Zane made me feel she was slipping further away from me. Spending the holidays with them was the last thing I wanted to do. Other than this recent winter break, I managed to steer clear of them by participating in various out-of-state internships.

Damon's eyes revealed a deep understanding. "I'm angry at those other people, not you," he clarified, his voice dropping for a gentler one. "And I'm angry at myself. Wish I could've been there for you. Or at least been there to stop them from taking advantage of you."

I stilled at Damon's insinuation. "What do you mean?"

"It should have never happened," he lamented, his voice heavy with regret. "You were only fifteen."

"You attended boarding school. Are you really telling me the first time you had sex was at eighteen?"

"People in boarding school were my age. Everyone at college is a lot older than you," he countered, his frustration seeping through. "They should've known better. They got away with it on a technicality because you were also in college. They thought you were on equal footing when it couldn't have been further from the truth."

I struggled with Damon's sentiment. "Everything was consensual," I insisted.

"You can't give consent at fifteen."

His conviction clouded my mind. "That's why you hate Eli—" I cut myself off upon catching Damon's icy glare. "That's why you hate the RA from Cornell?" I restated, though the irony wasn't lost on me.

Damon believed Elijah preyed on me. However, hadn't Damon done worse by drugging me, marrying me, and trying to knock me up?

As always, Damon seemed to pluck my thoughts from the air. "Don't compare what we have with him. It's different. You're my wife, and we'll be together forever. It's not just about sex between us."

I didn't know what to say or how to feel. Damon claimed he did all this to be with me, not to hurt me. He was justifying erratic behaviors while simultaneously beating up others for lesser crimes. "That makes it okay?"

"You're an adult, and we're evenly matched. Whereas when you lost your virginity, you were a kid who suffered some great losses. People preyed on your vulnerabilities because you're so damn beautiful. It was the only way they could have you because you were out of their leagues, and they knew it, too."

"That's crazy."

"You think so?" Damon challenged, his voice laced with conviction. "Rose is twenty-one, the same age Dankworth was back then. How would you feel if Rose had sex with a fifteen-year-old?"

Disgust rippled through me instinctively. "She'd never do that. Gross."

"Exactly," Damon affirmed triumphantly.

I was stumped to find out I wholeheartedly agreed with Damon. Until now, I never considered what Elijah did was wrong. He was perfectly nice and asked me for permission. He did the respectable thing by offering to stay the night and buy me breakfast the following morning. I turned him down when he asked me out.

On some level, I guess I knew it wasn't cool for a twenty-one-year-old to pursue a fifteen-year-old. If the roles were reversed, I'd never partake. The idea of hooking up with a fifteen-year-old repulsed me. Despite my ambiguous moral foundations, it wasn't a threshold I'd cross. It was the same reason I respected Sophie for approaching me after I turned eighteen. The thought brought forth another lurking suspicion I'd been grappling with.

"Did you know about the threesome before going to the party?"

Damon shook his head. "Sophie figured out I had feelings for you and decided to create drama by springing the threesome on me."

"How did she find out?"

"After I overheard Sophie sniffing around about you, I asked her to stay the hell away." The edge in Damon's voice returned. This time, it was pure jealousy. "It only piqued her interest, and she approached you anyway."

"Then why did you come to my room?"

"I told you. I recently found out what you did on your mother's anniversary. I went to that party to stop you from sleeping with someone else and memorized the layout of the house. When Sophie texted me at the party to meet up, she sent the directions to your room. I realized she had gone back on her word and propositioned you. So, I wrecked her car."

It should've freaked me out, but for some reason, laughter tumbled out of my mouth instead. It turned out Damon was the kind of crazy I had been searching for all my life.

CHAPTER THIRTY-FIVE
DAMON

Poppy was slick by the time I settled between her thighs, my unbuckled belt skimming her bare legs. I had vowed to make her crave me, except I was the one who couldn't go a few hours without her. My insides were exploding from the frustration of withholding sex while I let our bodies recover. She couldn't even walk last night, and my dick was beyond chafed.

Poppy suggested we keep ourselves occupied with a movie marathon, *Twelve Gruesome Murders,* followed by *Thirteen Gruesome Murders.* Although, in her opinion, the sequel was too mainstream.

Poppy left halfway through the movie to use the bathroom. I cornered her when she returned, pushing her against the living room wall.

My sanity had taken yet another hit. A bomb had been ticking away inside me, ready to detonate. I kissed her fervently and ground her into the wall so hard that she fought back for respite.

"Damon," Poppy moaned.

"I think we've waited long enough. Don't you? I can't ease you into it this time. I need you too much," I growled, hurling her sweater above her head and discarding it on the floor. I slid her panties and leggings down to her thighs.

The head of my cock rubbed against her sex. Her cunt was tighter to enter, with her leggings around her thighs. Her glossy eyes shone with lust as I stretched her to accommodate my size. I was already too big for her, our significant size difference playing a factor.

Instead of easing her into it, I dove inside her like a beast. It had been half a day since we had sex. The little time her body had to recover was instantaneously destroyed.

"Fuck," Poppy gritted, breathing harshly through her mouth.

I pummeled her ruthlessly. I had become a madman since my first taste of her and thought this heat would simmer with time.

The opposite had transpired.

A scream sounded from the television, followed by the sound of a chainsaw and the hacking of body parts.

"Tell me what's happening in the movie." I could care less, but it was the perfect distraction from the pain in her tender cunt.

"The second victim is being chopped up on a surgery table," she panted.

I told her to keep paraphrasing the gory details while I was preoccupied. Poppy moaned a garbled version of the synopsis. She stopped talking when my hand went around her ass, parted her cheeks, and pushed a finger into her puckered hole.

"God." Her mouth hung open, and her eyes rolled to the back of her head.

"Fuck, you're tight."

I lost finesse and repeatedly plunged inside her with so much force that I could barely keep her up against the wall. At this point, it felt like nothing could stop this insanity.

The heavily glazed eyes staring back were stuck between pain and pleasure. She dug her nails into my back, which spurred me on. Finally, my index finger pushed inside her rosebud, and I thrust softly until it was all the way in.

"Oh, shit." Her body shook uncontrollably, legs wrapped around my waist. "Feels... so good."

"What's happening now?" I pressed.

"Now... he is... ah... he is fucking the dead body, mm."

Moving a hand between us, I stroked her sensitive clit. Her fussiness quietened at the sensation, replaced by new erotic sounds.

"Oh, shit," Poppy broke.

Soaking, wet tightness built as I rubbed her clit mercilessly. A silent scream from her parted lips leaked out, gaining volume, and it happened then. Poppy fell apart. My pace increased at the sight, rushing to the finish line with her. My hips knocked against her as I fought her back, thrusting her against the wall over and over until she spasmed.

"Fuck, baby." My wild groan was guttural. My world turned black, my heart hammering as if it might explode. With one final thrust, I spilled inside her.

I slid us onto the ground, turning Poppy over to lie on her back.

"Let me up," she protested when I didn't pull out.

"No," I said curtly.

"You do know that lying horizontal to get pregnant is a myth."

"Technically, it hasn't been disproven."

"Hasn't been proven, either," she countered.

I shrugged. "I'll take whatever increases my chances."

Poppy rolled her eyes but complied.

I only lifted off her slightly to stare at where we were joined. The sight alone could make me come a second time. "I missed this."

"It's been six hours," she said incredulously.

I laughed, glancing off to the side. The handcuffs dangled off the coffee table. I forgot about them.

Over the last few days, there had been no more handcuffs unless an emergency requiring my attention pulled me away from our home. Poppy was still a flight risk, but I allowed her freedom around the apartment.

Poppy was softening toward me; I could feel it.

The other day, I intentionally left out a butcher's knife to assess where she was in this relationship. Although Poppy swiped the knife when she thought I wasn't looking, she didn't attack me with it.

Eventually, I realized Poppy did it out of habit. She slept with a pocketknife inside her nightstand at her old apartment as well. It was for protection. She didn't want to rely on me to rescue her if someone broke into our home. Little did she know I'd never take such a risk when it came to Poppy. I might be the one monitoring the cameras inside our home, but security guards were stationed outside and could reach her within seconds.

Nonetheless, I remained on guard. I kept waiting for her to stab me and was stumped when nothing happened. There could only be one rational conclusion.

Poppy was in love with me.

Our love index was madness, I admit. However, Poppy not killing me for her freedom was as bold a declaration as one could expect.

So now, she enjoys autonomy inside our home. I didn't restrict her access in between rooms or conceal sharp objects. We still slept handcuffed together, but that was out of habit.

I didn't want to leave this bubble of ours. In here, our last names didn't matter, our families didn't exist, nor did their bickering. The investigation against me in Rayyan Ambani's murder was officially dismissed earlier today, citing a lack of leads. The Ambanis wouldn't take kindly to this defeat. At least Poppy and I remained untouched by the drama.

Things were going relatively well between us, or as best as they could go between a captor and captive. I knew it wouldn't be the case once our family got involved again.

"What's that noise?" Poppy wheezed against me.

I glanced at my phone, buzzing relentlessly on the coffee table.

I groaned. "I need to take this."

So much for our little bubble. My team was instructed to screen and intercept my calls for the month, only patching through the most important ones. Which meant something terrible had happened, requiring my immediate attention.

A few minutes later, I was proven right.

CHAPTER
THIRTY-SIX
POPPY

"This is ridiculous," I grumbled.

Damon handcuffed me to one of the posts of the bed because his highness had been called away.

"Sorry, baby." The crazy thing was that he genuinely sounded apologetic.

"If you're so sorry, don't handcuff me to the bed."

He brushed off my comment and pushed a remote toward me. "Feel free to finish the movie without me. I set it up to stream to the bedroom TV. I should be home in an hour." Then he gestured at an electronic screen on my nightstand resembling a mini-Smart television. "If you get bored, you can play around with this."

I eyed it suspiciously. "What is it?"

"It's a virtual assistant device I've been working on. It's still in beta testing, but it's good for organizing contacts, recipes, streaming movies, that kind of stuff. And you can call people from your directory."

"That already exists. It's called an Alexa."

"Mine's better. And it's called a Spawn." He puffed out his chest, making me smirk.

"Spawn," I immediately called on his evil creation. The screen spurred to life. "Call the police and tell them Damon Maxwell is holding me hostage."

Damon pulled a face. "Nice try. It's programmed only to call me."

"A kidnapper's dream," I retorted dryly.

Damon draped his arm around my shoulders and kissed my cheek. It was impossible to remain aloof when he showered me with physical affection. I'd rather hold onto my sulkiness because I didn't want him to leave.

It turned out Damon was right all along.

Yes, saving my company superseded Damon's psychotic behavior. But that wasn't all.

No matter how we got here, I couldn't deny the facts of the matter. There was no one better suited for me than Damon. We were matched in every way. Our routines. Our work. Our passion. Our ambition.

He didn't annoy me or require me to entertain him with endless chatter. What was more astonishing was the growing restlessness during the short intervals we were apart. Like when he left the apartment yesterday to pick up my favorite ice cream, I couldn't handle the separation because I missed him too much. I didn't want a repeat of that emotion.

What the hell was happening to me?

"Why do you have to leave?" I asked bitterly, hating myself for the pathetic weakness in my voice.

It made Damon smile. "I don't want to leave," he explained patiently. "But Paris is awake. He called and wanted to talk in person."

My head whipped in his direction. Damon told me everything that happened with Paris. "Why would Paris want to see you after what happened?"

"That's what I'm going to find out. I also need to remind him to keep quiet about how he ended up at the hospital."

I nodded.

If Paris went to the police about what Damon or I did, it wouldn't bode well for us. The matter was pressing. I understood why Damon had to nip it in the bud, but something was off.

Why would Paris want another encounter with the man who beat him to a pulp?

Damon leaned over to kiss me with such absolution that I forgot to care about my apprehensions. My fingers were trembling over his chest by the time he let go with a "Later, Ambani."

Reluctantly, he grabbed his keys and disappeared through the bedroom door.

Fifteen minutes later, I was bored out of my mind, the same emotion from yesterday returning in ten-folds. I hated these newfound emotions.

I gave in with an embarrassing ease. "Spawn," I spat through my lips. "Call Damon."

The device came to life, but nothing happened. What the hell? I didn't call the police this time and thought Damon's phone number had already been programmed.

After considering it for a moment, I tried again. "Spawn, call husband."

I rolled my eyes when the device came to life, announcing, "Calling your husband."

"Figures," I muttered.

Damon picked up by the end of the first ring. "Miss me already?"

"Is that how you answer all your calls?"

He laughed.

"Are you at the hospital?"

"Yeah. I just parked. Walking now."

"Alone?" Damon always had a security team following him in case of stalkers. Ironic, wasn't it? "Where is your team?"

"Watching over you," he replied easily.

I frantically scouted the bedroom for men who might be hiding under our bed or in the bathroom.

Of course, he knew what I was doing. "Don't worry, baby. I wouldn't let a bunch of horny men inside our apartment or watch my wife on a security feed. They are stationed outside in case of a fire."

It made good sense, but I couldn't shake the ominous feeling. Why would Paris call Damon after what happened?

"Tell me again why Paris called you," I pressed.

"He didn't. Someone from the hospital called. They said Paris asked for me."

"So, you never spoke to Paris?"

Something didn't add up here. Call it a wife's intuition, and no, I wasn't being sarcastic.

"No..." Damon trailed off momentarily. "What the hell?"

"Hello, Damon." I heard a different voice on the other end of the line.

My stomach dropped at the sound of the familiar voice.

Uncle Dev, Rose's father.

"Mr. Ambani?" Damon confirmed my suspicions. "Put the gun down."

Cold sweat broke out on my forehead.

Shit. Shit. Shit.

"Damon, you need to get the hell out of there," I whispered.

But Damon only spoke to the man in front of him. "Put the gun down, Dev. This isn't you."

"Do not engage with him, Damon," I warned. "Dev is an emotional man." Emotional men often make unstable decisions.

I banged at the post, trying to get the cuffs off me. It was futile. Dev had a gun, and I couldn't even call the police.

Despite my advice, Damon spoke to Dev with kindness. "You don't seem okay, man. Put the gun down, and let's talk about this calmly. We both know you aren't going to shoot me in broad daylight and get away with it."

"I don't care," Dev shouted, voice shaking. It sounded like he had been drinking. "You are the one who keeps getting away with it. I'm tired of it. You destroyed my family, yet nothing happened to you. I'm about to change that, and I don't care what happens to me after."

"Dammit, Damon. Don't try to be a hero right now. This man can't be reasoned with if he already went through the trouble of procuring a gun." I banged the cuffs against the post again. I kicked it, too, hoping to break it. If I could make it to the front door, I could yell for the security guards outside and tell them what was happening. One of them could call the police.

Damon continued to speak to Dev in a soothing voice, refusing to believe this was a lost cause. The philanthropist in him was winning, wanting to help a devastated father instead of caring for his own life.

I closed my eyes, wishing this nightmare away. The same uselessness I felt years ago when Papa was dying slammed through me. I was no longer that lost little girl, and I refused to let yet another man who meant the world to me die while I did nothing.

"There is something you don't know about Dev," I spoke into the phone softly, hoping Damon could hear me succinctly over the conversation with Dev. "Years ago, he had an affair with his sister-in-law, his brother's wife, Sonia."

I knew Damon was listening despite coaxing Dev, telling him everything would be alright.

"The investigation was officially dropped today," I continued. "And clearly, Dev has lost his mind as a result. Because the product of his affair with Sonia was Rayyan. Dev believes you killed his son on top of seducing his only daughter. Dev thinks you took both his children from him."

"What?" The shock was evident in Damon's voice. This was a buried family scandal only a few knew about.

"Who the hell are you talking to?" Dev barked. "Hang up."

I heard a shuffle before Damon announced, "Done."

However, the line didn't go dead. I imagined Damon had his Bluetooth on if he was just getting out of the car. He pretended to hang up, and Dev didn't verify, so hopefully, I could talk Damon through this.

"Listen to me carefully," I whispered, hoping Dev couldn't hear our conversation. "Dev has a bad shoulder from an old tennis injury. If he gets close enough, you need to punch his left shoulder and make a run for it. He also has an ACL tear on his right knee. He won't be able to follow you if you run fast enough and take cover. Please, Damon, don't be a hero right now. He has nothing to lose, so he will shoot you. The only chance you have is by getting the hell out of there."

But that wasn't Damon's style.

"I love you," he whispered right before the bang went off, the phone went dead, and my world went dark.

FATAL OBSESSION

Pulling the nightstand drawer open, I retracted the knife hidden inside. Call me crazy for sleeping with a knife by my bedside, but my suspicions had been proven right repeatedly.

My hand was rock-steady as I placed it on top of the nightstand, my wrist still encased in cuffs.

"Fear exists in your mind," I reminded myself. "It isn't real."

He is alive. He is alive. He is alive. I repeated the mantra until it became real to me.

With the butcher's knife raised high with my other hand, I spread my fingers so my pinky was the farthest from the rest. I only had one chance at this. A wrong strike would cause too much bleeding and render me useless. I couldn't do anything for Damon if that happened. There was a possibility of passing out if I lost too much blood. Nonetheless, I had to roll the dice.

"Mind over matter," I told myself. "There is no such thing as pain if you refuse to believe in it. Damon is alive and needs your help, so do this now."

I stuffed the remote into my mouth to have something to bite down on. Without a second thought, I brought the knife down with as much strength as I could muster.

"Fuck," I screamed.

It hurt like a bitch, but it didn't do the trick, so I slammed the knife down two more times until my pinky finger was severed.

Damn. Dismembering yourself was painful.

It's not like I had many choices. I called Damon repeatedly while testing numerous combinations to unlock the cuffs. His birthday. My birthday. The day we met. Our wedding day. Any combination that might be meaningful.

In the end, I realized Damon chose random numbers without meaning, anticipating my attempt to get into his head to figure out the code.

It was frustratingly ingenious.

Then his words from the first time he cuffed me rang in my ears.

The only way to unlock these cuffs without the code is by chopping off your fingers.

Blood dripped from my open wound, the blade of the knife glistening with the shiny red liquid. Struggling with the cuff, I managed to pull my hand out of the hole.

Finally.

Part of my severed pinky lay on the nightstand. I scooped it up and dashed into the kitchen to dump it inside a Ziplock bag, filling it with ice. A trail of blood followed my wake. Cursing under my breath, I snatched a kitchen rag and wrapped it tightly around what remained of my pinky.

You better be alive, Damon. I screamed in my head because the alternative was an option I refused to entertain.

Sliding my feet through the first pair of flip-flops I could find, I banged on the front door with all my might.

"Luke! I need your help!" I screamed. Luke was Damon's head of security. I met him on the flight to Vegas. If I had to guess, Damon wouldn't trust anyone other than Luke to watch me.

He didn't answer, though. No doubt, he was given instructions not to let me out of the house and to ignore my pleas for escape.

However, I also bet Damon told Luke he'd kill him with his bare hands if anything happened to me. I had to take the plunge and mimic a damsel in distress.

What the hell was I thinking?

My husband might be dead, and I just chopped off my finger to get to him.

I *was* a damn damsel in distress.

"Luke," I yelled at the top of my lungs. "I hurt myself badly. I chopped my finger off trying to cut a..." I was a terrible cook and couldn't think of anything I'd chop off other than Luke's dick if he didn't let me out right this instant.

"Are you okay, Mrs. Maxwell?" His response was immediate, concern laced in his voice.

"No!" I shouted. "I'm bleeding to death. We need to go to the hospital."

The door flew open. The man with the buzz-cut hair and dressed like he was auditioning for Men-In-Black appeared petrified at the sight to grace him. His gaze went to my hand, wrapped poorly in a bloody rag. Then he saw the butcher's knife I held in one hand and the bag of ice in the other with my severed pinky.

I held up the knife to his throat before he could say another word. "Take me to my husband right this second."

CHAPTER
THIRTY-SEVEN
POPPY

THE CONTINUOUS BEEPING IRRITATED MY EARBUDS, THE persistent sound piercing through my closed eyelids. The cacophony of voices only made it worse. Not the evil ones in my head constantly encouraging havoc but the ones outside.

Mom.

Her voice was mingled with that of a man I couldn't place. From the sounds of it, we were at the hospital, and he was my attending physician. They were discussing medical treatment and aftercare. Judging from their conversation, I deduced that I was heavily medicated. Despite wanting to set this place ablaze with the demands of seeing Damon, my lips refused to move. My eyes wouldn't open, either.

What in the fresh hell was this?

More importantly, where was Damon?

After completing his update, the doctor said sternly, "Mrs. Trimalchio. I have another important matter to discuss. The staff told me that your daughter's behavior today was unacceptable. Another outburst like that, and we'll have to consider the Psychiatric Ward."

Well, this brought back warm memories of every headmaster from my boarding school days.

"What did she do?" Mom asked tentatively.

"She broke a coffee table after we informed her that her husband wasn't admitted here and took down one of our attendees when he tried to inspect her injured hand."

"That's my Poppy." Mom gave a small laugh before quickly clearing her throat. "Sorry, that's not funny. I'll pay for the damages."

After I held the butcher's knife to Luke's throat, I disclosed what happened, demanding he take me to Damon. Luke was convinced I wouldn't jam the knife inside his throat. The cockiness was an overkill. I only refrained because he surrendered his phone and keys without a fight. I rushed to his car. Luke followed behind with my finger in a baggie. He tried to drive, so I was forced to threaten him with the knife again because he wouldn't have agreed to drive at the necessary speed of ninety miles an hour.

While I drove to the hospital, I called the police with Damon's last known location. I called the hospital, too. No one by the name of Damon Maxwell had been admitted. The staff claimed to have heard a gunshot, but it was ruled out as a car backfire when they couldn't locate a victim or a shooter on the premises. No one saw anything, and conveniently, no cameras were facing that part of the parking lot, either.

What was more astonishing was that Paris checked out of the hospital yesterday.

Luke dispatched his men, asking everyone to meet at the hospital and search the grounds. Meanwhile, I stormed the hospital in search of Damon. But Luke, the traitor, turned on me and forced me to get admitted for my severed finger—something about how Damon would murder him with his bare hands if anything happened to me.

Suffice it to say, I didn't go down without a fight. The last thing I remembered was turning over a coffee table. I'd scream this place down again if I could open my mouth.

"When can I take my daughter home?" Mom asked.

"We'll keep her under observation for a few days. Reattaching the finger was a simple procedure. But I'm concerned about her mental state."

"Is there anything we can do?"

"Try to keep her calm. I don't want to have to give her another sedative in her condition."

What condition?

There was a momentary pause on Mom's end. "Is there a way to stream Twelve Gruesome Murders on this TV of yours?"

The man sounded astonished. "Mrs. Trimalchio, I highly doubt a violent movie is appropriate right now."

"It calms her down."

The man sounded pissed off about the family of freaks he was assigned to. "I meant try saying things she might find comforting."

"Of course. Thank you, doctor."

Footsteps shuffled out of the room after a curt goodbye.

A familiar smell engulfed me as a pair of lips swooshed down to my forehead. "Oh God, Poppy. I should've been there for you."

I no longer cared about our fight. I barely even remembered it. It happened so long ago. My mind was focused on a singular pursuit.

I forced my lips to move, but no sound came out.

"Are you trying to say something, Poppy?"

I tried again but failed. Trying to peel my eyes open was no better. Dammit.

"Shh." A comforting hand soothed over my hair. "It's okay. Don't push yourself."

Damon. I could've sworn this time I said it, but again, no sound came out.

Luckily, Mom caught on. "I'm so sorry, Beta. We haven't been able to find him."

I suddenly wanted to sink back into the abyss I'd awakened from and have my consciousness returned only after they located Damon. Despite my closed eyes, something on my face must've warned Mom of my state.

"But you mustn't give up hope, Poppy. We have a search party led by the best detectives looking for him."

Everything turned numb inside me.

I was apathetic to Mom's news because I knew what they'd uncover. At best, they'd discover Damon's corpse because life had dealt me nothing other than the card of death. It was the only thing in store for me.

I didn't dwell on how Mom found out about my marriage or why she was suddenly concerned for Damon.

While I lay there, hoping to be anywhere but here, Mom tried to follow the doctor's advice, attempting to keep me calm. She paved the path by repeatedly expressing her approval of Damon and disclosing how she learned to accept him.

Mom recounted how Damon reached out to her the day we left for Las Vegas, assuring her I was safe and we were together. Ever since, he had been dropping by her house routinely, determined to win over Mom and Zane.

He showed up at their doorstep like a gentleman and informed them of our impromptu wedding, stating it was my idea, an act of rebellion against Mom. Damon had suggested waiting for Mom's blessing. However, I was insistent, and he could never deny me because he loved me too damn much.

His manipulations made my heart smile.

In the following days, Damon continued to drop by, allowing Mom and Zane to get to know him. He shared photos from our Gothic-themed wedding in Las Vegas. While Mom admitted it looked like my dream wedding, she was devastated over not being included. Zane and Damon reassured her that a grand reception in our honor would take place upon my graduation.

Damon, the perfect son-in-law, never snuck in to steal the picture frame from their house. If there was one thing all three versions of my mother—Piya Mittal/Ambani/Trimalchio—understood, it was true love. She saw it in his eyes. So, when Damon asked if he could take Papa's photo to surprise me, she showed him to my room. It sounded like he discreetly pocketed the frame before she could notice the missing picture inside.

During each visit, Mom begged him to arrange a meeting between us. Damon claimed I was still angry and to give me space, which she believed, given our last conversation. Nonetheless, he appeased her by showing her photos of us eating breakfast, watching movies, or going for a swim in the outdoor pool on his terrace.

Mom thought I'd never looked happier. It was enough for her to grant her blessing. The three of them had been working together since, trying to bridge the gap between the two families.

Mom's one-sided conversation abruptly stopped when Zane's voice drifted into the room.

"We found blood in the parking lot."

I didn't need to open my eyes to know what was coming next. The all-too-familiar rip in my heart ached the same, the one I had become accustomed to over the years. Darkness spread its black tentacles around my heart, reminding me it was here to stay.

"And?" Mom asked breathlessly, anxiety spiking in her voice. She thought I had fallen asleep due to my extended silence.

There was a long pause before Zane replied. "They confirmed it was Damon's blood. I think Dev shot Damon and hired men to bury the body."

The longing for the oblivion returned. I didn't fight it. I wanted it to pull me down into the pits, to consume me and erase this awful existence. How was I still here? I no longer wanted to be here, in this room, city, world. Nothing mattered anymore because deep down, I knew Zane was right. Damon was dead.

"No, Axel, don't say that. He's alive. He has to be."

"I wish I had better news."

"Please, Axel," Mom begged. "There must be something else we can do. She is our only daughter, and she won't survive his death. I can feel it."

"I'm sorry, Princess. Dev's gone, too. There are no more leads."

"Please, please, Axel. You have to do something," Mom pleaded through her tears.

"Shh. Okay. Okay. Let me have Levi track Paris. It's the only thing I haven't pursued yet."

"Paris?" Mom's voice trembled.

"Apparently, Dev was at the hospital visiting Rose when he saw Damon dropping Paris off. After Paris was discharged, Dev made a call out of Paris's room with an urgent request to meet with Damon. For whatever reason, Damon agreed, and Dev was waiting for him in the parking lot. Maybe Paris knows something."

Paris knew nothing. Dev must have figured out that whatever Damon did to land Paris in the hospital was bad enough to warrant a meeting. It guaranteed him the meeting that destroyed our lives.

The last traces of humanity left within me nurtured through the sheer determination of Papa's teachings, Mom's devotion, Rose's affections, and Neil's untainted warmth, vanished into thin air. Because they could never comprehend the true darkness inside me and love me unconditionally the way Damon could. I was too fucked up in the head for them, too full of sin.

That was why the universe couldn't allow me to have something good. The one good thing I had been granted after all these years was violently ripped away, just as I had always known it would be. And now, I was alone forever. This is how I was meant to be.

Returning to my old life felt empty. I didn't say this out of misguided notions surrounding emotions I couldn't feel. Instead, I was saying this because I was fully aware of my capabilities. I had known it to be true the moment the gunshot had gone off.

After a day of refusing food and water and conversation with the revolving door of relatives dropping by for a visit, Mom's agitation grew. I wasn't obstinate in hurting her. My will to fight was simply gone. I'd rather wither away than face the doom of the impending, gloomy news. This was one loss I couldn't handle. I wasn't equipped for it. I could survive everything else, even Papa's death, because I knew his legacy would live on in me when I became CEO. Damon's death was the final blow. I had been a fighter until now, but I no longer cared to live if Damon wasn't in this world to live in it with me.

Because Damon wasn't my chance at happiness, he was my only possibility for it.

∼

"Poppy, I know you don't want to hear this, but I need you to come back to me."

Mom was right. I didn't want to hear it.

"Please, baby," Mom pleaded for what seemed like the hundredth time while gently squeezing my uninjured hand.

Once upon a time, my mother's tears held immense power over me, and I'd go to great lengths to stop them from forming. But now, I was impervious.

My insides were numb. No one could touch me again with their words. I was an existence without purpose, something taking up space and oxygen without contributing anything worthwhile. They hooked me up to IVs after my refusal to eat or drink, surrounding me with wires from every angle. This felt like a giant waste of resources, too. There was nothing left other than this never-ending emptiness.

There was only one logical course of action.

I had to end it because a dead woman couldn't feel emotions. What was the point of inhabiting a body that took up oxygen, space, and resources without contributing positively to society?

Years ago, I had watched them cremate my father and then my grandmother, taking the best parts of me with them. For years after, I remained the lost little girl who couldn't move on from the loss. I was frozen. Then he came and thawed my world.

He saw me. The evil vile me and he loved me all the same. The only person who didn't turn his back on me no matter how black this heart had gotten. He loved my rotten heart even when there was nothing I could give him in turn.

And now, there was one thing I wanted to give him in return. Companionship.

I could join him in death and keep him company.

It was ironic. Damon had entered my life to prevent me from making this very decision. In the past, I would have never considered such an act. But now, it consumed my every thought because Damon happened.

Piercing blue eyes came into my life.

I got used to running my fingers through messy, dirty blonde locks.

The smell of burnt croissants while perched on his lap had consumed my senses.

The callous attitude he exercised about my fucked up mind couldn't be replicated by anyone.

The way he looked at me like I was his entire world. As if he couldn't bear to be apart from me. As if even a second away from me was torture.

Enough!

Stop it. Stop it. Stop it.

I spent most of my life seeking solitude, even in misery. But I didn't like the idea of Damon dead somewhere, suffering eternity in solitude. This life had turned meaningless without him. This was now the only meaningful thing I could do. Join Damon in death.

My fingers played with the scalpel I had swiped from the doctor's tray. Everyone had finally left my room. Some went to the ICU to visit Rose, others were in the cafeteria, and my mother was with the doctors. My cousins were loitering in the hallway, seeking respite from the oppressive atmosphere.

I twisted the scalpel between my fingers, feeling its coolness against my skin. It would be poetic if I slit my wrist, replacing the fading red marks left behind by the handcuffs. The thought brought a strange sense of comfort as I traced the sharp blade.

The only reason I hadn't sliced my wrist yet was because I wanted to live a few more minutes basking in the moments I shared with Damon.

Blue eyes.

The smell of burnt croissants.

Dirty blonde hair flopping messily over his eyes.

I shook my head. Enough already.

I could spend an entire lifetime within these memories, but Damon was waiting. And I knew he hated being apart from me for too long.

My thumb brushed against the two stacked rings on my ring finger, feeling the tattoo underneath—my real wedding ring. We had promised until '*death do us part,*' but no one said only one of us had to die.

Bringing my other hand forward, I pressed the scalpel against my wrist. Blood seeped out as I applied pressure, but before it could do any significant harm, it was snatched away from me.

"Don't even think about it," Zane warned in a steady voice.

CHAPTER
THIRTY-EIGHT
POPPY

Stupid, irritating Zane. He couldn't even let me die in peace.

"You do understand how selfish you're being, right? You'll kill your mother if you do that."

I said nothing, looking straight ahead. How did he know to come back and stop me?

Zane watched me closely for a few moments, twirling the bloody scalpel between his fingers. Finally, he walked over to the abandoned tray on the other side of the room to gather gauze and tape. He returned to my bedside, sitting next to me.

"What the hell are you doing?" Those were the first words I had spoken in two days. What was this, Zane, the nursemaid?

He ignored my attempt to pull away and spoke like we were old college chums. "Do you know why you bug me so much?"

I rolled my eyes. His attempts at playing nice left much to be desired.

"Because your mother will never love me as much as she loves you," he spoke without meeting my gaze, focused on cleaning the cut on my wrist.

"Yet when the time came, she chose you over Papa," I couldn't help countering.

"Your mother never chose me over Ambani. Nor did she choose Ambani over me."

A puzzled frown tugged at my forehead.

Zane spoke slowly as if explaining how the world worked to a child. "Piya chose to give you a better life over me. And while it brings me no joy to admit it, maybe she made the right decision. Just look at our relationship. I treat you the way my asshole father used to treat me."

"Then why do you do it?"

"Because you were and always will be the greatest love of your mother's life," he snapped. "What do you think Piya would've done if she came in here and found you with your wrist sliced open?"

Find the nearest bridge and jump off it. It was a cruel thought, but my mind instinctively went there. Mom wouldn't survive it if anything happened to me.

For the first time, I experienced an emotion I didn't think I was capable of feeling. Shame.

"You're an idiot," he declared for clarity.

"Thanks. Have you considered working as a phone operator for a suicide prevention hotline? I think you'd have a hundred percent success rate."

Zane appeared agitated, wrapping the gauze around my wrist tighter than necessary. "Do you think this is easy for me? I might fight you every step of the way, but I do admire you as a person. And I know that's Ambani's doing. You would've never turned out okay if I raised you."

There was nothing to say. We both knew the statement to be true. Papa showered me with nothing but love and support throughout my childhood. Nothing compared to it until Damon.

"My father was an asshole," he continued. "And look at what he turned me into. He didn't care about anything other than alcohol."

"You don't care about anything other than Mom," I pointed out.

Zane nodded thoughtfully. "Perhaps. But the sentiment only applies to me. Piya chose you every step of the way. It's impossible to compete with what she feels for you. Where do you think that leaves me?"

"That's my fault? You made my life miserable because Mom loves me."

"I wasn't trying to make your life miserable," he gritted between clenched teeth. "You might not believe this, but I did some of those things because I wanted you to admire me, too."

I didn't know what to make of Zane's admissions and stared blankly.

My silence made Zane uncomfortable. "Your mother might be dramatic at times, but she isn't controlling. She knew you didn't want to attend our wedding and suggested excusing you from participating altogether."

Son of a bitch. "Then why did you put me through it? That day was hell for me."

"Forgive me for wanting my daughter at my wedding."

Said the rational psychopath who cut out my dead father's face from my childhood photos.

"Piya didn't make any stipulations for a standing Friday night dinner, either," he continued. "I put the rule in place to spend time with you. I was trying to be a little bit better of a father than mine was to me. Did it never cross your mind that I was trying to get to know you?"

"No. Do you know why? Because you were blackmailing me."

With an exasperated breath, he said, "Sometimes you're just as dramatic as your mother."

I blew out an equally frustrated exhale. "You're telling me that you blackmailed me all these years because you loved me so damn much?"

"How else could I have gotten you to spend time with me?"

I didn't know what to say and rubbed my temples. Even his fatherly love was twisted.

Zane let out a relented sigh. "Piya once told me that you didn't need another father, and I'm starting to believe that works for us. I never wanted children, and you never wanted or needed a replacement father. However, there is one thing I could give you instead. I could be your ally."

My head whipped in his direction. "What does that mean?"

His eyes held untold mystery. "You'll find out soon enough. Meanwhile, we need to do something about your itchy finger syndrome." He pointedly glared at the scalpel.

"How did you know to come to this room, anyway?" I asked since everyone had dispersed after lunch.

Zane shrugged. "I had a feeling you'd try something like this."

My eyes met his steady gaze.

"We are cut from the same cloth, remember? If my sole connection to this earth were also gone," he was talking about Mom, "I'd consider the same. Why do you think I bought matching caskets with your mother? I refuse to live a moment longer if she died before me."

I huffed. "Yet you expect me to keep on living."

Zane took a deep breath. The hypocrisy wasn't lost on him. "It doesn't matter what I expect. You've got to keep living because you're better than me. Ambani raised you with all his damn moral high grounds. Do you think he would've wanted this for you? If your mother did the right thing by choosing to raise you with him, don't let her sacrifices go to waste. Be better than this." He tossed the scalpel onto the bed between us.

I eyed the sharp object meant to be my relief from this sweet Hell.

I would do anything for Mom, but Damon was waiting. I couldn't let him go through purgatory alone. "Like you said, we are cut from the same cloth."

Zane let out an infuriated rumble. "Then there is something else you should know. The doctors recommended against telling you because of your mental state. They thought it might worsen things, but this might finally snap you out of it."

A thick cloak of ominous premonition suffocated the room. I knew it was coming before he said it.

"You're pregnant."

My hand immediately flew to my stomach.

It had been four days since my pregnancy test, but we had a lot of sex three days ago. It didn't come as a surprise, only the most incredible news I had ever heard. Suddenly, all wasn't lost.

I had a new lease on life.

"If you loved him so much, is this how you want to end his legacy? Because if you do, then here." Zane grabbed the scalpel and placed it in my hand. "Go for it."

"Do I get a say in this?" A deep voice interrupted us from the door.

∼

Damon

My girl caught me staring at her from the doorway before screaming, "Damon!" and jumping off the hospital bed.

She forgot about the IV lines hooked up to her, holding her back. Poppy tore through them at manic speed, but I had already taken the five steps to reach her and scooped her into my arms. Blood from my right hand, where Dev shot me, dripped onto Poppy's black hospital gown. I bet Piya special ordered them to spruce up the room for Poppy.

Poppy straddled me, throwing her arm around my neck with legs wrapped around my waist. I kissed her neck and cheeks while my hands moved over her body to ensure this wasn't a mirage.

The gown was tied in the back, suited more for comfort than fashion. Her raven hair was in two braids, draping over each shoulder. Despite the pain shooting off my right hand, the heat radiating off her was a call that couldn't go unanswered.

She was so damn beautiful.

Every part of my body was in agony. There was a slight limp in my steps, too, but her embrace was magic. I was okay again. I could breathe again from just the sight of her after the grueling separation.

"Oh, look. You're alive, after all. Good for you." Despite Zane's attempt to sound bored at the status of my mortality, I detected a hint of relief.

"Poppy, I brought your favorite...Damon!" Piya gasped.

Piya rushed inside the room upon noticing Poppy in my embrace. She hugged us both but awkwardly disengaged when neither of us let go of the inappropriate display of public affection. We didn't give a fuck that her parents were in the room.

Piya was the one to break up the reunion. "Poppy, your eyes," she spoke in awe.

I pulled back to inspect my girl, gently setting her down on the bed with my arms wrapped around her. I didn't think I could separate from her again in this lifetime.

Poppy patted her cheeks drenched in moisture. "I'm leaking," she exclaimed, horrified. "What the hell's going on? Why are my eyes leaking?"

Piya laughed. "You're not leaking, baby. You're crying."

Where it should've been alarming, it seemed to make her mother immensely happy. Poppy was crying for the first time in her life, an emotion Piya never thought she'd witness in her daughter.

I stared at her, equally mesmerized. "You're crying," I echoed Piya's words. Brown, glossy eyes shined in the poorly lit room, more tears falling on her cheeks. It was beautiful, haunting, and utterly captivating.

She swiped her cheek with her index finger to gather a droplet, staring at the moisture dry against her fingertip. "Why?" she seemed to be speaking to herself, trying to determine the cause behind such an act.

A smile tugged at my lips. "Haven't you figured it out yet, little Spawn?"

She examined me thoughtfully. "Yes," she whispered, holding nothing back. "Because I love you, and I can't live without you."

I yanked her to my lips, kissing her with such absolution in front of my new in-laws that it could only be viewed as disrespectful. I couldn't find it in myself to scale back when Poppy threw her arms around my neck and nuzzled into me like she'd never let go, either. "I love you," I whispered back, though she had heard it a million times already.

This time, her parents took the hint. "Why don't we give them a moment?" Piya suggested.

"We'll gather everyone and bring them back here," Zane said over his shoulders before disappearing out of the room.

I saw the inquisitive look on my girl's face about gathering everyone, but she didn't question it. Instead, her hands roamed my battered body, taking in my ragged t-shirt, the dried blood around my lips, and the finger that was still bleeding.

"What did Dev do to you? Where did he take you?" she choked. Fuck, her tear-soaked voice made my dick hard. I could get used to this a little too easily.

I wanted to tell her everything but was distracted by the gauze wrapped around Poppy's wrist and her pinky finger encased in a mini cast. I shook my head with rage.

I held my fingers over hers. Though even an inch of her pain caused me severe mental anguish, it was poetic that we now shared the same injury. Part of my pinky was shot off by her Uncle Dev.

"It's okay." Poppy rubbed a hand up and down my shoulders when she noted the darkness brewing in my eyes. "They are just scrapes. I'm fine." Her focus was on my finger instead. "Tell me what he did."

I gave her another chaste kiss. "I will. I'll explain once everyone is here."

Fifteen minutes later, Poppy and I finally dragged ourselves away from one another after she disclosed what happened to her finger and the subsequent hospital visit. She insisted on calling a doctor to look at my wounds as well. They wanted me to get admitted, but there was no way in hell I'd leave her side. She was still hooked up to IV lines, and unless they could admit me to the same room, it wasn't happening. Eventually, a nurse took pity on the couple with separation anxiety and bandaged my superficial wounds. Luckily, it was a clean gunshot, and nothing was infected. I stood under the shower of Poppy's ensuite bathroom to wash off any remnants of blood while Luke was summoned to bring me a change of clothes.

Even the short separation while showering proved to be torture. When I returned to the room, I saw her browsing through a book.

"What are you reading?"

"*What To Expect When You're Expecting*. Mom just dropped it off," she replied callously.

I froze.

Poppy's gaze coasted to me. "Don't look so shocked." She raised a challenging brow. "Given how careful you were being, surprised is the last thing you should be feeling right now."

She was right. I took her face between my hands. "Is it true?" I asked softly. "You sure you're pregnant?"

"No, but I am," a man's voice drifted into the room. An older doctor wearing a stern expression, deep lines, and a furrowed brow examined my state. His eyes narrowed, and his mouth pinched in disapproval. "Young man, has anyone told you that you look like shit. You need to get admitted right away."

"I'm fine," I insisted. "I want to be here when you tell us what's going on with the baby. I'm the father," I told him, puffing out my chest.

He was unimpressed. "Of course you are." He looked me up and down, the frown stretching at the sight of my bruised face and injured body.

"He doesn't like us very much," Poppy whispered to me.

"She is right," the doctor replied without looking up from his charts.

"That's great. So, how's our baby?" I wrapped an arm around Poppy, beaming with pride.

Judgmental eyes perused us, convinced we'd be disastrous parents. Nonetheless, he gave us the necessary update. Baby was fine. No issues.

My hand didn't leave her stomach even long after he left the room.

I peppered her face with kisses, though there was some apprehension about how she felt about all this. "I hope this is good news for you, too, baby."

Poppy's expression softened, eyes locked on me. "The best news."

I leaned back to study her expression. "You sure you're happy about this?" I no longer cared about tricking her into this. After everything we'd been through, I wanted this to be *our* decision for *our* future.

"It was my new lease on life," was the only answer Poppy gave me.

I frowned, not grasping the reference.

She didn't let me look too closely into it, crashing her lips against mine.

"What the hell is going on in here?" A booming voice cut through our happiness.

CHAPTER THIRTY-NINE

DAMON

"What the hell is going on in here?" Nick Ambani stumbled into the room, glowering at Poppy.

No one else had been informed of our secret marriage. I had been working discreetly with Zane and Piya to mend the gap between our two families.

"Have you lost your mind?" Samar joined Nick. "What are you doing with a Maxwell?"

Poppy pulled back from our kiss. My arms instinctively tightened around her middle. She must've sensed I wouldn't let go anytime soon. Not only did she remain complacent in my hold, but Poppy didn't retract the arms wrapped around my neck either.

Shital and Sonia Ambani were the next to join the group, followed by Nick Senior and Yash.

Sonia stopped short upon taking in our intimate huddle on the bed. It left little to the imagination. "Poppy," she gasped.

Sonia was Rayyan's mother. She lost her husband a few years ago, followed by her only son. Of everyone in this room, she was the only person with the right to hold a grievance. Despite her misdirected anger, I wished her no harm.

She didn't feel the same and stared at Poppy as if she had stuck a knife in her back. "How could you, Poppy? Do we mean nothing to you?"

More people trickled into the room. They circled us like hounds. We sat on the bed in the middle of the room, surrounded by people who should be our well-wishers, not our enemies.

Shital glanced at Piya with accusatory eyes. "Don't just stand there. Say something to your daughter."

Piya was unfazed, standing tall and proud. "Sure." She turned to us and loudly said, "Congrats, baby."

"W-What are you doing?"

Piya looked Shital over coolly. "I believe congratulations are in order after someone gets married."

Anger burnt in Shital's cheeks. "W-What?"

"Poppy and Damon got married," Piya explained patiently as if talking down to someone who was having difficulty understanding her.

Nick Senior was ready to hit the roof. "When did this happen?" He glared at Poppy. "You can say goodbye to being CEO. None of us will ever vote for someone who turned their back on their family."

"We'll never acknowledge a Maxwell as one of us," Samar piped in.

Instead of calming the mob down, Piya threw gasoline onto the fire. "It doesn't matter whether you accept it. The doctors just confirmed the good news. They are expecting."

Everyone inhaled sharply at the news that an Ambani's fate was officially sealed with a Maxwell, followed by undecipherable insults and high-pitched grumbling all at once.

Piya spoke over the voices. "Perhaps Damon would like to say a few words on this happy occasion."

On the contrary, I planned on maintaining my silence during this exchange. The best way to handle bickering parties was to let them vent and fight it out amongst themselves.

Poppy glanced at me with a knowing look. She also wanted to see how this would play out if we gave them a voice to state their grievances.

"A Maxwell will never be accepted into this family," Sonia seethed, voice cracking. "They are always out to destroy us."

"Dev's the one who held Damon at gunpoint before kidnapping him," Piya countered.

Shital had enough. "This is absurd. My brother would never hold someone at gunpoint or take them captive. You don't seriously believe this, do you?"

"How could you turn your back on your family?" Sonia implored Poppy, stuck between bitterness and anger. "Did you forget this man killed my son? You'll give up your dream of being the CEO for a man who killed your cousin?"

"Actually," Zane walked into the room with my brother, father, and Sophie in tow, shocking everyone. I knew the other two would comply with my request for this meeting, but I had no idea how Zane convinced Dad to attend. "Poppy is to become the CEO of Ambani Corp effective immediately.

Or I'm pulling out my assets from your company, and Piya will start selling her stocks until Ambanis lose controlling share."

Zane wasn't a part of Poppy's family. Rather, he was sort of an independent contractor who was family adjacent. Nonetheless, I urged him to back us. For once, he came through to be the father Poppy needed him to be. At my advice, Zane invested his life savings into Ambani Corp, becoming their biggest client and throwing them a lifeline to help with their depleting business. They had to agree to his demands if they didn't want to go belly up. This was part of the plan we had concocted over the weeks.

"Furthermore," Zane continued, "Damon had nothing to do with Rayyan's murder. Rayyan died from a drug overdose."

"That's impossible," Sonia said, the irritation evident in her voice.

"It's true. He happened to be sitting too close to the edge of his terrace and fell to his death."

Therein lay the problem.

Rayyan fell off the terrace of his home that overlooked the ocean. His death was similar to Rose's misfortune. It was an unfortunate coincidence they both fell from tall heights, and I happened to have engaged with them right before the separate incidents. However, the family refused to ignore the stroke of misfortune involving the same man, especially a Maxwell.

Rayyan died the night of Poppy's eighteenth birthday. They went to a party, where I propositioned Poppy and ended up in an altercation with Rayyan. Poppy's rejection had pushed me to act rashly, and I made a blunder. I ended up at her place, waiting for her to come home so I could watch her sleep for a few hours. I was out on her balcony, inhaling a few angry cigarettes instead of practicing my usual caution.

Since Rayyan lived in Sands Point and the party was in the city, he was to stay the night in Poppy's guest room. Upon stepping inside, Poppy immediately noted three things that weren't how she left it, including the open balcony door. Luckily, she couldn't see my silhouette since I was off to the side, but she called security and her mother.

Piya freaked out, demanding both Poppy and Rayyan return to Sands Point. Poppy dropped Rayyan off at his house on the way to Piya's. She just didn't know I was following them in my car.

"Rayyan was on a lot of drugs and fell. This could have been prevented if you paid attention to how out of control he was getting. If you don't believe me, just take a look at what we found." Zane nodded at my twin.

Caden stepped forward with a folder in hand. He handed it to Sonia and spoke to her in a gentle voice, "We spoke to four different rehab clinics. Rayyan had been forced into numerous court-mandated programs for his drug usage, but he'd covered up his tracks for years. That is where he was whenever he told you he was going away on vacation."

Sonia gasped, her hand flew to her mouth, and her eyes widened in shock. She never believed the toxicology reports presented by the police. But the evidence was undeniable as she sorted through the documents and the photos of Rayyan checking in and out of various clinics. Despite the numerous rehabs and expensive treatments, Rayyan returned to his old habits after being released into society.

The wheels in Sonia's head were turning, wondering how well she knew her own flesh and blood. A morsel of my empathy extended to her. I had gone through similar emotions after Mom passed away. No one wanted to believe such a thing could be true about their loved one.

Sonia dropped the papers on the floor, causing them to scatter.

"I know this is hard to accept," Piya started softly. "But Damon didn't push Rayyan. Rayyan wasn't aware of what he was doing and simply fell. He had an ongoing drug issue. I know we don't want to believe the worst in our children, but that's the truth of what happened." Piya extended her arms for Sonia, but Sonia stumbled back just out of reach.

"No." Denial coated her voice. "That's not possible." She looked around frantically until her gaze landed on Sophie. "She." Sonia pointed at Sophie with an accusatory finger. "She saw Damon that night. Sophie saw him leaving the property."

Sophie, who had been quiet this whole time, had her gaze on the floor. Meekly, she looked up and addressed the room. "I-I thought I saw Damon that night," she came clean. "But it-it was dark, and I had a few drinks. Later, I realized that I was mistaken."

"No." Sonia shook her head, unable to accept the confession.

"When I realized my mistake, I tried to fix it. I told Damon I would retract my statement, but he asked me not to."

Sonia's jaw dropped, glancing at me. "Why would he do that?"

Piya stepped forward. "Because Damon didn't want to tarnish the Ambani name by letting everyone find out about Rayyan's drug problems. Rayyan was being groomed just like Poppy. If this information about the future leaders of the company went public, there would be no more shareholder meetings. So, even though Sophie was mistaken, Damon let it be."

"B-But it would've cleared his name," Sonia said, bewildered.

Piya shook her head sadly. "Damon's in love with my daughter. He knew hurting her family would only hurt Poppy. Damon did nothing other than protect the Ambani name at all costs. He knew the charges against him were fraudulent and wouldn't hold up in court. He thought it'd be the best way to protect Poppy and her entire family. That's the truth."

At that, Sonia dropped into an armchair near the door and broke down in tears. Everything she knew and believed had been turned upside down within seconds. She didn't know how to process it.

"You did all this to protect us," she forced a whisper out of her mouth. "Why would you do this?"

"The same reason he protected me." Dev emerged out of the blue, turning everyone's heads in his direction. "To save us from ourselves."

∽

I woke up tied to a chair, blood dripping from my pinky finger. It had been poorly bandaged with a rag, the scent of anti-septic difficult to deny. The rancid taste in my mouth left it dry, craving water. My eyes peeled open with great effort to take in my surroundings. There was no outside light coming in, and it smelled damp and moldy. We were in some sort of basement.

Dev circled my chair with a bat in his hand. His clothes were disheveled, and his wild eyes looked out of place on his grief-stricken face.

"Look who's finally awake," he spoke tauntingly.

"How long have I been here?" My voice was coarse.

"Twenty-four hours."

Shit.

Luke was instructed to check on Poppy if I ever went missing for more than six hours, and he was given specific instructions not to let harm befall her unless he wanted to pay with his own life. But I had a sinking feeling that after hearing the gunshot over the phone, Poppy wouldn't sit pretty.

When Dev approached me in the parking lot, gun in his hand, I knew I was facing a man who was on the brink of insanity. Nonetheless, I saw something in his eyes that Poppy couldn't see through the phone. The bleak emptiness of a man who had nothing left to lose.

I had helped many like him before. If there was something I understood, it was the deep isolation that led people down a dark path. Perhaps I had no problem ripping someone to pieces if they touched Poppy, but for some reason, I couldn't exercise the same wrath toward someone trying to hurt me.

Dev needed a second chance.

Correction. Dev wanted a second chance. He just didn't know how to ask for it.

Dev shot me but had no intention of killing me. The bullet hit the side of my hand, grazing over my ear to knock the Bluetooth off. If I had to guess, he hired men to sedate me and throw me in a car while I was momentarily out of commission. He couldn't have dragged someone my size down to this basement alone.

Allowing my eyes to sweep the room, I realized no one else was here. Dev wasn't cocky enough to think he could take me with just a bat. Which meant he had a concealed weapon that he planned on using.

But if he wanted to kill me, why fix up the gunshot wound, albeit somewhat poorly?

It hit me then. He wanted me to feel the same desolation he had been experiencing. Because somewhere deep down, he was someone's father, and murdering someone else's son was difficult for him to stomach.

But that didn't stop him from swinging the bat into my stomach. It sunk in, hurting like a bitch. I clenched my teeth, holding in the pain. He did it over and over, hitting me with the bat. However, a part of him was holding back. He purposefully avoided my head and vital organs.

"I don't hate you, Dev," I whispered. "You're grieving. What happened to you was terrible. No parent should have to watch their children suffer."

Dev leaned down to meet my eyes. I expected to find hatred in them, but all I saw was more of the same loss and destitution. It quickly vanished.

"You're right. And now, you'll never be able to do that to someone else again. I won't let you."

"I didn't hurt your daughter." I shook my head, closing my eyes. "Nor did I hurt your son."

Dev froze, not having expected my knowledge of their sordid family secret. Rayyan was his son.

"Poppy told me," I explained carefully. "We got married a few weeks ago."

His eyes widened as if I had said the apocalypse was coming. "She would never betray us like that."

"It wasn't about betrayal. I love her more than anything in this world. And what she loves the most is her family, including Rose. I wouldn't hurt anyone or anything that Poppy cares about. Deep down, you know I'm telling the truth."

Dev said nothing and just watched me with the agony only a parent could feel.

∼

Over the next two days, I talked Dev down from the brink. He'd hold up a gun when he let me use the bathroom or brought me food. There were times when I found him tending to my wounds. He was a broken man with no outlet for his pain. And in an impulsive move, he had decided to kidnap me.

I pitied him.

Regardless, I needed to get back to my wife to ensure she was okay. After Dev found out that Poppy was in the hospital, his conscience got the better of him. He tentatively released me, hanging his head in defeat, probably expecting me to lunge for the gun. He was shocked when I asked him for a ride to the hospital instead to see my wife.

I guess he never left the hospital, expecting to pay for his sins. When Piya and Zane gathered everyone to reveal Rayyan's past deeds, they didn't expect Dev to be in the vicinity.

"I-I never meant to hurt anyone," Dev started crying, blubbering endlessly. "I'm sorry. Oh god, I'm sorry. What have I done?"

I knew my wife was seconds away from lunging and choking Dev to death. I tightened my grip around her when she tried jumping off the bed.

"Don't you dare apologize," Poppy hissed, her hands turned into fists. "It means nothing after what you did to Damon."

I held her back as she struggled to get out of my hold. We were too close to the finish line to lose sight now. They had to believe Poppy and I were the wronged parties for their guilty conscience to take precedence.

My brother stepped forward menacingly, ready to launch his own attack. "You should be in jail right now. I'm calling the police."

"Everyone, calm down. I wanted Dev to be here."

Caden glanced at me with shock. "Have you lost your mind? This man shot you."

I held up my hand. My twin and I were as different as they came, but we could communicate nonverbally when needed. I silently asked him to stand down.

Loosening my hold on Poppy, I rose from the bed. "We are ending this feud, once and for all," I declared, leaving no room for discussion.

I walked up purposefully to Dev.

"You shot me. You held me captive. You thought I hurt your children when I did nothing of the sort. But I'm not pressing charges and choosing to forgive you."

His bottom lip trembled. "Why?"

"Because any anger I might feel wouldn't surpass my love for my wife." I held out my hand to shake his, calling a truce.

Dev's eyes shone at the gesture, and he lunged for my hand with both of his, breaking down with guilt-induced tears. "I don't deserve this second chance, but I will do everything in my power to earn it. I promise. And I'm sorry. I'm so sorry."

Everyone hung onto each of Dev's words. He had led the charge against the Maxwells for so long that they didn't know how to react.

Piya took the opportunity to step forward and shake hands with my dad. "I'd like to be the first to welcome you into our family and all the benefits that come with it." She said with a wink, tempting him with acceptance from the coveted inner circle. Dad was an easily dissuadable man, only interested in the glamorous association that came with the Ambanis.

Joe Maxwell shook Piya Trimalchio's hand, and with it, we officially ended this bitter war.

CHAPTER
FORTY
DAMON

Sophie shifted uncomfortably under Damon's intense glare, trying to determine why I asked her to stay behind. Everyone else left the hospital. Now that the news of our marriage had gone public, the next step was to work on an Ambani-Maxwell merger. Damon would leave Maxwell Corp and join Ambani Corp, taking his technology with him. His uncle would receive a hefty buyout, and Mom would pave the way for Joe to become the belle of every ball. Zane insisted I was to become CEO effective immediately, finishing my last semester of college on the side. Otherwise, he'd pull out his investments. Having an ally turned out to be a much better fit for us than a faux father-daughter relationship.

Everyone won, but one detail was yet to be ironed out.

Who did Sophie see on the night of Rayyan's murder?

Sophie's gaze shifted between me and Damon.

Damon agreed to this meeting despite how difficult it was for him to see me with a past hookup.

Sophie cleared her throat. She was careful never to look directly at me after Damon informed her it wasn't allowed.

Regardless, I needed a few private moments with Sophie. My gaze drifted to Damon pointedly, hinting for him to leave. "Do you mind?"

"Yes," he replied curtly, sinking further into the sofa of my hospital suite with me on his lap. Another power move to assert his dominance in case Sophie got any funny ideas.

His hand moved up and down my upper thigh, his mouth hovering over my neck. I must've turned my back on shame because I visibly shivered in his hold despite Sophie having a front-row view of our lewd behavior. My eyes rolled to the back of my head when he nibbled on my neck, the heady scent of his musk consuming my senses.

His hardness poked my ass. He didn't give a shit about the public displays of affection. Every damn time we were together, it felt like we were the only two people in this world. I don't know how I managed to rip away from his ministrations to focus on the task at hand instead.

This conversation would be tricky with Damon in the room. I couldn't openly communicate under his watchful eyes. I considered Morse Code when I was saved by the bell.

Damon's phone buzzed, and he cursed. "It's the office. I need to take this. News about the Ambani-Maxwell merger has been leaked. Everyone's losing it."

I hopped off his lap so Damon could step out onto the ensuite balcony. He made the "I'm watching you" motion with two fingers at Sophie, another silent threat to keep her hands off me.

His eyes were still trained on us from the balcony. At least he was no longer within earshot. It was the only private moment we'd get, and I didn't have the luxury of wasting time. I got straight to the point. "I have some questions for you regarding the night of Rayyan's death."

Sophie straightened in the plush blue-gray armchair. "Okay," she spoke tentatively.

"When the police first came to see you, why did you set my husband up by telling them you saw him?"

Her head lurched back. "I wasn't trying to set Damon up."

My disbelieving eyes narrowed. "Let's say I believe you," I drawled. "That you thought you saw Damon leaving Rayyan's house."

"I did," Sophie insisted with a bravado she hadn't shown in front of Damon.

My gaze roamed her mien, searching for traces of dishonesty.

Fuck. She was telling the truth.

My chest tightened, gravity pulling my insides down ferociously. It made no sense. Damon said he never followed me at Sands Point.

It took immense control to remain unmoved and continue the conversation. "Why would Damon still be friends with you after you ratted him out to the police?"

She frowned, puzzled. She thought Damon and I were in cahoots about this and had no clue of my ignorance over the matter. "I-I don't understand. I did everything Damon asked of me."

"Explain."

Sophie sighed. "I had a hunch Damon liked you since the day he threatened me for expressing an interest in you. That's why I organized a threesome. I thought if he worked you out of his system, he'd stop snapping at the rest of us. And he wouldn't care if I shoot my shot with you." Sophie winked at me.

I rolled my eyes. If Damon were to return to the room this instant, he'd wreck another one of Sophie's cars.

Similar thoughts must've crossed her mind, and Sophie's boldness waned. She gestured at my ring finger. "Obviously, circumstances have changed. I didn't realize how obsessed he was with you."

"What does that have to do with Rayyan?"

"I've known Damon my entire life and knew he couldn't have killed anyone. But he especially wouldn't hurt your family. You mean too much to him. I heard about what happened at that party and assumed Damon stopped by to apologize to Rayyan for punching him."

"You are certain of your convictions."

Sophie shrugged. "Damon was the one who told me that I needed to be honest about what I saw, which was Damon leaving Rayyan's house. A man who did something wrong wouldn't have asked me to be truthful."

"But the deposition you provided painted him as a killer."

Sophie appeared confused. "I wasn't trying to paint Damon as a killer. When I told the police I saw him leaving Rayyan's place, I didn't know there had been a death or that it was connected to a murder investigation. Otherwise, I would've never implicated Damon. I tried retracting the statement, but Damon told me not to bother. I didn't realize he was taking the heat to protect your family."

But Damon only protected one person in this world.

Me.

"Tell me what you saw."

"I was home alone that night when I heard a scream from Rayyan's house. I called the police, and when I looked out the window and into Rayyan's yard, I saw Damon exiting the house."

My heart stopped. Damon was there. He was there the night of Rayyan's death and told Sophie to fabricate the details.

"So why did you lie in front of my family?"

"I told you. Damon's my oldest friend. I know he isn't capable of murder. He explained the situation and told me he needed your family to trust him."

"Damon was there," I reinstated in a small voice.

The room turned quiet following my declaration. Sophie watched me, trying to assess if she said too much. Perhaps I wasn't meant to know those little pieces of information.

Before she could open her mouth, the balcony door slid open, and Damon stalked back in, shoving his phone in his pocket.

Sophie's mild gaze bounced between Damon and me. She had no idea of the bomb she had dropped. "Well, I should get going," she said mildly, rising to her feet.

Damon flicked his eyes over her briefly before focusing on me. I don't know how I forced my head into a nod.

Damon tensed almost imperceptibly at my composure. "You okay?"

I gazed at him longingly before throwing my arms around his neck and wrapping my legs around his waist.

Damon truly was the only one capable of loving me.

∼

"Come on, do one bump with me."

I rolled my eyes as Rayyan did a line of coke off the ledge of the terrace. The warm summer breeze whipped hair around my face, the crashing ocean waves sounding like white noise. What could've been a tolerable experience was ruined by Rayyan's insipient presence.

He jumped onto the ledge and sat on the edge of the terrace, his legs dangling over the side with the blue expanse of the ocean below him.

Idiot.

"You'll fall to your death," I warned. "Get down from there."

He didn't listen, and I cursed myself for coming here. It was out of my loyalty to Rose that I kept Rayyan in check. She knew Rayyan was her half-brother and, unfortunately, showed him more kindness than he deserved. That's why I agreed to let Rayyan stay at my house after the party. However, some asshole broke into my apartment.

At Mom's persistence, I returned to Sands Point, dropping Rayyan off on the way. He insisted on a nightcap, and I stayed to ensure the asshole didn't tumble to his death. He had a habit of doing coke on this terrace, a terrible place to be when you were barely lucid. A drug addict with a home overlooking the ocean was a recipe for disaster.

Ugh. Kill me.

"Aww. Don't look so miserable, Poppy," he said mockingly.

"I wouldn't have to if I wasn't here," I retorted.

It made him laugh, and he suddenly turned philosophical. "You know, everyone fears you because they think you're the big, bad. But you're just a little goth girl who acts tough."

"Oh yeah?"

"Obviously. I mean, just look at us. I'm going after your dream job, and you haven't done a thing to fight me. I'll be CEO by the time you graduate."

I snorted. "There is no reason to fight you, Rayyan." I gestured at the ensemble of drugs sitting on the ledge. "You'll be dead by the time I graduate from college. You're digging your own grave, and I have a front-row seat to it.

Trust me, I'm enjoying the show of your slow demise. I'd rather extend your misery than allow you a quick death."

Instead of being offended, Rayyan threw his head back and laughed wholeheartedly like it was the cutest thing he'd ever heard.

Whatever. Rayyan's opinion of me made no difference to me. As I said, he was digging himself an early grave. I just wished Rose would see it, too. In her heart, she believed he could be saved and needed our help.

Rookie mistake.

Rayyan did another bump. When I tried to take away his magic powder, he screamed up a storm. God dammit.

My loyalty to Rose forced me to help Rayyan. She wouldn't like it if I allowed him to plummet to his death. Ugh. Family was the worst.

"Okay, how about we hop off that ledge now? Go to sleep so I can be done with babysitting you."

"You're such a buzzkill. Bzz. Bzz." Rayyan was coked out of his mind and garbled nonsense.

I checked the time on my phone when I caught something out of the corner of my eye. Perhaps it was my imagination, but I could've sworn I saw a shadow in his bedroom.

Almost as if someone was watching me.

"Did you invite a girl over by any chance?" I asked, trying to make out the figure.

Rayyan snorted, zonked out of his mind. He really shouldn't be sitting on the edge of that terrace. "Probably my sister coming back for revenge."

"Huh?"

The maniacal laughter got louder. "It's a secret."

"Whatever. I need to go. Can you please get off the ledge first? I don't need you dying on my watch."

Rayyan held up both hands as if in surrender, looking out into the ocean. "Alright. Alright. I'll tell you. Remember when Rose was found beaten outside Uncle Dev's house?"

I sighed. "How can I forget?" Rose had never been the same since the incident. It ruined her life. She feared the dark and always looked over her shoulders. At times, she couldn't even string two syllables together. Fear had overtaken her existence. After a momentary pause, I said, "You know that Rose is"

"My sister?" The laughter grew louder, his body moving from side to side. This freak was officially creeping me out. "Of course, I know, dear cousin. That's why I tried beating her to death, but that security guard came to her rescue and ruined everything. If only that bitch had died, I could've become Uncle Dev's sole heir and inherited all his stocks." He was slurring his words and had no idea what he was saying or who he was speaking with.

I bent to gather my purse off the ground. "Bye, Rayyan. And remember, you're an idiot."

Rayyan didn't turn to face me. "Next time, I'll finish the job and kill the bitch."

I sighed deeply.

I placed both hands on his shoulder blades and pushed him off the ledge. I slung my bag over my shoulders and turned away, listening to Rayyan's last scream on earth as he fell to his death.

∽

EPILOGUE

~

Poppy

THE RICH LEATHER SCENT FROM THE CHAIR WAFTED INTO THE air as my fingers trailed over the luxurious dark brown material. There was an aphrodisiac to this touch like it was meant to be mine. It smelled like power.

My tongue darted out to lick my bottom lip. Damon smirked from the other end of the long conference table, watching me with the same lustful eyes as I was watching the chair. We finished prepping for our first official meeting since the merger. Damon left Maxwell Corp, taking his patented technology with him. The clients that left Ambani Corp flocked back to us as a result. Damon even changed his last name to Ambani and assumed a position on the board. I wanted to share the co-CEO title with him, but he refused, claiming his dream had been to watch me sit in the head chair and rule the world.

How many husbands would do that on top of covering up their wife's murder?

No, I didn't regret killing Rayyan. He would've died within a few years anyway from drugs but might've killed Rose before leaving this earth. I had no choice but to take care of the problem.

Nonetheless, it bothered me that Rayyan's death saddened Rose. I owed her for both Damon and Rayyan and vowed to make things right once she was lucid.

More so, it bothered me when the blame for the murder fell on Damon. I pursued Sophie, leading a charge to reverse her deposition. But my husband was a few steps ahead of me.

He always cleaned up my mess, never once berating me for my terrible impulses. No evil too great could turn Damon away from me, not even murder. For the longest time, I feared he'd find out and would want nothing more to do with me.

Unbeknownst to me, the opposite was true. Damon put multiple safeguards in place so I wouldn't end up in jail. He was willing to take the fall if they fell through, leading the suspicion away from me.

That beautiful lunatic.

I bit my lower lip, salivating after him at just the thought. Hunger lit in his eye at the small action. If we didn't have a meeting in two minutes, he'd defile me on this table right now. I couldn't look away from him even as the rest of the members filtered into the boardroom, exchanging pleasantries.

One of the junior interns, a cousin of mine, went around pouring fresh cups of coffee for everyone. I smirked, watching him return to the same chair I used to sit in once upon a time. My palm unknowingly rested on my abdomen, craving the day the baby inside me would do the same. They'd climb the ladder until reaching the very top.

I scanned every inch of the room, taking in every detail of this monumental moment. I wanted to capture and preserve it. My fingers hovered over the tattoos on the back of my neck, hidden underneath the perfectly tailored black suit, so Papa could witness our dreams come true. My crown-shaped engagement ring glinted with premonition as I pressed my palm onto the chair to pull it out. I waited until everyone was settled before sinking into the chair slightly bigger than the rest.

With my back ramrod straight, my posture exuding authority, I looked over my empire.

"Let's begin."

∽

Damon

I glanced at my nightstand, frowning at my vibrating phone. It was late. My wife was out cold, given that it was past midnight.

Poppy had been a trooper throughout the pregnancy, training her body not to experience morning sickness. However, sleep deprivation was where I drew the line. I wanted her to sleep a full eight hours every night. She countered with six. Finally, we settled on seven.

With a quick peck on her cheek, I grabbed my phone and found Caden's name flashing on the screen.

I picked it up immediately. My twin, the doctor, knew better than to call a pregnant woman's house after midnight.

"What's wrong?"

He didn't beat around the bush, either. "Don't freak out."

Famous first words.

There was a bad premonition in the air. Caden had done a few erratic things in the past, which led me to ask, "What did you do?"

"I took Sleeping Beauty, and I need you to cover for me."

∼

Continue the Tales of Obsession Series with Rose & Caden's Story inspired by The Titanic. Turn the page to find out more about a Bonus Scene.

AFTERWORD

Thank you for giving my books a chance. This Romeo & Juliet retelling has been a passion project of mine, with a nod to my favorite female character, Wednesday Addams. You'll also find some Easter egg banters inspired by C.C. and Niles from The Nanny.

A review for an author is like leaving a tip for your server. If you enjoyed this retelling, consider writing me a review on Goodreads or Amazon. Once I reach 1000 reviews, I'll write a bonus scene for Poppy and Damon.

In the meantime, don't forget to preorder Rose & Caden's Story, inspired by The Titanic.

Sign up for my Newsletter or find me on Facebook for signed paperbacks, giveaways, and more.

ACKNOWLEDGMENTS

A massive shoutout to my lovely Beta Team. Thank you, Ashley, Alexis, and Tori, for working through the holidays for me.

A big thank you goes to my editors for taking on this massive project.
Developmental Editors: Theresa from Fairy Plot Mother & Erin from The Word Faery
Copy Editing: Jenny from Editing4Indies & Bianca Williams
Proofreading: Angie from Lunar Rose

About the Author

Drethi is a dark, contemporary author and prefers to write anti-heroes. Drethi's stories will always have angst, obsession, and a dark twist. Though toxic love and darkness are major players in her books, romance is still a priority. Stay tuned for future releases by signing up for her Newsletter.
Connect with the author directly:
Linktree

Also by Drethi Anis

THE QUARANTINE SERIES
QUARANTINED
ISOLATION
ESSENTIAL
THE QUARANTINE BOX SET 1-3 & BONUS SCENES

THE CHAOS SERIES
ORGANIZED CHAOS
DISCORD

THE SEVEN SINS SERIES
LUST

5000 NIGHTS OF OBSESSION
FATAL OBSESSION
TALES OF OBSESSION BOOK#3

Printed in Great Britain
by Amazon